MAGIC UNLEASHED

Hall of Blood and Mercy Book 3

K. M. SHEA

MAGIC UNLEASHED
Copyright © 2020 by K. M. Shea

Magiford Supernatural City is a registered trademark of K. M. Shea LLC.

Cover Art by Natasha Snow Designs
Edited by Deborah Grace White

All rights reserved. No part of this book may be used or reproduced in any number whatsoever without written permission of the author, except in the case of quotations embodied in articles and reviews.

This is a work of fiction. Names, characters, places, and incidents are either the product of the author's imagination, or are used fictitiously. Any resemblance to actual persons, living or dead, or historic events is entirely coincidental.

ISBN: 978-1-950635-09-2

www.kmshea.com

For my Champions.
You are the wizards of House Shea.

CHAPTER ONE

Hazel

"Again!" I strengthened my magic shield and braced myself, digging the heels of my boots into the grassy turf of House Medeis's front lawn.

Felix hammered at me with a chunk of ice that was almost bigger than me—which, given I could only break five feet tall when wearing heels, wasn't quite as impressive as it sounds.

My shield held, but the ice did push me back a few inches. I pulled more raw magic through my blood and added it to my shield constructed of my blue tinted magic, then leaned into it, pushing back.

The ice gave, but Mr. Baree was on me next with a wave of *molten lava*.

The lava hissed and popped, slapping against my shield with the consistency of thick sludge—though the grass underneath and around it went up in flames.

I kept my expression even—it was only two weeks ago that Mr. Baree had finally stopped asking me if I was okay after every attack he made. If I gave him an inkling that his lava freaked me out, he was going to stop and apologize for at least five minutes.

Last came Franco—Felix's older brother—and Franco's wife, Leslie. Leslie wielded a spear wrapped in fire, while Franco stood just behind her with a crossbow. Franco shot first, the bolt of his crossbow glowing blue. Rather than aiming at me, he'd hit a spot in my shield that had been weakened by the ice and lava. The bolt stuck to the shield and made a tiny crack, though it didn't poke all the way through.

My right hand buzzed—I was both holding and maintaining a sword made of electricity magic. I hurriedly tossed it in the air as I forced more magic into my shield just before Leslie jabbed her spearhead at the little crack Franco's bolt had created.

Even though it was cold, sweat dripped down my spine from the effort it took to hold my shield up. I leaned my forearm against my shield and caught my lightning sword with my free hand.

Felix created three stakes of ice that narrowed into a sharp point, then slammed them at the weakened spot of my shield.

I held it for the first two, but the last one broke through, making my shield crackle. I gritted my teeth, but it took me a couple moments to restore it.

Franco crouched on the ground and shook his head. "I gotta say, Adept. You are a powerhouse."

I pushed a frizzy lock of blond hair that had escaped from my ponytail out of my face. "You guys broke through that time—those were some impressive attacks!"

"But it took four of us to match you." Leslie frowned as she peered down at her spear. "And we've had years with our level of magic, but you haven't even been unsealed for half a year."

"Maybe, but all of this is different from what you learned when you were first taught magic." I gestured around with my lightning sword.

Scattered across the front lawn, the rest of the wizards of

House Medeis were focused on practice, too. Off to the left, Momoko was going through some of the newly minted attack and defensive formations with half a dozen other wizards. A shout from her and they'd scramble from a straight line to a V position, their magic-forged shields linking up to create an impassable wall. Closer to the long driveway, Mrs. Clark and Mrs. Yamada—Momoko's mom—were using some bushes and magic to test just how thick a magic-reinforced bush had to be to stop a car. Farther back it looked like some House Medeis wizards were working on a seemingly average ball of electricity that exploded into a lightning storm on contact.

None of this was even remotely normal for regular wizards. A good fireball was the typical fare for our kind. What we were practicing was a heck of a lot more effective—and deadly.

"Yeah, I'm not convinced." Felix used his shirt to wipe sweat off his face, slightly mussing his movie-perfect, golden hair. "Unless those vampires fed you something weird, you've gotta admit you're a near genius at this stuff."

I stared Felix down, daring him to push the subject of vampires. When he guiltily looked away, I tapped my lightning sword on my thigh, shedding sparks on the bright red and orange leaves that covered the lawn. The sword wasn't really good for anything, even though when I first tried creating it I had high hopes I could use it like a Taser. (Spoiler, it didn't work like that.) The lightning sword was just another way for me to hone my magic while I did my best to coach my House through practice. It took a lot of concentration to keep up, so I figured it had to help my stamina. "I have the Paragon's book."

The Paragon was the top fae in America—but if you asked him he'd be sure to stress that he was a representative only, and didn't actually rule all the fae courts.

I met the Paragon during my time at Drake Hall, and he had lent me a book to study. I'd been forced to leave the book behind when I left Drake Hall, but a couple days after my

Ascension ceremony he showed up with the book and shoved it in my arms.

"Yeah, but you can't even read that old book." Felix—who was shockingly beautiful for a human, even a magical one—blinked, flashing his long eyelashes. "The words are so faded you can only look at the pictures."

"And it's responsible for most of the attacks I'm teaching you." I pointed at him with my lightning sword. "And don't forget, I practice for an extra hour during the day while everyone else is at work."

Even wizards had to make money somehow. Most members of House Medeis worked in libraries or at one of the local museums—though we had two accountants, a computer programmer, and, my favorite, an electrician. Officially, my career was Adept. I had to manage House Medeis and the wizards who had sworn to it, and I served as the contact with magical society. (In other words, I had to make sure all our paperwork was filed correctly, and I was slightly involved in local politics.)

But this meant I could make my own schedule. And since I knew firsthand how important it was to be battle-ready, I made time to train alone so I could keep improving and didn't stagnate as I taught the rest of my family everything I had learned from...

I shook my head, cutting the thought off. "You should switch with Momoko's group and practice battle formations," I said.

Mr. Baree raised his thick eyebrows, revealing the soulful brown of his eyes. "And you'll let a new group hammer at you?"

"I'm the only one who can take multiple attackers at once," I mildly pointed out.

Mr. Baree frowned. "While I understand, don't overwork yourself, Adept. We're safe now. Mason can't make trouble anymore."

Mason had been a senior wizard of House Medeis, but he turned on me when I first inherited the House several months ago, in spring, after my parents died. He attempted a coup, and the only reason he didn't succeed was because I made it out and took shelter with the most feared vampire in the Midwest, Killian Drake.

Killian had kicked me out in late summer, and I'd come back to the House and beaten Mason in combat, earning my place as the rightful Adept. Mason hadn't agreed, and tried to kill me once the fight was done and my back was turned, so I eliminated him in self-defense.

I stared at my magic-forged weapon, which crackled and vibrated against my palm. "He can't. But just because he's gone doesn't mean the danger is over. He had allies, after all. *Lots* of allies."

Felix scowled, and Franco and Leslie exchanged looks.

Leslie stood straight and raised her chin, reining in the flames so they once again danced around her weapon of choice. "Again, then, Adept?"

"Adept?"

I turned around, a smile blooming when I saw Great Aunt Marraine picking her way across the front yard.

Strictly speaking, I wasn't related to Great Aunt Marraine, or any of the House Medeis wizards. They swore fealty to the magical House and to me, and then fell under my protection. But I had grown up with them, and I considered them my family, Great Aunt Marraine especially so.

Great Aunt Marraine waved a clipboard—the papers clipped to it were a stark white in the dimming light as the sun threatened to set. "A moment of your time, if I may?"

"Of course." I turned back to my training group. "Pair up, and switch on and off raising a shield and attacking."

Franco playfully saluted me. "Whatever you say, Adept!"

"I'll attack." Leslie shot-putted the butt of her spear at her husband's gut. Franco wheezed and folded in half when he didn't raise a shield in time.

He coughed. "Couldn't give me more notice than that, could you?"

"Not if you choose to make light of a very serious matter."

"Okay—AHH! Stop jabbing that spear at me, woman! I get it, I'll take it seriously!"

I chuckled as I turned to Great Aunt Marraine and let my magic shield flicker and die out. "What's up?"

The older woman flipped through her papers, pausing only to fix a button on her bright, fuchsia pink jacket. "You missed your afternoon update, and I don't want you working after dinner, so I thought I could get you caught up now before you're finished for the day."

Since Great Aunt Marraine was old enough to be my parents' grandmother, she hadn't started training with everyone else in the House—though she knew all the formations and helped me set up traps around the perimeter of the property. Instead, she took on more of a secretarial role because I was swimming in more paperwork than my parents had ever faced.

When I Ascended—the ceremony where an Adept officially bonds with their magical House so they can use it and share magic at will—House Medeis had drastically grown. We'd gained another floor of the mansion, and another wing had popped out of the ground. Typically, the size of a House is correlated to the power and esteem the wizard House receives in supernatural society. House Medeis was now the second largest House in the city of Magiford, and one of the largest in the Midwest. As a result, our rank among wizarding Houses had skyrocketed...which meant I was a lot more involved in politics than I ever wanted to be, and brought on a new wave of paperwork.

Great Aunt Marraine waded through the papers for me and helped explain what all the legalese really meant.

"What new paperwork and forms have been inflicted on us today?" I flicked my sweat soaked bangs out of my face as I felt the heat from my wizard mark die out as the magic-sensitive tattoo faded back into my skin.

"There's a new applicant looking to join House Medeis."

"Really?"

"Yep." Great Aunt Marraine tapped the paper. "It seems like she's serious about it, too."

Once word got out that House Medeis's rank had exploded, we had a bunch of applications from other wizards to join. That had mostly died off since everyone found out that joining House Medeis meant you had to listen when the crazy Adept demanded you get up before 6 am every morning to fit in a workout with the specially hired martial artist and weapons trainer, and attend a mandatory magic practice session in the evening.

Strangely, though, we'd gotten a steady trickle of serious applicants among the fad chasers. So far we'd welcomed five new wizards into our ranks, and all of them had one thing in common…

"She comes from Michigan. She's obviously willing to relocate, but we'll have some extra paperwork for her since she's a sixteen-year-old."

"She's *sixteen*?" I yelped. "Doesn't she have a guardian?"

"Her aunt, yes." Great Aunt Marraine peered down at the paper. "She has the necessary guardian permission form, where the aunt says they'll relocate here together, if that's acceptable. The aunt is a regular human."

Wizards, you see, were regular humans, except we could use magic, which came with some benefits.

I scrunched my eyes shut, already afraid I could predict what brought the youngest applicant we'd received yet to our doorstep. "Her parents are…?"

"Dead," Great Aunt Marraine confirmed. "In her essay explaining why she wants to join us, she said they died in an 'accidental' magical skirmish. She wants to join House Medeis because she also wants to be able to protect and learn more about magic beyond the...I believe she called it the 'party tricks' most wizards perform today."

Yep. That was the gut check. Everyone who genuinely wanted to join House Medeis had all suffered in some way, or lost someone they loved because of a fight among supernaturals.

As if she could sense my thoughts, Great Aunt Marraine slightly shook her head, making her plump cheeks shake. "This is all your doing, Adept. Word spread when you vowed that House Medeis would no longer be passive, and that we would train and study so we could protect with great ferocity." She paused. "And I think it's the applicants like this one who prove that your vision for House Medeis—your desire for a wizard House that can stand up not only to other wizards, but the other supernaturals as well—is needed."

Wizards are considered bottom feeders among magical society. Since we're humans, we're really weak compared to races like werewolves, and we are ridiculously fragile and slow compared to vampires. But I wasn't content with the excuse of our humanity anymore. When I'd stayed with Killian and the Drake Family, the vampires had shown me just how strong I could be even though I was a human. (And then they'd dropped me, but that wasn't a memory I needed to revisit.)

"Schedule a meeting with her," I said. "I can do a phone conversation first, and then she and her aunt can come visit House Medeis if that works out."

"There's no need for a phone conversation," Great Aunt Marraine said. "She's already here in Magiford. She and her aunt requested an in-person interview first thing tomorrow morning."

"Oh." I blinked, surprised at the enthusiasm.

Great Aunt Marraine patted my back. "She already looks up to you, dear. It seems to me she's going to do everything she can to join us."

"Okay. That's...great," I said slowly.

"I received a report that two Drake vampires were attacked

today in Chicago." Great Aunt Marraine spoke so quickly I couldn't get a word in. "It was the work of fae, given that a magic item went off in their faces. Thankfully, there were no fatalities—although the vampires were pretty badly injured. I couldn't get their names, sorry."

"Great Aunt Marraine." I yanked my hair free from my ponytail as I tried to cover up my frustration. "You don't have to give me these reports on the Drake Family. In fact, I have emphatically told you I *don't* want any news about them!"

Great Aunt Marraine laughed with the sly, carefree chortle of a senior citizen who knows how to manipulate her grandchildren. "You *say* you don't want to hear about it, but you can't hide your heart from me, Adept. I helped change your diapers!"

She playfully swatted at me with the clipboard.

I held in a groan. Avoiding a topic seemed to be my favorite way to avoid something that pained me, and that applied to the Drake Family.

I wracked my brain for a subject that would make my crafty great aunt drop the vampires, then paused. "Today is Tuesday…so tomorrow is Wednesday…" I let a slow but enormous smile creep across my lips. "Is everything ready for tomorrow?"

Great Aunt Marraine's smile turned devious. "Oh, yes," she said. "*Everything* is ready, as per usual."

"Fantastic." I took in a deep breath, almost purring in my joy. "I *do* look forward to our weekly trip to the Curia Cloisters. It's so important to visit the wizards responsible for governing us, and to voice our concerns as citizens."

"So very important." Great Aunt Marraine agreed.

We smirked at each other for a few moments before erupting into cackles. Wednesdays were such fun, because it brought retribution to those who backed Mason in the most painful of ways—legal ones.

CHAPTER TWO

Killian

For the second time in recent weeks, I strode through the halls of a building so overwhelmingly luxurious, it was almost obnoxious.

I sneered as I passed a chandelier studded with real diamonds. This place reminded me of Versailles in its peak—bloated in its own wealth and self-importance.

I wouldn't make the drive to Chicago and visit this luxurious abode if it didn't have something I wanted badly: a library.

Specifically, a library filled with some of the oldest and most well-recorded vampiric texts.

The yappy vampire who accompanied me as guide almost frog hopped to keep up with me. "Is there anything I could help you find, Your Eminence?" He had to be on the young side—for a vampire. He was dressed in a suit and clutched a bowler hat, but the vampires who had greeted me wore clothing that was popular during the European Renaissance.

The building was owned by an ancient Elder who rarely surfaced from his room, and hadn't left the building in decades.

His Family was one of the oldest in the Midwest, and well respected, even if they were practically leader-less these days.

While the Elder's absence politically irked me—it was a problem I'd been battling since before I became the top vampire political figure in the region—I was somewhat relieved it meant I only had to deal with his toadying Family and servants and not be plagued by wistful grumbles of centuries long past and years that were remembered with more fondness than they deserved.

It seemed to me that all too often vampire Elders forgot how recently indoor plumbing had been developed.

"Are you searching for a specific record or text?" the twitchy vampire asked as I barged into the private library.

"No." I studied the shelves. "Leave me."

"Y-yes, Your Eminence." He scurried out, seemingly relieved to be dismissed.

I turned in a slow circle, letting the graveyard-like silence of the room envelop me.

It was a dark, dreary room. There was one window, but a heavy, velvet curtain was drawn across it—needlessly so since it was close to midnight.

The lights were so dimmed it almost felt like candlelight—it even flickered annoyingly like flames—but the rest of the library was decked out with all the decoration that I'd come to expect of the place.

There were books studded with jewels, a few original art pieces painted by some of the greatest artists the world had seen, ancient, alchemical instruments, a unicorn horn, and more.

But I wasn't interested in the useless collection; I was here for the books on vampire lore.

I had my own library at Drake Hall, but it wasn't nearly so specialized on vampire history and records. I possessed a great deal of books about wizards, fae, werewolves, and other supernaturals that I frequently went up against on the Regional Committee of Magic.

I put my back to the shelf of leather-bound, hand written books that I'd studied on my previous trip, and this time chose a bookcase that had several empty golden flasks and vials decorating its shelves.

I emptied two shelves, carefully placing the ancient manuscripts on a large table, and dug in.

I skimmed through book after book, espying all kinds of legends and details about my race, but hardly anything on the topic I was searching for—how we vampires could protect humans.

Most of our power only extended to working for ourselves. We healed fast, were among the fastest supernaturals alive, and were immortal.

But there had to be records of vampire Elders taking humans under their protection. Before the 1900s vampires had occasionally intermarried with other supernaturals and humans—that was how the supernaturally gifted vampire hunters came to be born.

The only problem was it seemed not many manuscripts about our relationships with other races—specifically humans—survived.

Probably because vampires were a race not prone to caring for other supernaturals, or even humans beyond using them as blood donors.

I set a book aside—concluding it was going to be useless—and barely refrained from growling.

This is stupid. I selected another manuscript from the pile. *I should assign Rupert or Julianne to research this instead of wasting my time.*

But I read on, skimming the manuscripts as I searched for any information. The thing that drove me to come here, drove me to read.

This was a chance, after all.

If I could figure out how to protect Hazel from the fae, I could reinitiate our relationship.

Although I had come to like the sassy, strong-willed wizard, I'd chosen to turn her out of Drake Hall and cut off ties with her when Queen Nyte of the fae Night Court sent me a letter that threatened Hazel's life.

Normally I would have ignored such a pathetic attempt at manipulation, but in this case there was some truth to the threat.

Hazel wasn't a vampire. While she could sense fae magic, a bullet could take her life in an instant unlike myself or any of my underlings.

Driving her out was the best option I had at the time. I planned to renew our relationship once I finally dealt with the Night Court, but since the fight had already lasted years it occurred to me Queen Nyte might continue to drag it out, so perhaps it was in my best interest to find a way to use vampire power to protect Hazel.

Unfortunately, none of the books I'd read ever mentioned such a thing, and I wasn't desperate enough to ask any colleagues. Doing so would bait them, and reveal my weakness for the mouthy wizard.

So I kept researching.

I skimmed the last book at roughly three in the morning—I couldn't delay going any longer. I still had the drive back to Magiford with Josh and Rupert—who had accompanied me here—and there was work I needed to complete back at Drake Hall.

But I paused when I flipped to a section about blood donors.

That's what we called the humans who offered their blood for a vampire to directly imbibe from them—blood donors. In return the human was often generously paid, and usually housed and fed free of charge.

There were older, less complimentary names for blood donors that we used to use—I had been alive for some of them. But while now blood donors were seen as more of luxury employees kept at an arm's length, back then they were closer to pets, and barely made the footnotes of most records.

The chapter in this aging book and its brittle pages was mostly about the care of a blood donor and how a vampire could stay safe while drinking.

But there was a tiny subsection that caught my attention.

Extending the life of your servants...

It dusted off a few foggy memories I had of encountering blood donors who had been highly prized by their vampires.

I had even met a vampire who had declared her donor was *the one*.

I was pretty doubtful that *the one* actually existed for any vampire who wasn't fanciful or dreamy, but vampires had a history of giving special treatment to the small percentage of humans and supernaturals who became important to us.

It wasn't talked about much, but we vampires could grant a slight form of eternal youth to those we drank from—as long as we lived, anyway. It wasn't easily granted. Firstly, because we didn't want humans or other supernaturals knowing we were capable of it. Secondly, because it meant secreting chemical compounds in our spit that were only present when we drank directly from a source, and it had to be done frequently enough to keep pumping that compound into the donor's body.

But drinking from blood donors was risky. Even the most careful vampires had to follow precautions, which was probably why the practice had fallen out of favor.

It's not real protection...but perhaps it could be useful for her.

I'd never drink from Hazel. No matter how deeply the wizard had dug her way into my mind, that was one line I wasn't ever going to cross.

But perhaps Celestina or one of my other underlings could.

The idea didn't sit quite right with me, but if I didn't get things settled with the Night Court soon I would have to start worrying about Hazel dying off of old age before I could bring her back into the fold.

Humans aged so quickly and seemed to die within the blink of an eye for a vampire. I had forgotten that in the sparkle of Hazel's warm personality, and the equally warm and rich smell that followed her around.

My phone buzzed—a stark reminder of the times I lived in.

I quickly replaced the books I'd searched, sliding the manuscript that contained the section on blood donors in last.

I rested my hand on the books. "Extending her life is a big risk for a wizard I've known for barely a breath."

I crossed the room and made it all the way to the door before I looped back, plucking out the book.

I'd borrow it for a few weeks and see if I could discern anything interesting from it. The Family wouldn't mind, and it would give me time to think of alternatives.

Hazel was important to me. I'd fight fae for her and let other supernaturals speculate that I'd lost it for her.

But drink her blood?

Never.

CHAPTER THREE

Hazel

The only reason my arms weren't shaking as I carried a reusable grocery bag filled with reams of paper was because I had done some weightlifting during my time with the Drake Family. (If Gavino, my trainer, saw me now he'd be so proud. Maybe. If Killian would let him be.)

I led Great Aunt Marraine through the maze-like hallways of the Curia Cloisters—which was a bit like a safe haven, meeting place, and town hall for the supernatural community rolled into one building. It was beautiful—the vampires and fae were pretty loaded with cash, so there was no way they were going to let a building they had to spend a significant portion of time in be anything less than gorgeous. But it was almost domineering in its austere beauty with cold tiled floors, white stone columns veined with what looked like gold, wood paneled walls, and statues and paintings of significant heroes to our society from ages past.

We made our way to the least ornamented section of the building—the home to us little guys in the savage pecking order that was our society—the wizard offices.

Since my arms were full I kicked the door open with zero regrets, even after the door hit the plaster office wall with a crack.

Three secretaries—two women and a man who was just a bit older than me—peered over the top of their horseshoe-shaped desk, paling when they saw me.

"Oh, no." The secretary who looked perfectly dressed in a black pencil skirt with an appropriately placid green blouse threw off her glasses and pressed her palms into her eyes. "I forgot it was Wednesday!"

"It's not me," said the rosy-cheeked secretary who somewhat resembled Mrs. Claus. "I took care of her last time. Bobby, you're up." Spry despite her elderly appearance, Mrs. Claus kicked "Bobby's" chair, making him wobble.

The young man looked like he was being sent to prison as he sank deeper in his chair. "Good morning, Adept Medeis."

I flashed all three secretaries my biggest smile. "Good morning! How are you three today?"

"Quite well, until now," the perfect secretary grumbled.

I set my grocery bag down and rested my hands on the edge of their desk. "Understandably. Can you tell me, has the council agreed to consider creating a law to punish other wizards for meddling in House inheritance?" I asked.

When Mason went after me, he had the backing of several Houses that were *supposedly* House Medeis allies. His friends did their best to track me down and stop me, but thankfully I found safety before they caught up. But once it became obvious they couldn't pick me off or force me to hand the House over to Mason, the conniving wizards resolved to get Medeis through sheer social pressure, and banded more Houses together to formally approve Mason as the Adept of House Medeis.

It shouldn't have been possible. House inheritance was a private matter—if the wrong person inherited the House, the building would flip out, and there would be some pretty severe repercussions.

And yet! Strictly speaking, while the other Houses—namely the Telliers and Rothchilds—had broken laws in their attempts to kill me, there weren't any laws against backing someone besides the Heir and attempting a coup of another House. (Mostly because no one had previously been STUPID enough to try it!)

The Telliers and Rothchilds had gotten spanked for their involvement with Mason. They were banned from the Wizard Council—the subcommittee that listened to all wizard issues, complaints, and requests—and they had lost a lot of ranks and been fined pretty heftily.

But while I would have preferred to make them miserable, what I really wanted was to get a law passed to make sure something like this couldn't happen again. And based on how uncooperative the Wizard Council was acting with putting such a law together, I was afraid they had plans for other Houses.

Magic was dying. Slowly, our society was being drained of our magic and dying out. It was why we came out to humans—because if we didn't do something fast, we were going to disappear altogether. (Not that regular humans knew that. It would give them a dangerous upper hand.)

But since magic was dying, our society was starting to show cracks in it. Mason was allowed to keep pushing because when he first tried to kill me, I had almost no magic—a dangerous thing for an Adept of a House.

There was no telling what else they'd allow if they felt it might expand our power as wizards or give us a bit more time before magic left our bloodlines entirely.

I, however, didn't care about any of that.

What Mason did was wrong. What the Wizard Subcommittee and my so-called allies had helped him do was *wrong*. And I was going to make sure it couldn't happen again.

Besides, what was the point of grasping for power and maybe surviving an extra generation if we had to ruin lives and harm people in the process?

Bobby cleared his throat. "You are referring to your request that other Houses be banned from involving themselves in House inheritance, yes?"

"Yes," I said with the patience and smile of a thousand angels.

He gulped. "I regret to say...you see, the Wizard Council has been very busy...what I mean is..." Bobby stared helplessly at me.

"They still won't agree to even look into such a law, will they?" I asked.

Bobby mutely shook his head.

Great Aunt Marraine patted my shoulder. "You'll win them over, Adept. Or they'll eventually give up when they realize resistance is futile."

Mrs. Claus looked alarmed as Great Aunt Marraine laughed.

I tapped my fingers on the desk. "It's fine! I have something for you, in that case." I crouched down and began pulling stacks of paper out of my cloth bag.

"They've discussed it, you know." Bobby stared at the growing stacks of paper with dread. "Adept Luna and Adept Bakersfield both pushed to at least draw up a draft of such a law."

I set another stack of papers on the desk. "But they were outvoted?"

"Yes," he glumly said.

"I figured as much—it's why I came prepared. These are all for the council members." I separated packets of papers that were so thick they had to be clipped, not stapled. "They are neatly organized for review. These complaints come from Senior Wizard Ed Clark, and Franco Clark regarding the treatment they received under Mason and House Tellier and House Rothchild. They've filled out the necessary forms and have included essays."

Bobby looked the forms over, then squinted up at me. "You have a document saved with all of this, don't you?"

"Bobby!" the perfect secretary hissed.

Great Aunt Marraine made a tisking noise. "Such a foolish boy."

Bobby turned to his coworkers. "But these forms always look almost identical! And the essays are almost exact copies!"

"The keyword is *almost*." I leaned over the desk, subtly invading his territory. "Franco and Ed have added a few of their own *special* touches to their complaints. And if the Wizard Council members don't address those specifics when they write up their reviews, I will drag this to the Regional Committee of Magic."

Behind me, Great Aunt Marraine chortled.

Bobby gulped loudly.

At least his reaction proved my method of payback was hitting them all in a sore spot.

Since the Wizard Council refused to do anything about House inheritance, I was slowly doling out complaints from myself and the members of House Medeis. I had written up the original form and essay and, as I had said, everyone went through and made a few minor changes.

This was the most painful—*legal*—method I could think of. The staff below the Wizard Council had to process the paperwork—which involved scanning, summarizing, notarizing, and placing it in public places. Meanwhile, all the wizards on the subcommittee had to read the complaints and write up personal reviews.

And I did this *every week*. Which meant week in and week out, they were reading the same story and forms over and over and over again.

Thankfully, this was the Curia Cloisters I was dealing with. I'm pretty sure if I'd been dealing with a human government, they would have thrown me out by now. But since there isn't a law against it, the Wizard Council couldn't stop me from doing it.

Bobby glumly started collecting up the thick files. "I'll send these to the members of the Wizard Council immediately, Adept Medeis."

"Thank you!" I said in a sing-song voice.

"Adept Medeis." Perfect Secretary cleared her throat. "While you are here, I have some official offers of an alliance."

"Oh goodie!" Great Aunt Marraine rubbed her hands together and shuffled over to the secretary, who was retrieving a few pieces of thick, creamy paper from a mailbox slot on the back wall.

Since House Medeis had grown so much and had risen so high through the ranks, we now had an official mailbox at the Curia Cloisters. Anyone who wanted to offer an alliance to us had to make the offer through the Cloisters. The official reason was to make sure the bigger Houses couldn't bully the smaller ones, but I'd seen how spectacularly that had failed. In reality I think it was just because the Wizard Council was nosy, and even if the members were rotated on a yearly basis you can bet they'd do everything in their power to try to make things easier on their own Houses.

"Here." Perfect Secretary passed the thick sheets of paper over. All of them had wax seals pressed into the bottom of the paper, stamped with the House's coat of arms.

Great Aunt Marraine fixed her glasses, then snorted. "Rothchild? They *dare* to ask us for an alliance? Hah!" She ripped the offer into thin shreds, then pulled out an envelope from her massive hand bag and put the ripped paper in the envelope. "We'll have to stop at a post box on our way home, Adept." She slapped a stamp on the envelope and scrawled out the address of House Rothchild.

I rubbed the back of my neck and smiled. "Sure! Sounds great to me!"

House Rothchild was forever on my black list for helping Mason, so being petty like this was a huge morale boost. (Plus, I figured it wasn't as awful as what I *wanted* to do, which was have a good slug out with their traitorous Adept, who supposedly had once been a friend of my parents!)

"Let's see...who else? House Nells, House Fischer—no, nope." Great Aunt Marraine casually tossed the offers aside.

I folded up my cloth bag, only half listening as she continued. "House Schnider, House Luna..."

"Wait, House Luna?" I asked.

Great Aunt Marraine retrieved the paper she had cast aside. "It seems so, yes. It's an official offer, but since Adept Luna is currently serving on the Wizard Council she requests that the alliance not start until January of next year, when her term ends."

Adept Luna supported my request to make some laws about House inheritance, and when I had gone before the Wizard Council to request that they officially name me as Adept—since I had been the Heir, even though I'd been turned out of the House by Mason—she was one of four wizards who had sided with me.

"Let's accept that one."

"Splendid!" Great Aunt Marraine swiped the offer. She pulled a manila filing folder from her purse and slipped the offer in it before returning her attention to the other offers, collecting them in a pile. She gave Mrs. Claus and Perfect Secretary a beaming smile. "As for all of these scallywags, you can tell them to go to—"

"Adept Medeis!"

Faintly recognizing the voice, I turned around. "Elite Bellus, good morning!"

Whispered murmurs of "Elite Bellus!" wafted through the office as the staffers stood and smiled at the Elite.

The Elite was the most powerful wizard in our region. He served on the Regional Committee of Magic, and frequently communicated with the Wizard Council—although he was officially banned from taking part in local politics as a check to his power, which is why he had been unable to help me.

He was a clean-cut man with a well-groomed goatee and silvery hair that he slicked back. Both his appearance and his clothes—navy blue slacks and a black sweater vest—gave him a sort of kind, professor-ish appearance, but really he had the mind of a steel trap and was as sharp as they come, even though he was kind, too.

"I thought I could catch you in here about now. Care to join me for a cup of coffee in my office?" the Elite asked.

I glanced at Great Aunt Marraine, who dipped her head to me. "Go ahead, Adept. I'll take care of everything here."

"Thank you." I gave her a quick side hug, barely escaping when she reached for my ear.

She—and probably every staff member present—was likely wondering how I came to be on speaking terms with the Elite.

Granted, I had spoken to him a lot after I got House Medeis back as I tried to unravel everything Mason had done. But that investigation had closed a month ago.

I waited until we were in the hallway—the door closed behind us—before I made my guess. "You have something you want to ask me about Killian Drake, don't you?" I wryly asked.

Elite Bellus smiled at me. "No, of course not! Well, perhaps indirectly."

When I stared at him he winked and beckoned me down the hallway.

To illustrate his separation from the Wizard Council, Elite Bellus had his own private offices with a much smaller staff—a secretary, two guards, and at least one aide were always floating through the front rooms.

When we entered, Elite Bellus took a tray that held two steaming mugs of coffee from his secretary, then led the way through a maze of desks and tables to his office.

Elite Bellus's office had a big window with a spectacular view of the lake that elbowed its way through Magiford. The water was dark, but still beautiful as the last of the red, yellow, and orange leaves fell off tall trees.

I plopped down in the overstuffed, plaid chair positioned in front of his massive desk—which was barely visible thanks to the stacks and stacks of paperwork he had scattered around the room.

"Still bearding the Wizard's Council, are you?" Elite Bellus offered me a tiny pitcher of cream.

"I'm not going to let them relax until they get an inheritance law on the table for discussion."

"And the more they resist?"

I grinned. "The more paperwork they're going to find waiting on their desks. So far we've only been lodging complaints about *Mason*. We can still register complaints on all the Houses that actively worked against me."

Elite Bellus laughed heartily. "I like your style. It's legal, but you're going to push until you force their hand—or drive them insane. Well done."

"Thank you. So. What did you want to discuss?"

Elite Bellus took a sip of his coffee, then slapped a folded piece of paper on top of the stack of folders closest to me. "I'd like to invite you to this."

I set my coffee aside and picked up the paper, unfolding it so I could see it was an invitation to an event. "A meeting?" I asked, reading the top line.

"Yes. A mixed group of magical races is giving a small presentation. Everyone from the Regional Committee will be there, and we were each allotted a number of extra invitations to give to the movers and shakers of our community. I'm choosing House Medeis as one of my invitees." Elite Bellus smoothed his goatee and offered me a sweet smile.

I glanced back at the invitation. "What's the presentation about?"

"An inter-species police force and local government. The group is from South Dakota, where magical races of any sort have had to pool resources to survive. They claim it has helped reduce fights, increase morale, their community has grown as a result—all the usual claims." He waved his hand, dismissing the achievement.

"You don't believe that it's beneficial?"

"Quite the contrary," Elite Bellus said. "I believe it's very beneficial—for those who can manage it. But every place I've seen it work has been small and overwhelmed. Everyone was forced together out of sheer necessity. It won't work here in the Midwest—or the majority of regions—because we don't have those outside forces at work. It's just a pretty dream for us. But Pre-Dominant Harka made some noise about it and insisted we fly them out to speak to us when she heard about them."

I stared at the invitation, trying to piece everything together. Why was he inviting me if he didn't think the talk would be useful? I mentally reviewed his description of the meeting, then sighed. "You want me to come because Killian is going to be there."

Elite Bellus gave me two thumbs up. "That's how your House was able to fly up the ranking charts—you're sharp!"

"What can you possibly gain by dragging me there?" I asked. "I already told you we didn't part on good terms."

Actually, we'd parted on terrible terms. Killian—being manipulative and untrusting—decided the best way to protect me from his Family's war with the fae Night Court was to unceremoniously kick me out. I figured out what he was doing, but it didn't matter. I didn't put up with being treated like that—even if it was because he was doing it for my good. *Especially* because he thought he was doing it for my good.

Killian had the habit of being a manipulative jerk, and I wasn't going to let him yank me around on a chain and make all my life decisions for me. Ever since I got House Medeis back I'd seen a vampire lingering on my street at least once every other day, and whenever possible I chased them off. I didn't want Killian Drake finding anything out about me.

"Even if you're mad at him, the fact is Killian Drake took you under his protection. Though it was a short amount of time, he doesn't extend his protection to just anyone—I've seen him watch vampires get arrested in front of him, and he doesn't even twitch. Somewhere in there, he cares for you. The way he paraded you around the Summer's End Ball is proof—he wouldn't lightly introduce you to society in such a way if he didn't intend to keep the connection."

I folded one leg over the other and wiggled my foot. "That's unexpectedly romantic of you, Elite Bellus."

"Hardly—I'm too logical to afford myself romantic nonsense where Killian Drake is concerned," he dryly said.

"But you still haven't said what you hope to achieve."

"Ah, yes." He brandished a finger in the air. "Given the topic, I suspect seeing you might throw him for a loop."

"And you want him thrown for a loop?"

"Indeed." Elite Bellus leaned back in his chair and picked up his coffee, taking a slow sip. "He's been an absolute bear since you left. If he goes to that meeting, he's going to reject everything they say for the sheer principle of it."

"Why would that matter?" I asked. "You just said you didn't think anything they talked about would work here."

"You are right. We'll never have the mixed subcommittees, but they have a few practices I'd *like* to consider. Big changes aren't possible, but if we start small, we might be able to push enough to see if we could benefit."

"If you want to change things," I grumbled, "you could start by suggesting inheritance laws."

Elite Bellus laughed hard enough to make his shoulders twinge. "You are right. That is something we wizards should look into. But I'm afraid I'm more concerned about our society in general, as it stands."

"Fine." I tapped the invitation on my leg. "You want me to come so you can hopefully throw Killian off, and then he won't reject everything the speakers talk about. I'll do it as long as it works into my schedule."

"Thank you, I'll be indebted to you," Elite Bellus said.

I smiled. "It will be interesting to hear the discussion. But why are you looking to change things here? Are you concerned with where it looks like we're headed?"

"Yes." Elite Bellus took another sip of his coffee—more out of habit than real desire, it seemed to me. "If we don't change our course things are going to get...messy. Besides, we already know what we're currently doing isn't working. Magic is still dying."

I narrowed my eyes. "You think the death of magic can be *stopped*? Everyone's been trying to fix it for years, and nothing has worked."

"I think its failure can be slowed," Elite Bellus corrected me. "I don't know if it will ever stop leaking out of our world—not since we let the elves die out. But it's dying at a faster rate than it was fifty years ago. If we can stabilize it, it will buy us more time."

I slowly nodded. "I see."

"Thank you for coming."

I picked up my cup of coffee and took a sip—holy cow did the Elite like a dark and bitter blend. I dumped enough cream in it to turn it into a latte. "Don't hold your breath—Killian might not react at all."

"Maybe, but I'd rather stack the deck in my favor."

I glanced at the invitation again. "Am I allowed to bring anyone from my House?"

"Of course! As Adept you should bring at least a few of your people. Now, why don't you tell me what kind of inheritance law *you* would propose?"

I took another sip of my coffee, then set it aside as I leaned forward. "I'm so glad you asked..."

———

Two nights later, I tugged my scarf tighter around my neck and leaned up against the House. "Block off the driveway gate and move the front rosebushes so they butt up against the front fence."

A swirl of magic, and the House complied, feeding off my abilities as it shut the driveway gate and reinforced it with boulders the size of laundry baskets. When it moved the rosebushes it almost looked like an animal was burrowing across the front yard. But even though the prickly bushes had lost their leaves and buds for the year, the branches would still make anyone think twice about trying to shimmy over the tall fence, or stick their arms through the gaps in the iron spokes.

"Good." I shuffled back a tiny step so my back bumped against the House's cold, stone covered exterior wall. "Now lock down the weapons and shift them to the basement."

From my perch on the third-floor patio, I had the perfect view of the locked, waterproofed chests of our practice weapons getting swallowed up by the ground.

The House pushed magic through me—making heat swirl in my wizard mark. The House trundled the chests underground, burping them out in the basement.

I felt a little lightheaded—which was usually a sign I was starting to hit my limits. I sat down on a window ledge and patted the House. "Excellent. Give me a few minutes, and we'll practice some more."

I picked up the packet of papers I'd brought outside with me for my down time and tried to turn a page, but it was hard to do with my gloved fingers.

If Great Aunt Marraine knew I was working she'd be furious, and unfortunately I was too short to be out of ear-yanking range. But I needed to go over these papers, and it was the perfect thing to do when I needed to take a break from practicing defensive maneuvers with House Medeis.

Since I was Adept, House Medeis and I could pull and push magic between us. It really upped my abilities—while I was on our property anyway—but it also took a lot of energy. I was trying to accustom myself to it and see if I could improve my stamina. It seemed like it was working—though it also might just be that the

House and I were starting to get the feel for each other and were working better together.

I squinted and held my packet up, trying to get some of the light that streamed through the window directly behind me.

House Medeis helpfully turned on a light above my head so I could see what I was reading—the monthly budget for November. (I gotta say, there was a lot more math to being an Adept than I ever thought.)

I stretched my legs out in front of me, resting my feet against one of the spokes of the tiny patio wrought-iron fence. A shadow passed over my papers as someone entered the empty room behind me.

Momoko stuck her head through the patio doorway. "Found a new spot to practice in, didya?"

Felix poked his head out just above hers. "Great Aunt Marraine is looking for you."

I grinned. "Why do you think I went through the trouble of finding a new spot?"

Felix and Momoko joined me on the patio—which was pretty small, so we were squashed together so we could all fit. I didn't mind the close quarters—I grew up with Felix and Momoko, and we'd been best friends since forever.

That's why it was pretty obvious the two of them were psyching themselves up to ask me something—I knew all their tells. Felix was leaning against the door and looking innocent—a sure sign he was up to something—while Momoko was staring at her hands and chewing on her lower lip.

"What is it?" I asked.

The two exchanged looks.

I was a little irritated that they had something they'd obviously discussed separately—we used to share *everything*—so I might have laced my voice with more sarcasm than necessary. "What, did you two finally confess your unending love for each other?"

Momoko gagged. "What? No! Ew! Gross."

Felix grimaced as if the idea physically pained him. "I stopped seeing *either* of you as females years ago."

"Really?" Momoko asked. "That's funny, because you seem a lot like a girl friend to me."

"You—" Felix forcefully cut himself off. He shut his eyes and exhaled loudly, then glared at Momoko. "That's not important. We have something we want to discuss. *Don't we*, Momoko?"

Momoko pushed some of her black hair over her shoulder, then pressed her hands together as she looked thoughtful. "Yes, that's right. Hazel...we're concerned."

"What, is this an intervention?" I laughed.

Neither of them joined me.

"When you first got the House back I know there was a ton of work you had to catch up on," Felix said. "But it's been weeks. You shouldn't have to work every second of the day anymore."

"I don't do work every second," I argued. "I eat and hang out with everyone!"

"You do. You make sure you talk to everyone in the House so no one feels left out, and you've worked hard to welcome the new wizards. But." Momoko pressed her steepled fingers against her chin. "The second no one is bothering you, you run off and do more work. It's like you're scared of being left alone with your thoughts."

"There's a lot of work that still has to be done." I set the monthly budget down again—having it sitting on my lap wasn't going to help my argument. "And I'll admit some of it is self-inflicted—like torturing the Wizard Council—but I want some clear-cut laws in place about House inheritance so this doesn't happen again."

Felix pressed his lips into a thin line, his angelic looks making him appear beautifully determined. "Let me rephrase what Momoko said. We know you're not acting like a crazed workaholic because you feel like you have to get everything done, but because you're trying to avoid thinking about Killian and the Drake Family."

Dratted childhood friends—I'd forgotten that *they* could see all of *my* tells, too! "I am *not* trying to avoid thinking about them." I sounded so fake, canned cheese seemed more genuine.

"Avoidance is your primary coping technique," Momoko said. "You did it all the time as a kid, and I know you did it some with your parents. You would have avoided Mason if he'd only gone after you, but since he involved all of us he riled up your endless honor and virtue so you were going to face him sooner or later."

I forcibly kept my expression blank—Momoko almost sounded like Killian. His favorite pet name for me was the Virtuous Idiot. *Don't think of Killian.*

"There—right now!" Felix crowded Momoko so he could poke my cheek. "You avoided thinking of the Drake vampires right then!"

"I was not—"

"There's a muscle under your eye that twitches just a little bit." Momoko joined Felix in poking me. "Which proves our point. Hazel, you've got to let yourself come to terms with the Drakes."

"There's nothing to come to terms with," I stiffly said. "Killian drew a line. I'm choosing to honor it."

"Oh, yeah, he drew a line alright. That's why we've got vampires loitering on our street!" Felix pointed to the shadowy figure standing on the street corner.

CHAPTER FOUR

Hazel

Since I had human eyes I couldn't tell which Drake vampire it was. I suspected it was Julianne—she was sent to watch us most frequently—but I hadn't paid much attention because I figured I'd wait to shoo her away until I finished my practice session with the House.

"You can't live like this forever," Momoko said. "You'll die of overworking yourself. You either need to forgive him, or let the Drakes go entirely."

"I'm not totally avoiding him, or I wouldn't be going to the meeting Elite Bellus invited me to," I pointed out.

"Or you're just shifty enough to know this will put the Elite in your debt, and you're going to use that to push for an inheritance law, which is really important to you," Felix said dryly.

"You two are horrible," I complained.

"We're concerned," Momoko corrected. "And besides Great Aunt Marraine and us, I don't think there's anyone in the House that can confront you. Even our parents feel like you're untouchable and some kind of perfect Adept since you freed us. Everyone loves you—they *adore* you. But they don't feel like it's their place to offer help."

"We don't care," Felix added. "Because we know you ate crayons in elementary school."

"That was an off year for me!"

Momoko grabbed my hand and squeezed it. "Just think about it. We're not saying you should call up Killian—we *don't* want you to call him up, actually."

"He scares the magic straight out of me," Felix grumbled.

"Just do whatever you have to do so you can live and be happy again," Momoko said.

I stared out at the front lawn. I couldn't really reply because they were right. I didn't like thinking about the Drake vampires and the mix of emotions it revived. I was still angry Killian felt he couldn't trust me, and his underlings' utter rejection of me after he'd sent me off had been a slug to my gut. I hadn't thought they'd cut me out so easily—particularly Josh and Celestina. We'd had so much fun together...

But I didn't want to think about it just then, so I did what I do best and changed the topic. "Maybe you're right, but regardless of how I felt about Killian, I'd still be out here doing maneuvers with the House."

"Yeah, everyone knows you want to turn this place into a fortress," Felix said. "Do you think one of the other wizard Houses will retaliate, or something? I mean, Mason's dead. There's not much of a point."

"It's not the wizards I'm afraid of," I said grimly. "It's the Night Court."

Whatever emotion it was that had Momoko puffed up, collapsed. She hunched her shoulders and sank in on herself. "You think they'll attack us? But Felix is right, Mason is dead. And fae aren't known for their unending loyalty—just the opposite, really."

"They hadn't been Mason's allies for very long, either," Felix added.

"Yeah, but there's still a chance they might come after me because of my association with Killian." I flexed my hands and resisted pulling on my magic, liking the hot, electrical burst of energy magic always brought along for the ride. "I met the Night Court Queen and her consort, and let's just say I wasn't particularly respectful to either of them. I want to be prepared."

Momoko cocked her head. "That's why you keep practicing with the House?"

"I should be practicing with House Medeis regardless. It's important to—"

"*Hazel*," Felix said.

I sighed. "Yeah. The fae might become a problem. I want to be ready if that happens."

We sat in silence, shivering in our jackets from the cold night air as the wind scattered some of the dead leaves on the lawn.

"Well." Momoko stuffed her hands in the pockets of her coat. "Now I feel like a jerk."

"She's still avoiding the Drakes," Felix drawled. "She just had a ready excuse for this particular instance."

"I *told* you we should have cornered her at breakfast," Momoko said.

"You only suggested that because you thought you'd be able to eat extra bacon since we figured this was going to be a long conversation."

Momoko sniffed and shoved her nose high in the air. "You never know, Hazel might have dropped her guard if she got to eat a lot of bacon, too!"

Felix bumped Momoko, but peered over her head so he could meet my gaze. "Look, we get it, Hazel. Your concern about the fae is probably a smart idea. We'll do anything you want to help you—and don't try to shoulder it all as your duty. We belong to House Medeis, too. It's our duty as well."

"But," Momoko held a finger up. "*Please* consider what we said, and see if you can sort your feelings out about the Drakes. We don't want you to keep going like this."

I tipped backwards, resting my shoulders against the glass pane of the window. "Fine," I agreed. "I'll think about it." *Eventually*.

The truth was, I didn't know exactly how I felt about everything. Right after I Ascended, I would have said I was ready to cut ties forever. But as much as I *hated* it, there was something reassuring about seeing the vampires lingering around our street.

I had to face Mason alone—or everyone would have doubted I ruled House Medeis by myself. But I was sick of our House being the only one pushing for change. I was tired of fighting alone.

Still. That didn't mean I was willing to renew my friendship with Killian. Oh heck no. Right now, I mostly wanted to strangle him with his stupid, expensive tie made to match one of his stupid, expensive suits. His actions still made me grind my teeth, and I didn't think I'd *ever* be able to look at Celestina and Josh the same again.

I let out a puff of air that turned into a cloud of mist in the chilly fall night. "Do you guys wanna watch me go tell a vampire to scram?" I asked.

"Yes!" Momoko popped to her feet. "It's always *hilarious*. You're so tiny, and an angry squeak from you sends those big, *armed*, deadly vampires running!"

"It's always a great sight for House Medeis's morale," Felix added. He struggled to open the door and slide through without bumping into Momoko. "Why do they leave? Franco said when he went with you once they bowed to you a little bit and called you Miss Hazel."

"Who knows?" I evasively said. I hid my face—and my tells, dang you childhood friends—by stooping over to pick up the abandoned monthly budget before I joined them inside.

I wasn't about to tell them that after my magic was unsealed,

Celestina and Josh pitted me against the other Drake vampires in *daily* battles, and that the title and bow were probably hangers-on from when I beat them. (Most of them, anyway. I thankfully never had to face Celestina or Josh.)

"Whatever. Vampires are weird," Momoko grunted.

"They are," I confirmed. "So let's go shoo off whatever spy Killian has planted outside."

"As you command, Adept!"

I groaned. "Seriously, you guys really are the worst!"

"We love you too, Adept!"

I PLOPPED down in the uncomfortable wooden chair, rocking it slightly, and rested my arms on the polished table.

"I wish they'd serve coffee at functions like this." Franco groaned and rubbed his eyes. "I am dying."

"It was a lot of information to take in." I peered at the notebook I'd taken a few notes in.

The group from South Dakota had already given a presentation—which had lasted three hours, not including the break we got at the halfway mark. They were finished now. The wizard Elite, the werewolf Pre-Dominant, the vampire Eminence AKA Killian, and the Winter Queen—who was acting as the fae representative on the Regional Committee of Magic starting in November—were supposed to publicly discuss the talk for a bit and give some closing remarks, but we still had five minutes left of our second break.

I glanced down my table. Everyone I had brought—Felix, Momoko, Franco, Leslie, Mr. Baree, and Mrs. Yamada—was already back from the bathrooms and seated in the wobbly chairs.

"I would have thought they'd get more comfortable chairs for this room." Felix scowled as he wiggled in his seat.

"Maybe the point is that they are uncomfortable, so you don't fall asleep," Leslie said.

The meeting was held in the Regional Committee Chamber—the largest room in the Curia Cloisters. Like the assembly hall, it was filled with seemingly endless tables and chairs, though pressed at the front of the room was a raised dais that held a big, grand table and cushy chairs Felix would love. When in session, that was where the Regional Committee of Magic was seated. All the other seats were set up for their staff, and for the observers. (They drew quite the crowd—though there were some politics mixed into that as I think every leader made sure a good show of their people came, for intimidation or something stupid.)

The chamber also had a second story for observational purposes, which was filled with all the werewolf representatives—who had really shown up tonight. Probably because Pre-Dominant Harka was so interested in this. Based on the amount of yawning I saw up there, it didn't seem like all the shifters shared her enthusiasm.

"Are we going to stay for the entire discussion portion of the meeting?" Momoko asked.

"I planned to," I said. "What time is it?"

Mrs. Yamada—Momoko's mother—checked her phone. "Nearly seven. I'm surprised the meeting lasted as long as it did, given that they started late in the afternoon."

"I imagine they hoped more vampires would show." Against my will, my gaze crept in Killian's direction.

He—and his retinue—were the only vampires present. Given that there weren't any younger vampires in attendance from the other Families, I was pretty sure this was a political statement on his end, and not a case of the vampire Elders being disinterested with life and society in general as they were prone to do. (Although he had only a handful of Drake vampires present.)

I was pretty sure the Elite's hope that my presence would rattle him was a huge failure.

Killian hadn't looked my way since I entered the room. And he didn't appear any different. His skin was always pale—though instead of the more ghostly shade of some of his cohorts, his skin was more of a snow-white. His eyes appeared black instead of the regular vampire red from this distance, and his hair was artfully mussed so he resembled a model in his designer suit, but that's how he always looked. The only difference I could see was that he had a five o'clock shadow, which was pretty unusual for him. I don't think I'd ever seen him any way besides clean shaven. But it's not like it made him look haggard—if anything he looked more model-like than usual.

Maybe I overestimated my own importance and he really did kick me out because he had no use for me...but he still could have had me sense when fae magic was used around him. That would have been dead useful in a fight with the Night Court.

"Good evening, Adept Medeis!" The Elite sauntered up to my table and leaned against it. "And greetings to those of the honorable House Medeis."

Even Felix looked cowed as he stared up, slightly open mouthed, at Elite Bellus.

"Good Evening, Elite Bellus," Mrs. Yamada said.

"Thank you for being my guests this evening!" He peered up and down the table at my escorts. "I'm glad you could make it."

"It's our honor," Franco said. He showed no sign of all the passionate statements he'd made on the way here, talking about how all of them were coming just because they were paranoid about me leaving without at least a couple of them to guard my back, and lecturing me for letting Elite Bellus use me to try to manipulate Killian. (Who, Franco had spent a portion of his lecture pointing out, it was impossible to out manipulate, so why was Elite Bellus even bothering to try?)

"What did you think of the talk?" Elite Bellus clasped his hands behind his back as he studied me.

"It was very interesting," I said. "It's wonderful to hear how communities have been able to successfully pull together."

Elite Bellus nodded, and kept staring.

I shifted in my chair; my butt was starting to ache from all the sitting. "I don't know that I picked up on anything you could immediately apply to Magiford," I cautiously continued—I didn't want to offend him, or the South Dakota crew. "But I did wonder if one or two of the smaller cities that are mostly occupied by those of us from the magical community could enact some of their practices—like a joint police force."

Elite Bellus smoothed his goatee. "I wondered as well. You know..." he trailed off and frowned.

I tilted my head, wondering why he stopped, when I tasted the distinct, floral-bathwater taste that active fae magic always gave off, and a second, stronger flavor of magic that felt old and wild. "Do you feel—"

The Curia Cloisters shook as though an explosion had rocked them at their very core.

I leaped to my feet, throwing my magic-made shield up in record time so it blocked both myself and Elite Bellus. The air around me hummed as the six House Medeis wizards copied me, creating their own shields. They moved around so we stood in a circle, all sides guarded.

Elite Bellus blinked slowly. "...What?"

"Other side of the room," Mr. Baree barked.

I swiveled my gaze just in time to watch Consort Ira of the Night Court raise a staff studded with a crystal and point it at Killian.

Purple magic swirled around the staff's largest crystal, then shot across the room at Killian.

He ducked, avoiding the magical blast, which punched a hole through the drywall of the far wall.

"Really? They're going to fight it out in the *Curia Cloisters?*" Felix snarled.

"Oh dear," Elite Bellus said. He sounded only mildly concerned as he watched the fae with a cocked head.

The crowd seemed spooked, but only those closest to where the Drake Family was seated bothered to scurry away.

Until the consort tried it again, this time narrowly missing a vampire standing at the back of the room.

Everyone lost it.

(Well, everyone except Celestina. She unholstered her firearm and took a shot at the consort—although she missed.)

Someone screamed, and tables and chairs were overturned as everyone ran for the door. Up in the second floor the werewolves were more orderly about leaving. They clustered around the Pre-Dominant, and were slowly backing out, their teeth showing as a few of them transformed into their giant wolf forms for good measure.

I turned to my people, our shields glowing bright blue as everyone streamed past us. "We have to get the Elite out of here."

Franco grimly set his shoulders. "Understood."

Momoko squinted at the direction of the fighting night fae and Drake vampires, but it was too bright from the magic to see much. "It seems like they aren't involving outsiders."

"I don't believe that," Felix snarled. "Why else would the Night Court attack them in the middle of a public forum in a building that's a neutral zone?"

"We should go out the side exit," Mrs. Yamada tipped her head, pointing to an unassuming side door. "The main doors are swamped."

"Right," I agreed. "Let's do it—moon formation, Leslie and Mr. Baree in escort mode."

My family snapped into position, the weeks of drilling making our movements precise and clean.

Together we created a half circle, and Leslie and Mr. Baree

moved to our unprotected side, ready to bodily push anything out of our way and open the doors.

"This way, please, Elite Bellus," I said.

Mr. Baree set a hand on the Elite's elbow and guided him away, making my request more of a command, but the Elite didn't seem to mind.

"Very well!" Elite Bellus slid two fingers into his mouth, producing three shrill whistles that were almost eclipsed by the hungry roar of fae magic smashing through a solid oak table.

We made our way to the side door in an ungraceful shuffle. Even with Leslie and Mr. Baree moving things for us, we had to navigate the aisles, and once a terrified fae—Day Court, if her sunshine blond hair was anything to go by—in a hurry to escape smacked into my shield with such force she actually ricocheted off it and hit the ground.

"What kind of magic are you using?" Elite Bellus mildly asked when we hit one of the main aisles and were finally able to pick up our pace.

"This side of the room is clear," Leslie shouted, ignoring the question. "Everyone's run to the main doors."

I glanced over my shoulder and grimaced.

Like terrified sheep, the crowd had flocked to the main double doors that had remained open, rather than using one of the four side doors, like we were.

We reached the door and Leslie opened it then stepped to the side as Mr. Baree thrust out his hand—encased with fire—and slid into the hall.

"Clear," he shouted.

We started to slip through the door, Mrs. Yamada going first, shifting so she could keep her shield up. Leslie followed her, and I frowned at the stampede at the main doors.

"Momoko," I called. "Can you open the two side doors over there?" I pointed to the plain wooden doors just a few feet away from the crowded entryway, where people were literally trampling one another to get out.

Momoko narrowed her eyes. Her wizard mark—a stark tattoo of spikes and bold lines—stuck out on her pale skin and eased up her forehead and down her cheek, stopping just at her jawline.

Momoko was one of my best precision wizards. She was great at using small amounts of magic for delicate tasks, and since she started practicing in the evenings with me, I'd had her target marks that were smaller and farther away.

Magic buzzed, and two gusts of wind popped the side doors open.

Momoko grinned. "Got it!"

I found I could breathe a bit easier as I saw some wizards peel off from the mob to run through the doors, a few fae scuttling behind them.

"Good. Let's go!"

Franco, Felix, and I were the last out of the chamber, backing into the hall so we could keep our eyes on the battle.

That was how I caught sight of the magic circle swirling on the ground beneath Killian and the five vampires that accompanied him.

Given its scale, I had a hunch it was the first spell we felt go off.

I shifted my eyes to Celestina, who was crouched next to Killian and shouting to Rupert.

Rupert, a sour-faced, red-haired vampire I had a bit of a history with, tried to step past the boundaries of the magic circle, and failed.

They were trapped.

A bitter taste filled my mouth, but I forced myself to step into the hall, tearing my gaze away from the fight as two Night Court fae threw crystal vials that shattered on impact and released noxious orange fumes.

In the hallway, my family had reorganized themselves into our half-circle formation, curling protectively around Elite Bellus.

"We need to travel in the opposite direction to everyone else," I said. "It'll be the fastest route outside."

"This'll be the best way." Mr. Baree pointed down the hallway—which was audibly quieter than the other direction, where everyone was shouting and screaming.

"Wall formation—Mr. Baree and Leslie combat ready," I ordered.

Everyone shifted around me, creating a solid wall with our shields at our backs so no one could sneak up on us.

I tugged on the magic in the air and summoned lightning to my hands. It crackled up my arms and shed sparks at my fingernails. Since I was the only one capable of using a lot of magic while keeping my shield strong, I stood in the center of the line with Leslie and Mr. Baree standing off to the sides, wielding blue fire around their fists.

"If you'll stand behind me, Elite Bellus," Mr. Baree mildly said.

The Elite watched us all with a curious gaze—it stressed me out that he didn't seem more concerned about everything.

"Let's go!" I shouted. We trotted down the hallway, turning off a few times so we spiraled away from the chamber.

We were in sight of a side door that opened up to the parking lot when someone shouted behind us.

"Sir!"

Three wizards dressed in royal purple and deep red charged down the hallways after us.

I glanced at Elite Bellus, who smiled. "They are from my House," he confirmed.

"Let them in," I said. "But we need to get outside."

Mrs. Yamada and Franco shifted to the side, opening a narrow space for the three wizards to pass through, closing the gap behind them.

The wizards crowded around Elite Bellus, giving us House

Medeis wizards curious looks as we prowled the distance to the side door.

Once again Leslie opened it and Mr. Baree darted through. He reappeared a moment later, fire still swirling around his hands.

"It's clear. It seems the Night Court and Drake Family are still fighting in the chamber," he said. "Out here it's only everyone who escaped."

I cautiously dropped my shield—Franco and Felix stepping closer together to block out the hole I left—and poked my head out the door.

Supernaturals were flooding out the back doors of the Cloisters, retreating into the parking lot in frenzied sprints.

It didn't look like anyone had been seriously hurt, and no one out here was fighting—though the occasional explosion that rocked the building was a pretty solid indicator that the battle was still going strong.

"I think we're good." I stepped outside into the nippy night air, my breath clouding when I exhaled.

The cold air seemed to knock some sense into people. No one was screaming out here—or jostling one another. A few fae had even formed a circle on the sidewalk to talk.

One by one, my family dropped their shields as they left the building, relaxing once it became obvious we weren't in danger.

"It was a deliberate attack, then." Elite Bellus scuffed his dress shoe on the sidewalk as Franco and Felix—the last of us—slipped out the door. "I wonder if the Night Court knows just what they've done."

"What do you mean, Sir?" one of the wizards from House Bellus asked.

"The Curia Cloisters are a neutral territory." Elite Bellus's mild look slipped into a cold expression with narrowed eyes. "By attacking the Drakes they've broken a treaty that's been held since the Cloisters were established." He glanced back at the building. "They're going to regret it—that's if the Drakes don't tear them to shreds."

"Hopefully no one got injured in the crossfire." Leslie bit her lip.

"I think the crowd was the biggest threat to itself." Franco dropped his arm over his wife's shoulders. "They were acting like a bunch of idiots."

"People tend to lose their sense of logic when frightened like that." I tapped my fingers on my thigh as I stared at the glass door we'd come through.

Elite Bellus glanced at his wizards. "Did you notify my wife?"

One of the wizards bowed. "She's on her way with a force of Bellus wizards. We also touched base with Pre-Dominant Harka. A werewolf force is roughly twenty minutes out."

Twenty minutes.

That was a long time during a fight.

"Thank you for your help, Adept Medeis and wizards of House Medeis," Elite Bellus said. "Seeing you work together was eye-opening, and I am thankful for the protection you provided."

"It was our honor," I said automatically.

Elite Bellus smoothed his goatee. "I may have to call upon you on a future date for some collaboration, but for now I think it's safe to assume the meeting is over. I'd head home if I were you."

"Of course. Goodnight, Elite Bellus," I said.

"Goodnight." He waved to us as he stalked off, his three wizards swirling around him, answering questions and swiping at their cellphones.

Once he was gone, I turned around to face my family. "I think that was a pretty smooth exit, great job everyone."

"It was *awesome!*" Franco affectionately ruffled my hair. "I finally get why you make us memorize and practice so many formations, Adept!"

"It was very effective," Mrs. Yamada agreed.

"Yeah," Felix said. "But maybe we need to get our Adept a

whistle? Everyone was so panicked it was pretty hard to hear orders."

"I think when Elite Bellus whistled he was signaling his people," Leslie said. "Maybe we should come up with a similar code?"

"Not just for formations, but locations, plans—it'll take work, but I think after today we know it will be worth it." Momoko rubbed her hands together, rapidly warming to the idea.

"Should Felix and I go pull up the cars, Adept?" Mr. Baree asked.

I looked back at the glass door, my stomach in knots.

Whatever spell held the Drake Family in the chambers, it had to be a powerful one. Normally I'd think the Night Court were idiots for trying to pen up vampires—they're more lethal in close combat than ranged—but it looked as if the trap was just around the Drakes. None of the fae had entered the trap. Which meant the only way the vampires had to fight back were their guns.

Don't get me wrong—they were dead shots, so the Night Court were in for a load of trouble. But over the summer the fae had given Mason a particularly old and powerful spell that I suspected was so ancient it was originally made by the elves.

If they tossed that to Mason—a lowly ally—it was pretty likely they had more spells like that in their arsenal. And if they dared to break Curia Cloisters laws to attack Killian, I was pretty sure they were going to make it worth the consequences and throw everything they had at them.

Celestina was with him, as were Rupert, Julianne, Josh, and Gavino. They'll be fine.

Something in my chest twisted.

It was Killian and his five against Ira and all the fae he'd brought. When I'd been leaving it looked like they had at least fifteen.

That wasn't a fair fight. And help would be a long time in coming.

It wasn't right.

I was still furious with Killian, and I really wanted to rip Celestina and Josh each a new one. But no matter how angry I was, I couldn't abandon anyone to an ambush like this.

"Get the cars," I confirmed. "I want all of you to go back. Call someone at the House, and as soon as you arrive put it on lockdown."

"Why are you talking like this? You're coming with us," Felix said.

I started walking backwards to the door. "I can't leave things like this. But go home and prepare the House. Depending how nasty the Night Court is feeling, they might decide to come bother us."

"Hazel!" Momoko shouted.

I could feel the extra tinge of fear in her voice, and I felt like a jerk for what I was about to do.

We had invisible wounds in House Medeis. If I was extra protective of them because of my baggage, they had become rabidly protective of me.

But I can't leave Killian and the Drakes like this.

"Be careful!" I spun around and yanked the glass door, slipping back into the building, which positively *reeked* of fae magic.

And so into battle I went. For a vampire I currently hated, to a fight I wasn't at all involved in.

And it felt so, so right.

CHAPTER FIVE

Killian

I tossed a table on its side and crouched behind it, Celestina doing the same to my right. "How many down?" I asked as I checked my handgun's magazine. It was empty.

"We've taken down four of sixteen, Your Eminence," Celestina reported.

I exhaled a curse—that was too few.

The table I was braced against cracked ominously when a forest green ball of magic smashed into it.

Shooting them was our only option. We were trapped in this magic circle they'd erected under our feet, which swirled and rotated so it looked like a vine-like pattern grew around us. We couldn't escape, and we couldn't get any closer.

I exhaled a second curse.

"How are we doing on ammo?" I asked.

"We each still have two to three loaded magazines," Celestina said. "Unfortunately, they raised a ward, and it seems like our bullets cannot pass through it."

"Josh?" I shouted for my Second Knight.

Josh slunk around the barricade of chairs he'd created and slid to a stop next to me. "Your Eminence."

"How's Gavino?"

Josh bowed his head. "His injury is grievous. They hit him in the belly. He'll survive if we can get out."

If.

It wasn't necessarily a given.

I'd been such a fool. Though I usually armed my people with great paranoia, I hadn't learned from the occasion with Hazel's degenerate cousin and the elf spell he'd dropped on us.

I should have realized what that spell meant and started carrying items to break wards.

How could I fail like this? How could I fail them? If Hazel...

No. I didn't regret sending her away. Hazel could have busted us out of this—possibly—but I didn't want to involve her, didn't want to risk her...

My gaze wandered from Josh to Celestina as another glass vial sailed over our heads and hit Josh's barricade, spattering a red liquid that slowly ate through the wood.

"We have to hold out," I said. "Pre-Dominant Harka and Elite Bellus were in attendance. They'll send forces, and our people will learn of it."

Celestina and Josh nodded, and the table groaned before its left side shattered into splinters.

"Get back to Gavino," I said.

"Yes, Your Eminence."

Even in the middle of a battle my First and Second Knights kept up with a title which—at the moment—I felt like I didn't deserve.

Josh crouched as he ran back to his barricade, ducking out of sight.

I reloaded my handgun's magazine, then propped my hand on the table for stabilization and shot twice, carefully spacing the bullets. If we could keep them wary, maybe they'd stop slinging so many spells—

Pink tinted magic rippled underneath Celestina. She barely rolled away in time before the magic clamped around her table like the jaws of a creature and swallowed it, pulverizing it into dust and slivers of wood.

I shot off a few more bullets, attempting to cover for my First Knight while she dove for new shelter. She barely made it behind a desk, tucking her feet in just before purple magic punched through it.

Celestina was thrown into the invisible wall of the spell that encased us, her face muscles grimacing in pain.

My table creaked ominously, and I edged out from behind it before it collapsed entirely.

We were losing, terribly. And things were about to get painful.

The thing about vampire healing was it could keep you alive even under constant injury for a long time.

I'd be able to survive just about anything the fae threw at me. My underlings, however...

"Gavino!" Julianne screamed, her voice high-pitched with terror.

A fireball consumed the barricade Josh had built. While he shot off his handgun, Julianne dragged an unconscious Gavino toward two tables Rupert had tipped on their sides.

As she pulled him along, a fae shot an arrow made of black-hued magic at the inert vampire.

Julianne swiveled him so she took the bolt to the side, rather than let it hit Gavino. She cried in pain and fell to her knees as the bolt disintegrated and magic racked up and down her body.

They weren't going to make it.

And I was powerless to stop this.

Snarling, I tried to slam my hand through the wall of the invisible barrier that held us captive.

The resistant magic burned my skin and made my whole arm

numb, but I gritted my teeth and pushed harder. The wall didn't give, but I could start to see strains in the magic, hairline fractures that spread through the barrier.

Keep pushing...

I clenched my jaw as I pushed, agony radiating from my hand up and down my body.

One of the fae turned their attention from blasting my cornered underlings to me, hitting me in the shoulder with purple magic that had a slick, oily feeling to it and burned like fire.

It burned my suit, but with my powers, my body quickly repaired the damage, producing an uncomfortable, bone deep ache.

I leaned into the spell, but although it was still cracking, the area I was affecting wasn't much bigger than my upper torso. But if I could just push through...

Rupert's shout broke through the angry hum of magic.

I swiveled, freezing when I saw Rupert collapse, holding his right shoulder. Dark, angry magic crawled up his throat and clawed its way across his face. The whites of his eyes were wide as he gazed at me, fear and pain filling his expression.

For a moment, the constant bombardment paused. I streaked across our limited fighting area and carefully scooped Rupert up and set him down behind the last remaining bit of cover with Julianne and Gavino.

Gavino was out, and Julianne whimpered as she hung her head, her hands clamped to her bleeding side.

I took her handgun from her thigh holster and stood upright, adding my fire to Celestina's and Josh's as we shot at the cowardly fae.

As Celestina had said, our bullets were stopped by whatever shielding spell they used.

"Hold your fire," I ordered as I jogged past a bruised Josh and bloodied Celestina.

When I reached the spot of our circle that was closest to the fae, I stopped.

Three fae were standing by a sword. This far away I didn't recognize it, but between all the gold and the glittering gems encrusted on it, it had to be a magic sword. Possibly even one of the holy swords the elves used to revere. How had Queen Nyte and her foolish consort gotten their hands on *that*?

If they used it, Celestina, Josh, Rupert, Gavino, and Julianne would die.

I raised my gun and wasted three bullets, trying to prevent the inevitable.

The shots hit their shield and fell to the ground with an audible clink as the sword started to glow.

Desperate, I turned around.

Josh had retreated back to the tables where Rupert, Gavino, and Julianne were. When he saw my face, he bowed his head, then loaded his handgun with another loaded magazine.

He knew what was about to happen.

I shifted my gaze to Celestina, who offered me a smile, her red eyes warm and proud. "I know you will avenge us, Your Eminence."

I wanted to say something, to tell her they all were going to survive. I wanted to roar. It couldn't end this way!

The magic in the sword throbbed in a wave even I, a magicless vampire, could feel. The humming noise increased, broken by crackles of raw power.

I backed up a few feet and shook my head. "No," I said.

"Get back behind the tables, Your Eminence. Please." Josh stood with Celestina, his expression calm.

Celestina rolled her shoulders. "The tables might shield you a little longer and spare you a bit of pain."

I set my shoulders. "I can survive a blast, even from a holy sword. You go."

Celestina's smile turned amused. "You know very well, Your

Eminence, there's no table thick enough in the world to save vampires of our caliber from that." She nodded at the sword.

"Please go, Your Eminence," Josh said. "We will remain here. They'll have to lower their shield for an attack of this size. We might be able to get some shots off before it's over."

No! This couldn't happen! How could I be so powerless to stop this?

Celestina and Josh had stood with me for decades—I couldn't...

Celestina winked. "It's been an honor, Your Eminence."

Josh bowed, and then they were gone, pressed against opposite sides of the circle as they tried to take up positions that would offer them the best line of sight.

It was said vampires didn't have souls. I never gave it much thought. It didn't matter to me because I didn't intend to die.

But now, I swear I felt my soul—or something deep inside of me—fracture.

The fae shouted words that were lost to the murmur of magic. They held books that started to glow, and the sword burned with such pure light I couldn't look at it.

Unwilling to retreat to the table, I backed up until I was lined up with Celestina and Josh. I was their sire. And while I had failed to protect them, the least I could do was stand with them while they passed on.

An explosion triggered the sword, and the air fell into smothering silence as light blasted from it, cutting a path toward our prison. It ate up the ground, disintegrating floor tiles and furniture in its wake.

And I could only watch.

Soon it was too bright to see anything. I lowered my eyes to half-mast and was just about to shut them and brace for unending pain and agony, when a shadow passed in front of me.

Sound cracked through the air with such intensity my ears rang, and my eyes snapped open.

Standing inside, near the front of our magic cage was a solitary figure. Her blond hair whipped in the raging wind caused by magic, and with her hands thrust out in front of her, she powered a blue shield of magic so large it encompassed about half the width of our prison.

Her arms shook, and her petite body trembled with strain as she held back the full blast of a *holy sword* with her shield.

Bolts of unstable magic ran up and down the length of the blast, blackening the ground and making the glass covering the framed artwork hanging on the walls pop and shatter. The air was hot, and flames sprouted at the spot where the attack from the holy sword thrust against the wizard's shield.

There was never any doubt in my mind who she was—there was only one wizard capable of this. But when she cast a look at me over her shoulder, it felt like the moment lasted a human lifetime.

Funneling so much magic that the edges of her black wizard mark were glowing *blue,* she lifted a cocky eyebrow at me. She inhaled deeply, her shoulders rising, then roared—audible above the thundering clash of magic—and leaned into her shield.

I'd cast her out for her sake, but she had returned to save *me*.

Hazel Medeis had come back.

CHAPTER SIX

Hazel

As I sprinted through the building I felt the pressure in the air increase. The floral taste of fae magic was overwhelming, but that foreign, ancient magic Mason had once attacked me with veined it.

Whatever Killian and his vampires were facing, it wasn't good.

I heard a few gunshots as I finally reached the chamber. I turned so sharply into it I slipped and smacked my shoulder on the door frame, but the stinging pain was the last thing on my mind as I stared at the battleground before me.

The Night Court had, as I had feared, penned the Drake vampires in a magic circle. It wasn't a problem for me—I'd probably be able to break in and join them because most fae magic didn't work on wizards. Unfortunately, that was the only thing the fight had going for it.

Rupert and Julianne were slumped behind two overturned tables. And I couldn't be sure, but I thought the motionless heap at Julianne's side was Gavino.

Killian, Celestina, and Josh were the only ones standing. The

First and Second Knights were hugging the sides of the magic-made cage, and Killian stood in the center, wearing an expression I had never seen on his face before. Was that...*fear*?

Three fae holding books began shouting. I blinked as I realized they surrounded a very fancy, bejeweled sword—it had to be an artifact. But when their books began to glow, I started to swear.

I hustled into the chamber, losing precious time scooting around chairs that had been tossed into the aisles either during the mob's frantic exit, or during the fight.

Hoping to move faster, I hopped onto a chair and then jumped from table to table, kicking pens and papers as I went.

I swore faster and faster when the sword crackled with light, and I felt the magic harbored in the blade.

Hurry! I have to reach them in time.

I jumped off the last ring of tables, my ankles jarring with the impact when I hit the ground, and the sword went off.

Unnatural silence fell over the chamber—the magic was so hungry it even ate up the patter of my footsteps. Light that had a clear, crystal-like veneer to it blasted from the sword, consuming everything in its path like a raging wildfire as it stalked toward its aimed target, the captured vampires.

Sweat dripped down my back and made my blue jacket stick to me like a second skin, but I threw myself into the spell that held the Drakes captive, releasing a puff of breath when I passed through.

The blast of magic from the sword pierced the very edge of the spell, and I streaked across the circle, skidding to a stop just in front of the sword's magical attack.

The heat baked my skin, and I was so glad Celestina and Josh had thrown the most hellish training I could endure at me, because I raised my shield so fast it was second nature to me.

I could sense the power in the sword, and the deadly intent that radiated through its blast, so I put everything I had into my shield and made it as big as I could manage. I had just enough time to tense for impact before the attack slammed against my shield.

The force of it pushed me back at least three feet before I leaned in with all that I had and was able to resist it.

It felt like my blood was boiling as I pulled so much magic into my body I couldn't see straight. I didn't need to, though. The sword blast was so bright it made my eyes hurt. Through the overwhelming contact it had with my shield, I felt the blast's reverberations as it, denied progress, shed bolts of magic.

Based on the angry hisses and the sheer amount of shattering glass that I heard, I was pretty sure this entire room would need a remodel after we were finished.

My hands were on fire as the sword's attack pushed harder, testing my shield's integrity and searching for a weak spot.

Every muscle in my body screamed with pain, and my skin felt rubbed raw from the amount of magic I was dealing with. But my shield held—thankfully. Faced with this much power, fae magic or not, if I let my shield fall there was no way I was coming out of this uninjured. The attack was that overwhelming, and that consuming.

I turned my head, trying to get relief from the horrible heat.

It took my eyes a few moments to realize I was seeing Killian standing some feet behind me.

His eyes were wide with shock, and for once his body language was open with his disbelief.

Hah. That will teach him!

I raised an eyebrow at him as I wondered why he wasn't on his phone or preparing to rain pain down on the fae. Because I *needed* reinforcements. My arms were shaking, and I didn't think I'd be able to hold the line much longer.

When the magic succeeded in pushing me back a step, I turned back around and leaned in. Sweat dripped down the side of my face, and the heat and pressure were unbearable. I gritted my teeth as I poured magic into my spell, fighting the squeezing sensation in my chest.

I can't hold on much longer...

Just when I thought my arms would give out, a blue shield slammed into place on my right side, reinforcing my spell and strengthening it. I barely had time to glance to my right and realize it was Felix before Momoko snapped her shield into place on my left.

With our magic converged, the pressure lifted from my arms, and our shield grew in size, humming with the low-throated purr of wizard magic.

"At your orders, Adept!" Momoko shouted.

I felt two more shields latch into place. I leaned forward to see who had joined us, and was not surprised to see Leslie and Franco on one end. A moment later, and Mrs. Yamada and Mr. Baree shored up the other side, and we formed a straight line across the spell-crafted prison.

Magic still raged through my body, but I no longer felt like I was about to sweat blood. My palms prickled, but I had stopped shaking, and our shields were an impenetrable wall. With the seven of us wizards working in harmony, our magic shields resonated, layering over one another, so soon even the heat from the spell was mostly blocked.

I laughed.

This is what I had wanted! This is what we'd practiced for, why we got up early and sweated and bruised ourselves every day.

So we could stand between danger and what we wanted to protect, and no one would be able to tear us apart.

"Medeis!" I shouted.

"House!" My six wizards shouted the word we'd chosen as our rally cry.

"Medeis!" I repeated.

"*House!*"

"V formation!" I yelled. "V formation, stepping forward into blast edge attack formation!"

"V formation!" Momoko shouted to my left.

"V formation!" Felix echoed on my right.

The orders swirled down the line, and Leslie and Franco backed up on the right side, while Mrs. Yamada and Mr. Baree backed up on the left, until we resembled an upside-down V.

My shield was back to taking the brunt of the attack, but the strain was minimal. With Momoko and Felix standing just behind me, their magic flowed into mine.

I wasn't alone. Not anymore.

The first step I took I had to push with every muscle in my body and fight my way forward. Same with the second. By the third or fourth step, we'd successfully started pushing the sword's attack backwards.

Each step was easier, and the blast of power that pushed down on us weakened. Soon we were jogging, leaving the magic circle and bearing down on the fae.

I couldn't see them behind the brightness of their attack, but I was pretty sure I could hear fragmented shouts from Consort Ira.

I grinned as I felt the magic in the blast weaken, and flicker, and sure enough, I caught a full yell from Ira.

"Stop the attack! They'll burn us alive with it!"

The blast from the sword grew less blindingly bright, and it lost about half of its power, finally giving me a good look at what we were facing.

Eleven fae were huddled together, horror flashing on their faces. The three fae responsible for charging the sword were hurriedly reading from books, but most importantly it didn't seem like they were using any defensive spell that was made out of the same ancient magic the sword was.

Perfect.

"Switch, *now!*" I yelled to my family. "Blast edge attack, go!"

Momoko, Felix, and I held our shields and pushed hard, forcing the fae to complete the spell that powered down the sword.

Mrs. Yamada, Mr. Baree, Franco, and Leslie burst forward at a sprint, cutting around our shield and falling on the unprepared fae.

Franco must have gotten their weapons from the cars, because he had his crossbow loaded and within moments had shot a fae in the shoulder. The rest of my family were wielding their weapons of choice as well.

One of the night fae tried to rush Franco, her sword flashing, but Leslie slithered between them and smashed the fae in the chest with the butt of her spear. She spun it over her head like a warrior princess, and then leaned forward with her whole body and almost eviscerated the closest book-reading fae.

Mrs. Yamada and Mr. Baree both waded into the action, Mr. Baree bearing a club spiked with nasty iron spikes, and Mrs. Yamada with her falchion sword.

The magic sword had successfully been turned off, so as Leslie, Franco, Mrs. Yamada, and Mr. Baree made a mess of the fae front lines, Felix and Momoko moved closer to me so our shoulders brushed. We dropped our shield spells and began charging our portion of the attack.

Ira roared in rage from relative safety at the center of the group. "Stop them! They're just *wizards*!"

But the fae had been fighting a distance battle with fae magic —which wouldn't work on us.

The fae fumbled as they hurriedly swapped their crystal studded staffs for swords and daggers. But by that time, the hair on the back of my neck was standing up with the charge of our joint spell.

A male dressed in fae knight gear, bearing a wicked-looking black sword, took a swipe at Mrs. Yamada. A female fae knight managed to give Mr. Baree a wicked cut on his forearm, but it didn't stop him from smashing his spiked club into her chestplate, crumpling it.

"Fall back!" I shouted.

Ira pointed to me. "Push our advantage!" he shouted.

It was his mistake.

Felix had his arm resting on my shoulder, and my arm pressed against Momoko's back. When she twisted her neck to grin at me, her wizard mark was still the dark color it had been when we had our shields raised.

"Now?" Felix asked almost lazily.

"Now," Momoko agreed.

Together we unleashed our intertwined spells, creating a lightning bolt blast radius that was the perfect size of the area the fae occupied. It rocked the Curia Cloisters and spawned cracks of thunder so loud, we temporarily deafened ourselves.

I had named this formation blast edge for a reason.

Lightning strike after strike pulverized the fae, crackling around them like a summer storm.

The fae scrambled to activate their magical items and raise their shields, but it was clear we had rattled them.

I didn't know for certain that we'd turned the tide until a particularly big bolt of lightning struck Consort Ira, and sent him flying. He bowled over a couple of his men, and they lost their ranks.

"Retreat!"

"Open a door to the Night Court!"

"We can't in here—they'll follow us!"

The fae bolted, abandoning their injured and sprinting through a side door.

I glanced over my shoulder just in time to see the spell caging in the Drakes fade from the ground and then evaporate entirely.

"Follow them!" I shouted to my family.

I took the lead with Leslie and Franco pairing up and taking their place behind me, and the others falling in line behind them so we made one straight line. We sprinted out of the chamber and down one of the long, snaking hallways, trailing the Night Court. Fae are naturally faster than humans, but these jerks were carting a lot of artifacts, so while they were putting distance between us it wasn't *too* much.

Franco, as if sensing my thoughts, shot a fireball at the fae party. Leslie followed his attack up with a carefully constructed fireball under one of the fire alarms, triggering the sprinkler system, which rained water down on the hallway.

It didn't bother us wizards too much, but it made the laden down fae slip and slide.

The fae made it out a door and rushed to open a gate to their Court on the front lawn.

The House Medeis wizards and I clambered outside, releasing a few more blasts of magic that the fae blocked.

A rectangular shape covered with black-ish purple mist solidified, and the fae started to pour through it.

I slowed to a stop and threw a few more lightning bolts at them, but it was over. They were gone.

And just barely in time. A blur raced past me, stirring my sodden hair.

Killian reached them as the last fae scrambled through the door, and it evaporated behind him, the mist disappearing in the haze of the night sky.

I finally dropped my hands—which I'd been holding fizzing electricity in, and turned around to face my family.

Mr. Baree's cut was still bleeding, but it didn't look like we had any other major injuries. In fact, everyone had humongous smiles stretching their faces.

"It worked!" Momoko squealed. She elbowed past Felix so she could hug me.

"That was brilliant!" Franco lowered his weapon, but couldn't stop grinning. "We worked so perfectly in time—all those practices paid off!"

"And that shield spell!" Mrs. Yamada wistfully tapped the hilt of her falchion. "It worked so *beautifully*! I can't believe such a useful form of magic ever slipped out of our training."

"We should talk to Elite Bellus about it," Leslie said.

"I'm sure after witnessing it in use, he'll be more open to the idea," Mr. Baree said.

"You guys didn't follow my orders," I said with a fake whine to my voice.

"That's because they were stupid orders," Felix said.

"We called Great Aunt Marraine, so the House is still on lockdown like you wanted," Momoko said. "But we couldn't let you go in there alone."

"Heck no we couldn't!" Leslie snarled. "You've fought alone too many times—and this is why you are training us!"

"You were perfect, Hazel. Exactly how an Adept should be." Felix ruffled my hair.

"Thanks." I laughed as I looked around the circle of wizards, but some motion just behind them caught my attention.

Josh and Celestina stood together, watching me with intense eyes that glowed crimson in the evening light. I couldn't quite read their expressions, but they looked pretty stoic considering what they must have gone through.

I felt more than heard Killian behind me. So I slowly turned away from my family to face the Midwest Eminence.

Annoyingly, he didn't look too bad.

His fancy designer suit was streaked with dust and a little singed, and he had a smudge on one cheek, and his hair was extra mussed. His eyes had a little more of a red light in them than usual, but as he stared down at me—and believe me, with our height difference I had to crank my neck to look up at him—he didn't appear hurt. He looked like a super hot villain who had just stepped out of a movie.

Intimidated a little despite myself—not because I was actually *afraid* of him, but I was a little afraid of what his reaction would be—I nervously twitched my shoulders. "Hey," I said, using one of the greatest openers ever. "I think backup—"

Killian swept me up, lifting me off the ground and crushing me against his chest.

It took me a few seconds to process it. It wasn't until the angry squawks of my family—who sounded like a flock of fuming parrots—broke through my daze that I realized Killian was holding me in his arms.

I stiffened, and my frustration and anger reared to life. "Killian—" I intended to rip him a new one, but I fell silent as I took it in.

Not that Killian was holding me in a dreamy way most girls would sigh over—I didn't care about that. Actually, I was pretty tempted to pull his hair for it.

No, it was that when I set my fists on his chest, intending to push off him, I realized he was shaking.

I hesitated and flatted my hands so my palms were smooth against his dress shirt as I tried to gauge him.

He had his head pressed against the nape of my neck, and took in a very slow and steady—but long—inhale. No rattling, no extra noises. His grip on me was firm—perhaps the tiniest bit tight—but his hands were steady, and he didn't react at all to the House Medeis wizards who were quickly raising their weapons.

He wasn't shaking with fear or leftover adrenaline like I was. Not a chance. Based on his body language, I'd guess he was shaking with barely repressed emotion.

I wasn't entirely certain what *kind* of repressed emotion. With his head still pressed against my neck I couldn't see his eyebrows—which were the best indicators of his current mood. But I knew it wasn't a great mix to have my wizards—who were overly protective—mixed with Killian—who was suspicious at best. (And that didn't touch his minions.)

I cleared my throat. "I guess now would be as good a time as any to tell you that you are a raging moron."

The House Medeis wizards quieted at my words, but I could feel their tension—and rage on the part of Felix and Momoko, who were probably staring holes into my back.

It was the right thing to say to Killian, though, who had frequently referred to my snark as the "amusing yaps of a puppy" when I first met him.

He finally peeled his head back, a hint of a smirk playing on his lips. "I guess," he echoed. "Though I expected you to first complain how close my hand is to your butt, given that you seem very protective of it."

Someone made a strangled gurgle—I'm pretty sure it was Mr. Baree.

"You are right," I said. "Move it an inch, and I will call down a lightning strike right here and now."

Killian raised both of his eyebrows. "It might be worth it—just to see exactly what makes you so defensive."

And just like that it was as if the past few weeks fell away. It was as if he'd never kicked me out, as if no time had passed at all.

Oh, no. He's not getting off that easy.

The smile fell from my face. "Put me down."

Killian's smirk slowly faded, and he studied my face, his eyes turning black in the dim light.

"*Now*," I growled.

Killian slowly set me down, letting my feet tap the cement before fully releasing my weight. "Thank you for your help," he said.

I shrugged. "The Night Court played dirty. Someone had to show them society isn't just going to sit by and let them break the law." I forcibly turned my back to him. "Leslie, check in with everyone back at the House, would you? I want to make sure no one dropped by to play."

"Yes, Adept."

"Are we heading back?" Mr. Baree asked.

"That depends." I shifted my gaze to the Curia Cloisters—the sirens were blaring, and even though the parking lot was on the other side of the building I was pretty sure I could hear the endless rumble of cars. It sounded like Elite Bellus's backup had arrived.

"What does it depend upon?" Mrs. Yamada asked.

I bit my lip. "Do you think my notes on the lecture survived that?"

Felix snorted a bark of laughter before he could muffle it. "Are you *joking?*"

I scrunched my nose at my much taller friend. "I worked hard on those notes! And you can bet Elite Bellus will call on us and want to know what we thought of the presentation, just to bug me."

"You might deserve it for all the paperwork you inflict on the Wizard Council," Momoko said.

"Hey, they could end that standoff any time," I reminded her.

"Hazel," Killian said.

I stiffened my shoulders. "What?"

"I want an alliance."

Against my will, my traitorous body spun around so I could face him. "You want *what?*"

Killian's eyes smoldered. "An alliance."

I laughed harshly. "You've got to be kidding. You kicked me out and called me useless, and now you want an *alliance?* Hah!"

"You knew I was lying about that." Killian slid his hands into the pockets of his slacks. "You said so as you stormed out of my office."

"That doesn't excuse what you did!" I curled my hands into fists, shaking with anger—and maybe a hint of betrayal.

I'm not sure if it was the fury in my voice or just their instincts, but Celestina and Josh appeared behind Killian. They weren't holding weapons or anything, but I got the feeling they were there just in case I decided to launch myself at him.

Killian shrugged. "I did it for your own good."

"You did it because you didn't trust me," I snarled.

"No." Killian stared at me, unflappable. "I did it because the Night Court fae threatened you. That's what the paintball attack in the mall was all about."

"You seem to think that your lying, manipulating, and scheming is acceptable as long as it's for a cause *you* decide is right," I said. "Newsflash, it's not! And you better get it through your head that I'm not one of your little minions who is going to fall in line and end friendships just because you tell me to."

That, I was somewhat satisfied to see, made Celestina wince.

Killian tilted his head. "You're still mad? Even though you know I sent you away to keep you out of harm?"

"Yes."

"I sent the Paragon to you to make it easier to fight your cousin, and attacked the Night Court while you fought him so they couldn't provide backup. If you don't believe me—"

"I already knew about that!" I felt magic jolt through me with my high emotions. "The problem is you didn't trust me! If you had told me we could have worked something out. But you're suspicious and paranoid, and you wanted to deal with it in your own way. That's fine for you vampires, but that's not how *I'm* willing to play."

"Very well. What, then, do I do to change your mind?"

"You have to apologize!"

"I'm sorry." He sounded about as convincing and sincere as a con man. "Now will you join in an alliance with me?" he continued.

"No!"

"I apologized."

"You had absolutely no sincerity, and you still clearly don't believe you were wrong—" I groaned and cut myself off.

"An alliance would be beneficial for House Medeis as well," Killian prodded, unable to let the topic drop. "The Night Court might have left you alone before, but after tonight there's no chance they'll let you off."

The distant sirens pounded into my head like nails. "I can't deal with this tonight."

"Come to Drake Hall tomorrow," Killian said. When I murderously glared at him, he added, "So we can continue this talk. I'd like to reconcile, Hazel."

"Yeah, and I'd like a pony," I grumbled.

"You'll come tomorrow?"

I glanced back at my wizards. They were all staring at me with great attention, but none of them showed any kind of reaction beyond curiosity and interest.

A sigh leaked out of me like I was a poked balloon. "Not tomorrow. We'll have to talk to Elite Bellus. We'll come over this weekend."

Killian slightly bowed his head. "We will prepare for your arrival." He lifted his hand and almost brushed my cheek before I recoiled.

"This weekend," I stiffly said.

It took a lot of willpower to turn my back to him and force a smile to my cheeks. "Let's go, House Medeis."

"Yes, Adept!"

"I'll run ahead and get the cars."

"Do you want me to dart in and see if your notes happened to survive?"

I had never been more grateful for my family. Since my nerves were obviously frayed, they enveloped me as a group and chatted brightly without expecting real answers as they bodily escorted me away from Killian Drake.

An alliance.

He wanted an *alliance*?

What on earth was he thinking?

CHAPTER SEVEN

Killian

Two nights after the attack at the Cloisters, I impatiently tapped a pen on my desk as I considered the conundrum that was Hazel Medeis.

She had sent me a curt message, scheduling a meeting for tomorrow evening. Which meant I had roughly twenty-four hours to figure out how to win my way back into her good graces.

It felt both ridiculous and refreshingly challenging. I hadn't worried about what any specific person thought of me since long before I became the Eminence. And now here I was, wondering how I could get one petite but powerful wizard to talk to me without annoyance crinkling the corners of her blue eyes.

I sighed and tossed the pen on my desk. "I'd say it's embarrassing, except—alarmingly—I'm more worried about the outcome than my prestige."

"You are referring to Hazel, Your Eminence?"

I glanced over at my Second Knight, who hovered in the open doorway of my office. "Yes."

"She has the fire of humans within her," Josh placidly said. "It allows her to be passionate about many things."

"Maybe in some cases." I leaned back in my desk chair, making the leather sigh. "But I suspect this grudge of hers has been nursed along because she's suffered a lot of betrayal recently." I narrowed my eyes at my desk. "She's known since the day she left Drake Hall that I was sending her off for her own good. And I suspect she knew the Paragon didn't drop by House Medeis when she was fighting Mason because he thought he should pay a social call."

"Perhaps someone ratted you out," Josh said.

"Of course they did," I snorted. "It's why I put all the bleeding hearts on guard rotation for her street. I thought Julianne was my surest shot, but I don't know for certain it was she who told Hazel about the raid we pulled off on the Night Court…"

"Even though Hazel knows your motivations, she's still angry with you," Josh said. I think he thought he was helping me organize my thoughts, but instead a dagger to my side would have been more comfortable.

"I'm not in that position all by my lonesome," I reminded him. "She's furious with you and Celestina as well."

"Indeed. Celestina assured me she had a plan to worm her way back into Hazel's good graces after she left, but apparently she was out maneuvered."

I shrugged a little. If I was going to be in the wizard's bad graces, I might as well have some company. "You are here to report on Gavino, I assume?"

"As you requested, yes." Josh straightened his shoulders. "He is up and walking around. It's been recommended that he refrain from training for at least two days, and no strenuous work outs for a week."

"Good. Make sure he and Julianne are kept off guard rotation for this week. And Rupert?"

"Is perfectly recovered," Josh reported. "Or so he would say.

He's still tight in the shoulders and drops his guard a bit in hand to hand combat, but I imagine by tomorrow evening he'll be back in perfect condition."

Tomorrow, that would be just in time to thank Hazel—which was sure to put Rupert in a sour mood given his dislike of her.

I went back to staring at my desk. "She's mad because she says I don't *trust* her."

"Ah, we have returned to the topic of Hazel?" Josh thoughtfully tipped his head. "Perhaps she does not understand that the small degree to which you *do* trust her is rare."

"Yes," I agreed without any intonation. "A small degree."

In reality I trusted Hazel far more than I wanted to.

A wizard's blood *reeked* to vampires—a self-defense mechanism because if a vampire actually did manage to drink a wizard's blood, they were then immune to that wizard's magic. The magic in the wizard's blood, however, was not very amiable and acted as built-in protection. As long as the wizard didn't trust the vampire, their blood would taste so rancid and disgusting that no vampire would be able to swallow. On the flip side, as long as a vampire didn't trust the wizard, the wizard's blood would smell like a rotting carcass, and if the vampire tried to drink it anyway, they'd get sick.

It was a tactic Hazel had used to her advantage before. When fighting a crazed, Unclaimed vampire she'd smeared her blood across its face, making it gag and stop attacking her.

Unfortunately for me, Hazel smelled *amazing*. It was difficult to pin down because she didn't even smell like prey. Rather, she smelled how sunlight used to feel before I was a vampire and it sapped my strength. Warm, caressing, and beautiful.

As delectable as her scent was, it was a dangerous thing for me. *Trust* was dangerous. The only silver lining to this was no one had any way of suspecting just how much I really did trust her.

I sighed and dropped the depressing line of thought. "She

wanted an apology, then said it wasn't good enough. She said it wasn't…" I frowned as I recalled her exact words. "Sincere?"

Josh blinked his red eyes at me, absolutely no help.

Maybe I should ask Celestina. But it weirdly seems like that would be admitting defeat—besides, Hazel is mad at her, as well, so Celestina obviously isn't that much more advanced in this area than I am.

"You sent her away for her protection, but given the alliance you proposed to her, might I assume you believe it's no longer needed?" Josh asked.

"She *badly* needs protection," I said. "Because she's an idiot who will run head first into a fight that doesn't involve her just because she thinks it's the 'right thing to do.'" The distaste I held for the idea made me furrow my brow. "But I'm willing to admit she's trained her underlings faster than I thought possible. She's only had approximately two months, and already they were fighting as a unit and were able to hold up magic-made shields that were strong enough to repel a blast from a holy sword."

"It was impressive," Josh said.

It was more than impressive; it was a game changer. With House Medeis united, it would take far more than bullets to attack her. Although they had lower numbers, if Hazel kept training her people and herself—I hadn't missed how massive her shield was, she'd come a long way since she last practiced in Drake Hall—they were actually the larger threat to fae.

Which was why the Night Court were more likely to attack Hazel at House Medeis now even if she had distanced herself from me, and there was no way I could allow that to happen.

I no longer needed to hold her at arm's length—forcibly keeping her out wasn't going to stop the Night Court from attacking her.

It irked me a little that all my extracurricular reading had been for naught—she didn't need my protection since she had her own. But I was glad she'd be safe. Or safer, at least.

It'd be a relief, to welcome her back, actually. It made me

sound like some sort of angst-ridden, newly-turned vampire, but I had missed her. A lot.

I abruptly stood. "She said I wasn't sincere," I repeated, recycling my previous observation. "So, I will drown her in apologies until she gets one that hits whatever vague requirement she's settled on." I smirked, pleased with the turn my thoughts had taken. "But I should be able to tip the scales in my favor with a bit of research. Call for Celestina...and Rupert."

CHAPTER EIGHT

Hazel

I was grumpy when we arrived at Drake Hall. Or really, I was irritated with myself.

My lungs twisted weirdly in my chest, and my traitor of a heart had me feeling *nervous*.

Seriously, it was enough to make a girl enraged! I was justifiably mad at Killian and his Family—Josh and Celestina in particular.

While Julianne and Manjeet had smuggled my beloved katana to me—which I now very pointedly had hanging from my sword belt—Celestina and Josh, the two vampires I was closest to, had followed Killian's orders and kicked me out without even a goodbye. Heck, sour-faced Rupert—who *hated* me—had even broken his orders to confirm that Killian had sent me away for my safety and had performed a raid on the Night Court to distract them while I attacked Mason—their ally—and reclaimed House Medeis.

And yet the two I trusted most had essentially painted me out of their lives.

So I was understandably furious with my fragile heart that was happy to return to Drake Hall.

I slid out of the car, shut the door, and leaned against it. A deep sigh leaked out of me as the vampires standing guard at the front door and holding sun-blocking umbrellas bowed to me and my retinue.

"You okay?" Felix's golden hair glowed like magic even in the weak, late afternoon sunlight.

"Of course."

"You don't have to do this." Momoko slammed the driver's door and marched around the front of the car. "Say the word, and we'll go home."

I pulled my wool coat tight, trying to ward off the chill of the frosty fall air. "No. If I can wrangle everything I want, an alliance with the Drake Family will be really advantageous. And since I've written off everyone who ignored us when Mason took over, our allies are slim pickings." I scratched my cheek and tried to casually grin. "Plus, I'm pretty sure we ticked off the Night Court enough that they may try and fight us. Once they get out from underneath all the regulations and punishments they've been slapped with for breaking the law and attacking while inside the Curia Cloisters, that is."

Momoko studied my face, then nodded. She stepped back, joining the other House Medeis wizards who waited on the sidewalk.

It was a small-ish group that had insisted on coming today. Momoko and Felix—of course—but Great Aunt Marraine had come as well, as did Mr. Clark—Felix's dad—and two middle-aged sisters who were new members of House Medeis. They were quiet but *powerful* wizards named April and June, who both shared similar tall and slightly stocky builds with high cheekbones and long eyelashes that rivaled Felix's.

I offered my people a smile. "Just remember, even if I shout at Killian, he's not going to hurt me or any of us. Probably."

Mr. Clark went pale, but everyone else nodded.

I climbed the first of the handful of stairs that led the way into Drake Hall, and both of the front doors were abruptly thrown open.

"Welcome, Adept Medeis and wizards of House Medeis," Celestina said. "Please come inside." She offered me her brightest smile, but since I was no longer in the middle of a battlefield, worrying a fae might kill her, I kept my expression neutral.

Not even a single goodbye, my thoughts taunted me. *Is she friendly, then, because Killian told her she had to be?*

It was a bitter tasting idea. One that made me nod my head and stare straight in front of me as I passed her and stepped into the painfully familiar mansion.

"There you are, Hazel." Killian sauntered down the ornate stairway that led to the second floor, a hint of a smile playing at the corners of his lips. "Welcome back."

He didn't stop at the base of the stairs, but moved so close to me it felt like he was invading my personal space. He offered me a bow that brought his head so close to mine if I had moved at all we could have touched foreheads, then popped upright and held out a bouquet of roses.

"I'm sorry." His voice was deep and throaty—almost a purr. And crowded this close to me, his entire being was overwhelming.

I almost reached for the bouquet automatically, but stopped myself at the last moment. "You don't give flowers to a potential ally, Killian," I dryly said. "That's something a boyfriend would do."

He waited until I met his gaze, his obsidian-red eyes glowing with a heat I'd seen before, in a garden located in a chunk of the fae realm owned by the Regional Committee of Magic. He'd given me an extremely unforgettable kiss that night, and the next time I got a chance to talk to him, he kicked me out of Drake Hall.

He might have thought his charming smolder would move me, but it only made me more determined.

It was not okay for him to kiss me like that, and then actively manipulate me and refuse to tell me the truth of what was going on.

"Where are we going to hold negotiations?" I asked.

Killian studied me for a few minutes, his expression unrelenting. "In the meeting room. You know the way."

I turned my back to him—instantly feeling a bit better—and smiled at my people. "Everyone ready?"

April and June exchanged confused looks, and Felix and Mr. Clark both were in danger of their eyes popping out of their heads. Sly Great Aunt Marraine looked unfortunately thoughtful, but Momoko studied me with a furrowed brow.

I awkwardly cleared my throat. "It's this way."

I led the way to the meeting room, smiling or nodding at the occasional vampire we "happened" to meet on our way to the chosen room.

The Drake Hall meeting room was a long, thin room that had a gigantic table slashing through the center, big enough for about half of the vampires at Drake Hall to sit around.

Some vampires were waiting for us, including two I was quite familiar with.

"Miss Hazel!" Julianne pounced on me, dragging me into a hug. "I didn't get to see you like the First and Second Knight, but they said you were incredible! Thank you for saving us." She had to hunch her back so she could lean down far enough to gently knock her head against mine.

I felt a little bit like a teddy bear being cuddled, but I returned the hug anyway. "I'm glad you're okay," I said. "How are Rupert and Gavino?"

Julianne let me go and rolled her eyes. "Rupert is doing so swimmingly he's back to himself, and Gavino—"

"Is right here." Gavino stepped out of the shadows cast by the closed drapes. "Hello, Miss Hazel."

He looked pale. Well, *all* vampires had a pale skin tone, but

Gavino's skin was so pale it made the bags under his eyes look like bruising, and the ridges of his face were a little gaunt. He'd been hurt pretty badly from what I'd seen during the attack. But for him to look this bad even with fae potions and his vampiric accelerated healing...he must have been a hair's width from dying.

I crossed the room and hesitated for a moment. But the truth was no matter how hurt I felt, I still cared for the Drakes, even though I should have known better. I gazed up at Gavino and started to shift, then smiled when he beat me to it and swept me up in a hug just like Julianne had.

I tried to squeeze him during the hug, but given my begrudgingly small stature and his massively broad shoulders—he was the biggest Drake vampire I'd seen, which made his fragile health that much more heartbreaking—it was pretty hopeless. "I'm glad you're okay," I whispered.

Gavino let me go and hunkered down so he could look me in the eyes. "Thanks to you, Miss Hazel. I owe you a great debt."

"No way." I smiled. "That's what friends do."

A collective sigh of relief slipped from every vampire in the room.

Confused, I glanced around, smiling and waving to Manjeet and a few other vampires I knew, then made my way back to my House.

Great Aunt Marraine smiled and patted my cheek when I rejoined the group. "You seem to be a great deal closer to the Drakes than I originally estimated," she muttered.

"It's not what you're thinking," I said.

Great Aunt Marraine snickered and shook her head. "Oh, after what I've seen I *very much* doubt that!"

Killian finally joined us, Celestina and Josh flanking him. "Please, sit down." He motioned to the table as he circled around to the opposite side.

I chose a spot with plenty of space on either side for my

fellow wizards. Unsurprisingly, Killian sat down directly across from me.

Three members of the kitchen staff bustled in, pushing carts laden with baked snacks and choices of drinks, which they unloaded onto the table.

I grabbed a homemade glazed donut and thanked the staff.

April and June followed my example and piled treats on a small plate, as did Felix. Great Aunt Marraine sipped at some kind of fruity drink that I dearly hoped didn't have alcohol or this meeting was going to be a lot more interesting than I wanted, and Momoko only took a cup of tea while Mr. Clark declined any refreshments—though he shook his head in amazement.

"This food is amazing," Felix whisper-hissed to me.

"Yep," I agreed.

"Shall we begin?" Killian asked.

I took a bite of my donut—which had the most delicious glaze that it made me instantly drool. "Yeah."

"Very well. I, Killian Drake of the Drake Family and Eminence of the Midwest, would like to extend an official invitation for an alliance between us," Killian said.

I ate another bite of my donut and critically eyed him—though it was pretty hard to be critical when I was eating heaven covered in a sugary glaze. "Why?"

"It would be beneficial to both House Medeis and Drake Family," Killian said. "In multiple ways, of course, but first and foremost it would give us a united front and shared forces and intelligence against the Night Court."

"You expect more trouble from them."

Up went one of Killian's eyebrows—the angle of it indicated he was somewhat surprised. "You don't?"

"I do." I watched his eyebrow return to its regular position as I ate the last bit of my donut—which I had eaten too fast and was now left feeling a little mournful at its passing. "I think we have a little time, though. They're going to get the book thrown at them for attacking you in the Curia Cloisters—particularly in the middle of a multi-race meeting. It's going to take them some time to recover from that."

"Agreed," Killian said.

"But we'd better use the time to our advantage and prepare for a war," I said. "Before I thought they'd just plague you for a few decades before giving up. But since they broke Cloister law…" I shook my head. "I'm pretty sure they aren't going to stop until they kill you, or until you crush them."

Killian's shrug was miniscule. "That is roughly what I've estimated as well. At worst, they'll declare war on us. At best, we might get a certamen."

Certamen was a super old term used to describe what was essentially a trial by combat.

In an effort to minimize loss of life among supernaturals and limit—if not outright ban—war between us, roughly a hundred years ago the movers and shakers of supernaturals had gotten together and come up with certamen.

With the drain of magic, war became dangerous for our entire community—which was already pretty fragile. Certamen was supposed to limit the slaughter because it was kind of like a cross between a duel—with all its rules—and a one-battle war.

Opponents were given one opportunity to face each other on the battlefield. The winner of the fight picked the terms of surrender for the loser, and whatever enmity or event that had pushed the two sides into the certamen was considered solved.

There usually were some casualties, but the numbers were tiny compared to the wars that used to last decades between feuding factions.

There hadn't been too many conflicts in the USA, so I had never met anyone who had taken part in a certamen before. They were more popular in Europe—I suspect because all the Houses, Courts, Families, and Packs over there had a much longer and far more bloody history with each other than we did here in the relatively young country of the USA.

"And," Killian continued, "you've made your House a secondary target by standing with me."

"I didn't stand with you." My voice was sharp, and I pushed my empty plate away from me. "What they did was wrong. It was illegal, dishonorable, and it risked the lives of everyone in that room. I stood against *them*."

"Perhaps," Killian said. "But you said we needed to use this time to prepare. I assume, then, that you agree to my proposal?" To his credit, Killian didn't look smug, or smirk, or show any kind of emotion that would show insincerity for an alliance. He appeared to be completely serious.

And I had to think he was.

Killian was brilliant. Even if he'd changed his mind and decided he wanted me around again, he wasn't oblivious to the way my much smaller group of wizards had turned the tides on the fae. We were worthy of his respect, and an excellent chess piece for him to use. He really did want this alliance.

Which was great, because I did, too—with some big caveats.

I glanced at Great Aunt Marraine, who was seated next to me and patted my thigh under the table. She'd gone through my list of requests with me line by line every day since she'd learned about the meeting. We could do this.

I took a deep breath. "I'll agree to an alliance, should you agree to my requirements."

"Name them," Killian said.

"I want a written, *signed* agreement that we'll share all information and intelligence we receive about the Night Court and their plans," I said. "You will not conveniently leave out any details, or fail to tell us about a new movement."

Again, up went an eyebrow. "You don't want me to act without your knowledge."

"Yes." My smile was brittle. "Because you've proven to be untrustworthy."

"Fair enough. What else?"

"I want Gavino." I held my breath and tried to gauge his reaction.

Killian narrowed his eyes. "*What?*"

"I want Gavino to live at House Medeis for six months, and work as a trainer for my wizards," I said. "During that time he won't be available for regular vampire duties—so you can't use him as your plant and yank him out whenever it suits you. But if we're going to a fight then we'll agree he should stand with the vampires."

Killian rapidly blinked, then looked quizzically at me. "You want him as a *trainer?*"

"House Medeis now has a large gym, including a pretty nice arrangement of weights and lifting machines," I said. "I've hired a martial artist and a weapons trainer who come by once or twice a week, but I want my people to have the same base fitness training I had. If possible, I'd also like him to train us in more self-defense maneuvers."

Killian turned to look at Gavino, who had first looked shocked and maybe a little terrified at my initial suggestion, but was now thoughtfully folding his arms across his chest. The big vampire nodded at Killian.

"That could be arranged, provided you're willing to make allowances so he *can* live at House Medeis," Killian said.

"We'll get him a blood delivery, and provide a room with the right kind of drapes to block sunlight." I sat straighter in my chair.

This was one of the demands I thought Killian would bargain to drive me down on—I figured at best he'd send Gavino over for a day or two during the week. I was a little giddy at the thought of having Gavino on hand to train us whenever we liked. Since we added to our numbers there were almost thirty House Medeis adult wizards, and I'd probably have him do some sessions with the teenagers as well...

"If you're willing, then I don't think it will be a problem," Killian said, interrupting my glee. "What else?"

For the next half hour I laid out my more strategic requirements—that we fight together but keep our Family and House business separate, and once the conflict with the Night Court was over the ties to our alliance would be looser—so he couldn't permanently insert himself into House Medeis business.

It was mostly boring legal stuff, with a few fighting provisions —we each separately commanded our people, blah, blah, blah. (We wouldn't have to bother with it usually, except this was Killian Drake. We needed things to be as clear and straightforward as possible, or he'd find a loop hole.) But there was one final requirement I *really* wanted, and I wasn't quite sure how it would shake out.

Killian looked up from the printed paper that had my list of requirements—as recorded by Julianne on a laptop. "Is there anything else?" he asked. "Or shall we draw the documents up?"

"No, I have one last requirement."

Great Aunt Marraine whipped her head around to look at me so quickly that the blue streak in her gray hair was a blur. She stared intently at me, and I could *feel* her confusion and apprehension.

I held in a wince—I hadn't dared to tell her about this demand. I knew she wouldn't go for it, but it was important.

I tried to seem relaxed and casual as I gave Killian a shallow, business-like smile. "I want to continue my training here at Drake Hall at least once a week for the next six months."

Great Aunt Marraine grabbed my thigh and squeezed, and I could hear the faint wheeze of air escaping her lungs.

Undeterred, I added, "If my presence is distasteful to the vampires at Drake Hall, I can be trained at House Medeis as long as skilled vampires come to teach me."

Since leaving Drake Hall, I had understandably stalled in my combat training.

My family was picking up on the magic skills I'd learned at Drake Hall—like the magic shield—at a much faster rate than I had. Part of that was I was able to actually *show* them what to do. When I'd been in their position, I was blindly feeling about with only pictures from a book to help me.

But I wasn't satisfied with my current level of fighting. And while I could keep working on my magic abilities since the Paragon had dropped off the book, I really needed the combat experience the Drake Family provided when I practiced with them. And sadly Gavino wasn't going to cut it, or I wouldn't have to ask for this.

"That's acceptable." Killian stabbed a straw into a blood pouch and sucked it down quickly. "It will work well with my requirement."

I warily eyed him. "And that is?"

Killian smirked, losing the business-like manner he'd held on to since we sat down. "*My* requirement is that once a month, during these next six months while you are getting training and support, you have to stay at Drake Hall."

CHAPTER NINE

Hazel

Mr. Clark stood up and knocked his chair over. "*What?*"

Momoko narrowed her eyes and murmured to me, "He's joking, right?"

"That's not happening," I snarled.

Killian held up a hand. "Wait a moment and think about what I've said. I'm asking you to stay at Drake Hall, and you already want to be here to receive training. If you keep a room here, it will be easier for you—and if you want to bring some of your wizards with you we'll clear out rooms for them, too."

"You can't suddenly demand that I spend a week with you every month," I warned him.

"I understand," Killian said. "The length of your stay will be up to your discretion, but I will require a minimum of one night per month."

"There's something fishy about this." Though Felix spoke in a lowered tone, I knew the vampires still heard him with their superior senses.

I combed a hand through the wild mess of my blond hair. "Why?" I asked.

"You are referring to?"

"Why do you want me to stay?" I pursed my lips as I studied the vampire. "Everything I've asked for has a clear reason. What do you get out of this?"

Killian's smile turned bemused—but not smug. No, it was almost...sad? "Isn't it obvious, Hazel?"

He stared at me with such intensity, my nerves made me look away. "I agree to your terms," I said.

Great Aunt Marraine grabbed my hand and squeezed it. "Adept, are you sure about this?"

"Yes," I said. "Though he'll try to boss us all around and might have a go at making you all wear suits whenever you're here, he's not going to physically hurt us. He'll suddenly turn colder than a prissy mean girl in high school, but we can roll with that."

"Such an admirable depiction of me," Killian mused as he considered an unopened blood pouch.

"You'll have the papers drawn up?" I asked. "We'll have to register them through the Curia Cloisters before we can sign them."

Killian glanced at Julianne, who bobbed her head. "It's done. Julianne will correct and format the contract. I'll give you a copy before you leave, and submit a second copy to the Cloisters."

I sagged a little in my chair, relieved that negotiations were over.

Killian had given in to everything I wanted—probably a ploy so he could get his one night a month. I wasn't exactly moved by that request. It was more like I was wondering how he was going to use it—because Killian never did anything just for the heart of it.

"Splendid!" Celestina clapped her hands once and beamed at me and my wizards like a benevolent fairy godmother. "Since we're going to be working so closely together for the foreseeable future, please allow me to give you a tour of Drake Hall as our esteemed guests!"

My retinue doubtfully looked back at me, and I felt like a mom giving permission for her kids to go play. "You guys should go," I said. "It's a big house, and if any of you come with me for my weekly practices, you'll want to know your way around."

"This way!" Celestina made her way to the door, resembling a tour guide.

I don't think it had occurred to my family to wonder why the Drake Family's First Knight—in other words the strongest vampire after Killian—was playing tourist with them. I was pretty sure it was because her warmer, tawny skin tone that hadn't lost all its color when she turned and her bright personality would make them lower their guard faster. (Her personality was a tactic that had worked on me, after all.)

"Hazel," Killian said. "Would you join me in my study?" His faint British accent was ever so slightly pronounced. But I couldn't see anything in his expression that would indicate why.

I glanced at the door, making sure the last House Medeis wizard cleared the room. "Sure."

"Really?" Killian blinked down at me. "I thought I'd have to try harder to pry you away from your family."

"I'm pretty sure I know what you want to talk about," I said. "And we'll have to discuss it eventually. We may as well have at it now while I know they're occupied."

It wasn't that I didn't appreciate my family's tight defense. But to make this alliance work I needed to draw clear boundaries for Killian, and given our...murky history, I didn't really want anyone listening in, just in case he decided to drop the bombshell that we —a wizard and vampire—had kissed.

Inter-supernatural romances weren't outlawed or anything—it was the offspring of vampires and humans that became the first vampire slayers, and the descendants of werewolves and humans had become werewolf hunters. But nowadays it was a taboo—and had been a taboo for a looong time.

Some of the races had pulled back to "protect the purity" of their bloodlines. (Give me a break.) Otherwise, it was more of a political thing, done so each race could solidify their power base. They couldn't have us intermingling—it might make it harder when we had to fight for laws and favorable outcomes for our own people.

"Very well," Killian said. "You know the way."

I raised my eyebrow at him, but left the meeting room and made my way through the maze-like mansion to his study.

Killian's study was a blend of decadence, militant tidiness, and technology.

Austere bookshelves filled with tediously sorted magical books guarded the walls, but there was also a shelf dedicated to a giant TV, a tablet, and a laptop. The tall walls had some kind of damask wallpaper, but the wooden floor was covered with a surprisingly plush rug.

He'd gotten new chairs since I'd last been there, and now there was a comfy-looking sofa in a corner that previously had been occupied by a statue of a rearing horse.

I flung myself into one of the new chairs—which was soft and cushy—then peered expectantly at Killian. "All right. I'm here. Let's talk."

Instead of sitting himself at his desk, Killian stood next to it, his eyes narrowed. "You know why I sent you out of Drake Hall."

"We've covered this," I said. "Yeah, I know that you did a raid on the Night Court to keep them busy so they couldn't help Mason when I attacked him, and yeah, I know you sent the Paragon to my doorstep to ensure a fair fight, and yeah I know you kicked me out because you knew I was a prime target for the Night Court. Can we stop rehashing this?"

"Then I'm confused," Killian said. "If you know all of that, why are you so angry with me?"

"Your motivation doesn't excuse your behavior."

"But I apologized."

"Not very well," I muttered.

"But everything worked out for the best," Killian persisted. He leaned against his desk and tilted his head as he studied me. "And you've never been this angry before—not even when I dropped you off the balcony."

I almost grinned at the memory—I'd been terrified and furious at the time, but the balcony incident had helped break the ice with the other Drake vampires, and had been my first real step toward friendship with them. At least it had been when I thought we were friends.

"Hazel."

I reluctantly dragged my eyes up to meet his gaze.

He stared at me for several long moments, and something in his expression tightened before he adopted his slightly arrogant look he usually only used in political situations. "Is it that you can't admit I was right?"

"*Right?*" I exploded out of my chair. "You think you were *right?* You *lied* to me! You could have just told me what was going on, but instead you decided to manipulate me. Things could have turned out so differently if you had just *told* me the fae were making stupid threats! But no, you didn't trust me enough to stay with you, to be safe—to even handle *myself*! I'd worked like a dog to become a better wizard and decent in a fight and thought I'd won myself a place in this wretched hall, but you took everything because you didn't think you could tell me the Night Court was scheming! Which—newsflash!—is *all they ever do*!" I snarled.

"If you think I'm so incompetent you should have just told me. Instead you chose to do everything behind my back and nudge me into what *you* wanted to do because obviously I can't be trusted! And you'll never trust me, because you don't trust anyone that's not a vampire!"

When I finished my tirade I heaved a few breaths, and Killian looked thoughtful. I reviewed what he'd said, compared it to the slant of his eyebrows, then pointed a finger at him. "And you just did it *again*! You manipulated me into yelling at you!"

"It's hardly my fault you were so reluctant to share," Killian pointed out. "And I can't correct my mistake if you don't tell me what I did."

I angrily threw myself back down in the comfy chair. My magic had spiked a little with my emotions, so now I was hot and somewhat miserable since I'd ripped the wound open again.

"It seems that you were most offended by my lack of trust," Killian said. "Which isn't quite true. I trust you a great deal more than you would think."

I gave him a withering glare. "Now that's the stupidest lie you've ever tried to tell me."

"Except it's true." Killian thoughtfully folded his arms across his chest. "However, I don't trust anyone—vampire or otherwise—at the level you seem to desire."

I opened my mouth to interrupt, but Killian must have guessed what my retort would be. "Not even Celestina and Josh," he said. "They are comrades that I treasure, and they are probably the most capable at guessing what my plans are, but I don't tell them."

I folded my fingers together and stared at him.

"It's very...difficult for me to trust anyone," Killian continued. "I didn't become the Eminence by good sportsmanship. Vampires in general tend to be distrustful—it's in our nature, and frequently enforced upon us. When you live as long as we do, you are inevitably betrayed again and again, and after a while the bitterness tends to seep into even the most kind-hearted of vampires." Killian sighed. "Though I am admittedly worse. For my own safety, for the good of vampires, and to achieve my goals I've learned that deep trust is a luxury I can't afford."

I plucked at my warm sweater, pondering my response. "In your position, trusting someone would be difficult. However, the way you manipulated me isn't okay. It's not healthy, and I won't take it long term. You really hurt me. Even though I had a hunch I knew what you were doing, you ripped me from the friends I'd made—from *you*—and dumped me on my own without any warning. That's toxic, and I'm not going to experience it again."

Killian pressed his palms together. "What does that mean?"

"It means either you trust me more and *tell* me what's going on, or, once we take care of the Night Court, we will have an alliance of formality, not friendship," I said.

Killian cocked an eyebrow. "That doesn't seem fair. You're asking me to go against instincts and experience."

"It's the price of my friendship, Killian," I said. "Trust me, or we'll both be miserable."

His expression was thoughtful, which shocked me. I didn't think he'd actually care quite this much.

But it was about time to lighten the moment, so I inhaled deeply and forced myself to perk up. "And I still want an apology—a *real* one," I stressed.

He snapped on a caressing smirk. "But all of my apologies are real," he insisted.

"Well they're not at all convincing," I grumbled.

"If I apologize properly, you'll forgive me?"

I thought for a moment. "No. I already have forgiven you—now that everything is out there."

"Then why is trust still an issue?"

"Forgiveness means giving up my anger at your actions. It doesn't mean there are no consequences to your actions," I said.

"How very inconvenient."

I rolled my eyes. "So sorry you don't get to have *everything* you want."

"There is another matter we should discuss."

"Hm?" I lazily glanced at him, then tensed.

In the stark light of his office, he looked more vampiric than usual with his eyes glowing red and his slight smirk revealing one of his pronounced fangs. His eyes were usually closer to a shade of obsidian veined with rubies, and typically only intensified when he had stronger emotions—whether he was feeling murderous or smug. AKA, things looked shaky for me.

I sat up and eyed him. "What?"

"I was informed that we ought to *define our relationship.*" Killian pushed off his desk and strolled closer to me.

I cleared my throat. "Who told you that?"

"Research, and some sources."

"Research?" I blinked, confused. "What is that supposed to mean?"

Killian stood so close to my chair his legs brushed my knees, and he thoroughly ignored me. "Where, then, do we stand?"

"Not very close together." I pointedly tucked my legs up onto the chair.

His chuckle was smokey. "That isn't quite what I meant."

I squirmed in my chair, aware that this could end badly.

I wasn't an idiot. I was *painfully* aware of how handsome Killian was, and I was competent enough to know he hadn't kissed me on a lark. But I was also intelligent enough to know that if we couldn't get the trust issue worked out, things would end badly. And I would be the one to pay the price. I didn't love by halves—it was why Killian's lack of trust hit me so hard, same as Celestina and Josh's rejection.

"Nothing changes," I blurted out. "Until we fix our issues."

Killian thoughtfully studied me. "You mean until I show that I trust you?"

"Yes."

"Your butt is still off limits to me, then?"

"*Yes!*" I bristled at him and sank deeper into the chair as if it could protect me. "Why are you so obsessed with my butt, anyway?"

"Mere curiosity. You are profoundly protective of it, so I imagine there must be a reason for that."

I groaned and mashed my palms into my eyes. "You're the *worst*."

Killian laughed again. This time, it wasn't quite so throaty, and his eyes didn't glow so much—though he still didn't move.

I leaned my head back as I studied him. "Is it really okay for me to borrow Gavino? I mean—if he doesn't want to come he doesn't have to."

"You're allowing him an honor he's sure to hold over every member of my household," Killian dryly said. "He's more than fine with it. And yes, I can lend you Gavino. I'm surprised you didn't try for Josh or Celestina."

"I didn't part well with them."

"You fault them for their loyalty to me?"

"No. I was hurt by the way they treated me as I left." I sighed. "They could have at least said goodbye, or wished me luck —*anything*."

"Ahh," Killian said. "Well, I'm sure you will have ample time to discuss it now that we have our alliance."

"I don't want to discuss it," I muttered.

"You are willing to forgive me, but not my First or Second Knight?" Killian raised both eyebrows. "I don't know if I should be concerned or rejoice at the preferential treatment."

"It's not preferential," I said. "I expected scheming and manipulating from you—you don't even try to hide it. But Josh and Celestina treated me like a real friend, and then ripped that from me. Since they weren't scheming like you, it revealed what they really thought of me."

"I wouldn't say they weren't scheming," Killian said almost dismissively. He glanced at the door behind us, probably hearing something I couldn't.

"What is it?" I asked.

"Your *dear* Great Aunt Marraine is giving Rupert a tongue lashing in the hallway for sneering at your family," he said.

I hopped to my feet. "We better intervene," I said. "Or they'll be at each other's throats."

"Fine, but I have one last question for you," Killian said. "If you were still angry with me, why did you agree to meet and discuss an alliance?"

I paused with my hand on the doorknob. "I was mad at you, and I knew we needed to define our boundaries...but I'm *furious* with the Night Court for attacking you guys in what was supposed to be neutral territory."

"Ahhhh." Killian smiled. "Your virtues stirred up righteous indignation, I see."

"What?"

"Not to worry. It seems I ought to be thankful to the Night Court for provoking your champion-like tendencies." He joined me at the door and gestured for me to continue. "Now, let us go save our wayward kinsmen."

"Great Aunt Marraine is a lot of things. I don't know that I would ever call her wayward. Pushy, yes. Opinionated, for sure. Stubborn, heck yes. Naturally, I assume this means she and Rupert will be *besties*."

"What an auspicious start to our alliance."

"Totally."

The following week I puttered with two refrigerated blood packs as I waited for Gavino to arrive at House Medeis.

I'd learned more about blood refrigeration in the past few days than I had ever wanted to. Apparently, an extremely accurate fridge was required for the blood, because if it froze the red cells burst—something vampires didn't appreciate in their food, apparently.

I mentally went down my checklist as I adjusted the shades in the room.

I'd chosen what everyone called the "front parlor" to welcome Gavino. It was a little more ornate than I wanted since it had an onyx fireplace—which was lit and crackling—a fancy tiled ceiling I had been informed was called a "coffered ceiling" (Momoko, it seemed, was a secret HGTV fanatic) dark wooden paneling on the lower portion of the walls, and antique furniture. However, it was also the least sunny sitting room at this time of the day, and I wanted to make sure Gavino felt comfortable. We'd probably be talking for a while—I needed to explain to him some of House Medeis's...eccentricities, and my family was going to pass through so they could slowly introduce themselves to him one at a time instead of overwhelming him at dinner.

The doorbell for the driveway gate rang.

"I'll get it!" Felix thundered down the hallway to greet our vampire guest.

I gave one last look at the snacks I'd put out—some crackers and cheese, though Gavino usually just nibbled at human food so I didn't know if he'd really want to eat—and turned to the parlor door just in time for Great Aunt Marraine to bustle through.

"How nice!" She appropriately cooed, cupping her plump cheeks with her hands. "Your little vampire friend will feel quite welcome! We'll all make sure of it."

"He's not exactly little," I said.

"Oh, pooh," Great Aunt Marraine wrinkled her nose at me. "Everyone is little to the likes of me." She winked, flashing her neon pink eyeshadow. She'd changed her dyed stripe of color in her silvery-gray hair from blue to pink, and had adjusted her wardrobe accordingly.

"How so?" I asked, though I got distracted when I felt the warm but dry touch of House Medeis mentally poking me.

Great Aunt Marraine chuckled. "At my age, you realize just how small the world is. Why, I—"

The House poked me again. "I'm sorry, Great Aunt Marraine, could you give me a moment? The House wants something." I expectantly turned to the wall.

"Oh. Well. The House is important," Great Aunt Marraine rambled uncharacteristically. (She was never one to lack words, but usually she had a point she was driving you to, so this was a little odd.)

I filtered her out as I tuned in to House Medeis.

Since my Ascension ceremony at the very end of summer, my relationship with the magical House had drastically deepened.

Previously I had to guess how it was feeling and what it wanted—which wasn't too much of a problem since it was very clear on speaking its mind. If it was mad, it might express this by taking away all hot water from me, or by sending a raccoon down a chimney, which it had done once when I was a kid and broke a window but blamed it on the next-door neighbors. (Let me tell you, after that I was an *extremely* honest child. Nothing traumatizes you quite like taking an angry, sooty raccoon to the face.)

Now, House Medeis could communicate by adding its own little twists to the magic that freely oozed around in the air. That was how it told me that two others had arrived with Gavino—vampires, presumably—and that both Felix *and* Momoko were escorting them in through the side door by the kitchen.

Thankfully, the House didn't seem displeased with their presence, though it was paying special attention to them. (I'd have to make sure I warned Gavino about taking off his shoes, or the House might take it upon itself to "teach" him.)

Great Aunt Marraine rattled on, which made me suspicious because she usually went quiet the second I said I needed to speak to the House.

What is she trying to hide?

I heard footsteps in the hallway, and a smile bloomed on my

face. "Gavino!" I jogged to the doorway. "I'm so happy you're...here."

Gavino—big and hulking—grinned playfully at me as he dragged a rolling suitcase and had a garment bag slung over his shoulder—for his suits, probably.

Behind him, however, were Celestina and Josh.

CHAPTER TEN

Hazel

Celestina wore her brightest, most inviting grin, and even Josh had dusted off a rusty smile for the occasion.

On a hunch, I swung around to give Great Aunt Marraine an accusatory look.

She beamed sweetly at me and bustled out of the room. "Dear me, I'm turning into an old woman who prattles at inconvenient times. Since our guest has arrived, I'll take my leave. Though I must say it will be exciting to have such a strapping young man in the House!" She winked as she passed Gavino—who released a bark of laughter.

At a loss, I could only stare at her back as she retreated, her pink, checkered dress a bright spot in the hallway.

"We'll just leave, too." Momoko started to sidle away. "We wouldn't want to cramp your reunion."

"Oh, no you don't." I grabbed Momoko by the hood of her sweatshirt. "Do you care to tell me why neither you, Felix, nor Great Aunt Marraine is shocked to see the Drake Family's First and Second Knights?" I snarled.

"Uhh, not really," Momoko said.

Felix, carrying a wooden tray that had several more blood pouches balanced on it, ducked past me to get into the parlor. "It was Momoko's idea," he said. "We came up with it when Celestina gave us the tour of Drake Hall."

"Thanks for the support, Felix," Momoko growled.

"It was obvious Celestina knew you really well." Felix set the blood pouches on an antique card table after finding some coasters. "The whole tour was peppered with stories about you. We told them to come with Gavino so they could talk to you since you were obviously avoiding them."

I glared at my childhood friend, but it was Momoko who whispered, "I think there was a misunderstanding, Hazel. And while I get that they hurt you, I know you love them enough to want to know what really went down. We arranged this for your sake."

I again glanced at Celestina and Josh, then sighed and released Momoko. "Come on in."

The three vampires trooped in after Momoko and me. I plopped down in what Momoko had informed me earlier in the day was a "Rococo revival sofa with a mahogany veneer." Frankly, I didn't know what that meant besides EXPENSIVE, DO NOT BREAK! (I hadn't realized how much antique furniture was in the House until I suddenly became responsible for it. I was going to have all gray hair by the time I turned thirty.)

I thought Momoko or Felix would sit next to me, but they lingered by the fireplace, letting the vampires take the seats around the card table.

"Thanks for agreeing to come here to train us, Gavino," I said once everyone had settled.

Gavino laughed, his steely voice gruff and deep. "It's my delight. This will be a vacation for me."

"I certainly hope it will be comfortable enough for you. I have a bedroom picked out for you—I can show it to you once we finish here," I said.

He nodded, then glanced at his superiors.

Josh still had his rusty smile on, but Celestina had knit her eyebrows together in her concern. "We're sorry," she blurted out. "It didn't go down the way it was supposed to. We—I—messed up."

"I assume you're talking about my escort out of Drake Hall?" I asked.

Celestina winced. "His Eminence was expressively clear that you needed to leave with no strings attached so you'd go win back your House."

"And the best way to achieve that was to act like a jerk?" I politely inquired.

"I went overboard," Celestina said. "But I knew why the Eminence didn't want you around."

"And you agreed with him?"

"Yes, no." Celestina made a frustrated sound and rattled a few sentences off in disgruntled Spanish.

"I believe what my superior is attempting to say," Josh cut in, "is that she was deeply traumatized by the events at the mall."

I stared at the black-haired vampire, and said, "What," in a flat tone.

"It's true, Hazel," Celestina said. "I don't think you understand how terrifying it was to have the fae threaten to target you with weapons you couldn't feel—unlike their magic. Weapons that we would be able to react to, but not in time to save *you*."

I pinched the bridge of my nose. "Does the entire Drake Family like to act like haughty know-it-alls and then use heart-twisting motivations to excuse their behavior, or is that just an upper management thing?"

"We're not trying to excuse our behavior, but rather explain it," Josh said. "As much as I like to create witty quips and lighthearted statements about the unstoppable hunger of death that will eventually consume the world with its gaping maw, the prospect of losing you was daunting for myself, and Celestina."

"That's why we agreed when His Eminence decided to send you away. You're my friend, Hazel. As selfish as it makes me, I also didn't want to risk losing you." The sincerity in Celestina's red eyes was almost painful to witness as she knit her fingers together and perched at the edge of her seat. "But Josh and I planned for ways to reach out to you! They just all…failed."

I tapped my fingers on my thighs. "Neither you nor Josh ever came here for guard duty—though I suppose Killian couldn't do without his First or Second Knight in times like this."

"It was your sword, actually," Celestina said. "I purposely left it and the Paragon's book back at Drake Hall. I planned to take a detour to House Medeis on my way to the Night Court's stronghold that night so I could give you your katana before you fought Mason. I thought it would give me a chance to explain a little bit of what was going on. And I figured that after you won your House back, I could wait a few days and then bring you the Paragon's book as my second excuse to connect with you. By then we would have received more intelligence on the Night Court, and I could tell you exactly how Killian was protecting you."

"I already know about why Killian did everything he did," I said. "From a very unlikely source."

Celestina nodded. "I expected as much—particularly once I found out your sword had gone mysteriously missing directly after you left, as had the book."

"The book was the Paragon's doing," Josh added. "But the sword was a surprising act of rebellion in the face of—what did you call us? 'Upper Management'? Anyway, it was the work of a Drake vampire."

The duo stared expectantly at me.

"I'm not saying anything about that," I said.

Celestina nodded. "As we expected. Regardless, we wish to apologize—we made a grave misstep in handling this matter."

"It was not our intention to hurt you," Josh said. "We are sorry for any pain we might have caused."

I sighed—when they explained it like that, could I really be mad at them? "Next time this happens, would you guys just *tell* me what's going on? The mental games aren't necessary. I'm a pretty reasonable person."

Celestina shook her head. "There won't be a next time."

"That's hardly realistic. I love you guys, but I know you'll choose Killian every time—which I can understand. As long as you don't ice me out again."

"Agreed," Josh said. "But he's not going to let you go a second time."

"I doubt that."

"You don't think he is that desirous of you?" Josh asked.

Gavino had been calmly sipping a blood pouch, but abruptly choked on it and started coughing up a storm.

Similarly, Felix dropped a massive unlit candle he'd swiped off the mantle. It landed on his foot with a painful crack.

"I think Killian is a very wily vampire who is stuck in his ways and prone to thinking he knows best about everything," I dryly said. "As long as he is so distrustful, it's only a matter of time before he tries to manipulate me instead of just telling me what's going on. But that's between Killian and me."

Josh looked thoughtful, but Celestina merely shrugged. "If you wish it. But are Josh and I forgiven?"

I smiled a little. "Yeah. I forgive you. But you still didn't answer me. Next time—"

"If there is a next time, we will choose Killian as you said, but we promise to speak frankly with you," Celestina said.

"That's all I want." I glanced over at Momoko and Felix—who were inspecting Felix's foot. "Does the peanut gallery have anything to say about this?"

Momoko batted her long eyelashes. "No. Why would we?"

"You felt strongly enough about it to invite them here."

"And we don't regret it," Felix confirmed.

"Should I go tell Mrs. Clark to expect extra guests for dinner?" Momoko asked.

"Good point." I swung my gaze back to my vampire friends. "You guys can stick around for Gavino's introduction if you like. After I show him around and the family gets a good gawk at him, we figured we'd have dinner."

"We would love to join you," Celestina said.

Josh squinted slightly. "Do you also have a no-weapons rule at the dinner table?"

"No. Why? Do you think you aren't safe here?" I frowned, disturbed by the idea.

"Not at all," Josh assured me. "Rather, I have a new hidden dagger I wanted to try wearing, and it's located inside my boxers—I do not think your family would appreciate such a show."

It was apparently Felix's turn to choke. He exploded into a rattling cough.

I tapped my cheek. "What good does the hidden dagger do if it's in your boxers?"

"That is the point I was hoping to test," Josh said. "Thus far it has been an unsatisfactory experience."

"I see. Either way, it's fine." I tipped my head as I felt the whispery touch of the House. "Gavino, I'd recommend you finish your blood, because my Great Aunt is about thirty seconds away from barreling through the door with the first round of wizards for you to meet."

"Yes, Miss Hazel."

I started to stand, but paused midstep. "Oh, and Celestina, Josh?"

"Yes?" Celestina asked.

"Thanks for coming to apologize."

THE FOLLOWING WEEK Celestina came back to House Medeis to pick me up for my first bi-weekly training session.

"You know, I have a car." I tightened the laces of my running shoes and glanced at my escort. "You didn't have to drive me."

"Nonsense," Celestina said. "It's cheaper to carpool."

"Killian *does* remember that I'm not staying at Drake Hall this week, doesn't he?" I asked suspiciously.

"Of course," Celestina soothed.

Unconvinced, I twisted around in my seat to look behind me.

Momoko sat in the back seat, making a thorough inspection of the car's fancy leather interior. "Wow. Being old must pay really well."

I smirked at her. "Not all the Drake vampires have Celestina's sense of humor, you know?"

Momoko blinked. "But I wasn't being funny."

I slightly shook my head and glanced out the rearview window. A black SUV followed behind us—it contained Felix, Franco, and Rupert.

I had hoped the mischievous wizard brothers would keep their mouths shut, but based on the way the car was angrily veering around the road, I'm pretty sure Rupert was close to homicidal.

"Rupert must be having fun," Celestina chirped with innocence.

"Do you think he'll refrain from killing them?" I asked.

Rupert's car abruptly slammed to a stop, then raced after us again moments later.

"He learned his lesson when he harmed you," Celestina assured me.

"Yeah, except the Clark brothers are about twice as bad as I am." I reluctantly faced forward again, recognizing the rolling countryside, which was cast in long, blue shadows as the sun hovered just over the horizon. Soon, I could spy the wrought-iron fence that divided Drake Hall from its neighbors.

Fleetingly, I remembered their friendly neighbor who'd given me a ride right after Killian kicked me out. "Hey Celestina," I said. "Do you think we could stop in and see Leila sometime?"

"Certainly." Celestina glanced at the clock. "She should be home right about now."

"Do you really think we could visit her right now?" I asked. "Shouldn't we call or something?"

"It's not necessary. Leila and her family are used to unexpected visits from us," Celestina said. "The dogs know she gives out treats, so if their handler isn't paying attention, they slip through the fence to visit her."

She cruised past the dragon gates that barred the way to Drake Hall, and kept on driving.

"Huh, I'm surprised Killian puts up with that," Momoko said from the backseat.

"I'm pretty sure he doesn't care what the dogs do as long as they are healthy and well cared for," I said. "He mentioned he got them just to inflict mental warfare against the local Alphas."

"Correct!" Celestina laughed as she pulled into a gravel driveway and drove up to a quaint, ranch-style house. A beautiful chicken coop was nestled next to the house, and hens that were a reddish-brown with flecks of white clucked at us in lecturing tones as they watched from the coop door.

Out back I could see pastures marked with white, wooden fences, and a small barn that had to be a stable since Leila—holding a bright blue leadrope—was exiting the building with a beautiful horse in tow.

The horse was a chestnut color with reddish brown hair and stockings on its legs that were so white they practically glowed in the dim sunset. It followed placidly behind Lelia as she waved once we parked the car.

"Hey, Celestina. Did the dogs get out again? They haven't made their way over here, yet."

"For once I am not here about our wayward pets," Celestina said. "I brought you a guest."

Leila curiously peered at me, then smiled again, making her dazzling. "Hazel!"

Man, that fae blood is dangerous.

"Hi, Leila." I cautiously approached her—that horse she was holding on to was ginormous—and gave her a side hug. "It's great to see you again."

"Hello! I assume it's safe to wish you a welcome back to the neighborhood?" She pointedly tossed her head in Celestina's direction and watched Rupert park and throw himself out of the car.

"Kind of," I said. "I'm not staying here, but Killian and I are talking again."

When Leila had taken me back to House Medeis after Killian kicked me out, we had swapped numbers, and I'd given her a shortened version of our history, so she was vaguely aware of the problems that had stirred up House Medeis, and that I had stayed with the Drakes for a while.

"*Why*," Rupert snarled, "are we *here*?"

"Hey, Rupert!" Leila waved to the red-haired vampire, and curiously watched Franco and Felix climb out of his car. "Hanging with humans, huh? That's pretty rare for you."

Rupert gave her a withering glare.

Leila chuckled. "Awww, you're just as precious as usual."

Rupert's eyes bulged, and I wondered if today would be the day one of us pushed him over the edge into a homicidal maniac.

I glanced at the horse again—which was watching Rupert as it twitched its lips—and smiled. "I wanted to thank you again for your help, and let you know I'll be hanging around."

"That's wonderful!" Leila's grin amplified the brightness of her violet-blue eyes—one of the reasons why I suspected she had fae heritage. "It's pretty rare for anyone besides vampires to go in and out of Drake Hall, so I'm so happy for the Drakes in particular."

Rupert's right eyebrow twitched, but Celestina nodded her agreement.

"Oh, I'm sorry—I'm being rude. Momoko, Felix, Franco, this is Leila. Leila, meet Momoko, Felix, and Franco—they're wizards who belong to House Medeis."

"I remember you mentioning her," Felix said. "Thank you for bringing our Adept back to us." He offered Leila a glittering smile that rivaled her own.

"Of course! I'm glad I happened to be in the right place," Leila said.

"You still haven't visited House Medeis," I reminded her. "We need to fix that."

"For sure! Oh, and you should come over sometime if you ever need a break from all the training that goes on over there." She gestured vaguely in the direction of Drake Hall.

"You could stop in at Drake Hall whenever you wish, Leila," Celestina chimed in. "You do have an open invitation."

"Really?" I whipped my gaze back to Leila. "That's pretty rare."

"It's not as impressive as it sounds," Leila patted her horse's muscled neck when he lipped her shoulder. "The vampire in charge of the dogs has me come over a few times a year for a training refresher for them."

"You're a dog trainer?" Momoko asked. "That's awesome!"

"Oh, no I'm not really a trainer—not for any animal." Leila slung her arm over the horse's shoulders. "But I've got some fae blood, so animals that interact with me for long periods of time tend to be smarter than average."

Ah-hah! I was right—and I didn't even have to be rude or nosy and ask!

Franco scratched his chin as he studied Leila. "I didn't know that was a common fae trait."

"I don't know that it's common," Leila said. "Not all fae have it. But I won't lie, it's really fun!"

Celestina slightly bowed her head. "We Drakes are grateful you are willing to use your talent on our behalf."

Rupert made a noise of dissension in the back of his throat and pointedly looked away.

An ominous thud followed by the clatter of buckets spilling onto the ground filtered out of the barn.

Leila swung around to face the shadows of the open door. "Again? Really, Bagel. Do you have to be *that* nosy?"

It sounded like a couple dozen more buckets and bins were turned over before a small donkey emerged from the stable.

He brayed—a noise that sounded like car brakes screeching combined with a sea lion barking, only at a decimal level that was almost loud enough to break your eardrums. When he brayed his whole body jiggled with the force it took to make the noise and suck in enough air. He blasted his bray at us for a few moments, then flattened his long ears, poked his nose up in the sky, and gave us a donkey smile.

"Sorry, that's Bagel," Leila apologized. "You can ignore him. He's a little stinker and gets out all the time, but he won't go anywhere. He probably just heard us and decided to come say hello."

Bagel's fuzzy gray-brown coat made him look extra huggable, and even though he might have just deafened me, the dimple in his velveteen muzzle and the way he flicked his boney tail was too cute to hold anything against him.

I, apparently, wasn't the only one who thought so. The horse Leila held on to nickered at the fuzzy newcomer.

"Don't encourage him," Leila scolded.

Bagel meandered out by us, alternating between flashing his donkey smile and straightening his ears so we could admire them.

"He's so cute!" I stroked his neck, laughing as he visibly preened.

"He's spoiled rotten," Leila wryly said. "He thinks he's God's gift to the world. I'm sure he believes he poops gold." She rolled her eyes. "It's fine!"

Leila's horse companion shook his head, making his halter jingle, and Bagel lipped my arm.

"We should get out of your hair—but we have to make plans soon." I reluctantly gave the donkey one last pat.

"Sounds great. Take care—and welcome back." Leila waited until Rupert had turned his back to her, then called in a musical tone that sounded as sweet as candy tasted. "Bye-bye Rupert, I'll miss you!"

When he visibly shivered she snickered, then turned and led the giant horse back to the stable. "Come on, Bagel."

Bagel erupted into a series of loud brays, but he dutifully followed after Leila.

Felix and Franco exchanged smirks, then jogged after their vampire driver.

"Rupert, wait up!" Felix called.

"Yeah." Franco's voice was *too* innocent and happy for him to be anything except gleeful. "You've been holding out on us! You didn't tell us how friendly you are with other humans!"

"I feel so wounded!"

The pair caught up to Rupert and walked on either side of him, matching his pace even though he was essentially speed-walking.

Momoko, Celestina and I trailed after them, making our way back to the cars.

"She seems nice," Momoko said. "But I'd never want to get caught between her and Felix—that's too much dazzling good looks for a regular person to handle."

"Yeah," I agreed. "I was kind of wondering if he'd see her as competition, or a potential ally. It seems like they'll be allies. I don't think that bodes well for Rupert."

"It's good for Rupert to encounter frustration," Celestina said. "It fosters character."

I started to laugh, but up ahead Rupert grabbed both Felix and Franco by the collars of their shirts, and dragged them down. "Get down!"

CHAPTER ELEVEN

Hazel

I was already on my way down, but Celestina—being so much faster—yanked Momoko's feet out from under her, dragging her down, and half covered me with her own body before I even hit the gravel driveway.

Pebbles mashed my cheek, but I didn't dare raise my head. "What is it?" I whispered.

An arrow struck the ground about a foot away from me. The arrowhead glowed green for a moment, and I felt the floral sensation of fae magic. "Break the arrows!" I shouted. "They're laced with magic."

I yanked the arrow out of the ground and snapped it in half.

Momoko wriggled her arms out in front of her and got a shield up. "What formation, Adept?"

"Sphere!" I let magic filter through my blood, then jolted up into a sitting position, raising a shield of my own so our magic snapped together, creating a spherical shield as we were back to back. I was relieved to see Leila had made it to the stable with

Bagel and the horse, and hadn't yet ventured back out—hopefully we could end this before she did.

"Celestina, where are they?" I asked.

Momoko and I shuffled to keep the spherical shield intact, but I now faced the front so I could see Felix and Franco pull off the same balancing act with Rupert between them.

"There." Celestina pointed to a tiny copse of trees where the driveway turned onto the road. "Two archers."

"If we scare them out of their cover, can you and Rupert safely nab them?" I asked.

Celestina's smile was cruel. "Certainly."

"House Medeis," I shouted, getting the Clark brothers' attention. "Mark!"

I nodded to Momoko. She dropped her shield and created a green colored sparkler of magic over the trees, marking our target—hopefully Leila and her parents wouldn't be too upset that we were about to kill their landscaping.

I waited for Felix's and Franco's nods, then shouted, "Release!" and dropped my shield.

I shot off a lightning bolt big enough to make the surrounding buildings shake. Even with my eyes shut, the light still burned my eyeballs, and my eyes watered as I heard the other wizards releasing their own volleys.

The noise that was most blessed to my ears, however, was the sound of someone cursing in fae.

"They're out." Celestina was gone before the words were completely out of her mouth. She and Rupert closed in on the two archers as they staggered out of the blackened and—in some portions—burning trees.

They slammed the fae to the ground with enough force to make their bones rattle, and I'm pretty sure they half-suffocated them.

I was relieved to see they didn't immediately kill the fae—that probably meant they were going to hang on to them for use in political maneuvering. Maybe parade them in front of the Regional Committee of Magic or something. Though Rupert seemed to be having a little too much fun shaking his victim.

"Hazel." Celestina offered me a friendly smile as she pushed down on the fae's throat, making him gurgle. "Could you check with Leila if she has any rope we could use?"

"I'll do it." Franco saluted Celestina then trotted off to the barn. "Excuse me, Leila?"

Momoko and I moved to stand with Felix, bringing us much closer to the nearly comatose fae.

"I thought that went pretty smoothly." I cringed when I glanced at the smoldering trees. "Well, mostly. I might have overdone it with the lightning."

"I used fire—I thought it would scare them but wouldn't burn much." Felix gazed up at the branches burning on a few trees. "It seems I was wrong."

Momoko snorted. "Instead of standing there you could always put it out."

"Good point." Felix's wizard mark surfaced again, covering most of his forehead and cheek. A twist of his hand and he dropped water on the trees, putting out the fires with a loud hiss and a cloud of steam.

"What are you going to do with them, Celestina?" I took a step closer, but stopped when Rupert gave me a quelling sneer.

"The Night Court is already in trouble for breaking the bylaws and attacking in the Curia Cloisters," she said. "We shall use this pair to further press their illegal actions."

"I've got some rope!" Franco jogged back outside, holding up a fistful of twine used on hay bales. "The scratchiest stuff Leila could find."

"Excellent." Celestina dragged her sagging fae upright. "We'll secure them, phone in for reinforcements, and Rupert will drive you all over to Drake Hall."

Rupert puffed up like an angry cat. "Wait, why do *I* have to drive them? Why can't I stay here and you take the rat—take them home?"

"Are you questioning my orders?" Celestina sounded pleasant, but her expression must have been pretty terrifying because Rupert turned whiter than usual.

"No, First Knight," he mumbled. "I'll take the wizards to Drake Hall once the fae are secured."

Rupert's fae seemed to come out of his addled state, so he gave him another good shake while Celestina tied up her fae attacker and called home.

Us wizards stood together, gossiping with Leila—once she joined us—and casting anxious glances at the singed trees.

But by the time the first Drake vampire showed up—jumping the wrought-iron fence—and Rupert herded us to his car, it had occurred to me there was something about that fight.

It was the first real time we wizards had fought *with* vampires, and we'd rocked it.

The vampires had given us an early warning, but we'd covered them from the magic that would usually pose a big threat to them. We'd also been able to flush the fae out, and the vampires with their superior speed took the baddies down before I'd even blinked.

The Drake vampires were an incredible fighting force on their own, and House Medeis wizards weren't slouches, either. But together? ...Maybe the Night Court was right to be afraid of us.

"Did you know Rupert gets eye twitches when he's really annoyed?" I trotted at Killian's side as we made our way down to the gym. "It's *so* fun to watch!"

Killian raised an eyebrow at me. "You were attacked by fae archers, and the most interesting observation you make out of the entire event is that Rupert has poor muscle control?"

"It was pretty uneventful." I held my katana in place at my side so it wouldn't smack my leg with my fast steps—since Killian was so much taller I usually had to scramble to keep up. This light jog was a pretty slow pace for him. "We took the fae down in like a minute flat."

After nearly crashing on the short drive over—Rupert didn't appreciate it when Momoko tried to fish a leaf out of his hair while he was pulling into the driveway—we made it to Drake Hall.

Instead of discussing the attack, Killian insisted I prepare for training, and listened to a verbal report before escorting me downstairs. (The other wizards were sent to the kitchen for a snack. Momoko assured me they would find me after getting a bite to eat, but I ate here every day for the entire summer. I knew there was no way I'd see them again until it was time to go.)

"That may be, but it shows the Night Court hasn't given up yet," Killian said. "To their detriment. I intend to hang Queen Nyte with political ramifications for this until all fae in the region can't move in the mess of red tape."

"Can you really do that?"

"I am the Vampire Eminence and on the Regional Committee of Magic. Since *they* broke the rules, there's not many who can stop me." Killian stretched out his fingers and clenched them. "The Paragon might, but I intend to keep him out of the fight."

"That's thoughtful of you," I said. "But I suppose, you are friends." I cleared my throat and kept my eyes straight ahead.

I could *feel* Killian's gaze on me, but I chose to ignore it, because otherwise that would mean looking at him.

For the first time I'd ever seen, Killian wasn't wearing a ludicrously expensive designer suit.

Instead he was in one of those fancy, moisture-wicking t-shirts, and black jogger pants. He looked like a fitness model, and I was willing to bet that when he did train, he never sweated a drop. (Not fair! As a wizard my temperature always ran hotter, and whenever I trained with the Drakes they turned me into a sweaty mess.)

I didn't want to ask him about the fitness clothes, or give him the satisfaction of seeing me eye him, so I kept my eyeballs facing forward and my mouth shut.

"The Paragon and I are *not* friends," Killian stressed.

"Sure you are," I said. "That's why you don't want to involve him in this mess."

"No, it's not." Killian insisted.

"Just keep telling yourself that."

Killian opened the door for me, conveniently letting me slip in front of him.

"Thanks," I started. "So are you..." I slowly trailed off as I got a good look around the gym.

Every time I'd trained here, there were *at least* five other vampires working out—whether that meant lifting weights or practicing combat over in the padded section.

Today, there was no one.

The gym was deserted.

I sucked my neck into my shoulders and felt my nerves crackle to life. "What's going on?" I reluctantly shuffled around so I could suspiciously peer up at Killian.

He smiled at me and gestured to the ground.

I looked down, and my hackles rose at the red and white rose petals that were scattered on the floor, making a trail over to the thickly padded section of mats. I returned my gaze to Killian. His smile turned bemused.

"You want me to follow the petal trail?" I guessed.

"Of course."

I followed the petals, which wound around a few pieces of weight lifting equipment, and—as I had guessed—eventually ended up over on the mats. The white petals stopped about halfway there, so the only petals in use were red. That was why, when I got to the mat, the message spelled out in petals looked so disturbingly like blood spatters I had to look twice.

"*I'm sorry*," I read the words. I stared at the flower petals before I dared to ask, "Is this another apology?"

"It is."

"Is there a reason why you keep going for a romantic vibe?"

"I'm certain I don't know what you mean," Killian smirked.

I inhaled deeply and started massaging my temples. "Where did you get this idea?"

"I assigned Rupert the task of watching several human chick flick movies. He said this method usually returned wayward males into the good graces of their significant others."

"Why would you make him do that?" I asked. "You could have just asked Celestina!"

"I did ask Celestina what bribe she recommended," he said. "She suggested what she called a spa day and insisted she'd go with you as your protection detail, which meant the day was probably more for her than you, so I discarded the idea."

I set my hands on my hips. "Ah."

"After hearing Celestina's suggestion, Josh wanted me to get you a gun."

I raised a finger in the air. "I definitely don't want that."

"I figured as much. Julianne suggested a sword."

I made an appreciative noise. "Not a bad idea."

"You really would forgive me if I got you another sword?"

"I already told you I forgave you." I looked around, hoping for a broom or something to sweep the petals up—I now understood why all other vampires were conspicuously absent.

"But we aren't back to the way we were," Killian persisted.

"I told you just because I forgave you doesn't mean there aren't any consequences."

"Hazel." Killian moved to stand in front of me, forcing me to look at his well-defined muscles that were visible through his shirt, which made me realize just how much his suits hid. (And how much he had to train. Seriously, did he ever sleep? As long as I had been around I'd only seen him work all night, but he had to do some serious training by himself to have that kind of muscle definition. Also, it made me suspect he was really vain, because wearing a shirt this tight was totally unnecessary and not appreciated given the tiny amount of definition I'd managed to achieve with all of my work. Was it getting hot, or was it just me?)

Killian's eyes were a little more red than usual. "If you just tell me what I have to do to fix this, it would make things easier."

"And I told you, I just want you to trust me."

Killian made a frustrated noise that sounded like a growl. "And you want proof of that trust?"

"Yes."

Killian narrowed his eyes. By the way he'd fallen silent, I had a feeling he wasn't happy with my response.

Too bad! I didn't care, buwahah!

I folded my arms across my chest and looked down at the blood-red flower petals again. "This looks like a murder scene."

Killian studied the flowers with too much interest. "It does bear a startling resemblance."

"Should I go find a broom to sweep them up with since whoever is training me hasn't shown up yet?" I did a few torso twists as I looked around.

Maybe there's a broom in the locker room...

"I'm training you."

CHAPTER TWELVE

Hazel

I froze mid-twist. "Say what?"

"I'm going to be your trainer."

All the muscles in my body went slack. "You've got to be kidding me."

"Since you insist you are only available for training twice weekly, it is important that your sessions *count*," Killian said. "Thus, I decided you should learn from the best."

I squinted up at him. "I don't believe you. Is this revenge for something?"

Killian raised both of his eyebrows. "I am merely giving you what you asked for in the terms of our contract."

"Hah! Likely story!" I shook my finger at him. "Come on, what is it really? There's no way you intend to waste your time like this."

"Any time spent with you is never a waste."

I whipped around real quick and put my back to him so he couldn't see my blush. "I still don't get it. Celestina and Josh were amazing trainers. They've got to have an endless supply of things they could teach me. This seems awfully...lame to make you train me when I'm so bad with martial arts and I'm still a newbie with my sword—not to mention I've only covered the bare basics with guns."

"True," Killian said. "But since we have limited time, we're not aiming to make you a martial arts expert or a sword master."

"What do you mean?"

"We have six months to make you a better fighter," Killian said. "And while Josh and Celestina are superior to you in many ways, given the additional training you've undergone of your own volition these past weeks, you'd be able to take them in a fight if allowed to use your magic."

"You can't know that," I scoffed.

Killian smirked. "You've held the majority of your training practices on your front lawn. There is very little I *don't* know about your current fighting condition."

I scrunched my nose at him. "Talk about getting your underlings to do your dirty work."

"And quite effectively so." Killian stretched his arms out as he studied the matted area. "I'm thinking a practice match is in order."

"Practice—are you out of your mind? You'll squash me like a bug!" I wouldn't put it past him to start the match without my approval, so I hastily pulled magic through my blood, making heat crawl across my face as my wizard's mark surfaced.

"I'll hold back," he assured me. "But you shouldn't. Use everything you've got—though I'd appreciate it if you didn't trash the place. The Curia Cloisters is still getting repairs done from that storm you conjured."

"Momoko and Felix helped—it's one of our new strategies." I kept my magic rolling as I copied Killian and started stretching. "You know, when we finally do start having confrontations with the Night Court...I think it might be most effective if we didn't keep our forces entirely separate, but had them fight together—or at least had some of our best fight together."

"Why would you say that?"

"When we were attacked at Leila's it worked really well to have two of us wizards paired off with a vampire. We could protect our vampire, but Celestina and Rupert were able to sense the fae more easily since they didn't bust out magic right away. And once we wizards flushed them out, it was easy for Celestina and Rupert to subdue them."

Killian tilted his head in thought. "It's an idea that has merit. It will be interesting to see what my First Knight reports. Fighting with wizards is perhaps a little more intimidating for vampires than you realize given your friendly familiarity with the Drakes who inherently trust you."

"What do you mean?"

"I mean a stray lightning bolt could do great damage, particularly if it was cast by a wizard trained by you, which makes them more competent than most."

I snorted. "Yeah, and you can recover really fast from pretty much any magical attack. But I know what you mean. There are a few members of my House who wouldn't be thrilled to have a vampire at their back when you guys could snap our necks before we realize what's going on."

"And yet, here we are, about to enter a practice match together." Killian grinned at me.

I shook my head. "My trust in you isn't the issue, Killian. You're the one with the trust problem."

He stared at me for several long moments. An emotion simmered in his black-red eyes, but his eyebrows weren't at all slanted, so I didn't know how to read it.

Well, if he wasn't going to start us off, I'd take the advantage of being prepared. I unsheathed my chisa katana, wrapped it with electricity, and raised my shield. "Ready?"

Killian nodded sharply, and backed up a bit. Then he disappeared.

I shifted my shield to my back and created a ring of fire around me, spanning from my feet to the outer edge of the circle, which I had precisely calculated to be longer than Killian's arm so he couldn't yank me right over the top.

Killian darkly chuckled, and I caught sight of him to my left. "Not bad." He threw something at me.

I ducked, but caught sight of it flying over my head, confirming it was indeed a dagger. (Where had he kept that?!)

Killian effortlessly leaped over me. I crouched even lower, avoiding his hand when he tried to snag my arm, and managed to stab my katana upwards.

It missed him by a mile—of course, he was too fast for that—but he had to take two steps when he landed instead of one to maneuver himself for the blur of his next charge.

I tried to rock out of the awkward crouch I'd been backed into, when I heard my shield crunch behind me, then felt something smack me across the back.

His legs, I thought as I fell into my own flames. *I forgot to calculate for kicks with his freakishly long legs.*

I scrambled to my feet. My own magic couldn't hurt me, but since I was knocked out of the center, I was now within distance of—

Killian snagged me by the collar of my shirt and twitched me out of my fire. Flower petals ground in my clothes, but I wasn't done yet!

I stabbed at him with my katana.

He dodged, but it was a feint and an ill done one as I only used one hand.

I reached behind me with my free hand and grabbed Killian's wrist, then let the electric buzz of magic flood me. Lightning danced across my skin, crawled up my arm, and lashed out at Killian.

He yanked his arm free, but before I could move he used the toe of his shoe to flip me over and plant a foot over my throat.

I was about to struggle despite the pressure, but I looked up... and my entire body grew paralyzed.

Killian was smiling—not a smirk, or the bright grin he flashed whenever he wanted to irritate me, or even the fond/affectionate smile he occasionally trotted out. This was a slightly unhinged, or maybe battle-crazed smile. His eyes were as red as blood and glowed with excitement, and his lips pulled back in the unsettling grin with both of his fangs bared.

Something deep within me wailed that this was the face of death. Even though I knew Killian wouldn't *physically* hurt me, years of conditioning kicked in, and my fight-or-flight response screamed to life. I wanted to run, but he had me pinned down like a bug. My heart pounded louder and louder as I stared at the face of a predator.

Killian's grin grew and he started to hunker down by me, but I flinched, and he must have seen something in my face. He froze for a second, then backed off so fast there was a breeze with his exit. He retreated to the far side of the mats, giving me plenty of room.

I sat flat on the mats for a few moments, trying to get my heart back to normal. It took a few lungfuls of air, but eventually my shakes subsided and I could peel myself off the ground.

Killian waited until I was sitting up. "You did well. Your speed has increased a lot since you first started your training."

I shakily stood and bought myself a few moments by brushing mashed petals off my clothes. "I lasted longer than I thought I would. But how on earth did you get through my shield to kick me?" I shook my head, shaking off the last bits of fear stamped in me.

"I went in at an angle at the side." Killian gave me the side eye, keeping his body pointed away from me, but carefully watching me.

I offered him a smile and rubbed the back of my neck. "I'll have to work on curving the shield more to stop that."

He hesitantly nodded, then straightened his shoulders. "When you dodge you give up too much space. You were half flattened on the ground when I jumped over you—that puts you at a severe disadvantage. Don't retreat so much—it will give you an advantage so *you* can attack them easier."

"Gotcha."

"Let's practice a few dodges, and at the end of the session we can give the practice match another try."

I retrieved my katana and shook out my arms. "Sounds good to me!"

"Very well. Let's begin."

———

ALTHOUGH I WAS the Adept of House Medeis, and we got along really well—it was a miracle the House happened to agree with all the changes I was making, they're infamous for hating that sort of thing—it still *loved* playing tricks on me.

Like now. I tried to pull the chain on a ceiling fan to toggle the fan off, but the House kept lowering the chain and then raising it whenever I made a jump for it.

My fingers just brushed the fancy pendent that ended the switch, and the House yanked it out of my grasp.

I set my hands on my hips. "I will burn scented candles in *every room* and stink this whole place up if you don't turn off the ceiling fan."

The flooring squeaked, and around me the House groaned.

"I don't care if it's fun!" I narrowed my eyes and did my best to channel the look my parents used whenever I'd been particularly disobedient. "It's late fall! There's frost on the ground, the sun is barely up, the heater *just* turned on, and I'm freezing! Turn. It. Off!"

Something in the ceiling fan clicked, and the blades of the fan slowed down, cutting back the breeze that whipped the icy cold morning air through my room.

I glanced at the alarm clock by my bed—5:30. I still had a bit of time before I needed to get ready for the morning practice. But after all that jumping around, it'd be useless trying to sleep again.

I stuffed my feet in my slippers and shrugged on a warm sweater. I was about to head to the kitchen for a very early breakfast, when something rang in my room.

It took me several long moments to recognize it was a ringtone, but not of my regular cellphone. It was the one Killian had given me in summer.

Even though I had my regular cellphone back and used it as my primary number, when I'd gone to Drake Hall for the alliance negotiations, Killian had insisted I take the phone with me.

The vampires were the only ones with the number, so I usually left it behind, which is why I had to scramble around my room to search for it, eventually unearthing it from under a pile of workout clothes.

I gaped at the name displayed on the screen, but hurried to answer it. "Killian?" My voice broke, making me sound squeaky.

"Good morning, Hazel."

I suspiciously peered around the room, feeling weirdly awkward. (I couldn't tell you why—Killian had barged into my room a number of times when I was in Drake Hall, and when I first swore loyalty to him as a servant I was wearing fleece pajama pants with sheep on them. It doesn't get much more embarrassing than that.) But I skirted across the wooden floor of my bedroom and hopped on my bed. "You're up late. Isn't this when most everyone is usually going to bed at Drake Hall?"

"Except for the vampires on patrol, yes," Killian said, sounding extra British-y, which meant something was bothering him. "I usually stay up until the sun has risen. No use giving it more allowances than it already takes."

I leaned against the headboard, kicked my slippers off, and shoved my feet under the covers. "How very like you. Is something up?"

"What do you mean?"

"You called for a reason, right?" I yanked the covers of my bed up higher. "It's not like we haven't seen each other in a while. You just beat the snot out of me yesterday in our second training session."

Killian was silent.

"Is...is everything okay?" I hesitantly asked.

"I've been thinking about what you said."

I wrinkled my forehead as I tried to recall what conversations we'd recently had that might bear a phone call. The most likely culprit was the conversation Celestina and I snickered over in front of Killian while I stuffed my face with cookies right before I left after training.

"You confirmed Josh had a human fling years ago? How'd you pull that off? Was it a *Twilight* thing and werewolves were involved?"

"I was referring to when you said you needed proof that I trust you," Killian dryly said.

"Oh. Um, what about it?"

"I believe I have found sufficient proof for you."

I stared at the framed picture on the wall—the last family photo I'd taken with my parents. "Okay, I'll bite. What's your proof?"

"Your scent."

I tried to process his point, but it felt like my brain was filled with syrup. "I'm sorry, *what*?"

"Surely you know that wizard blood reeks to vampires."

"Yeah."

"Unless the vampire trusts the wizard."

"Double yeah." I furrowed my eyebrows—was he seriously calling me at 5:30 am to school me on the particulars of *my* blood?

"To me...you no longer smell."

I had to replay the sentence three times in my mind. "Like, I don't have a scent?"

That would be less surprising—Celestina and a number of Drake vampires had already told me I no longer stunk, and I had a neutral scent.

"I never said that, only that you don't smell."

A long pause stretched between us, and Killian continued. "You now smell...amazing."

It was shocking, pleasant, and a little eerie to hear. I was used to reactions like Rupert's—disgust and gagging. Most of the vampires in Drake Hall had stopped scrunching their noses at me a while ago, and they said I smelled neutral to them—neither good nor bad.

But *Killian* fully trusted me to the point where I no longer smelled bad, or even just neutral, but "amazing"? I was happy to hear it, but it was so unexpected...

"Really?" I slowly said. "Celestina said I don't have a scent to her."

Killian's voice was a little raspy. "I imagine it's not the same for me, because I trust you more. Your scent is..."

I could sense Killian needed a lighthearted moment since he seemed to be having trouble talking—another thing I hadn't really experienced before—so I made suspicion line my voice so thickly it was obviously an act. "If you say I smell like dinner I will pull your tie so it's lopsided the next time I see you."

I got my desired result, and Killian chuckled. "You don't smell like food, at all. Your scent is more evocative of feelings. It's very warm and welcoming and..." There was another long pause. "I think it reminds me how sunlight used to feel before I turned. I didn't know I even *remembered* the feeling until the day your scent switched."

I wriggled in my bed, feeling oddly bashful. "And when was that?"

"After you fought Solene at the Curia Cloisters."

I stretched my memory to that time. I only dimly remembered the first few days after the fight because I was so hopped up on fae potions, but I did recall that around then Killian suddenly seemed inclined to sniff me occasionally, and continued to do so until he kicked me out.

It supported his claim—he'd take the chance to sniff my wrist or neck whenever possible, which are pretty definitive actions, and certainly not something he'd planned months in advance. (There was no point to it. Even if he did swindle me into believing he trusted me, if he ever tried to take a bite out of me my magic would make him throw up if the trust wasn't mutual.) I didn't think he was lying about it, but it was still pretty surprising.

"Can you believe my claim?" Killian asked, his voice cutting through the silence.

"Yeah, it's so...unexpected. If you were lying to manipulate me you'd come up with something more believable," I admitted.

"I'm aware that this doesn't exactly support my case, given that you've smelled this way to me for some time," Killian said. "You want assurance that I will always act on that trust."

"Killian..." I stretched my toes out under my bed covers until the arches of my feet ached. "I know you're a vampire, and you've had lots of time to solidify your thoughts and actions. I know how you got into the position you currently have. I'm not asking you to change overnight. I just...expected better of you. And I hoped that you trusted *me* as a person enough to know you didn't have to screen your actions from me, because I'm not in this for the politics of it."

He was silent for so long I actually had to pull my phone back and make sure the call hadn't been disconnected.

"Killian? Are you there?"

"Yes." He exhaled deeply. "It's just that I perhaps see a little of what you've been complaining about. Your scent is proof, but I don't think it offers the assurance you want."

I opened my mouth to tell him that actually, I was pretty convinced, but his next sentence made all activity in my mind halt.

"So instead I will tell you my species' greatest weakness."

Weakness? Wasn't it magic? That was the only real way to take vampires down in battle...it's why fae stood a better chance of killing them than a werewolf. But that's common knowledge...

"...What?" I asked, more than a little confused.

Killian must have been in his office—I could hear the unique creak of his chair through the phone line. "Although human blood taken directly from a donor offers greater nutritional value, a boosted amount of energy, and increased powers, feeding is a very dangerous process for a vampire."

"Huh?" I said in my continued intellectual greatness. "Don't you just have to...*bite* them?"

"Actually, drinking fresh blood is quite easy," Killian assured me. "But after we've eaten, we fall into a catatonic state. We're completely helpless, and at the mercy of whomever we fed off."

Hold up, hold up, hold up...WHAT?!

"It's the only time in our lives in which we are truly helpless," Killian said. "When we sleep it is only fleeting, and it is nearly impossible to get us drunk or addled with drugs because we will naturally wake if we feel or sense something. We cannot do that when we feed off a human—our senses are dulled and our muscle control is shot as our bodies process the rush of nutrients. Because blood pouches and packs don't give us the same rich nutrients, they don't produce the...contentment we experience after taking blood from a blood donor. If we are injured and near death of course our reactions are slowed then, but the stretch of time after we've fed is the only instance in which we are truly comatose."

I was shocked. If Killian was being honest, he'd just told me the most effective way to kill his kind. Not him, of course—he only drank from pouches anyway.

"How have you been able to hide this from the rest of us supernaturals?" I asked. "Or am I really just that out of touch?"

"It's not something we advertise," Killian said. "And previously it was why we often killed or imprisoned those we fed from—a horrible reflection on us, but the honest truth." He sighed. "We've learned to cover it to a certain extent by limiting how much a blood donor sees. After a vampire feeds, in most Families the blood donor is immediately removed by other vampires. But…"

"That still leaves you open to attack from other vampires," I realized in a flash of insight. "Because even if the blood donors don't know, the vampires involved will, which means planning a rebellion or war is a lot easier to pull off if you can get a feeding schedule."

"Correct."

Slowly, my brain restarted, booting up like an ancient computer. "So…that's why you don't feed off blood donors." I could almost hear the "turning on" noise in my mind. "The vulnerability?"

"Correct," Killian said. "A number of ancient and great vampires throughout history were killed after feeding. It's one of the most common ways for a truly powerful vampire to die."

"Huh." I picked at a fuzzy on my bedcover. "And that's why you say you don't trust Celestina or Josh like I thought. Because you don't trust them enough to stand guard for you while you drink."

"Exactly."

I stared blankly at the wall, struggling with the immensity of what Killian had just shared with me.

"You're quiet," Killian said.

"I'm sorry, I'm just trying to process this. It's...this is huge."

"It's satisfactory proof, then?"

"Yeah, for sure." Guilt prickled at my conscience as I slouched in my bed. "I'm sorry, I didn't mean to tear such an important secret about your *whole race* from you."

"It's fine." Killian's voice was surprisingly calm. "You're a virtuous idiot after all. You won't even share this information with your House, and I'm aware you'll die before you share the news—your honor is too overwhelming for you to do anything else."

I was silent for a few moments. "You really don't trust Celestina or Josh to guard you?"

"They would never betray me," Killian said with confidence. "But that doesn't mean they wouldn't accidentally reveal a detail that could eventually spark my downfall. I have a lot of enemies—and some of them are vampires. It's natural that I have many who would love to kill me if given the chance, so it is better not to."

"It's still pretty sad," I said. "I hope one day you'll feel differently about this."

"It is what it is."

"Well, I'll call us even," I said. "Thanks for trusting me, Killian. I won't tell anyone. And I hope this means next time you'll *tell* me when you have a plan that involves my participation?"

"Yes."

I nodded, even though he couldn't see. "Good," I said. "That's all I really wanted."

"You are a simultaneously complex but simplistic creature."

"I'm a wizard, it's in my nature." I glanced at the clock—it was a little after six. I was officially late for practice. "Are you going to be okay?"

"You seem to be under the illusion that telling you this has somehow wounded me." His voice was amused. "Does that mean now is a suitable time to bargain?"

"Bargain for what?"

"Your bu—"

"Okay, and we're done," I interrupted him, guessing where he was going to take the conversation in an effort to prove just how fine he really was. "I get the picture. Thanks for calling, Killian. I'll see you at our next practice session in three days?"

"Perhaps sooner," Killian said.

I pulled the phone back to stare at it for a moment again. "Huh?" I said. "What do you mean?"

"Good morning, Hazel," Killian said before he hung up on me.

I stared at my phone some more, then shook my head. "I guess he wouldn't be a vampire if he wasn't so *mysterious*," I grumbled.

I clawed my way out of my bed and almost skidded out as I hurriedly threw on workout clothes. Although I rushed into a normal morning, I was well aware of the warm feeling that cushioned my heart.

Killian really did trust me. And I was pretty sure this was going to be a turning point for his Family, and my House.

The following day, we House Medeis wizards had just finished our early evening practice and were in the process of getting cleaned up for dinner when the doorbell rang.

I paused in the middle of yanking a clean shirt on. "House Medeis...who is it?" I cautiously asked.

I felt magic swirl around the property and return, bringing back the familiar and enviably cool sensation the House used to represent vampires.

"Huh." I finished tugging the shirt on and stepped into my slippers. "Did Gavino invite someone over?" I slipped into the hallway as the doorbell rang again. "I'll get it!" I shouted loud enough for my family to hear.

"'kay!" Someone—Momoko, I thought—shouted back.

I shuffled down the stairs and made it all the way to the front door where I swapped my slippers for shoes and opened the door, revealing a clutch of approximately twenty vampires crowding the sidewalk, with Killian at the front.

CHAPTER THIRTEEN

Hazel

"Good evening." His voice echoed across the empty lawn. "May we come in?"

I stomped my way down to the sidewalk. "What the heck are you *doing* here?" I glanced at his retinue, who were carrying duffle bags and various power tools.

"You said to tell you next time I had a plan that involved you." Killian shrugged, his shoulders barely moving. "It's next time."

"And what does that mean?" I unlocked the gate that blocked the brick path that trooped up to the House.

Celestina, armed with a drill, stared expectantly at me over Killian's shoulder.

"Yeah, yeah, come in." I waved the group in, but grabbed Killian by the arm. "Except you—you have to explain this."

"As you very well know, I am paranoid," he said.

"Uh-huh, I'm following you."

"So it makes me...*apprehensive* when you are away from Drake Hall," Killian said.

I pressed my lips together. "I live in a magic House with nearly thirty adult wizards, and you're *apprehensive*?"

"Would you rather I say it makes me unbearably anxious?" Killian smirked, looking calm and controlled—the exact opposite of what he supposedly felt. "And paranoia often doesn't make sense," he added.

The Drake vampires had slowly made their way across the lawn and were loitering outside the House—although they eyed it, and one or two of them were taking notes on sleek tablets.

"So, what, you're moving in?" I asked.

Killian perked. "That's an option?"

"*No!*"

He gave me a look of disapproval. "You know you are perfectly welcome to move into Drake Hall, but it seems wizards are not as good hosts as us vampires."

"You're paranoid, so what do you intend to do?" I eyed Julianne, who was measuring the front porch with a measuring tape.

"I'll have my people test it. I'd like to know what you're dealing with and shore up whatever weak spots we find."

"Define shore up."

"I have some wards I intend to install—that sort of thing."

"Oh." I blinked and relaxed slightly. "That'd be nice."

Killian raised his eyebrows. "You don't object?"

"Nah." I spun around to shout at his vampires. "Just don't do anything to the House without asking me first—it will get offended!"

Josh gave me a bow. "As you wish, Miss Hazel."

The vampires scattered. A few went around each side of the House, two retreated back to the gate and started walking the property line, one trailed off to carefully inspect the gates, and Celestina and a few others had taken it upon themselves to start scaling the outside of the House, climbing up the walls and perching on any outcropping they came across to take notes.

"I am pleasantly surprised." Killian stood so close his arm brushed mine as he watched his people work. "I thought you'd object."

"To free wards? Never—those things are expensive." I smiled indulgently at my House. "Besides, it's probably better if you experience for yourself how well-protected we really are if you are *that* 'anxious.'"

Killian made a noise of amusement. "Your doubt wounds me."

"I'm totally sure."

The House sent a pulse of magic that rippled beneath my feet, stirring waves of curiosity and worry.

I crouched down, and patted the lawn. "It's okay, House Medeis," I murmured. "They're friends."

I watched Josh use a sword as a yardstick to measure a window, and I suddenly remembered I was not the only resident of House Medeis. "Shoot—I've got to warn everyone!"

I sprinted across the lawn, jumped up the porch stairs, and flung the front door open. "Hey guys, we have some vampire visitors! No cause for alarm, okay?"

"How splendid." Great Aunt Marraine waddled out of the kitchen with a warm smile. "Have Joshua and Miss Celestina returned—my stars." Her eyes widened when she saw the vampires sweeping the property.

"Killian brought a crew here," I said. "They're checking our defenses for us. Could you tell the others?"

"Yes, of course." Great Aunt Marraine pursed her lips, and for a moment I worried she was upset with me for letting so many vampires in. "This is quite the problem, Adept," she said, confirming my fears. "I don't know if we have enough blood packs for everyone!"

I sagged in relief and laughed. "It'll be fine."

She shook her head. "This is a sign that we should increase our blood delivery order. Although it's possible we may end up wasting some blood packs then if we don't often have visitors of a vampiric nature..."

"It's fine," I assured her. "I'll take whatever ones are almost expired to Drake Hall and feed them to Killian."

"I am glad I can be your garbage disposal." Killian's dry voice came from directly behind me.

"Sounds fun!" Great Aunt Marraine said. "I'll leave you kids to it and go tell the others." She winked at me with a lot more suggestion than I liked, and made for the main staircase.

"Why did she wink?" Killian asked, his breath stirring my hair.

"I have no idea." He was so close I almost smacked into him when I turned around. "Yeah, so I wanted to ask about the power tools. What are they for?"

"Weak spots."

"Ah." I awkwardly rubbed the back of my neck. "Yeah, see that's the thing about having a magical House. As long as I'm doing my job it can self-repair for the most part."

"Oh?"

Celestina and Josh appeared behind Killian's shoulder, joining us in the front hallway. "Your Eminence," they murmured.

Killian glanced back at them. "Did you find something?"

"No," Celestina said. "We wanted to procure permission to conduct our search inside as well."

"Yeah, go for it," I said.

Josh nodded and retreated back to the porch. "We have permission to enter," he shouted.

"You were saying the House is self-repairing?" Killian asked.

"Yes," I said. "It's because of the magic in it—it renews the House. That's why it needs an Adept—the Adept keeps the magic flowing and provides extra power. In return the House is capable of magic wizards can't normally perform on their own."

"If it's damaged, how fast does it repair itself?" Killian asked.

I frowned a little as I searched my memory. "You know, I'm not sure. I never really thought about it."

"Then we ought to test it." Killian pulled a handgun from its holster, which was hidden by his suitcoat.

"What? *No!*" I leaped toward him and tried to push the gun back under his jacket.

Killian easily peeled my hands off. "It's something you should be aware of." He racked his gun, pulling the slider back to load a bullet into the chamber. "For safety's sake."

"You just want to try shooting the House to see if it will react," I hissed.

"Perhaps," he acknowledged. "I haven't had the pleasure of actually seeing House magic in such close quarters." He narrowed his eyes. "I am very *anxious* to see if it's worth all the sweat and blood you have pushed into this ancient place."

Yeah, that was pretty rich considering he was probably older than the House. But obviously, he wasn't going to give up.

"Fine. It's your head on the line." I held my hands up and backed off. "But the House has a personality of its own, Killian. You really *don't* want to tick it off."

"Is that so?" Killian said in a factual tone. He flicked off his handgun's safety and nonchalantly shot the floor.

Slivers of wood sprayed the air, and instantly the ground parted beneath Killian's feet, sending him plunging into the basement. The wood floor sealed up behind him, repairing the bullet hole, making it look as if nothing had happened.

I turned to Celestina. "Please allow me to express my congratulations on becoming the new Drake Family Elder."

Celestina stiffened in alarm. "You believe the House will kill him?"

"Nah." I shook my head and laughed. "It probably has him locked in a closet somewhere in the basement. But he's not going to get out until it's no longer quite so mad at him. Ahh, well. Serves him right." I folded my hands behind my head and stretched out my shoulders as I wandered in the direction of the kitchens. "I wonder what we're having for dinner..."

Celestina hurried after me. "Do I have permission to search the basement for His Eminence?" Her voice was tight with alarm.

"Celestina, you can chill," I said. "The House won't kill him. I invited you guys onto the property, and it knows better than to murder my guest."

Celestina glanced worriedly back down the hall.

"If you try and help him it's only going to make the House worse," I said. "Besides, he asked for it."

She briefly furrowed her eyebrows. "You swear to me he's fine?"

"He's safe." I pressed my hand against a wooden doorframe, confirming my guess, as I swung into the homey kitchen. "I'm positive he wouldn't define his current status as fine, though."

"What do you mean?"

"Let's put it this way. One time when I upset the House, it re-routed a gutter and dumped stale rainwater on me." Something banged deep in the basement, and I nodded. "Yep. He's safe alright."

"Very well." Celestina still looked a little worried, but she offered me a pale smile. "In that case I better continue with our testing."

"Good luck," I said. "Come back here if you get hungry for human food—and I think we have a few of Gavino's blood packs to spare," I said.

Celestina nodded and left the kitchen, almost colliding with Gavino on his way in.

"Giving my food away, are you?" Gavino grinned. He leaned against a countertop and winked.

"Yep. So do you wanna make a bet how long the House will manage to keep Killian hostage?"

There was another bang below our feet—I'm pretty sure it was the sound of another bullet firing.

Gavino didn't even blink. "Nope," he said. "Not interested at all. If I place a winning bet, I'm pretty sure His Eminence will be quite offended."

I cackled and affectionately patted the House, which seemed to purr in response.

There was a gigantic crash that shook the floor a little, but the House seemed pretty smug, so I was betting Killian Drake—the most powerful vampire in the area—was still stuck.

Well, he wanted to know exactly how safe House Medeis was. This was an *excellent* way for him to find out.

About an hour later, Killian emerged from the basement. I wasn't surprised to see he looked barely disheveled, and not noticeably meeker—but the House is magical, not a miracle-worker I suppose.

"Did you have a nice time *testing* the House?" I asked.

Killian straightened his suitcoat. "It's suitable enough, I suppose."

I cracked a smile. "I believe you that you came just to test our defenses."

Killian scoffed. "Of course that's why I am here. Or do you presume to believe the ancient prejudice about my people and dark, damp corners, which would mean I *enjoyed* crawling around the dirty basement?"

The House creaked ominously.

Killian narrowed his eyes—which were an ominous, shiny black color—at the wall opposite him. "Just try it," he taunted.

I patted a door as I passed it, taking a few steps closer to him. "He doesn't mean it," I told my House.

Killian stiffened and looked prepared to run his mouth, so I was quick to interrupt. "There was a possibility you came out here just to nose around a House. I'm sure plenty of wizards will see it that way and theorize you're trying to find a weakness you can exploit."

"Houses already have dreadfully huge weaknesses," Killian said. "They are called wizards—such a pathetic bunch. But I suppose House Medeis would be far more difficult given the firepower of your people." Killian thoughtfully rubbed his jaw, then flicked his eyes at me. "But this is hardly my first time in a House."

"I figured you'd visited House Bellus since you're the Eminence," I said.

Killian nodded and shrugged. "And a few more besides. But because your kind seem to forget things have not always been this way, I expect they would forget that it used to be more acceptable to co-mingle." He studied me for a few moments. "You said there was a possibility I came for information—did you really think that was why I am here?"

"I wondered," I said honestly. "All the Drakes you brought with you have been extremely genuine in their desire to test the House, so I didn't think so…but you usually have layers to your actions so I thought it was a possibility. But now I know it wasn't that at all."

Up went an eyebrow. "Oh?"

"You wouldn't have shot my House if you were here for any other reason besides testing it." I scuffed my foot on one of the Turkish rugs that ran up the hallway and stared at the bright design. "You were deliberately pushing it. If you wanted information you would have coddled it. Thank you for being honest, Killian. It really means a lot to me." I forced myself to raise my eyes and smile up at him, even though it made me a little uncomfortable.

This was an important moment. I needed to show that I understood what he was doing, and I was thankful. (Let's just call it what it is, positive reinforcement. And I was going to reinforce the crap out of this particular behavior.)

I smiled at Killian, fighting the urge to blush as he unashamedly stared back at me, the red in his eyes dimming to a simmer.

I eventually broke and dropped my eyes to the shoulders of his expensive suit. "Is that...*cat hair?*" I squinted, doubting my eyes. "But we don't even have a cat here—"

"Since you are no longer doubting my motives, I will take advantage of this moment and invite you to a meeting in two days."

Surprised, I backed up a step. "Where? And why?"

"It's at the Curia Cloisters. And why? Because you won't move back to Drake Hall, so if I wish to see you I am better off dangling bait like this meeting in front of you."

Another blush scorched my cheeks, and I wanted to elbow him, but I was pretty sure he was trying to lure me into that, so I held my ground. "No, I mean why are you holding a meeting? What is it for?"

"I've called an assembly of sorts for the vampires," Killian said. "It's not regional, strictly speaking. I sent invitations—or perhaps it would be more accurate to call them summons—to the local Families, and any other Family that might be tempted to take revenge on the Night Court for their actions."

"You're going to talk to them about going to war?" I asked.

"I'm going to attempt to talk them *out* of it," Killian said. "The last thing I need is for this to become a regional war between vampires and fae. Previously I thought it was inevitable, but since the Night Court attacked in the Curia Cloisters I'm hoping for something less...*drastic.*"

"That makes sense," I said. "But I assume that means you're going to use the Families to pressure the fae in other ways?"

Killian smiled and his fang teeth gleamed. "Precisely."

I tugged on the hem of my shirt as I reviewed his words, then nodded. "Okay, I'll come. My House will insist on sending some wizards with me, though."

"Naturally," Killian said. "You may bring Gavino to act as your guard as well if you wish."

"Yeah, that might be good for Gavino," I said. "He's been a great coach, but I'm sure he'd like to get out of here for a while."

"I doubt that," Killian said. "Coaching your wizards is a vacation compared to some of the past assignments I've placed him on."

"What do you think is worse than this?"

"There was a three-day period where he and a team tracked a rabid Unclaimed through the sewers. I am certain he'd tell you that was far more foul."

"Ew, yeah, I'd agree." I shivered. "Great Aunt Marraine has thrown together some snacks, and is serving blood pouches in the kitchen. Do you want me to snag something for you, and you can start listening to Celestina's and Josh's reports?"

"After overhearing you conspiring to feed me expired blood pouches, I would prefer to choose my own, thank you," Killian dryly said.

I grinned unashamedly. "Might be a smart move on your end," I admitted. "The kitchen is this way."

I started to turn, planning to lead the way up the hallway, but I paused when Killian held out his hand.

He watched me, some of the red igniting in his eyes as he waited for my reaction.

Do I take it? Or is that giving too much too early...

There was something both tired and guarded in his expression—in the set of his mouth and shoulders.

This is hard for him, I realized.

There were still hidden depths to him, and he was absolutely layering his actions. (Although the sappy invite did make me blush, there was a chance he would use my presence as a shield against the others—a way to show them they didn't need to fight because his attack dog was on the job.)

My eyes drifted to the cat hair on his suit.

But he's trying. He's fighting ancient instincts and basic vampire behavior to trust me.

I swallowed hard and took his hand.

His touch was as cool and soothing as always to my hot skin, and a gloating smile settled on his lips.

I was tempted to stick my tongue out at him, but something told me I'd regret that action, so I pulled on his hand. "Come on, Mr. Suspicious. The kitchen is this way."

Killian allowed me to pull him along, and just before we got to the kitchen he lightly rubbed the top of my hand with his thumb in a caressing manner.

Yep. Those instincts he was fighting were *alllll* about trust.

Because Great Aunt Marraine was obsessed with time—more like morbidly curious about the vampires—we arrived at the Curia Cloisters almost an hour before the meeting started.

That gave us plenty of time to select our spot in the assembly hall—the same room I'd punched a hole through the ceiling in when I took out Solene, the Unclaimed vampire who had taken it upon herself to go on a murdering spree.

Great Aunt Marraine had campaigned heavily to sit in the balcony area—I think she wanted to be able to freely gawk at all the vampires—but I'd won the battle, so we were all safely seated in comfy, padded chairs just off to the side of the dais where Killian would sit.

Gavino, Julianne, Manjeet, and Josh all sat with us—they were why I had pushed so hard for our selected spot. I wanted the extra security they would provide—though I wasn't worried about a vampire trying to drag one of my wizards off as a snack. (Our blood would repel them better than a can of mace.)

Since we still had plenty of time, I ventured off to make a pest of myself in the Wizard Council offices for a few minutes.

I got a very satisfying reaction—lots of moans, and a secretary on the verge of tears promised she would *make* a Wizard Council member review the laws I was suggesting they consider—so I left there in a pretty good mood with a hop in my step and a smirk on my lips as I moseyed my way through the Cloisters, heading back to the assembly hall.

"Adept Medeis?"

Surprised, I swung around. "Elite Bellus, hello."

Elite Bellus smiled warmly. "Here for the vampire meeting, are you?"

"Yes. I assume you heard about my alliance with the Drakes?"

"Adept, everyone in the *Midwest* knows about it."

I laughed nervously. "Yeah, I should have expected as much. How have you been since the attack? I only saw you briefly when we had to come in to give our official statements about everything that happened."

Elite Bellus gestured for me to keep walking—since I was so much shorter than him my normal paced walk was practically a stroll for him—then clasped his hands behind his back. "I'm quite well. Please allow me to thank you again for getting me out of the building safely. Once things have calmed down some, I mean to lodge an official request that you display your shield technique for House Bellus."

"I'm glad we could help," I honestly said. "It's the reason why we train so hard."

"Yes," he acknowledged. "I did want to talk to you a little about the attack. The Night Court is facing some pretty hefty accusations."

"I imagine Cloister officials were not happy that they breached the neutral territory agreement."

"Absolutely. They've been smacked with the worst fine I've ever seen in my career as the Elite. But they're actually getting the most grief from other fae Courts."

Puzzled, I peered up at Elite Bellus, scrutinizing the twinkle in his eyes. "Seriously? Why is that?"

"Because their actions were so inexcusable and indefensible, it immediately pitted werewolves and wizards against them," Elite Bellus said. "Normally it's us versus Killian so we can try to keep him from overpowering us all. But breaking the Curia Cloisters' safe haven law is inexcusable. If we let them get off without feeling much pain, our careful balancing act in supernatural government might collapse. We can't afford that, so we must make it obvious we won't allow this to happen in the future."

"Which means you're siding with Killian," I said.

"Exactly." He smoothed his goatee, and a quirk of a smile made it slant oddly. "Already one law and two motions that were set to slightly benefit fae were struck down. The entire fae community is feeling our displeasure, and as such they're going to mete justice out on the Night Court even if it means backstabbing their distant brethren."

"What can they do?" I asked.

"More than any of us." Elite Bellus chuckled. "Several of the Courts have broken trade agreements and various treaties with the Night Court. But I believe the biggest positive impact will be on the Night Court's plans for war."

I furrowed my brow. "I'm sorry...*what*? In what case can a war *ever* be considered a positive thing?"

"It's not," he assured me. "Rather, it's a positive thing because I believe the other Courts might have stomped out that notion. If the Night Court chose to declare a full war on the Drakes it would be a PR nightmare for the fae—the criminal Court attacking the noble vampire Family, that sort of thing. Killian would have a field day with the spins he could put on it, and the Courts know that."

"I don't think Queen Nyte is going to give up just because of the bad publicity," I said.

"She wouldn't," Elite Bellus agreed. "But the other Courts are basically holding a sword to Queen Nyte and Consort Ira. My sources tell me they've delivered an ultimatum—challenge the Drakes to a certamen, or swear to stop attacking. The Winter Queen nearly killed Consort Ira when you and the others were attacked just outside Drake land. Truthfully I think the only reason the other fae *didn't* kill him is because they're not sure yet if they mean to let Queen Nyte live."

I whistled lowly. "Wow. That is big. And based on your wording, I assume if Queen Nyte *does* challenge Killian to a certamen, the other Courts won't help?"

"Correct!"

I tugged on the sleeve of my crisp, Medeis-blue jacket. "I can't say I'm thrilled with the idea of fighting in a certamen against the Night Court, but that will really limit the casualties, and it's by far the best outcome we could hope for."

Don't misunderstand, certamen were still dangerous. (Magic duels are *still* duels, after all.) But certamen were more about short-term strategy, and were very, *very* final. If the Night Court lost, they'd have to leave us alone. For good.

"You think Queen Nyte will decide on a certamen?" Elite Bellus asked.

"Well, yeah." I blinked as we turned up a different hallway. "She's a fae. They can't lie. If she swears she won't attack the Drakes anymore, it means she'll have to stick to her word. And Queen Nyte doesn't strike me as the type to just give up."

"Indeed." Elite Bellus sighed. "It would be better for her Court if she did. But the Night Court was troubled long before she was crowned and killed her husband."

I didn't know what to say to this—I was in no position to talk politics. Even if House Medeis had recovered a lot of the respect we'd lost over the years, I was pretty set against the fae queen. So I settled for awkwardly nodding.

"I assume the Eminence knows all of this," Elite Bellus abruptly said. "His spies are far better than mine, and most everyone owes him in one way or another. But would you please pass along my observations, and tell him what I've said?"

This reeked of politics. It went against my better judgment to get involved in this kind of thing—plus it sounded like more *work*. I had enough on my plate, I didn't need extra. "That sounds like triangulation," I said. "It's against my policy to act as a go between and let both sides use me for their benefit." I thought for a moment then added, "Unless I get something for my troubles."

"You want House Medeis to rank higher?"

"No." I scoffed at the Elite. "I want what I've always wanted. A law about House—"

"—inheritance," Elite Bellus finished for me. "I should have seen that one coming. But I'm afraid that's beyond my reach, though I will try to use my influence."

"Yeah, yeah." I swatted my hand at him. "I'm still not playing messenger-girl. If you want to play politics with Killian you should go do that yourself."

"I'm not actually playing politics," Elite Bellus said.

I sourly stared up at him.

"At least not the way you think I am," he quickly amended.

We had reached one of the side entryways to the assembly hall. If we followed the hall as it turned, it would lead us around to the front. I could hear the wispy voices of a few vampires—their tones dry and brittle like old paper—but I couldn't make out any words. Feeling reasonably safe, I stopped, tucked myself against the wall, and peered up at the Elite. "Then please, enlighten me."

"This is an attempt to reach out to the Eminence," he said. "And I am not afraid to admit I am using you. If you deliver the news he'll be likely to recall my connection to you, and perhaps look more favorably upon what I intend to eventually offer."

"Uh-huh. You're not winning any points right now..."

"But I want him to look favorably upon me not for the sake of *my* political career, but for the relationship wizards have with vampires." The Elite cocked his head as he studied me. "I saw a recording of you fighting the fae at the Cloisters—the way you shielded the vampires and then struck at the fae was genius. But I am more interested in the verbal statements that were submitted about your encounter with the fae just outside Drake lands."

I relaxed a little—I'd half feared he was just buttering me up because he heard Killian and I were once again...whatever. It seemed that wasn't the case. But I didn't know exactly where this was headed, so I kept my eyes narrowed.

"I heard how you worked well with the vampires—covering them and flushing out your opponents, whom they were then able to capture." The Elite smoothed his goatee some more. "It—and the talk we heard that promoted supernatural intermingling—got me thinking. Perhaps we've been coming at this from the wrong angle."

"You mean survival?"

"Yes," the Elite said. "What if helping each other is the best option, rather than fortifying our own individual races?"

CHAPTER FOURTEEN

Hazel

I shifted, weirdly feeling challenged by the idea. "I guess it's obvious that our current efforts aren't really yielding anything—magic is dying off faster than ever."

"Exactly," the Elite said. "I wonder if it's because we lost something in our separation. If you hadn't been trained by the Drakes, you never would have bended your magic in such unique ways."

"That isn't wholly right," I confessed—I didn't want to mislead *my* leader. "Technically, I learned the shield you so admired and my other techniques from a book the Paragon lent me."

"That even furthers my point," Elite Bellus said. "You learned about magic from the fae because you were staying at Drake Hall, being taught methods of physical defense by vampires. You are a product of intermingling supernaturals—or at least your magic is. House Medeis has returned to its proper bloodline because they gave you the necessary teaching so you could take your House back."

"I guess that's true."

"It goes even deeper than just you," he continued. "You took your teachings to your House, and as a result were able to shield the Eminence and his vampires when they were attacked in the Cloisters. If you hadn't learned your particular style of magic, the Eminence was the only one who would have made it. His underlings—including his First and Second Knight—would have died. And *that* is what interests me."

"That we saved Celestina, Josh, and everyone?"

"No. Well, somewhat. I was specifically referring to the fact that your friendship changed the future of both the Drake Family and House Medeis." He pressed his lips together, his kind and handsome face turning grim. "And right now, we need some changing futures. Thus far, not much has changed for the better—except for House Medeis's return and the Drake Family's survival."

"I think the fae may play a bigger, positive role than you think," I said.

"You say that despite the Night Court's attempts against you?"

"I was thinking more of the Paragon," I admitted. "I think he's like you, and he wants to change our future." I hesitated.

In a conversation with Killian, the Paragon had said he was looking for something. Based on how reluctant he was to tell Killian, I was pretty sure he wouldn't want me telling the Elite. And while I would loyally serve the Elite and help wizards however I could, I wasn't about to sacrifice the Paragon when he'd only been kind to me.

Besides, Elite Bellus was an important-enough figure, he could talk to the Paragon himself.

"I don't think the Paragon is hanging around the Midwest just for funsies," I carefully said. "He might be another excellent ally."

Elite Bellus studied me for a few moments. "I see. Very well. Thank you for the recommendation. I shall make an appointment to speak with him. Though he is technically more important than

Killian, I am man enough to admit he scares me less, and is much more friendly." He glanced slyly at me.

I copied one of Killian's signature looks and raised an eyebrow. "That means you're still hoping I'll talk to Killian for you?"

"I am!"

I sighed. "I'll mention to him you're re-thinking some previous positions. But I'm not going to play mind-reader and tell him what you want. You'll need a seer for that."

"An opening from you will help pave the way." Elite Bellus peered at me with an appraising expression.

He had looked at me similarly at the Summer's End Ball. Recalling our conversation from then, I was quick to say, "I'm not Killian's *one*, you know."

"Mmm." He casually glided over my somewhat defensive statement. "Regardless, an opening is all I need. For now."

"Fabulous," I drawled. "If that is all, I need to slip out. I am pretty sure the meeting is going to start soon, and I want to take my seat."

"Naturally! Thank you, Adept Medeis. I appreciate your aid in this matter." Elite Bellus winked at me, then strolled back the way we'd come, whistling as he went.

I watched him for another moment, wondering if I had made the right choice, then slipped into the assembly hall through the side door.

The room was by no means full, but it didn't look like many vampires were lingering outside the main doors, so the meeting would probably begin soon.

I picked my way through the chairs, ignoring the red eyes and pinpricks of white fangs that flashed at me as I made my way to House Medeis's spot. A few vampires sniffed then hissed as I passed, irritated by my foul-smelling blood.

I wasn't too concerned—I could clear the room with a few drops of my blood—and I knew from my training that between my magic and fighting skills, I could get the drop on the average vampire. Possibly even a few Elders—the Family leader.

I caught Great Aunt Marraine's eye and waved when I was just a few steps from our chairs, but Killian intercepted me, stepping in front of me.

"Are you ready?" he asked.

"Yep. I've got some things to talk to you about, but I'm guessing we don't have time?"

"You can tell me as we take our seats."

"*Our* seats?"

Killian nodded at the dais—which was positioned to be the center of attention in the room. At the top level of the dais was a fancy desk with *two* chairs.

"I am not sitting up there with you," I said.

Killian frowned slightly. "Why not?"

"I'm not going to let you use me as a method of intimidation, and I don't want to get dragged into vampire politics!" I growled.

Killian actually heaved his eyes to the ceiling. "I don't want you to sit next to me for political reasons. Really, you're starting to be almost as paranoid as I am."

"What possible reason could you want me up there with you?" I demanded.

"Did I not say I was inviting you because I *missed* you?" Killian stressed. "That's why I want you sitting with me."

I uneasily rolled my shoulders—we were getting back into territory I wasn't totally comfortable with because we'd never really taken the time to define what we were. (We never had the chance—or we hadn't, until we'd resumed our...friendship?)

I glanced at the chair. "Okay, but what is everyone else going to think?"

"What I *want* them to think, and what I'm attempting to display."

"I *knew* politics were wrapped up in this somehow," I muttered.

"That was your cue to ask what I'm attempting to display."

"Fine. What are you attempting to display?"

"That we're equals."

His response surprised me so much my balance actually wobbled for a moment. "I'm sorry...*what?*"

Killian adjusted his cuff links and grinned slightly at me. "I'm the Eminence. No one sits on the same level as me. If I was trying to make a statement that you were under my power I'd tell you to stand with Celestina. But by giving you a seat next to me, I'm stating we're on equal footing. It will show just how highly I think of you."

I had to admire Killian's sharp intellect and the way he could understand politics. More and more it seemed to me he wasn't the tyrant of the Regional Committee of Magic just because he was powerful and intimidating. Rather, he understood power structures, and how to communicate without words.

Normally, that might make him even *more* scary.

I mean you have a fabulously rich vampire who rules over his physically superior race uncontested and is generally feared. Why not just throw in genius-like brains for good measure?

But this actually reassured me. Because Killian would use his same ridiculous intellect against the Night Court.

Still musing on the implications, I thoughtfully pressed my lips together and glanced out at the vampires.

Pale faces and glassy red eyes stared back at me.

"And," Killian swept a hand through his hair, showing how relaxed he was despite the stares, "if you sit next to me, we can talk to each other and increase the fear we inspire together without anyone knowing I'm just asking you how long you fed my underlings expired blood packs."

"Huh?"

"I talked to some of the kitchen staff this week about a few... plans. They mentioned missing how you rotated the fresh and old blood packs in the fridge for them."

"Oh. Yeah. Okay, fine," I massaged my forehead and hoped I wasn't going to regret this. "Let's do it. But now I want to know what shady plans of yours required input from your kitchen staff."

Killian flashed his fangs at me and sauntered off to the dais without replying.

I waited until I caught Great Aunt Marraine's eye again, then motioned after Killian.

The sassy old woman wriggled her eyebrows at me then smoothed the bright pink stripe in her silvery hair.

I shook my head at her, then hurried after Killian.

Instantly my phone started buzzing. I glanced down at it to see it was a message from Momoko and Franco, who were seated with Great Aunt Marraine and the two other wizards who had opted to come, April and June.

A quick swipe silenced it—I was pretty sure I didn't want to know what that duo had to say to me right now—and I climbed up the short set of stairs.

Killian had really planned his attack—there was a steaming mug of tea and a cup of water waiting for me, as well as a little bowl of fancy European chocolates.

"Nice." I plopped down in my chair, which was so big and ornate it felt like it swallowed me. "Are you ready to hear what the Elite had to say?"

Killian stabbed a straw through a blood pouch. "If I must."

I blabbed a summary of my conversation with the Elite—focusing on the fact that the Night Court was in trouble with the other fae, and staying away from Elite Bellus's thoughts about intermingling. (That was a different conversation for a different day, preferably over the phone when Killian could try and charm me with his smokey voice but not touch me and set my brain on fire.)

"Interesting," Killian said when I finished.

I watched him as I peeled a shiny wrapper off a chocolate. "He said you probably knew all of this already."

"I did." Killian steepled his fingers and studied me. "But that he gave you the information anyway is very curious."

I shrugged. "I gave you the message, so as far as I'm concerned I have nothing more to do with it. How is the turnout for the meeting?"

He stirred, his eyes glittering as he gazed out at the vampires he represented. "We have representatives from twenty-nine Families. Most of them are local, some of them are just *annoyingly* nosy."

I stared out at the vampires—it looked like there was closer to a hundred vampires than twenty-nine. "I assume that more than one representative is attending per Family?"

"Yes. It seems most Families sent between two to four reps each. Eleven Families only sent representatives. For everyone else, the Family Elder is in attendance."

"Those are pretty good numbers, right?" I asked. "Considering you said it can sometimes be hard to get the Elders to start moving."

"You make them sound like large boulders that merely need enough momentum to build up speed." His left eyebrow twitched in irritation. "If only that were so."

Killian had previously explained to me that one of the biggest dangers for a vampire Elder—the upper crust of an already dangerously superior species—was the tendency to grow apathetic in their old age. He said he thought it was caused by the weariness of life—of seeing kingdoms rise and fall, and history repeat itself again and again while they were forced to lose everyone they loved—but it usually amounted to the Elder never leaving their home, or possibly even falling asleep and never waking.

This dangerously left the younger vampires without proper leadership, and meant that those making the decisions weren't always vested or thinking clearly.

"More Elders attended today because even in their feeble

stupidity, they dare not miss this meeting as there is a possibility it will become a war council," Killian said.

"What?" I nearly rocketed out of my over-sized chair. "What happened to leaving them out of it and a war being the worst-case scenario?"

"I never said *I* planned for it to become a war council," Killian said. "Obviously, I'll be aiming to redirect them, and that was why I spoke with my kitchen staff and learned of your blood-pack rearranging habits."

"Are you thinking of throwing a party or something?"

"Given the seriousness of the topic, there will need to be a follow up meeting. However, I can communicate that I am unworried about a war and keep their nerves down if I pose the meeting as more of an informal dinner party at Drake Hall."

I thought for a moment or two. "I think I understand. When Solene-the-murderous-Unclaimed-vampire was on the loose you kept things formal and tight by having meetings here at the Cloisters. Now you want to convey the opposite, hence the party at Drake Hall."

"Precisely."

Appeased, I leaned back and took a sip of the warm drink—some kind of green tea with a faint blueberry flavor.

The assembly hall doors swung shut, and Celestina took up her position in front of the dais, then bowed to Killian.

He gave her a nod and leaned back in his chair, looking almost royal as a small smirk twitched on his lips.

Celestina squared her shoulders and faced the gathered vampires. "I, Celestina Drake, First Knight of the Drake Family, call this meeting of local Families into session, under the judgment of His Eminence Killian Drake."

"So it will be," the vampire attendees chorused together.

"As it was stated on the invitation," Celestina continued, "we are here to discuss the actions of the Night Court after they attacked His Eminence here in the neutral territory of the Curia Cloisters, on the night of..."

I inclined my head slightly in Killian's direction and hid my mouth behind my mug. "Why is Celestina doing all the talking? Don't you have to run this thing?"

"Why should I when I have a charismatic First Knight who can do the work for me?" Unlike me, Killian didn't try to hide that we were talking. His voice was hushed, but he openly swiveled his head to look at me and ignored Celestina's review of the attack.

I set my mug down—there was no sense hiding if he wasn't going to. "It has to be literally part of your job description."

"The best part about being Eminence is that no one can actually tell me what my job description *is*," Killian said. "That's the point of doing all the work to climb to this position."

I scoffed. "You did *not* do all of the work of getting this spot because you were sick of people telling you what to do."

"No, but it is an added bonus." Killian's smirk turned mischievous before his expression cleared all together. "I have Celestina run the meetings because it's the easiest way to gauge their reaction. When I don't speak and remind them I am present, they're more likely to run their mouths and say what they're really thinking. I want that because if they're really that stupid they may say something I can use against them, and at the very least it lets me see what they really think rather than only seeing them react in fear of *me*. For a leader, listening is far more important than shows of power."

I frowned so deeply I could feel my forehead wrinkle. "You did that the night I burst in on the vampire meeting."

"I did," Killian confirmed.

"I didn't even notice you were there. I nearly died when you spoke."

"It is a very effective tool."

I grudgingly nodded, and returned my attention to Celestina's run-down.

The vampires listened patiently to her recount of the Curia Cloisters attack, but I could see signs of anger swirl by the time she moved on to describing the fight at Leila's place.

Some of the younger-looking vampires—and by 'younger-looking' I mean they wore clothes that appeared to come from historical periods after 1910 given that all vampires had that waxy ageless look to them—fidgeted and started to get squirrelly, while the more middle aged vampires—those dressed in clothes from early AD centuries—pursed their lips and began to mutter to one another.

I studied the vampires that I *thought* were Elders—the male vampire in a toga was obviously one, as was the vampire dressed in black and white robes that looked Chinese to my uncultured eye, and a vampire that resembled a Viking. They were more guarded in their reactions, but they couldn't stop the red of their eyes from glowing in anger.

Regardless how he got his position, it was clear Killian was respected enough that the vampires were deeply offended by the attack.

"The instances have been recounted." Celestina wove her long fingers together and folded them in front of her. "What, then, do you have to say?"

There was silence for about two moments before a female vampire wearing a ruffled blue dress that made her look like a model from the 50s leaped to her feet. "We ought to attack them!" She shouted. "How *dare* they accost our Eminence in neutral territory! Let us storm their castle in the fae realm and slaughter them all!"

"You said it, kid!" A vampire with a thick black mustache and equally thick eyebrows leaped to his feet, his polka dot tie askew. "We oughtta smack some sense into those no-good fae—give 'em a good pop!"

Killian watched for a moment more, then leaned in close to me. "It is worth noting," he whispered, his breath tickling my ear, "that the Elders for these outspoken, young vampires are absent."

"You mean they wouldn't say this if their Family Elder was around to rein them in?" I asked.

Killian nodded slightly, then returned to lounging in his chair.

A woman in a Japanese kimono snapped a fan shut. "What has been the reaction from the other fae Courts?"

"They are unhappy," Celestina reported. "There are political ramifications for breaking Cloister law, of course. It is believed that they are putting pressure on the Night Court, but we cannot say to what extent."

"A war, then," a vampire shouted. "Against all the fae in the Midwest!"

"Hear, hear!"

"Yeah!"

As Killian had predicted, it looked like the most excited vampires were all younger. Only about ten or fifteen percent of the vampires present seemed eager to fight. The rest sat back with narrowed expressions.

Killian let it carry on for a few minutes before he spoke. "There will be no war between fae and vampires."

Instant silence—it was almost like magic.

Killian slowly dragged his gaze across the room, his dark eyes slicing through the attendees with the finesse of a sword.

The only noise I could hear was my own breathing. Everyone was absolutely still.

"If we declare open war on all fae Courts it will lead to an unnecessary, large-scale conflict that will only waste resources and lives." His voice was pitched extra low, but I'm pretty sure even the vampires tucked in the farthest corners of the room could hear him as if he stood next to them. "It is possible the Night Court may elect for a certamen or a duel of one degree or another," he continued. "But any physical conflict will be contained—

only involving the Night Court, the Drake Family…and House Medeis."

Whispers rolled through the room, and more than one jaw dropped.

"Wizards, Y-your Eminence?" the vampire in the toga said in a strangled voice. "You're trusting *wizards* to join the fight?"

"Of course," Killian said. "Adept Medeis protected my First and Second Knight in the Cloisters. She and her kinsmen sheltered my underlings when they had no way to defend themselves. I am gratified by their help, and I know they will be key players in the coming conflict."

"What about us?" a vampire somewhere in the back demanded. "The Stewarts have served you loyally, yet you will not allow us to join the fight?"

"The Beckets have served even longer than the Stewarts!"

"As have the Romeros!"

Killian barely narrowed his eyes, but I felt waves of power explode from him. His eyes heated like coals, and all the vampires were slammed back against their chairs, seemingly by his raw presence. "*Enough.*"

Again, there was silence.

Killian held them there, his immense powers hovering over us. I'd never met a fully transformed dragon shifter, but I had a feeling this was what it felt like—the impression of teeth and an icy death that pressed down on you from above.

He finally spoke. "I said no other Families would be involved in the war. I did *not* say I had no use for you."

Collectively, the vampires leaned forward.

Killian waited a few moments. "I want the fae to feel our displeasure. The other Midwest Courts have let the Night Court run amok for too long. But we must express our anger in a *controlled* effort. If we push too hard they'll feel backed into a corner and lash out. We want them angry with the Night Court, not half-convinced we are heading to war."

Some heads nodded, and a few smug looks conveyed Killian was getting across to his listeners.

"Do not avoid fae businesses or places commonly occupied by them. Rather, go there and discuss your disappointment with the attack and what it may mean. If you have any fae Court allies, invite them to a meeting where you happen to mention how shamed the fae must be by the Night Court's criminal and brash actions. Subtly needle them. Make them feel *uncomfortable*."

His words stirred the vampires. They exchanged thoughtful glances with one another, and a few even leaned in to whisper to one another, nodding with excitement as they started hatching their plans.

Killian waited for a few moments, tilting his head at the soft hush of whispers. "When you go out, keep watch and listen. Learn as much as you can, not just about the actions of the Night Court, but the fae in general. If there is a fight I want you there. A disagreement in public? I expect a report on it. I want eyes and ears on the fae, watching their every move.

"Because there is great value in information, we will hold a meeting again," Killian continued. "But I intend for it to be more informal—a party, of sorts."

Weirdly, it seemed the promise of a party satisfied the few vampires that had been holding out. Some of them straightened with interest, and soon all the red eyes in the room gleamed with interest more than bloodlust.

"Details concerning the matter will be emailed to you," Killian said in a very final tone. He leaned back, and whatever hold he had over them released.

Family representatives clumped together, exchanging hushed observations. An energy in the room that had been absent when they first arrived pulsed through the air.

I wanted to shake my head, but I was pretty sure that wouldn't look great since I was sitting next to Killian, so I sipped my tea and ate another chocolate. I couldn't believe how he was manipulating the vampires—and they had to know it!

Once the buzz of discussion grew loud enough, I leaned closer to Killian and whispered, "That was impressive. You practically have them eating out of your hand with the promise of a single party, and by inviting them into social warfare."

"They aren't that loyal to me, really." Killian shrugged. "But they respect power, and the majority of them—excluding the Elders who have their heads in the clouds—are aware I've solidified our grasp of power, and kept back the steady erasure of our kind. Many of them personally hate me, but they'll still help out of a sense of duty and sheer understanding."

"But you're using this as a way to energize them and fortify their connections with one another," I said.

Killian settled his forearms on the arm rests of his chair. "Vampires are a conniving bunch. If I leave them to their own devices they'll either get themselves killed, or start killing off one another. It's better to give them an objective they can mutually work toward, that won't turn into a double-edged sword. It would be a disaster if the fae and vampires all went to war, and in the upset I'm certain at least two Elders would attempt to kill me for my position."

I rubbed my eyes. "I'm really starting to understand why you have trust issues."

"Does that mean you'll expect less from me?"

"*No.* It just means I understand how you got to be this way." I shot him a glare.

He offered me a smirk. "How very sweet of you." He reached out and snagged my hand, raising it to his lips to kiss it—though I was pretty sure it was all just a cover to smell my blood.

"Are you sure it's really wise to act like this in front of all these Families?" I asked.

Killian shrugged. "I don't care what they think of my private life," he bluntly said. "And they all know better than to voice whatever objections they might have."

My cheeks heated when he kissed the inside of my wrist—because of course he would.

I awkwardly cleared my throat, but I didn't yank my hand away from Killian even though I weirdly itched to. "Do you think the Night Court will really challenge you to a certamen?"

I felt Killian's lips morph into a smile as they were still pressed against my wrist. "Oh yes," he purred. "I'm counting on it."

CHAPTER FIFTEEN

Hazel

I felt a breeze at my back.
I strengthened my shield and morphed the field of blue flames that surrounded me into hissing bolts of lightning, making them as big as I dared in hopes that I'd fry my attacker's guts.

An infuriating chuckle, and something slammed into my stomach.

I wheezed and folded over the wooden staff that was still pressed into my gut—of course he'd thought to use wood instead of metal!

I fumbled, but grabbed the pole and incinerated it with flames so hot they turned it into ash.

"Temper, temper," Killian taunted.

I created a veritable ice rink around his feet, then shoved some magic into the ground, making the flooring pop and creak.

It was supposed to make him slide into the ice and fall. Instead he jumped, becoming a blur and disappearing.

"Not again." I dropped my lightning field and swapped it out for thick sheets of ice that were so cold they groaned.

"Tsk, tsk. You still have so many openings."

I followed Killian's voice up to the ceiling, where he casually dangled off a hanging light.

He was in that predator mode again—the one that made my instincts scream and gave me goosebumps.

I felt my hair rise on the back of my neck as he laughed, his fangs flashing.

He let go, dropping down on me.

I released a jet of boiling water off over my head and scuttled to the side, but he was already there.

I locked my legs and tried to turn, but I slammed into his chest.

Before I knew it, he had me on my back, his thumb pressed down on my throat. Just a little bit of pressure in the right place, and he could kill me.

His grin was wild and a touch savage, and his eyes were bright red as he leaned over me. "Too slow."

I flinched.

He froze and was off me about two seconds later.

He stood on the other side of the mats, rolling his shoulders as he watched me, all signs of his wildness gone. Instead his black eyebrows were furrowed slightly, and his eyes were once again almost a ruby obsidian shade in their darkness.

I stayed where I was.

Not because I was scared, but because I was so *mad*!

Since we'd made up, I had been coming here three times a week, and I still wasn't seeing any improvement!

My stamina wasn't a problem—I never had the *chance* to be pushed into magical exhaustion because he could beat me so quickly. And it didn't seem like sword techniques or refined martial arts skills were really going to help me either because it was my goal to keep him away from me.

It's strategy. He's seen everything, so he's prepared for every bit of magic I throw at him.

I wanted to pound my fists on the mats, but that seemed pretty childish. So I made myself take what Great Aunt Marraine liked to call—and preach endlessly about—calming breaths.

Inhale...exhale.

Inhale...exhale.

I don't think there's a strategy I'll be able to find in a book that can defeat him—he's so old he's most likely seen it. It's not just that he's good at strategy, but that he's had a lot of experience. How could I use that to my advantage? What could I do that could throw him off balance because of all that experience?

"If I frightened you that much, I can ask Celestina to finish practice with you." Killian's tone was flat and expressionless, as was his face when I peeled my back off the ground to peer up at him.

"Huh?" I said.

"If facing me in a match scares you that much, you can have a different partner for the remainder of the day." His words were a veneer of politeness I hadn't heard from him in ages.

"It's fine." I scrambled to my feet and brushed off my workout pants. "I was just...thinking."

"Hm." Killian eyed me, then paused and turned in the direction of the door with a curious expression.

As usual for our training sessions, the gym was empty, but someone must be on their way if Killian's reaction was anything to go by.

"Is someone out in the hallway?" I asked.

He blinked. "Yes."

Celestina burst through the door, slammed it shut behind her, and leaned on it. "Your Eminence, Adept Medeis," she wheezed. She tried for a smile, but the door buckled, nearly bowling her over. "There is an unexpected...*guest* who is demanding to see you both."

I frowned and took a few cautious steps closer to Killian. "A guest?"

"Indeed!" Although Celestina kept her tone pleasant, it was obvious she—the Drake Family First Knight—was struggling desperately to keep the door shut as someone pounded on the other side.

"Let him in," Killian said. "And then you may go."

"Him?" I echoed.

"Yes, Your Eminence." Celestina stepped back from the door, which blew open with such force I think it might have made a dent in the wall.

In stormed the Paragon, his white mustache drooping past his chin, his long, silvery hair wild and disheveled, and his robes—an impressive silk brocade with embroidered feathers that I swear *moved* across the fabric—were wrinkled.

He drew himself up, sticking his craggy nose high in the air like a pouting kid. "You two are so mean!"

I blinked, internally replaying the Paragon's words because they were so random and weird that I had to be mistaken.

Nope. I didn't think I was.

I furrowed my brow and looked up at Killian, who had a similar expression and was looking down at me.

"What is he talking about?" Killian asked.

"Something to do with the Night Court, I guess?" I offered.

"*What is he talking about?*" the Paragon mimicked in an irritating, high pitched voice. "I'm talking about *you*—" he pointed a finger at Killian, "and *you*—" he moved his finger and stabbed it at me. "Being so wrapped up in each other you ignore me!"

I furrowed my eyebrows deeper, but Killian pinched the bridge of his perfectly straight nose and slightly shook his head.

The Paragon continued his rant, planting his hands on his hips. "You're terrible friends. Terrible!" He shook out his robe, his lips jutting out in a pout. "You're worse than two teenagers who have just entered a relationship! Killian, how old are you? Well beyond the years it is acceptable for you to act twitterpated.

Shame on you for leaving me high and dry just because your girlfriend is back!" he scolded.

I *had* been thinking that the Paragon was going to give himself a headache if he kept this tantrum up much longer, but he might have had a point—not the one he thought he did, but a point for me.

I mean, when he called me Killian's girlfriend, a stupid part of me did feel stupidly giddy. I was losing it! If I wasn't careful, I'd soon be doodling hearts whenever I thought about Killian.

I gritted my teeth and forcibly collected myself into what I considered a more proper reaction of slightly irritated bewilderment. "Are you seriously here to complain that we're having fun without you and you feel left out?"

"Yes! I mean, no!" The Paragon drew himself up again. "I mean I've been slumping around this stupid city for *days*, waiting for you two to come ask me for help with the Night Court! And you never showed!"

Fat crocodile tears that I was 99% sure were dramatized glazed the Paragon's eyes as he melodramatically wiped them. "I stood in the ice cream aisle for an *hour*. My hands got cold! And I'm now banned from the library!"

"Really?" Killian picked up his smartphone from the chair he'd left it on. "I'll have to make a note of that."

"Is that all you're going to say?" the Paragon demanded, taking large shuddering breaths like a woman in one of those silent, black and white movies. "You horrible man! Aphrodite was right about you!" he hiccupped, then erupted into sobs.

"You wanted us to seek you out for help with the Night Court?" Killian asked.

"Yes!" the Paragon spat. "You've bothered me with hundreds of other minor things! Naturally, when it counted I assumed you'd want my help as well! So much for believing we were such close *friends*!"

"So I was right!" I brightened. "I think it was when we visited you for the book that I said you two were friends, and you both got disgusted with me and claimed you weren't."

Killian scoffed. "It's because we're not."

The Paragon drew back, as if Killian had slapped him. "How *dare* you say that?!"

Now that I knew what really had the Paragon complaining, I found the situation a lot less confusing and a whole heck of a lot more entertaining.

Killian, however, didn't seem to share my amusement. "Stop grinning," he ordered. "You're only feeding into his dramatics."

"But this is an occasion to celebrate," I said.

Killian warily eyed me. "Is it?"

"Yes!" I winked at him. "It's so hard for you to make friends after all."

Killian's brow lowered by several degrees, and the black in his eyes seemed to grow. "You're even worse than he is."

"It's okay, Paragon." I ignored Killian and moved to pat the Paragon's back—earning me a suspicious gaze from the Eminence. "I understand the situation now."

"I'm glad to hear *someone* does!" The Paragon used his beard to wipe his face off—after all of this I wasn't just suspicious that the Paragon wasn't as old as he looked, but completely certain he was way younger than he chose to appear.

"I'm sorry you were waiting for us," I started. "But even before Killian and I had really...er...made up," I stumbled slightly, trying to name the re-adjustment to our relationship that we still hadn't quite given a name to, "we talked about you and agreed we couldn't ask you for help or advice in this, or the fae might see it as you giving us special treatment."

It was the truth—and even more startlingly it had been Killian's idea.

I'd been all for pumping the Paragon for information, but Killian had strongly opposed the idea. I had assumed it was because of his trust-lacking ways and he believed the Paragon would betray us and tell the Night Court we'd talked to him. But after the meeting with the local vampires at the Curia Cloisters, it was more likely he was telling the truth and not only did he want to avoid enlarging the possible conflict by involving the Paragon, he was attempting to shield his friend from picking sides by simply evading him all together.

"No one would get upset," the Paragon scoffed. "The Night Court has gotten itself on everyone's 'to be hated' list with their idiotic actions and the legal and political repercussions it's harvesting them."

"Yeah," I agreed. "But the other fae Courts might feel a *bit* resentful if the Paragon—*their* national representative—were to help a vampire Family and wizard House defeat a fae Court, no matter how much Queen Nyte deserves to be walloped."

The Paragon itched his nose for several moments. "Yes," he finally said. "That sounds about right. But! You could have told me!" He went back to poking a finger at Killian. "Especially you! You barged in on my life at all sorts of inconvenient times as long as you were fighting with your precious over here, and now that she's back I am suddenly ignored? So cold!"

"You visited the Paragon while we were fighting?" I asked.

"We weren't actively fighting, we were in a disagreement," Killian said.

"Hmph." The Paragon leaned near and spoke in the loudest whisper I'd ever heard. "See how he's trying to nit-pick to distract you from answering your question? Classic avoidance technique."

Killian shot the Paragon an annoyed look. "If you're so upset I wasn't visiting, you could have just *called*, like a normal supernatural."

"I," the Paragon snootily adjusted his spectacles, "am above such pettiness. Also, my cellphone doesn't always work in my pocket realm."

I reclaimed my chisa katana—it seemed like practice was over, because I didn't think the Paragon was going anywhere soon.

"Would you like to join us for coffee or tea—or blood, in Killian's case."

"He can wait until you leave." Killian checked his cellphone. "You said you were leaving in half an hour."

"Maybe I don't want to talk to you," the Paragon snidely said. "Maybe I just want to talk to Hazel since she *understands* me."

Killian narrowed his eyes. "If you are implying—"

"For heaven's sake, no!" The Paragon rolled his eyes. "I am not trying to put the moves on your beloved, so don't chip your fangs gnashing your teeth. My gosh, as if I'd think of a *wizard* like that! No offense."

"None taken," I said. "You're too old for me anyway."

"Oh, you think he's younger than I am?" The Paragon nodded at Killian. "I have got news for you, sister. He—"

"*Fine*," Killian sighed. "I'll call for refreshments."

The Paragon brightened. "No need! We can go to my place. Hold on!"

The sneaky fae had his unicorn coin purse out before Killian could refuse, and snapped it open.

Wind swept through the gym. I clamped my eyes shut when they started to water. Magic rippled around us, the wind died down, and when I opened my eyes we were in the Paragon's study —which was settled in his private pocket realm in the fae realm.

The study was stuffed with gorgeous wooden bookshelves, almost to the point of feeling overcrowded, but it was such a unique blend of old magic and human tech toys that it was always fun to visit.

A statue of a unicorn carved out of a crystal was settled on a shelf with a sleek video gaming system.

His desk—made out of a *living* tree—held stacks of books older than America, and what looked like one of the first iPod models.

Vials filled with curious liquids were lined up neatly on spice racks, and beneath them was an empty carton of Chinese takeout.

As always, the most noticeable thing about the study was the enormous velvet pet bed. It had changed locations from a bookshelf to the open mouth of a dragon head statue that was about the size of a pony. Lounging on that bed was a gloriously hairless sphinx cat.

Today she was rolled up like a giant, pink egg, her head tucked almost invisibly under her body.

"Hello, Aphrodite," I said.

She unearthed her head, revealing ears so big they were bat-like. She gave me a friendly "*Mmert*", and stretched, jiggling the tiny gold bell on her collar—which appeared to be embroidered with real gold.

"Aphrodite!" The Paragon scratched her chin and cooed over her. "Help me pick out a tea for my guests!" He scooped up the hairless cat and carried her across the study to a locked cabinet.

Killian hovered so close to my shoulder I could feel that perpetual air of coolness that followed him. "What are you intending to feed us?" he asked.

"I'm making you a loose-leaf tea." The Paragon tapped the lock of the wooden cabinet. The lock clicked open and the doors swung open, revealing rows and rows of canisters covered with gauzy blue silk. "You should be honored! Tea is a fae specialty we learned centuries ago from the elves themselves! We don't often make it for outsiders—*I* certainly never have!"

The Paragon set Aphrodite down inside the cabinet. "There you go my angel, find the best one for them," he said.

Aphrodite glanced back at us. "*Mert?*"

"Yes," the Paragon said. "For the both of them."

The cat twitched her long, bony tail, then started sniffing tea canisters.

What is going on?

Before I could ask, the Paragon beamed at us. "Not only am I bestowing this treasured drink upon you, but Aphrodite herself is picking out the flavor and mix! Such an honor is not often bestowed!"

Killian looked pained. "Your cat is picking out the tea?"

"Indeed!" the Paragon cackled. "She has superior taste, and it is always such fun to drink and discover what she has selected for the day."

I'd been watching the cat brush her pink nose on a few canisters as she prowled the shelf. "You mean you don't *know* what she chooses?"

"Goodness, no! That would ruin all the fun!" The Paragon swiped a canister of tea off the shelf and shook it at us for emphasis. "You see I have the brew time and water temperature labeled on the outside, but the tea flavor is only recorded on the bottom of the lid. I purposely bought the same containers so I can't tell them apart, and as long as I refrain from looking at the lid it's a pleasant surprise from Aphrodite to me!"

I had never before seen Killian's forehead look so wrinkled. "You have the mental capacity of a donut," he said.

"I don't know." I kept watching Aphrodite—she'd abandoned the shelf the Paragon had put her on and jumped down to a lower one where she was carefully sorting through tea canisters. "I think it's kind of cute. Look how hard she's working for us!"

"She's a cat," Killian said. "She doesn't care what we drink."

"You're such a doubter—and a downer!" the Paragon scolded.

Aphrodite sat down and curled her skinny tail around her feet. "*Mmert.*"

The Paragon whirled back around to face his pet. "You've decided on one?"

Aphrodite pawed at a canister hiding behind the front row.

The Paragon extracted it and held it out for her inspection. "This one?"

"*Mmert.*"

"She has chosen!" The Paragon briefly held the tea over his

head in a dramatic show, then shuffled off to a nearby machine that looked like a weird version of a coffee brewer.

He hummed under his breath as he scooped several tablespoons of the tea leaves out, dropping them in a metal basket.

"What did the cat choose?" Killian asked.

The Paragon harumphed in irritation. "Did you not listen to a word I said? It is meant to be a *surprise*!" He pointedly picked up the container, waited until Killian was watching, then shoved it back into the cabinet of identical containers and shuffled them around.

"Idiot," Killian muttered.

"Child!" the Paragon shot back.

"*Mmert*," Aphrodite said. She hopped onto the Paragon's shoulder, clearing the cabinet so he could relock it and shuffle back to the machine where he loaded the metal basket into a glass pot of water placed on an electric boiler.

"What is that thing?" I asked.

"It's a tea maker!" The Paragon beamed at me. "You select the temperature and brew time, and the machine will make the tea to these specifications, see?" He pointed to a tiny screen where he changed the time and temperature, then pressed a button.

"The Dominant—that is the top werewolf in America—gave it to me last Christmas at our secret Santa gift exchange. Best gift I ever got!" The Paragon smiled.

The machine buzzed, and within a few seconds the water started to heat.

"How can you claim this is special?" Killian scoffed. "You don't even brew the tea—you use a machine!"

The Paragon brandished the tablespoon at Killian. "Silence, doubter! You will realize how foolish you sound once you taste the heaven Aphrodite selected and I personally brewed for you."

Killian looked thoughtful. "A donut is too good for you," he finally said. "You're as mentally stable as a computer in need of updates."

The Paragon scoffed as he retrieved two mint green teacups and saucers that had beautiful gold edging and delicate gold flowers painted on the sides. "Ingrate. Aphrodite, don't mind him."

I also frowned when I watched the Paragon place the two cups down by the machine—which whirled as it lowered the metal basket containing the tea leaves into the hot water. "Why are you only getting out two teacups?"

"Because I'm not drinking this, naturally," the Paragon said.

"*What?*" Killian growled.

"Aphrodite chose this tea for *you two* specifically," the Paragon said. "I can't go trampling her careful choice and imbibing it myself. Now please, sit down."

I thought for a moment, then sat down at the tiny but ornate tea table the Paragon pointed to. I gratefully claimed the smallest chair, which didn't swallow me up, but looked up when I felt Killian's eyes on me. "What?"

"You're falling in line with a meekness I find surprising."

I shrugged. "I live in a magic House. The idea of a cat picking out my tea is hardly anything to get my sword belt twisted over."

"See? Hazel has a grace and maturity you lack," the Paragon said.

Killian turned around to face his friend. "You laced it with something, didn't you?"

"Nonsense!"

"Hazel, don't drink it," Killian said. "Who knows what he put in it?"

"You overly suspicious vampire." The Paragon rolled his eyes. "This is why it's so hard for you to make friends! Oh—it's done!"

The machine beeped and raised the basket out of the water.

The Paragon gave the pot a good swish, then poured the tea—which was a distinctive pink color—into the teacups. He set them on the table and stared at Killian until he sat down in the chair next to mine.

"Very good." He peeled Aphrodite off his shoulder and set her on her pet bed.

Killian raised an eyebrow. "Are you just going to sit there and watch us drink?"

"Goodness, no. I made a mobile Starbucks order which should be ready any moment." The Paragon pulled a smartphone out of the sleeves of his robe and peered down at the screen. "Don't touch anything valuable, I'll be back in a jiffy. I have a door rigged into my favorite Starbucks cafe—I can't wake up without my caffeine. Toodles!" The Paragon pulled a unicorn pen from the same sleeve and popped off the cap, disappearing with a puff of fog.

CHAPTER SIXTEEN

Hazel

I selected my teacup and saucer, sliding them in front of me. "He's a good friend for you."

"He is *not* my friend." Killian picked up the tea cup and gave it a whiff.

"Can you tell what flavor it is?" I gave the steam rising from my cup an experimental sniff. It had a sweet, almost fruity scent.

"Given that I have not devoted myself to sniffing tea leaves as a daily activity, I can't say I know what I'm smelling. There's a hint of chocolate and strawberries, but those are the only scents I can be certain about." Killian suspiciously eyed his drink.

"Bottoms up?" I held up my teacup.

Killian stared at me.

I shook my head and clinked my teacup against his. "You need to get out more." I took a sip of the hot tea, taking a few moments to try to pin down the flavor.

Killian was right. It had the tangy taste of tart strawberries that hadn't quite ripened, the smooth richness of chocolate, and an underlying floral taste.

It also made my tongue tingle. Which I was pretty sure wasn't normal. Did fae swirl magic into their tea mixes?

I took another sip, then curled my tongue. "It's good," I confirmed. "But there's something about it..."

Killian narrowed his eyes. "This is why one always has to be careful when they accept hospitality from fae. They can't lie, but they're deviant and frequently homicidal." He took a cautious sip—which actually was a pretty big indicator of how much he trusted the Paragon. I'd only seen him eat human food on *extremely* rare occasions. Usually he was all about blood packs.

I sipped my tea and leaned back in my chair, relaxing. "You know, I like it better the more and more I drink it."

"It is surprisingly good," Killian said.

"I didn't know you liked tea."

"I don't." His forehead wrinkled slightly as he stared at his cup. "Which is what makes this tea even more dubious."

I laughed, and then struggled to hold my teacup still so I didn't spill any on my practice clothes.

Killian smiled, looking the most relaxed I'd seen him since we started our training session. "I missed your laugh, you know. When you were gone."

The sudden change in our discussion surprised me a little, but I set my teacup down on its saucer with a quiet clack. "There were a lot of things I missed—about you, the other Drakes, and Drake Hall in general."

"It's not going to happen again."

I peeled my gaze from my teacup. "What's not going to happen?"

"I'm not going to let go of you again," Killian said. "So why do we keep dancing around whatever we are?"

I stared at Killian, a little shocked, but my reply dropped from my mouth seemingly without my consent. "All right. But what are you picturing we're going to end up as?"

Killian's smile turned cunning. "I'll take it all."

I blinked. "...what?"

In the span of a heartbeat, Killian was out of his seat, and had his hands planted on the arm rests of my chair as he leaned into me. "I want everything," he said. "Whatever you'll give me. If that means friendship, we can stay there. But it seems to me you're willing for more..."

"I'm not your *one*," I said, more as a test than a coherent statement.

The term *the one* had been thrown around a few times regarding Killian and me. It was basically the vampire equivalent of soul mates, *the one* they would love the rest of their days. It was super romantic, but I wasn't that far gone to believe Killian thought of me like that.

Killian shrugged. "I doubt such a thing truly exists these days, and I'm not particularly inclined to care about it."

Yep, that was just about what I expected.

"How romantic."

"Just because I don't think you're my destined *soul mate*—a sappier, more unlikely thing I've never heard of—doesn't mean I don't deeply care for you." Killian leaned closer and closer and rested his forehead on mine while he scooped me from my relaxed position so I sat on the edge of my seat. "I've never particularly hidden how I feel about you. And I'm fairly certain you feel something for me as well."

I wanted to think straight, but my brain wasn't cooperating. It was doing mental hiccups, which was super irritating, because I was trying to string together a cohesive thought while it was busy noticing how Killian was drop dead handsome.

FOCUS!

"Yeah, okay, but there's a lot to unpack there." I pinched my thigh to try to clear my mind, but it didn't work. "We can't just jump into anything. You're a vampire, and I'm a wizard. It might be—no—it *is* considered taboo for us to be together. There will be lots of political...stuff, as a result. Of us. If that were to happen."

I was babbling, why was I babbling? My tongue still tingled a little from the tea—was that the problem?

A dark chuckle escaped from Killian. "Do you *really* think I care what others will say about us?"

"No," I agreed. "You're too selfish." I slapped a hand over my mouth. "I didn't mean to say that out loud," I confessed with my hand still over my mouth.

"You're not wrong." Killian shrugged his broad shoulders, which unfortunately fascinated my already addled brain. "I can also use my power to stifle most upsets we might face—except for you, of course." He narrowed his eyes at me.

"Hey, right back at you, Mr. Paranoia," I snorted. "I would love for us to work something out, but while we have enough trust for a friendship, I'm not that far gone to believe there's enough trust between us to establish something as deep as...whatever. No matter how hot you are, if you only trust me about as much as one of your underlings, it wouldn't work. There's too much on the line—for both of us."

Why did I say he's hot?! What is wrong with me?

He smiled disarmingly and brushed the spot on my cheek where my wizard mark appeared if I used magic. "You think I'm attractive; that's a good enough start I suppose."

"No touching, no, none." I tried to wave him off as I gave my brain a kick.

Killian smirked. "You might be most adorable when you're flustered, did you know that?"

I stared at Killian in disbelief. Why was he being so honest all of a sudden?

Did he catch a cold or inhale something weird? Did we both *catch something?*

Something tickled my thoughts, but it escaped before I could grab it.

Of course, it was then that the Paragon reappeared with a pop of magic.

I was still seated on my chair, and Killian was still leaning over me. We were frozen—I in horror, and Killian in sheer indifference.

The Paragon, toting what looked like a venti sized Starbucks drink, beamed when he saw us. "Oh, it appears to have worked! What a *wonderful* choice, Aphrodite! As usual, you know just what tea to pick."

"...Huh?" I said.

"*What?*" Killian said, murderous.

"Aphrodite." The Paragon motioned to his cat—sitting in her pet bed positioned in the dragon statue's mouth—and plopped down in the empty seat at the table. "She picked out my '*lovers' summer*' tea for the two of you."

Killian straightened. "I thought you said you didn't check the label?"

"For me." The Paragon took off his spectacles and tossed them on the table. "Of course I was going to read what she picked out for the two of you! I need to know what she thinks you're lacking." He took a swig of his drink. "Ahhh, that's good stuff. Anyway, in this case, she must believe you need to rekindle your romance."

When our gazes swung to the sphinx cat, she yawned, displaying a mouthful of white teeth.

"You're joking," Killian said.

"Not at all. Aphrodite is very intuitive. She knows just what people need! Just last week she picked out a very appropriate tea for the Day King when he dropped by to complain. I call it '*calm the heck down.*' A few swigs and he was sleeping like a baby!"

"Wait." I narrowed my eyes as a few facts came into sharp focus. "Then Killian is right. Your tea *is* laced—with magic!"

The Paragon gave me a huge smile.

"No wonder it tasted flowery! That was fae magic—I thought

something was off. Fae mental magics are harder for us wizards to resist, so that would explain it." I groaned and massaged my head, until my mind caught up with me. "Wait, you *laced* our *drinks*!"

I leaped out of the chair and launched myself at the Paragon, who gave a high-pitched squeal of fright.

Killian caught me midair. "What was in the tea?" he said between clenched teeth.

"Barely anything at all." The Paragon retreated to the far side of his study, cowering by Aphrodite's dragon statue. "Just a hint of magic—barely enough to make you two relax and speak your minds. But the magic is only there for the first two or three sips. And the effects are very short lived—only a minute or two!"

Killian set me down, but left an arm resting on my shoulders, and together we stared the Paragon down.

He rolled his eyes. "It's such trace amounts it's not even illegal! Just being around Mr. Studly here is more likely to juice you up given the pheromones vampires ooze. I just wanted to give you two an opportunity to talk." When he glanced back at us, the light in his eyes was tired and ancient, matching his sham of an appearance. "What you two have is rare. It pained me to see you at odds when friendship between supernaturals is so unheard of."

Killian narrowed his eyes. "How easy is it for the fae Courts to find the next Paragon?"

The Paragon squeaked.

I exhaled deeply. "Shall we just forget that conversation ever happened?" I asked Killian in a lowered voice.

Killian released the Paragon from his gaze and glared down at me. "Why?"

"Because our tea was spiked?"

"It doesn't change what we said." Killian's eyes heated a little. "Why can't we continue?"

"Uh, how about because we're in the middle of a face off with the Night Court?" I wrinkled my nose at him, surprised *I* was being the practical one for once. "Can't we just keep dancing around...us, for now? This isn't an ideal time to try and hash it out."

"That sounds like a convenient excuse driven by your tendency to avoid things that upset you."

"No it's not! Wait. Well, maybe," I admitted. "But it's also the truth." I hesitated and bit my lip. "But can't we just wait until we finish dealing with the Night Court? If we changed what we are, there would be a lot we'd need to settle and..." I trailed off, glancing at the Paragon, who was doing his best to disappear. He seemed wholly engrossed with petting his purring cat, but I didn't really want to keep going with him standing so close.

Call me a coward, but I *needed* time to figure this out. Pursuing a relationship with Killian wasn't going to be the kind of casual dating I'd done so far in my life. There was no way I was jumping into it when I was in the middle of the most stressful, challenging, and awful year of my life. And I still wasn't quite so sure we were right for each other, even if we had feelings. There was that lack of trust between us...

Killian thought for a moment. "You're not saying no."

I eagerly nodded. "Just not right now."

After a few unnerving moments of silence, Killian nodded. "Fine. I'm willing to give you time. It seems I'll have to find a way to satisfy your nearly insatiable desire for trust, anyway. *However.*"

Ugh, he can read me a lot better than I like.

When I met his gaze, his eyes glowed faintly red, and he leaned in again. "I'm not going to let you escape, Hazel. If you keep trying to run from this issue just to avoid pain, I won't stand for it."

It was difficult to swallow. "Deal," I squeaked.

"It's a good thing I'm such an ancient, elderly fae," the Paragon piteously said. "So I can't overhear any secret whispers between you two."

Killian briefly took my hand and squeezed it, then shifted his eyes—now markedly blacker—to the Paragon again. "If you try to feed me magic again, your *cat* will be left as the next Paragon." He returned to his seat, all elegance and death.

"My mistake." The Paragon picked his way across his study. "Next time I'll warn you. Though I dare say Aphrodite would make a better Paragon than you'd expect. She has more sense than half the fae."

That didn't strike me as a very Paragon-esque thing to say about your own people, but the Paragon hardly looked at all like a fae as he slurped his drink and itched his nose. "So, are you two ready for me to drop some truth missiles on you as the kids say these days?"

"Truth bombs," I corrected.

"Whatever!" He swatted a hand at me, but when I grinned, he didn't smile in return. He pulled his bushy eyebrows together. "I apologize, for some of what I have to say may bring you...pain. You in particular, Hazel."

"What, are you going to insult wizards some more?" I attempted to joke.

"No," the Paragon said. "If only the situation was so straightforward and innocent that hurt feelings were all we had to worry about." He sighed and knit his fingers together.

Aphrodite hopped out of her bed and sauntered over to us, pushing her bald head into the Paragon's robes and purring.

"Regarding the Night Court," the Paragon began.

"Don't tell us anything that will have political repercussions," Killian slid in before the Paragon could continue.

The Paragon scooped his cat up and held her like a baby, patting her bare rump. "What we are about to discuss cannot leave the room. Not because others might retaliate, but because it's dangerous knowledge, and if word gets out of what I do know, I'll likely lose the trail I've been following for years."

"What is it?" I asked.

The Paragon squeezed his eyes shut. "I don't believe the Night Court is acting entirely alone."

"*What?*" Killian asked.

The Paragon winced. "Or perhaps, it would be better to say I suspect the Night Court has backers—and they are not fae."

"What do you mean?" I asked. "Supernaturals don't work together, typically. If anyone is supporting the Night Court they *must* be fae."

"Not necessarily." The Paragon leaned back in his chair and set Aphrodite down on his belly. "The Night Court has been bankrupt for years. They haven't had a decent ruler in decades. Even before you revealed Queen Nyte had killed her husband, the Courts of this area were not overly fond of the Night Court, although they used to be considered one of the most powerful in the region. They had shaky alliances at best, and those relationships have only deteriorated since Queen Nyte and Consort Ira have proven to be idiots in their dogmatic pursuit of revenge against you."

"No one likes them," I interpreted.

"Precisely." The Paragon rubbed Aphrodite on the top of her head. "And yet *somehow* they have come to possess countless elven magical items—artifacts considered priceless and precious. Artifacts that they have no way of being able to afford—indeed, there are only a handful of Courts and nobles who could afford such things, and somehow the Night Court came to possess them? Unlikely."

Worriedly, I glanced at Killian. "Could it be another vampire Family who wants to destroy you?"

Killian shook his head. "No. It doesn't follow the correct pattern. No vampire would buy elven artifacts—they are too dangerous for my kind, and we have no natural defense for them, unlike you wizards. It's possible a Family could be giving them funds, and the elven items are merely how the Night Court chooses to act, but even that is extremely unlikely. The conflict has gone on too long, and before the Cloister attack the Night fae were a threat, but not a large enough one to actually be serious. If a vampire wanted me out, he'd be better off finding one of the few remaining vampire slayers, or hiring a werewolf and wizard team. Fae are too treacherous and naturally too dangerous to a vampire. Wizards technically are a bigger threat, but only if they train as Hazel has, which as we all know simply doesn't happen. As such, fae are the natural enemy to a vampire."

"Solene worked for the Night Court," I pointed out.

"She was one Unclaimed vampire who was frightened and angry—which makes anyone easy to manipulate," Killian said. "A vampire with the means and desire to kill me would not be so easy to manipulate."

I winced at the casual way he mentioned his own death.

"I don't believe a vampire is behind this either," the Paragon said.

"Who could it be, then?" I asked.

The Paragon stared at his cat. "I don't believe the important aspect of this question is who, but rather why." He raised his eyes. "I don't believe Killian was targeted, or that this backer has a real desire to get rid of him. I think the true target was the Night Court."

"Wait." I held up my hand to stop him. "I don't think I'm following you. You think the people who backed the Night Court are actually after the Night Court?"

The Paragon fussed with his robe, pulling it partially over Aphrodite. "I cannot say their motive for certain. But I've been tracking them for some time during my search for...something. But they have a pattern." His hands twitched. "They prey upon the weak and those who are in danger. Vampire, fae, wizard, shifter, it doesn't matter what type of supernatural it is. They target the most desperate Courts, the lowest Families, the weakest Packs...which is why I believe this also involved Hazel."

Every nerve in my body felt like it was on fire, but I made myself stay sitting as I listened to the Paragon. There was only one possible way that could hook me into all of this, and it made me grimace just to think of it. "You think they backed Mason."

"Possibly. Have you had a chance to look over the statements and testimonies taken from the Telliers and Rothchilds?"

"Yes," I said. "They all said Mason approached them about the leadership of House Medeis. He offered them funds and promised a stronger alliance if they helped him." I hesitated. "I have no idea where he got the money. Great Aunt Marraine and I tried to follow a paper trail. In the end we assumed it was an inheritance from his parents—they died several years ago."

"My theory is that these mysterious backers are attempting to pick off the weak, or use them to implode local politics," the Paragon said. "Inciting a rebellion in a wizard House would match their general pattern as it could *only* bring destruction and ruin to the House once you were gone given the House's close ties to its family line."

The Paragon absently petted his cat. "Once Mason failed his backers, I suspect they doubled down on their investment in the Night Court. But since Queen Nyte attacked you in the Cloisters, I suspect the backers have packed up. The attack was too flashy and unavoidable. It's no longer possible for the Night Court to implode from the inside since Killian will likely have the legal right to clean house so to speak. So the backers have moved on. Given that they don't seem to be widespread—they pick up and move back and forth between single locations instead of spreading out like a large organization—I think they can't afford to be involved in a fight with multiple front lines. Hazel joining you, and the wizards and werewolves politically backing you, put a strain on them. I suspect."

"Who are they that they have the funds to cause all of this chaos?" Killian asked. "And how have I not heard of them before?"

The Paragon shrugged. "We haven't been able to pinpoint the activity to any particular person or even a specific supernatural race. The Dominant, the Ancient, the Magister, and myself are keeping an eye on the situation," he said, referring to the top werewolf, vampire, and wizard officials in America. "But thus far we don't have much to go off—just whispers and traces of rumors. We're *trying* to find supernaturals who could help us, but frankly it's not a top priority." He rubbed his chin, grumbling when he tangled his fingers in his long, drooping mustache. "We're far more concerned with the inevitable death of magic than these backers. They are a grease fire compared to the raging wildfire that awaits us if magic collapses entirely."

Killian drummed his fingers on the table. "So they are gone. What do you expect us to do, then?"

"Nothing. I'm not telling you because I wanted action, but because it seemed worthwhile to warn you." The Paragon hesitated and hugged Aphrodite close. "And because...Hazel...there is a possibility your parents' deaths were not an accident."

My heart sputtered. "What do you mean?" I asked in a shaky voice. "They died in a car crash."

"And within three weeks you had a coup on your hands?" The Paragon shook his head. "Mason was too well prepared for it to be a coincidence."

My spit tasted metallic and bitter. "You think they were murdered...to kick off Mason's coup?"

"It is a possibility." The Paragon cowered a little, then hesitantly offered me his hairless cat.

I wanted to burst into sobs and scream—I'd thought it wasn't fair my parents were taken from me when I was so young, but even just *thinking* that it might not have been an accident after all made their deaths that much crueler and more terrible.

"*Mmert*," Aphrodite said.

I reached out and took her with shaking hands.

I wasn't expecting to really feel comforted by her—even if she was a sweet cat, the hairless thing kinda freaked me out to be honest.

But Aphrodite climbed up my lap, planted her front paws on my chest, and leaned in, settling just over my heart. She purred, flooding me with warmth and assurance.

A moment later, Killian slid a hand across my shoulders. "I'm sorry," he murmured in my ear.

It was hard to swallow, but I made myself do it. Aphrodite's warmth gave me the courage to look up at the Paragon and meet his sad eyes. "Are you sure you don't want us to help, at all?"

"I simply wanted you to be aware. I'll tell the Elite and the Pre-Dominant eventually. But I believe the two of you deserve to know." He hesitated. "But if you really wished to bar the way for whoever this shadowy enemy is so they are not tempted to return to Magiford..."

"Obviously we do." Killian's usual smokey smooth voice was rushed, and his barely noticeable British accent was just a little stronger.

The Paragon took in a deep gulp of air. "Then I'd try to foster a working relationship with the other supernaturals—at least, as much as possible."

Killian stared at him. "You're joking."

"Not at all."

"Then the Elite, or some other bleeding-heart leader put you up to this," Killian said.

"Allow me to point out how very hypocritical it is to say that when you are openly courting a *wizard*," the Paragon stated.

Both he and Killian looked in my direction.

I forced a weak smile to my lips. "He's got a point."

Killian's blank expression shifted to a slight smile. He leaned in and lightly kissed my cheek, then whispered into my neck. "But you are special and unique. It's why we are this way."

The Paragon delicately coughed. "Yes. Ahem. If you could stop accosting Adept Medeis long enough for me to finish what I was going to say, I'd appreciate it."

Killian sighed in irritation and sat back in his chair. "Fine. Out with it."

"I didn't mean to say you had to politely discuss politics and create a more joint force or anything," the Paragon said. "Rather, if you can be socially polite, that would be an excellent start." He gestured to the two of us. "When you attended the Summer's End Ball together, that did wonderful things for both vampires and wizards. Repeat that, and I sincerely believe it will help."

"You want us to be socialites?" I asked.

"Of a sort," the Paragon acknowledged. "I will admit this is a bit of an experiment. I've never seen these shadowy people back away from a fight so fast, and I'm inclined to think it's because of the two of you."

Killian sighed. "I already have a party scheduled at Drake Hall. Originally it was supposed to only be for vampires, but I suppose I can expand it to include other supernaturals. It will be easy enough to convince the vampires that we'll use the occasion to look benevolently down on the fae to remind them of their shame. And I imagine it won't be a total loss. It will provide me with the chance to observe the leaders of society in a place where they cannot hide."

"Doesn't that defeat the point?" I asked.

"Nonsense," the Paragon said. "Considering supernaturals only seem to mix at funerals and parties pertaining to the Regional Committee of Magic, it will be a magnificent step forward, even if he does it out of a less than pure motivation. Besides, he'll have you to smooth things over."

"I don't know about that." I cleared my throat. "But, Paragon...thank you."

He blinked owlishly. "For asking Killian to host a party?"

"No. For telling me about my parents." I squeezed my eyes tight, relaxing when Aphrodite affectionately smashed her head under my chin, and I felt Killian's cool fingers slide between mine. "I appreciate...knowing."

"Of course." He bowed his head, and hesitated when his face was pointed down at the table. "And I know you didn't want any tips against the Night Court, but I think it's safe enough to point out to you that if you can topple Queen Nyte and Consort Ira, the Night Court won't give you any more problems."

"Are you sure about that?" I asked. "Wouldn't it just make them hate us more?"

"Quite the contrary." The Paragon shrugged moodily. "A Court swears absolute fealty to its monarchs. Without a ruler, it's nothing. And any new ruler unlucky enough to be dumped with the stinking pile that is the Night Court will be very anxious to distance themselves from Nyte and Ira's legacy."

"Perhaps," Killian said.

"More like for certain." The Paragon sighed and switched his gaze to staring at the ceiling. "Most of the time I hate my job. But it's times like this that I hate my people, too. They can be so *ugly*."

A painful silence stretched through the study. Surprisingly, it was Killian who broke it.

"What are *you* doing with a love tea, anyway?" He frowned at the Paragon. "I can't imagine anyone wanted to date you with this crusty appearance."

"I beg your pardon!" The Paragon puffed up his chest. "I'll have you know I am quite popular! Or—that is to say—I was very popular in my youth!" He laughed sheepishly.

"When was that?" Killian asked. "The American Civil War?"

"As if you have room to talk Sir 'I-hail-from-Britannia-and-probably-shook-hands-with-King-Arthur-and-am-now-robbing-the-cradle'!"

"I hope that cat of yours *bites* you."

"Dream on!"

I listened to the two bicker, perfectly aware it was a performance just to distract me. And as Aphrodite continued to purr, I did actually feel a little better.

My parents were dead. The how or why wasn't going to change that.

But if the Paragon was right about all of this, I was going to do everything in my power to protect Magiford *and* the Midwest, and to make sure nothing like this happened to another wizard again.

CHAPTER SEVENTEEN

Hazel

Two weeks later, during a Drake Family dinner, I was so tired I could barely put a forkful of mashed potatoes into my mouth.

I'd had a grueling practice with Killian—and I wasn't doing any better against him since I still hadn't come up with a method to subvert all his experience and knowledge—and then pulled a second practice with the ten Medeis wizards who had come with me and fifteen Drake vampires.

Both Killian and the Paragon seemed to take it for granted that we were going to have some kind of fight with the fae—a war at worst, a certamen at best. If that was true, I wanted my people familiar with vampires so there wouldn't be any mistakes in the middle of the fight.

It had actually turned out pretty fun, and I got to practice shielding Celestina and Josh while they ran amok.

The downside was I was so tired, walking out to the car was going to be a challenge. (And I had a feeling I was going to be hurting tomorrow.)

"Are you okay, Miss Hazel?" Gavino knelt next to me in concern—he had come with our group to consult a fellow vampire on a few different weight lifting routines for some of my younger wizards.

"Yeah, just tired." I tried to swallow a yawn, but it erupted, making my jaw crack.

Julianne watched me with concern from across the table. "I'd be tempted to feed you coffee, but aren't you back on a human sleeping schedule? I imagine you'll want to go to bed when you get home."

"Partaking in caffeine at this hour will open the mysteries of the universe and allow you to see things as they are," Josh said.

Momoko studied him, then bluntly said, "*What?*"

"I mean to imply if she drinks a caffeinated beverage at this hour, it will likely make her loopy," Josh said.

"Ah." Momoko nodded. "Truth."

"I don't need it," I said. "As long as I don't have to drive home we'll be fine."

Josh whipped out his smartphone. "I'll summon one of our drivers."

"Don't you dare," I warned him. "The last Drake you had take me home insisted on coming inside for a safety inspection, and then Mrs. Clark decided to feed him a blood pack and this disgusting blood pudding she's been working on making for you all. It took me three hours to kick him out!"

"Celestina!" Great Aunt Marraine called down the huge dining table to the First Knight who was almost on the opposite end. "I wanted to ask you if you have been overwhelmed and could use assistance in scaling up the party now that Killian has invited more supernaturals."

Celestina smiled and flipped the braid of her dark brown hair over her shoulder. "I have been prepared for such an occasion, so I mostly have the matter well in hand. I would like to consult you or Hazel for a few of the wizard House invitations, however."

"Of course!" Great Aunt Marraine raised her glass of wine with a happy gurgle. "I'd be delighted to help!"

"Gavino, can you review my form on the new weightlifting exercises you gave me earlier this week?" Felix asked. "I'm experiencing a bit of back strain, which has me thinking I'm doing something incorrectly."

"Of course!" The big vampire stood and moved down a few chairs to slide into a new seat. "I should take you down to the gym here—we have a few machines House Medeis doesn't have…"

Friendly chatter roamed up and down the dining table. I was pleased to see my people were sitting near each other, but all of them were conversing with a vampire or two.

When I first started coming here for my training they'd stay in the kitchens and insist we go immediately. And now they're willing to eat with them. I don't know if it's because Gavino has been hanging around, or they've just been here so much it's comfortable, but it's a good thing.

I glanced at the vampire seated on my left—the only one at the dinner table not involved in a conversation. "How's it hanging Rupert?"

The red-haired vampire gave me a withering glare. "What do you want?"

I slapped my hand over my heart. "So defensive! Anyone hearing you might not think we're friends!"

Rupert sipped his wine glass of blood. "If you're talking to me for appearances, Medeis, I assure you it isn't necessary."

I cleared my throat. "Actually, I wanted to thank you."

He tipped his head back slightly and studied me with puckered lips. "What for?"

"For the conversation we had after I Ascended," I evasively said. (I was pretty sure Celestina genuinely wanted to know who the leak was and give them a good 'scolding.' I wasn't going to put Rupert through that just because he was the most honest Drake in the Family.)

"You were pretty thankless at the time," Rupert sneered.

"Yes, I am aware of that. But knowing did help." I pushed my fork across my plate. "I know what a sacrifice it was. And what could have happened if you were found out." I glanced over at the vampire. "I mean it, Rupert. Thank you."

Rupert studied me for a few long moments, then slightly bowed his head. "Of course, Miss Hazel."

Normally the title made me grit my teeth—all the vampires had taken to calling me Miss Hazel once I beat them in a practice match. It was a sign of honor or something. But Rupert using the title was more of an...admittance.

Previously we'd always been on rocky ground because Rupert didn't much like humans in general, and seemed to have a special hatred for wizards. I don't know if it was Killian's influence, or if he had just mellowed over prolonged exposure, but I was glad he was less prickly these days.

"I hope having a clutch of wizards in Drake Hall hasn't been too offensive to your nose?" I winked as I slathered butter on my twice baked potato.

"One or ten of you hardly makes a difference," Rupert scoffed. "And at least your underlings have the good sense to not *bleed* everywhere and stink the place up."

I laughed. "Just wait until Killian makes you visit House Medeis during one of our practices. We get pretty banged up sometimes."

"Perhaps you ought to think of retaining a fae potion brewer on your payroll," Rupert grunted.

I half smiled as I watched the vampire take a measured sip from his glass. "You're a good egg, Rupert."

Rupert rolled his eyes. "I'm a vampire, not a dragon shifter."

"I know, but—"

Rupert tensed and abruptly twisted around in his seat so fast he almost snapped the back off.

Most of the vampires scrambled to stand, but all of them dropped their friendly conversations and stared at the door.

"Your Eminence," they murmured.

I had to peer around the back of my chair—it was too high for me to see over it—and saw Killian at the door, studying the pile of weapons Josh routinely left there whenever sitting down for dinner.

"What do you need, Your Eminence?" Celestina asked.

"Nothing." Killian's eyes were their usual shade of dark obsidian, but his mask of cold arrogance seemed a little cracked as he looked up and down the massive table. "I...nothing."

The room was suffocatingly awkward in its silence. I cleared my throat and leaned farther over the side so I was more visible. "Hey, Killian! Do you want to come sit with us?"

Killian hesitated, which was enough for Rupert.

The red-haired vampire swan dove out of his chair, scrambling to get free. He tugged on the lapels of his suit coat, then bowed. "If it would please Your Eminence." He motioned to the chair.

Killian remained rooted to the spot, an uncertain expression flitting through his face.

"Come on." I patted Rupert's chair in an invitation. "Sit."

Killian rocked into motion, slowly approaching me.

Rupert snatched up his glass of blood and fled. It had been the only thing he was eating, so Killian's spot was bare but clean. Unfortunately, the kitchen staff had already left, so no one had a plate to give him—but I didn't think he really wanted to eat human food anyway.

April offered her empty wine glass to Manjeet, who filled it with blood from a pitcher and lunged to put it in front of Killian.

Killian nodded in thanks and tapped the stem of the wine glass, but otherwise didn't touch it.

I smiled and looked around for some help to kick off all the conversation, but my dinner mates were failing me.

Most of the vampires were watching Killian, their eyes glazed over with hero worship. Only those farther up in rank—like Josh and Celestina—looked worried.

Celestina's tawny forehead was lined with wrinkles, and Josh—sitting two seats down from me—was writing something on a tiny notepad.

"Josh," I whispered. "What are you doing?"

"Writing my epitaph," Josh whispered back. "Because the end of the world has arrived. Time will soon collapse and all will sink into the ocean. The sign has appeared."

My head sagged on my neck at my hopeless and foolish desire for help.

"If the end of the world has come," June started, "what point is there in having an epitaph? No one will be around to read it."

Josh paused in the middle of writing a word. "This is true…"

Murmured conversations kicked up, softening the tense atmosphere.

I turned back to Killian and offered him a grin. "Hey."

He was glancing around the room, but when I spoke he shifted his attention to me. "Hello."

It seems like asking him why he's here would scare him off. I think he'll be most comfortable if I act like he eats with us all the time instead of making a big deal over it.

"Do you want some of my twice baked potato?" I asked.

Killian doubtfully eyed my plate of food.

I took a forkful and hummed in pleasure. "I don't mind sharing, but I won't be sad if you don't want any." I waved my fork at him. "Your kitchen staff are amazing. A-maz-ing!"

"I recall you singing their praises previously." He relaxed slightly, leaning back into the chair.

"Hey, you have no idea what a sacrifice it is to offer you my food." I wriggled my eyebrows at him and took another forkful. "This twice baked potato is worth a fight to the death."

A quirk of a smile tugged at the corners of Killian's lips. "Obviously I mean a lot to you."

"Yes," I nodded without thinking. "Wait, no! I take it back!"

Killian laughed and stared pointedly at my fork.

I made a loud, long suffering sigh and took a forkful of my precious food, then presented it to Killian.

He leaned forward to accommodate me, eating directly off my fork.

Down the dining table, one of the Drake vampires I had only seen a few times gaped at us. "What? Did he just—" He wheezed when Tasha, another Drake, smacked him upside the head.

A few other vampires bulged their eyes at us, and there were more than a couple dropped jaws.

Besides Celestina, Josh, and Gavino—who had all been present at the Summer's End Ball, where I had fed Killian a forkful of my dessert—the House Medeis wizards were the most nonchalant. They just shrugged and went back to their conversations.

(Don't get too impressed, they didn't know how rare it was for Killian to eat human food, or that it took a near miracle to get him to share plates or anything like that.)

Killian sipped at his glass of blood while I cut into my balsamic glazed steak tips—one of the many reasons why my wizards now fought over who got to come with me to Drake Hall.

"Any news about the Night Court?" I asked. "It's been a long time since they attacked you. I would have thought they'd have to have taken some kind of action by now."

Killian pointedly stared at my plate, so I moved my water glass and shifted the plate between us. "My sources tell me they *had* come to a decision, but apparently it upset the fae community when I followed the Paragon's advice and sent invitations to the Courts for the party. The Night Court wasn't invited, obviously, but I was told the Day King nearly had a brawl with Consort Ira this morning. I believe we have effectively backed them into a corner."

I offered him my fork. He took it and picked at my steak tips.

"You *aren't* going to attack the Night Court, right?" I asked.

Killian finished his bite and handed me my fork. "There is no reason to. Politically speaking, I have the upper hand. And if the Paragon is right and I can level this experience to use as a way to foster even just a slightly friendlier relationship with other supernatural races beyond vampires, it might be one of the best things that happened to my career."

"I could see that." I returned to my twice baked potato. "But I prefer to interpret it as friendship will only help us supernaturals."

"You would." Killian tilted his head. "Are you just going to ignore it?"

I squinted at him. "Ignore what?"

"Your salad." Killian pointed to the kale salad I'd been industriously avoiding.

"Yes," I said.

"You should at least try it."

"It's *kale salad*. Do you have any idea how awful that stuff tastes?"

"The kitchen staff prepared it for you."

"I don't like kale."

"You need to eat a complete diet given the exercises you put your body through."

I set my fork down. "Are you legit telling me to eat my vegetables?"

Killian smirked. "Perhaps."

"Fine. Then you try it first!" I set the salad bowl in front of Killian with a smirk.

"I don't get nutrients from regular food." Killian tapped his wine glass, making the thick blood ripple.

"Doesn't matter," I said. "If you want me to try this stuff, you at least have to suffer through a mouthful, too!"

Killian smirked, but ate a leaf. He kept his expression aloof, even though pretty much everyone was gaping at him now. (I guess a vampire eating kale was enough to shock my wizards, too.)

"You are right." He set the kale salad in front of me. "That *is* awful."

"At least your staff made a really good dressing for it." I sadly began consuming the hateful salad.

"Killian." Great Aunt Marraine—of course she was the only one daring enough to call him Killian to his face besides me—waved at him. "I must say I am delighted you decided to join us this evening!"

Killian smiled politely. "You are being too kind. I hope my presence isn't ruining the fun you were all having."

"Nonsense!" Great Aunt Marraine said. "You are such a dear boy. Of course we would be glad to see you!"

Rupert—who had roamed farther down the table since he'd been voluntarily displaced—choked on his glass of blood.

Killian laughed—not the smooth, charming one he'd started using on me, but the one he trotted out whenever I had a particularly good insult for Rupert or did something he thought was hilarious. "Thank you, Marraine," he grinned.

Great Aunt Marraine chuckled. "As long as you show your handsome young face more. I'm sure your people miss you!"

Celestina's unflappable smile cracked just a little, and I thought Gavino's eyes might pop out of his head.

"And you must promise to come have dinner with us at House Medeis sometime," Great Aunt Marraine continued. "I make a mean pot roast!"

Killian slightly bowed his head. "I shall do that."

Satisfied, Great Aunt Marraine turned her attention back to her previous conversation with a rather shell-shocked vampire.

"You know," I finished my last bit of kale and then eagerly finished off my potato, "she's going to hold you to that. Now every time she sees you she'll ask when you're coming for dinner."

To make plate sharing easier, Killian had slowly been edging closer. It wasn't until now, however, that I realized how close he was when he slipped an arm behind me, resting it on my lower back. "Then let's pick a date."

It was so tempting to lean into him. Even though the temperatures were cooler, I was still *hot*, and just sitting near Killian was pleasant. But I made myself sit upright.

Not yet. We promised, I reminded myself.

I cleared my throat and forced a smile. "That's pretty cute. Most people would think you actually *like* Great Aunt Marraine if you're willing to come to dinner."

Killian twitched up an eyebrow. "Of course I like Marraine," he said. "She is amusing and is excellent at keeping you in line."

I actually set my fork down and studied him.

He rolled his shoulders back. "What?"

"I was just thinking...this summer I don't know that I would have believed anyone if they told me you would come to like wizards."

"I liked you." He swooped in to grab my fork, but he didn't really seem to be hungry because he just flipped it between his fingers.

"I hardly counted," I said. "Besides, I was just an amusing toy to you in the beginning. I never thought that would spread over to other wizards."

Killian shrugged. "I was wrong." He took a casual sip of blood, but I wasn't fooled.

"Thanks, Killian."

He raised an eyebrow. "For what?"

I reached out and squeezed his hand that he was using to play with the fork. "For trying."

His smile was warm, but it turned mischievous as he leaned in. "If I keep up trying, we'll have to see where we end up, won't we?" He smirked, then shifted his attention to Josh.

"Any news from the patrols?"

"No, Your Eminence. All is well."

"Adept, is everything okay?" Felix wriggled his eyebrows at me. "You're as red as a tomato."

"Shut up, Felix," I growled.

Momoko and Felix snickered, and I tuned in to my plate of food with a determined zeal.

I THOUGHT GETTING ready for the Summer's End Ball had been an ordeal. Boy, was I stupid.

Now that Celestina had a House of wizards to tap, getting ready had become a group thing.

About half of House Medeis was going to attend Killian's party, and *all* the women who were coming were in cahoots with Celestina, so of course it was an all-day thing that involved manicures, pedicures, and getting our hair styled.

It was fun, but when they made me skip dinner, insisting there would be refreshments served at the party, I started getting a bit hangry and the glitter wore off. I held it together, though.

Celestina was glowing with joy as Momoko helped her with her hair, and the cute little high-school gal that had recently joined House Medeis was laughing with Julianne as the older vampire helped her with her makeup.

It was really special to see the two groups effortlessly mingling.

A prickle of guilt stabbed at me, too. I'd perhaps been a little too hard on Celestina, Josh, and even Killian. They were obviously making a big effort to welcome us wizards.

Maybe trust doesn't mean they have to tell me everything, but it's more about working with me instead of trying to push and manipulate me—even if it's for a hidden good.

I shook myself a little—I didn't have time to go all philosophic when guests were due to arrive any minute. "I'm heading down," I announced to the room.

Celestina checked her cellphone. "I'll be right behind you—I need to be there to direct the valets."

"Don't rush, we've got some time!" I smiled then slipped out of the massive bathroom and meandered through the bedroom that was littered with dress bags, the rumpled clothes we had arrived in, and backpacks stuffed with everything we'd need to spend the night. (Killian was getting his first Rent-a-Hazel night, tonight. Mostly because I knew the party would last until dawn, making it easier to collapse in my old Drake Hall bedroom instead of trying to get home while exhausted.)

Killian had given us ladies full run of the room. Given the larger patio, and the humongous bathroom that was well beyond what the rest of the vampire bed/bathrooms looked like, I was willing to bet this room was meant for visiting vampire Elders, or possibly if Killian ever took a...wife?

I'd say it was for his *one*, but it seemed Killian didn't think that was a real thing. There were still lots of vampires who got married and lived happy lives even if their spouse wasn't *the one*. And given our discussion in the Paragon's study it seemed like Killian had romantic aspirations for us, but I was a human. A *wizard*, even.

And dating a wizard was sure to bring lots of trouble on Killian's political career. I wasn't certain he'd realized that yet, which was one of the reasons why I had asked that we wait to talk about our...whatever until after we resolved the issue with the Night Court.

I made my way down to the second floor and all the way to the double spiral staircase that would dump me on the first floor, just by the main entrance, where I promptly got cold feet.

Killian is throwing a party for society, and I'm attending as his official guest and date. What the heck am I doing?

I made myself take a few of Great Aunt Marraine's 'calming breaths.'

Inhale...exhale.

Inhale...ex—*this isn't helping.*

I walked in a tight circle like a nervous horse.

Why did I let him talk me into this? I didn't want to get involved in politics. I just want to protect what's important to my House...but that means protecting the Drakes.

I groaned and almost rubbed my eyes before I remembered my eye makeup.

There was an end table with a big, fancy gilded mirror set off to the side.

I hurried over to it, inspecting my painstakingly applied makeup for any smears.

The smoky eyeshadow and perfectly executed cat-eye eyeliner —compliments of, surprisingly, Great Aunt Marraine—were still pristine.

A quick once over confirmed I was still in one piece. Momoko had curled my hair for the occasion, only pulling a few pieces back from around my face and pinning the tendrils to the top of my head.

My dress style was a little more on the simplistic end. It was— as Julianne had informed me—a mermaid style, which meant it was fitted through the shoulders, torso, and hips, but loosened up into a slight flare starting at the knees and dropping to the floor. It had taken a lot of strenuous arguing between me and Celestina, but she'd gotten me a dress that only had cute straps—unlike the vampires who all wore full sleeves. (I knew better, I was going to roast with the number of people coming tonight.)

But the style of the dress was simple because the gown's fabric was jaw dropping. It was a pinkish-peach color, but the embroidery on the chest, waist, and mermaid skirt was beautiful, golden sun patterns. And when I say the details were gold, I don't mean yellow, I mean they were *gold*. Like the precious metal, gold. It must have been enchanted, because the gold portions of the dress seemed to glow like a rising sun, and it really brought out the sun-streaked platinum of my blond hair.

Take the dress and match it with the diamond earrings and gold, diamond heart necklace Celestina had dressed me in, and I honestly felt like a Disney princess. (Which was way more fun than I was willing to admit.)

I didn't have my trusty book/rock stuffed clutch tonight, but that was because Celestina had showed me a small, unnoticeable slit in my dress designed to give me access to a thigh holster. She had wanted me to take a handgun, but I hadn't received enough gun training from Josh to make me comfortable wearing one on my thigh, so a dagger it was!

"You look beautiful." I jumped a little and turned around, but I had recognized the voice, so I was already smiling by the time I saw Killian.

CHAPTER EIGHTEEN

Hazel

"Thanks," I said. "And thanks for buying the dress. Again."

Killian smirked playfully. "Of course. I can't have any supernaturals calling me a cheapskate date." He was fiddling with his cufflinks—as all handsome men seem prone to do once stuffed in a tux.

I determinedly bustled up to him and fixed them for him so I wouldn't have to witness his moody-model pose anymore. "Tonight we have to smile and play nice."

"I know," Killian said.

"I *know* you know. I'm reminding myself," I said.

"If you just focus on how handsome I am you'll be so distracted tonight you won't think of anything else," Killian offered.

I patted him on the chest. "I could torch your tuxedo coat." My wizard mark burned as I wove flickering blue flames through my fingers.

Killian's smirk deepened. "You want to see me without a shirt? Oh my, Hazel, you'll turn this moment into a scandalous liaison."

I rolled my eyes. "When I learned about vampires, nobody ever bothered to tell me how *vain* you all are."

"Would you rather I use the term salacious?"

"I'd rather you be humbled," I stressed.

"Where would the fun be in that?" Killian prowled closer, sliding into my personal space. "Then I couldn't make you blush—which, along with the rising sun and the peace of night, makes my life complete." The slant of his eyebrows fought for a moment, revealing that he was barely keeping from laughing at the horrible line.

I burst out into super unattractive, snorting, laughter. "You got that from Rupert's reports on all those romcom movies, didn't you?"

"I might have, yes."

I wrinkled my nose as I tried to stop laughing—I couldn't cry from laughing, or I'd smear my makeup! "If you really wanted to get me to swoon you could just stand there and smolder."

"Are you implying you love me for my looks and not my 'great personality'?" Killian's voice was dead serious, but his onyx eyes had the faintest red glow to them, so I knew he was having fun. "And they say it's men who value outward appearances!"

I almost started snorting all over again, but the doorbell rang, and I froze.

Drake Hall couldn't have a normal, cheerful doorbell—certainly *not*. It had to have this deep, chiming tone that sounded like a church bell that you could hear from nearly *any room* in the mansion.

"It sounds like the first guests are here." I almost wiped my sweaty palms on my dress, but stopped myself at the last minute. "Are you ready to go greet them?"

"No." Killian raised both of his eyebrows at me. "That's what I have a First Knight for!"

"You can't possibly make Celestina receive all the guests at *your* party," I said.

"I'm the Eminence," he said. "Who is going to tell me I can't? Besides I'm very busy."

"Doing *what?*"

"Admiring you."

I snapped my fingers and pointed at him. "There you go, much better."

His grin turned a touch debonair. "Does that mean your butt will finally be available for viewing now?"

I sighed deeply. "*I'm* going down to greet your guests."

"Fine." Killian shrugged. "Just make sure you position yourself right there." He pointed to a red dragon painted across the marble tile of the front foyer. The dragon just so happened to be placed so my back would face him if he stayed up here gawking.

The first guests entered through the door, Celestina gliding forward to meet them.

I recognized Elite Bellus and his wife, the Adept of House Bellus.

"Okay," I agreed.

Killian blinked in surprise. "You're finally giving up?"

"Not at all," I assured him. "Because you'll be there with me."

Killian raised an eyebrow. "And how do you propose to accomplish that?"

"Like this." I leaned over the stair banister and shouted, "Elite Bellus, Adept Bellus, we're so glad you could make it!"

The wizard couple looked up to the second floor where we stood.

"Well played," Killian growled.

I smugly smiled. "Thank you!"

"Adept Medeis, how good it is to see you again!" Elite Bellus called back to me.

I patted Killian's forearm. "Come on. Let's get going."

"If you insist." He grabbed my hot, sweaty hand, his fingers instantly cooling mine when they intertwined.

Together, we went down to the main floor with big smiles, ready to greet guests and enter the political ring.

THE PARTY PROCEEDED SMOOTHLY—BETTER than what I had imagined anyway.

Since the guest list had suddenly expanded, a caterer was called in to help relieve the kitchen staff, and the food was *phenomenal*—particularly since they had a werewolf, fae, and vampire on staff, assuring the food tasted as exquisite as it looked and smelled.

Celestina had hired a stringed quartet to play in the Drake Hall ballroom. One of the parlors had been converted into a game room—and no, I don't mean for gambling or anything. When I sashayed through there earlier in the night I saw a few fae playing checkers, some vampires engaged in a rousing round of old maid, and a huddle of werewolves and wizards playing Clue.

The gardens were open—Celestina had ordered a number of propane patio stand heaters so the fae and werewolves could stand outside and admire the gardens and green spaces in comfort. I saw a few wizards escape out there as well, probably driven out by the heat.

I also had the great pleasure of being near a group of werewolves when they heard a few of the Drake dogs bark happily, and it was hysterical.

I was still snickering to myself as I picked my way around the outside edge of the mansion, waving to the patrolling Drake vampires.

Yeah, I was one of the wizards who had been driven out to the gardens by the high temperatures inside. Rather than immediately venture back in, I was looping around, intending to re-enter at the front doors and give myself a chance to cool off in the crisp, bordering on freezing, night air.

Fall and winter were intermingling now, so there was frost on the frozen ground, but it felt *amazing*.

Just as I reached the well illuminated entrance, I saw someone familiar waiting on the sidewalk that bordered the driveway.

"Leila?" I called.

Leila—her black hair plaited into a gorgeous braid and wearing a purply-blue that brought out the violet hue of her eyes—slowly turned around and smiled. "Hey, Hazel! Great party—especially the food!" Her happy expression and her supernatural beauty—which looked even more fae-like in the darkness of night—were an odd juxtaposition. You usually didn't see fae so...*open*. Though she looked so beautiful it probably was a good thing. If all the fae walked around like this it would be a lot harder to be wary of them.

I carefully navigated the stairs so I could join her on the sidewalk. "Leila—you look gorgeous! And yeah, the caterer really went all out. Did you try any of the raspberry mousse?"

Leila shook her head. "No, I stuffed myself on an affogato—I'm a sucker for coffee, and I *love* ice cream."

I clapped my hands in glee. "Then you need to try the tiramisu! It's to *die* for."

"I wish I could! Unfortunately, I'm just waiting for one of the boys to bring my truck around." Leila made a face. "It's time for me to go home."

"I hope you had a nice time—no one bothered you, did they?" My shoulders started to rise—I probably looked like an angry kitten arching its back, though. (I felt extra short next to her willowy frame.)

Leila laughed. "Not at all. Everyone was very welcoming—I had a great time talking with Felix and your Great Aunt Marraine. I even snuck out to see the dogs."

"Was that why they were barking? I was near some werewolves when they started up, it was the best thing ever! I don't think I've ever seen a werewolf look so sour." I tilted my head. "But are you *certain* you don't want to come back in for some more food? I'm serious, the tiramisu is that good."

Leila's smile faded a little. "Thanks, but I'm good. Look...I wanted to talk to you a little about the Night Court. I know I mentioned when you dropped by that I have some fae blood in me. Fae don't attack me, but I have no intention of ever pledging myself to a Court, and I can't say I've ever really enjoyed any interaction I've had with their kind."

Hmm... "Their kind," was it? That was pretty telling considering she was gorgeous enough to be half fae. Apparently it was an unwanted association.

"I'm so sorry," I said. "I hope they behaved themselves tonight?"

"Oh, it's fine!" Leila's smile was back. "I'm way too small a fish for any of the fae who are here tonight. Just being near them is a little...uncomfortable?"

"I think I know what you mean. When I first came to Drake Hall my nerves were shot in about two weeks after being around vampires all the time when I feared them so much." I slightly narrowed my eyes as I studied Leila.

Fae were known for meddling, and depending what Court her fae blood came from, I could see someone feeling it was their duty to bring her into her heritage, whether she wanted it or not.

No wonder she tried to avoid them.

I had missed it when she drove me to Magiford, but now that I got the chance to really study her, I could see in her eyes and the set of her eyebrows and mouth the same quiet desperation I'd nearly drowned in when I first became Adept.

I better change the topic. There's no sense making her hash out her personal problems on the front stoop. I'll invite her over sometime to see House Medeis, or she can come visit the dogs again.

I glanced back at Drake Hall, desperate for a new conversation topic. "I'm glad you came, though! I wish I had seen you earlier. We could have done a dessert tour together."

I grinned, and Leila returned my smile, but it was only for a moment.

"I actually wanted to talk to you, and I think now is as good a time as any." She glanced up at Drake Hall and down the driveway, but there was still no sign of the valet with her truck.

"It seems like it's pretty inevitable that the Drake Family, House Medeis, and the Night Court are going to clash." Her words were almost musical as she rushed to speak. "I'm assuming it's going to be in a certamen duel, because I don't think the Night Court could last against the negative publicity of a war. Either way, I imagine you're planning to focus on specifically taking down Queen Nyte and Consort Ira?"

"We've been told if the leaders of a Court topple, the Court itself won't keep fighting," I carefully said.

"It's true," Leila said. "Fae swear an oath to their king or queen. But the fight will be harder than it sounds because Queen Nyte and Consort Ira will order their people to protect them."

I sighed. "I was afraid of that. Of course I'd like to avoid conflict, but if it's inevitable, I want to have the least number of casualties possible—for *both* sides."

Leila relaxed minutely. "I hoped that would be a concern for you. Then as someone who knows the way fae think, I suggest you sucker punch them."

"What do you mean?" I asked.

"Fae are diabolical. Vampires at least follow codes of conduct, but fae are like quicksilver, always adjusting for their own selfish good. They are ruthless and awful, and the only way you'll really be able to surprise them is by using something they think they know against them," Leila said. "You nailed the Night Court in the Curia Cloisters because they took it for granted that no one would help the Drake Family. And it was effortless for you to get the fae who attacked you on my parents' property because they still didn't grasp how powerful House Medeis is. But Queen Nyte knows, now, what vampires and wizards together are capable of, so you can't count on that being your surprise play. You need to take something that they believe with every ounce of their being, and twist it on them."

"You are suggesting a surprise attack?"

"Not really." Leila twitched the end of her braid. "More like… in a sword fight. You need one surprise move that will give you the opening to finish your opponent."

I grinned widely. "Now that is a metaphor I understand!"

She laughed, then straightened when headlights trundled down the driveway. "I think that's finally my truck."

"Thanks for your advice, Leila," I said. "I'll keep it in mind."

Leila offered me another smile—this one more relaxed. "You're welcome. I'm just an observer—I don't know anything about Court life, and I'm not a strategist. But I've witnessed fae cruelty enough to know how they think. Good luck—with whatever happens."

I waved as Leila climbed into her truck and pulled away, watching until her tail lights disappeared into the trees that screened the snaking driveway.

She'd voiced some of the concerns I already had.

If it did come down to a war—or even just a certamen—I didn't want a bloody conflict where vampires, wizards, and fae were sacrificed. I was hoping we'd be able to come up with a strategy that hit Queen Nyte and Consort Ira and either captured them or, if it came down to it, eradicated them.

I'd been trying not to think too deeply about it—we didn't even know for sure if the Night Court would challenge us to a certamen or declare war. But Leila's warning served as another reminder that we were dealing with a different type of supernatural. Facing them would require a different kind of strategy from facing off with vampires.

I frowned thoughtfully as I turned and started up the stairs that led back into the mansion.

But how could we get that surprise factor...attack during the day, maybe?

"You are looking rather thoughtful, which frankly is a bit frightening."

I laughed as I looked up from the stairs. "We meet again, Elite Bellus! I hope you and Adept Bellus are enjoying yourselves?"

"Given that I left my wife cackling with Pre-Dominant Harka as they trashed some of the werewolves in a game of Pictionary, I'd say we are." He laughed as I joined him on the top stair, and together we slipped back into Drake Hall.

"I'm surprised by the number of attendees," I admitted. "We gave them pretty short notice, and Celestina said almost everyone accepted the invite."

I didn't know if it was because they were curious since Drake Hall had never held a party for supernaturals besides vampires, or because they didn't want to miss the possible politics, but that so many supernaturals had come was a pretty big deal.

"In general, it seems the party is a tremendous success," Elite Bellus said. "I'd say Killian has solidified his position as the wronged-party-who-is-unfailingly-innocent." He glanced down at me. "He wouldn't have been able to pull it off without you, you know."

"If you're implying I am Killian's accessory used to soften up his image I'm afraid I'll have to challenge you to a killer round of Pictionary," I warned him.

We strolled across the foyer, and Elite Bellus waved to a few wizards who offered him slight bows. "You have softened him up, but not in the way you're thinking," he said.

I furrowed my brow. "What do you mean by that?"

"He's slower to bring his brutal brand of justice down," Elite Bellus said. "A year ago, he'd react to any threat that showed even a *hint* of surfacing. If it were pre-Hazel Killian, this party wouldn't have happened, and he would have brutally attacked the Night Court and likely killed Queen Nyte and Consort Ira. There would have been a scuffle between vampires and fae, but he would have used the situation to his advantage politically."

We stopped next to a fountain Celestina had brought in for the occasion—she said something about needing it to "provide peaceful ambience." (It seemed like she was pretty concerned about everyone's stress levels at the party, because the string quartet had a very specific list of calming music they could play, and there were lavender candles burning *everywhere* in the mansion.)

"I don't know," I said. "He's still pretty cut-throat. He's only biding his time, you know."

"Most everyone figured as much," Elite Bellus grunted. "But it's not that he won't fight. It's...well...it's the new law he passed about the Unclaimed. Everyone thought he'd tighten his control over all the Unclaimed vampires after that one almost killed you at the start of summer. But instead he gave them a provision so they can band together and actually survive." He snapped his fingers. "It's mercy. You've brought at least a little mercy into his previously do-or-die thinking."

"Maybe that's true." I appeared to smooth the skirt of my dress, but really I was feeling for the reassuring line of my thigh holster. "He used to complain whenever I asked him to refrain from killing someone," I said. "But don't get me wrong. If someone comes after House Medeis or the Drake Family, I'll be right behind Killian when we get them."

"Yes, I've witnessed that firsthand." Elite Bellus smoothed his goatee. "Which brings up the real matter I wanted to discuss with you. Your future."

For a moment, I felt like a high school student who had been called to the guidance counselor's office. "I'm sorry...what?"

"I propose that in the next year, you should join my office."

"Elite Bellus..." I struggled for a moment, trying to figure out how to phrase the next part. "You *do* remember that I'm Adept of

House Medeis, right? I've got enough things I have to sort through, I really can't take on a job, too."

"I wasn't suggesting you work as a staff member!" Elite Bellus laughed, a jolly noise that reminded me a little of the way my dad used to laugh. "I'm asking you to be my protégée."

CHAPTER NINETEEN

Hazel

"Your protégée?" I parroted.

"Exactly." He smiled slyly. "I'm a long way off from retiring, but it's considered standard for the Elite to start training his or her protégée a decade before handing over the position. Given that you are rather young, no one will mind if your training lasts a few years extra, and I think you'll be useful and fun to have around."

My heart slammed in my chest. "Wait, are you seriously saying you want me to be the next Elite?"

"I am. The wizards will have to vote on it when I finally do retire, of course. But that's the merest formality. There's never been a protégée who wasn't approved in the Midwest. And I have a feeling your approval rating will be even heartier than normal," Elite Bellus said.

I didn't know what to think—or say! I had never imagined becoming the Elite. The job had always been way beyond my reach when my magic was sealed, and it was a much bigger deal than I had ever planned on being!

"Why would you think everyone would approve? If anything, I'd assume no one would *want* me as the Elite," I finally managed to say.

"Nonsense," he laughed again. "The staff overseeing the Wizard Council will probably cry with relief since it means you won't be able to meddle in local politics once you make Elite. But everyone else will be even happier since you've got the Eminence trained, which means wizards might stand a better chance at getting their voices heard."

"So you want me to be your protégée because of my connections," I said. "Not because of my skills or who I am."

"I said that's why other wizards would approve your appointment." Elite Bellus tapped his nose. "I didn't say it was why I wanted you as my protégée."

"Then why *do* you want me as your protégée?"

"Because we need change, and you've done it." He slid his hands into the pockets of his suitcoat and nodded. "In roughly half a year you've managed to form a deep friendship with the most lethal vampire Family in the region. You've turned your House around and have entirely changed the core basis of what your people believe in—*without* any backlash. If we want to save magic, we need to start working faster. You're a unique mixture of open-mindedness, action, and perseverance to do what needs to be done."

He hesitated, then added, "Though it would be a lie if I didn't admit I'm hoping you'll be able to muzzle Killian in the meetings. And don't think I haven't noticed how you've got the Paragon buddying up with you, too."

I nodded slowly as his words sank in.

I still didn't really know how to react. A part of me knew he was right. With everything I'd gone through since spring, *something* should have imploded on me. But neither the House nor my family had objected to the huge structural and philosophical changes we'd gone through. And no one had threatened me after

Killian and I took our alliance public. I didn't know how much of that was actual skill on my end, or sheer luck.

Besides, I wasn't an idiot. The position of Elite came with *a lot* of extra responsibilities. I wasn't sure I wanted to sign up for that.

I glanced at Elite Bellus, who offered me a smile.

I drew my shoulders back. "I'll think about it."

"Excellent!" He took my hand and pumped it in a firm handshake. "That's all I can ask for. Now…to find my wife." He turned to survey the crowd meandering through Drake Hall.

"You think she finished her Pictionary game with Pre-Dominant Harka?" I asked.

"Absolutely. It wouldn't take long for those two to trash those puppies." He raised his chin as he tried to peer above the crowd. (Or I assumed he was peering above the crowd. The only time I'd ever been high enough to experience that was when Gavino had me slung over his shoulder when we were breaking into a magic-guarded vault system owned by a dragon shifter.)

"If I see her, I will tell her you're looking for her."

"I'd appreciate that. I'm sure I'll see you later." He took a few steps away from me.

On an impulse, I called after him. "Elite Bellus, I have one last question."

He turned on his heels. "Yes?"

I hesitated, wondering how wise it was for me to ask this question. "Would it really be ethical for me to be considered for the position of Elite if I still had a strong alliance with the Drakes?"

"You mean the werewolves and fae might be concerned that you and the Eminence would team up on them?" Elite Bellus frowned and scratched his neck. "I can see how on paper that might appear to be a problem, but anyone who has seen you or heard of your behavior will know better. You're a rock, Adept. You won't do anything if you don't believe it is right, and that belief doesn't extend only to wizards, but beyond. Or you wouldn't have stepped in to save the Eminence even when the two of you were still feuding. You're...virtuous."

The moniker actually made me smile as it reminded me of a certain vampire. "I see. Thank you."

Elite Bellus waved. "Of course! Please do think about it. And once all of this settles, you can bet I will expect an answer. Good evening, Adept." He disappeared into the flow of the crowd, leaving me standing alone by the fountain.

I rolled my neck, trying to relieve some of the strain I was getting from all the tension—maybe Celestina's worry about stress wasn't too off target?—when I felt a familiar presence behind me.

"It seems unreasonable that I have to scent you out like a blasted werewolf in my own home." Killian tugged on my hand, maneuvering so when I turned around to face him I stepped into his arms.

"Hi, Killian. What are you doing?"

Killian's lips hovered just above my neck. "I am mentally weighing up if I can get away with kissing your neck or if you'll fish out that dagger I know Celestina got you."

I squeaked when his lips brushed my neck.

"No blade? I'll take that as a good sign," he chuckled into my ear.

"Did you need something?"

"Mm, yes. You."

"*Killian.*"

"I meant that sincerely." He leaned back just enough to give me some breathing room, but kept his arms slung around my waist. "The Paragon showed up. We need to go greet him, or we'll have a wretchedly difficult time getting him to leave because he'll be crying about what poor friends we are."

"We *would* be poor friends if we didn't greet him. Where is he?"

"Of course you'd side with him. You're excessively kind-hearted." Killian indolently shrugged. "And I believe he's near the door to the gardens."

I didn't think much about it when Killian let me go and held my hand as we made our way through the mansion, a pathway magically opening up in front of us.

But when the Paragon saw us and his expression lit up, it wasn't until he spoke that I thought about Killian's relaxed grasp.

"What's *this*?" The Paragon dragged out his words and wriggled his eyebrows. "Adept Medeis, are you finally accepting your role as future lady of the Drake Family and official monster tamer?"

I squinted at the Paragon. "Did someone spike your drink?"

He rolled his eyes and fanned his face with his free hand. "As annoyingly oblivious as ever. You do realize that you can't waltz around with *Killian Drake* holding you like you are a treasure and think people won't read into it, don't you?"

"We're not talking about this until…other matters are resolved," I said.

"That's what *you* think!" The Paragon laughed. "He's just going to use this time to campaign his way into your life so by the time you do have to define it, it will be too late! It's one of the oldest tricks in the book, and I am mildly disappointed you fell for it."

I forced a smile. "I know precisely what he's doing, Paragon."

"Oohhh, I see. So this is a trap so he will commence his campaign allowing you to snag him in return? Well done—now you're thinking like a fae." He nodded in approval.

I looked up at Killian. "Did you follow any of that?"

He shrugged. "I generally don't bother to follow what the Paragon has to say given that he is an idiot. This time, however, I gathered he thinks we're a couple. Because that suits me, I will approve."

I groaned and stared up at the ceiling. "Why is the supernatural high society obsessed with love and who is dating whom?

There are much higher stakes than whether or not we're dating, and frankly I find it *disturbing* that it's everyone's main concern."

I might have let a little more of my irritation leak into my voice than I meant, because the Paragon patted my arm in sympathy. "There, there, my dear," he said. "I dare say people only care because you're a wizard and he's a vampire. We haven't had a cross-race romance in *ages* to coo over. You're a modern Romeo and Juliet…if Romeo had political finesse and fangs and Juliet was capable of snapping someone's head off."

"I'm not that strong. I think I'd have to fry them with magic," I said. "But that's not the point."

"Then what *is* the point?" the Paragon asked.

I helplessly looked up at Killian, hoping he would help me out of the hole I'd dug myself.

He let go of my hand only long enough to tuck an arm around my shoulders, instantly lowering my body temperature by a blessed degree or two. "We came over here to welcome you to the party, and all you've done is rile Hazel up. That's a new low for you, isn't it?"

"Oh please." The Paragon snorted. "I'm not even trying."

"I was more referring to being a poor friend than your general existence as an annoying gnat of a person," Killian said.

"Oh…oh." The Paragon shot me a wounded look, which was kind of a weird expression given his ancient appearance. "In that case, I must tell you how pleasant I find this party! Drake Hall is so charming—certainly much better than when I last saw it and your underlings were so very pesky."

"You mean the last time when you barged in without permission?" Killian stated in a dead tone.

"Paragon, how is Aphrodite?" I asked, desperate for a change of subjects.

"Her beauty continues to shine on!" The Paragon beamed. "I took her portrait just today! Do you wish to see?"

"No, we do not," Killian firmly said.

The Paragon ignored him and rummaged through his pockets, pulling out his smartphone to show me a picture of the cat.

She was sitting on her pet bed, wearing a purple onesie with a hood and floppy rabbit ears.

Can I just say it? That cat puts up with *a lot*.

"Paragon, I hope you will allow me to intrude upon your conversation so I may thank our gracious host." A fae approached us, handsome and bright.

He had the smooth beauty and willowy build of the fae, but the fine lines around his eyes made him look somewhere in his early forties. His hair was the burning gold of the sun, and his robes were made of gold and red silk, with a massive golden belt and a small gold crown that appeared to legit be on fire.

This had to be King Solis of the fae—there was no mistaking the king of the Day Court. (It might have helped that he had three nobles trailing behind him, all of them wearing the rising sun crest of the Day Court.)

Killian glanced at the fae as he joined our circle. "I hope you have enjoyed yourself thus far, King Solis?"

"Indeed, I have." King Solis's smile seemed almost mechanical, and I didn't miss the way he warily flicked his eyes around the room. "Your Family has been receptive, and the aesthetic is pleasing."

Fae couldn't lie, so they were really good at using flowery words that mean nothing. Talking to a vampire was upsetting because you knew they could kill you and you couldn't stop them. Speaking with a fae wasn't much better, because if you weren't careful they could get you to legally agree to letting them slit your throat.

The Paragon was the only fae I'd ever met who was straightforward and blunt. *I wonder if that was why he took on the appearance of an ancient man. He has the mannerisms of someone much younger and I suspect he probably is younger than he appears, but his front lets him avoid the typical fae mean-streak because most people brush his honesty off as old age.*

"I am honored you came," Killian purred. "We would have missed the delicate charm of fae among the cleverness of wizards and the loyalty of werewolves."

"Yes. It seems supernaturals are quite comfortable here." King Solis watched Pre-Dominant Harka laugh with another Alpha, and a fine line creased his forehead. It seemed the Paragon's suggestion was right on—the fae didn't like the idea of the other supernaturals getting comfortable with the Drakes.

King Solis cleared his throat, and his expression returned to his forced smile. "It speaks well for our society to see the esteemed Paragon chatting with the Eminence and..." The fae king hesitated when he looked at me.

I bowed a little. "Adept Medeis—of House Medeis."

King Solis tilted his head back. "House Medeis is the Drake Family's wizard ally, is it not?"

Ohhhh, someone was fishing for information. *Let's see if I can help put the fear of God in them...*

I laughed and leaned playfully into Killian's side. "An ally? That's such a formal word. I suppose I fall in that category though. We had to bother with a formal alliance to make everything clean, of course, but I think it's safe to say House Medeis and the Drake Family are much more than mere allies."

Killian must have sensed what I was driving at, because he played along. An arrogant chuckle escaped from his lips, and he moved his arm so his hand was visible on the top of my shoulder, where he rubbed my skin with his thumb. "That reminds me...I neglected to ask, did Celestina prepare enough rooms for your people tonight?" He talked in a quiet tone that was more of a whisper, but based on King Solis's expression, he obviously heard what Killian had said.

"We're fine," I whispered back to Killian. "Momoko is

doubling up with me in my bedroom, but Celestina had plenty of guest rooms for everyone else."

King Solis's smile didn't budge, but a second fine line appeared on his forehead. "It seems you share a friendship. How commendable."

The Paragon snorted and looked to the side like a jaded teenager. "What?" he said when King Solis stared at him. "Are you really that innocent that you think they're just friends? Hah!"

King Solis's smile sputtered out, and he glanced behind him at one of his courtiers.

The tallest of the three whipped out a cellphone and started typing furiously on it.

It seemed our message was received.

I was a little surprised the Paragon joined in on our act—it was a pretty big indicator of just how concerned he was about those shadowy backers he told us about.

"I see." The king's smile was back, and his voice crackled with the warmth of a bonfire. "What a good omen for the vampires and wizards. But it seems I've taken up enough of your time. If you'll excuse me."

The Paragon was focused on scratching his drooping mustache. "Yeah, bye."

Killian smiled, flashing his pronounced fangs. "Please alert me if there is anything in the party not to your liking. I hope you enjoy the remainder of your time here."

Rather than answer and bind himself to Killian's promise, King Solis smiled and slightly inclined his head, then drifted off.

When he was about halfway across the room he kicked his pace up a few notches and booked it over to the fae queen of the Winter Court—who was easy to pick out because she was dressed entirely in white with shades of light blue and gray.

The two tipped their heads together as they spoke, and soon courtiers from the Winter Court were typing away furiously on their phones.

I had to purse my lips slightly so my smile wasn't gleeful. "I'd say that's a checkmate?"

"Checkmate, bingo, and goal," the Paragon cackled.

"Well done, Hazel," Killian whispered into my ear.

I rolled my shoulders, trying to push him into giving me space. "Now we just wait and see if the Night Court takes the bait, right? Do you think we'll find out by the end of the week?"

"Good heavens, no," the Paragon snorted. "You'll find out by the end of the *night*!"

CHAPTER TWENTY

Hazel

I was ready to tap out around 3:30 am, but the night was still young for the fae, werewolves, and vampires.

Most of the wizard guests were in the process of leaving, and about half of my family had retired. (Great Aunt Marraine, of course, was still going strong.)

I was forcing myself to stay awake, because I didn't know when I'd be needed as a prop, and if the Paragon was right and the Night Court made their move tonight I was going to be awake for it!

I retreated to the kitchens for a bit of peace and quiet and—most importantly—coffee.

The kitchens were quiet—most of the food had been served. The catering staff were only offering desserts and tea, which they prepared in a parlor room closer to the ballroom for convenience, so it was pretty abandoned.

The only noise was the gurgle of the coffee machine. I held a white mug with great zeal as I patiently waited.

Hopefully this will perk me up a bit.

"If you wanted an iced coffee to cool you down, I'm sure one of the staff members could make one."

I muffled a yawn. "Hey, Killian. And nah, this is fine. I just need to get some caffeine in my bloodstream if I want to make it."

I felt him stand behind me. He was off a little bit to the side, and he leaned forward to rest his palms on the kitchen counter.

I gave him a hard stare. "This is *not* going to be the gardens version 2.0."

"Of course not," Killian said. "We're in the kitchen. Kissing you here would be a very different experience, particularly because anyone stupid enough to try and follow me here who is not a member of my Family will be disemboweled."

I rolled my eyes. "You're *so* romantic."

"That is not a no."

I laughed a little, but the coffee machine beeped. I happily filled my cup and dumped in triple the creamer I normally used, then took a deep sniff.

Ahh. Heaven.

Killian watched me, his dark eyes glowing a faint red.

My coffee was too hot to drink, so I set it on the counter. "Why do you keep trying?" I asked.

Killian blinked. "I'm afraid I don't understand."

"We agreed in the Paragon's study that we'd talk about this after everything was over with the Night Court. Why are you still hinting and flirting?"

He popped one eyebrow up and smirked slightly. "*You* might think the Night Court is an all-consuming worry, but I've lived a lot longer than you. I am well aware that when it comes to my priorities, you top the list."

I wanted to rub my eyes, but I'd horribly smear my makeup, so I settled for awkwardly rolling my shoulders. "But I'm a wizard."

"And that is precisely why the notion that I am as...*fond* of you as I am makes this, as you would say, a big deal." He stood up straight and twined a piece of my curled blond hair around his finger. "I recognize that you have chosen to focus on the Night Court for now. I'll respect that decision, but I'm going to take every opportunity I can to remind you of what comes next."

He was too close.

My heart was rattling around my chest again, smashing into my lungs so it was kind of hard to breathe.

Killian's wide smirk softened into more of a hint, and he leaned down.

I settled my hands against his chest and my eyes drifted shut, and just as his lips touched mine I heard the kitchen door slam open.

"Your Eminence—I, er, forgive me, but—"

Killian sighed—the noise almost snake-like. "Naturally." He abruptly straightened, then smoothly turned to face the door, tugging me along so I was pressed into his side when we faced Gavino together. "I could have him killed," he said conversationally.

I scooped up my mug of coffee and took a loud slurp. "You can't," I said. "You're lending him out to me and House Medeis, and we wizards happen to like him."

Killian narrowed his eyes. "Then at the very least I could shoot him."

Gavino—always pale—turned snow white. "I'm sorry, Your Eminence, but the First Knight said this couldn't wait."

My heart—which had previously been doing cartwheels—froze. I gulped. "The Night Court?"

Gavino nodded. "A Night Court noblewoman is here with a message for you, Your Eminence."

Killian's eyes glowed blood red. "In that case, we can't keep them waiting, can we?"

"Not this time." I took another slug of my coffee as I remembered Leila's warning—our best bet was to catch them off guard.

"I'm coming with, but I think I'd rather have them believe our relationship is unequal."

Both of Killian's eyebrows shot up. "That ship sailed when you and a small team of your wizards massacred them."

"Maybe not," I said. "They know we're powerful, but they might think that we're just your henchmen."

Killian thought for a moment, then nodded. "It won't hurt to try. At the very least it might be amusing to see how it plays out. Let's go."

A final sip of my coffee and I abandoned my mug on the kitchen counter, slipping out of the kitchen after Killian.

Gavino waited by the door until I had passed through and brought up the back end. "The messenger is at the main entrance. The Drakes on patrol escorted her to the front door, but I believe the First and Second Knights are with her now."

Killian nodded, and stalked through his house. Supernaturals cleared out of his way, driven by the pressure even I could feel oozing off him.

I made sure I walked just a little behind Killian, my shoes clicking whenever we left a rug and marched across tile, hopefully looking not very intimidating.

We reached the foyer where, as Gavino had said, Celestina and Josh stood with the Night Court fae. Josh had a sword out and pointed at the representative, but Celestina looked deceptively benign in her gorgeous dress with her pretty smile and no visible weapons.

The fae delivering the notice was obviously from the Night Court—she had their coppery skin, and her hair was an ashy blond hue. She was wearing a dark blue tunic and held a thick sheaf of paper sealed with a glob of black wax, and was doing considerably well at hiding her nervousness. (Her expression was blank—it was her tendency to flick her eyes at Josh's sword that gave it away.)

When she saw Killian she bowed. "Eminence," she murmured.

"You have a message for me?" Killian asked.

"I do." She handed over the papers, keeping her eyes downcast as Killian ripped through the seal.

It grew suspiciously quiet around us, so I glanced back, confirming that a few of the fae kings and queens—including the Day King and the Winter Queen—had drawn closer to the entrance and were watching carefully.

Killian read the letter, then handed it over to me.

I only glanced at it and struggled between a sigh of relief and tensing in anticipation. It was one of our best-case scenarios. Queen Nyte challenged us to a certamen.

I won't bore you with the details—because of their tendency to tell half-truths and leave out important pieces of information, fae tend to be very detailed and long winded. (Seriously, they're worse than lawyers.)

Queen Nyte went on and on about how she was requesting a duel because Killian had dishonored her in accusing her of killing her husband—never mind that he'd been *right*—and since he had no honor this was the only possible outcome unless he accepted her terms of surrender, blah, blah, blah.

Her terms of surrender were a joke—she wanted a certain amount of money that ranked in the *millions*, as well as Killian to step down from his role of Eminence, and a bunch of other stuff that was never going to happen.

I couldn't help the snort that popped out of my mouth when I read it. I glanced up at Killian, who shook his head in a long-suffering way.

"Queen Nyte wished to express that she will expect your answer within two days," the courtier said. "Or else—"

"That is unnecessary," Killian interrupted. "I'll give you my reply now. I look forward to meeting Queen Nyte and Consort Ira on the battlefield, and as the recipient of the declaration of a certamen, I will choose the place and time our duel will commence."

The fae bowed. "I will deliver the message as you have spoken." Celestina opened the foyer door for her, revealing the team of vampires waiting to escort her off the property.

The foyer practically whistled with the amount of whispering going on. A few fae slipped deeper into the mansion—probably to inform those who hadn't seen the display.

The Paragon popped out of the crowd like a groundhog and scurried his way up to us, eagerly rubbing his hands together. "That worked well," he said. "You finally have your resolution!"

"Yeah, now all we have to do is win a duel," I dryly said.

Killian held out his hand, so I gave him the letter. "It's what we expected, and it's a better scenario than an actual war," he said. "Primarily because now we can finally—*legally*—crush Nyte."

Josh gave a happy sigh. "In preparation of the certamen, I'll take an inventory of my weapon collection for the House Medeis wizards after the party."

I brightened. "That actually sounds great! We have weapons, but I'm pretty sure yours are a higher caliber."

Josh bowed his head. "I would be honored to inspect your collection and personally choose weapons for your people."

"After our first strategizing session," Killian said. "For now, we have to proceed with the party. We wouldn't want to appear *worried* over the likes of Nyte."

"Right you are," the Paragon said.

Killian stared at him. "Which is why you need to get lost."

"How could you say such a thing?"

"You're a fae. You could be taking information back to Queen Nyte."

"Oh, please," the Paragon snorted. "You know I dislike her as much as you do. You're fixing a problem I frankly didn't want to get involved in. Good luck to you! But, I see your point. We'll talk later." The Paragon waved to us, then scurried off, disappearing back into the swirl of the party.

He passed by Great Aunt Marraine, who was waddling toward me with great determination.

I patted Killian's arm. "You go ahead. I think I have some questions to answer."

"Good luck." Killian leaned over and pressed his lips to my temple, and was then off. Gone before I could protest.

"Hazel, did my old ears deceive me?" Great Aunt Marraine asked. "Are we really entering a certamen?"

I smiled widely. "We are."

TWO NIGHTS LATER, about half of House Medeis and twenty or so Drake vampires were closeted up in the dining room, which had been temporarily converted into the war strategizing room because it was the only place in the house with enough room that wasn't obnoxiously large, like the ballroom.

Killian stood next to a huge smart board—one of those electronically connected white boards, which had been installed that morning—and was reviewing some of the finer details of battle preparation for the group.

"All vampire troops will be given a sample of Queen Nyte's and Consort Ira's scent, in hopes that it will make them easier to pick out," Killian said.

Tasha raised her hand and spoke only when Killian nodded. "Is it really necessary? Won't we slaughter most of the troops?"

I made a negative noise in the back of my throat, and my family shifted and balefully eyed our allies.

When the vampires turned so they could look at me—I was sitting at the fringe of the wizard group—I straightened my shoulders and cleared my throat. "That's not necessary, and it's not how House Medeis operates. We'll fight to win, but we're not going to go in with the mindset of maximizing bloodshed."

"Agreed," Killian said. "I'm not interested in upsetting the sensibilities of our fine allies." He nodded at us wizards. "But it's also not a good look on us. We're going into a duel—something that hasn't happened in the Midwest in a long time. Currently we have the moral advantage—Nyte challenged us after breaking deeply held Curia Cloisters laws. But if we create a bloodbath with our win, we'll be hated."

The vampires looked thoughtful and satisfied enough with the explanation.

"Because we have to be aware of the political ramifications of *how* we defeat the Night Court," Killian continued, "we're going to stack the deck in our favor both by our strategy, and by choosing the time and place of the battle."

A certamen wasn't like a typical battle fought in a human war. It was supposed to be an alternative to war and gave two sides the chance to hammer at each other and find a decisive victor—presumably with some casualties, but not the mass bloodshed that would result from a full-on war.

Because of supernaturals dying out, over a century ago our society came up with a bunch of rules and regulations for certamen that were supposed to minimize bloodshed and keep society more...*polite*.

This meant we'd be dealing with a specific framework.

After one Court/House/Pack/Family challenged another to a certamen, the accused were allowed to choose the time and place where the battle would take place. (I'm pretty sure the original creators of certamen were a bunch of crusty old British vampires who came up with these rules after living in a time of dueling, but it worked.)

Allies weren't always allowed to enter the battle—another attempt at minimizing bloodshed, and political consequences. But Queen Nyte—in her anger—had been stupid enough to declare a certamen on both the Drake Family and House Medeis by proxy. Probably because we wizards had so thoroughly trashed her people in the Curia Cloisters, and she wanted to prove she could effectively fight us."

Gavino raised his hand. "We'll be fighting at night, then?"

"No. We have our wizard allies to think of, and they don't see well in the dark." Killian glanced at the smart board, which was currently displaying pictures of Queen Nyte and Consort Ira. "Ideally the fight will begin at sunset. It will give the wizards enough light to see by, and won't hinder us much. But that will put a time limit on us. We'll want to defeat Queen Nyte and her consort by the time night falls, or we'll lose our advantage."

Now it was Celestina's turn to raise her hand. (Not gonna lie, it was pretty cute to see Killian posing like a teacher and his vampires obediently raising their hands.)

When Killian nodded, the First Knight stood. "It seems the best strategy will be to target Queen Nyte and Consort Ira, capture them, and demand their surrender?"

"Indeed." Killian casually rested his hand on the bottom rim of the whiteboard. "That is the tentative plan, given that it will provide the least bloodshed and the fastest win."

Mrs. Clark slowly raised her hand, sitting a little deeper in her chair when the vampires flicked their eyes in her direction.

"Yes, Mrs. Clark," Killian said.

She straightened, her mouth making an 'o' shape in her surprise of Killian knowing her name.

(I wasn't surprised. Mr. Paranoid probably had flashcards made so he could recognize all of my people on sight. Which was kind of touching if you thought about it.)

"What if we capture them and they don't surrender? Presumably they'll be executed, but what about the rest of their troops?"

"In fae Courts, the ruler's orders are absolute," Killian said. "But once that ruler is no longer alive or in power, the fae are no longer obligated to follow those orders."

Momoko chewed on her lip. "So the fighting will stop once we take out those two rats?" She spoke quietly, and probably only meant for us wizards to hear.

But vampire hearing was a thing, so Killian said, "Yes. If we provide a proper motivation, they will definitely give up. Fae are selfish things. They have no desire to die for monarchs who are no longer around to protect them."

Manjeet raised his hand. "Then I imagine we will need a specific strategy to capture Queen Nyte and Consort Ira, given that they will probably spend the bulk of their resources protecting themselves."

"Exactly. I haven't settled on a strategy quite yet," Killian said. "But I do believe it will involve intermingling wizard and vampire forces. Wizards are capable of shielding fae magic and in some cases breaking it, while vampire troops are more skilled at whatever offensive strikes we decide to go with." Killian glanced at me, which I knew was my cue.

I stood and joined Killian by the smart board. "That's why we'll be holding daily joint practices," I announced. "Allowing us to grow familiar with the process of fighting together."

"Our strategy will shape and take form as we discover how we best move together," Killian said.

I hesitated, then added, "Although I personally would like us to experiment and try new things."

All eyes in the room shifted to me. It was a little intimidating, mostly because I didn't know what I was talking about and was going entirely based off what Leila and the Paragon had said. "After speaking to several fae, it seems the way to best minimize bloodshed would be to catch the Night Court off guard—as we wizards did at the Curia Cloisters."

A vampire I recognized but didn't know by name raised his hand. "Wouldn't it be easier to overwhelm them with our combined forces? With wizards shielding, we vampires will have an easier go of it."

"It's probably the most solid strategy," I agreed. "But if we can surprise them and catch them in a way they didn't expect, they should be easier to handle. Fae are prideful and deeply believe in their own intellect. Surprising them would ideally make their forces crumble."

There were several long moments of silence—I hadn't even mentioned this idea to Killian.

"A strike team might be a good base design to work with." Celestina tapped her fingers on the leg of her chair as she thought. "If we could get a well matched team they could cut through the Night Court army, straight to the queen and consort."

"We could try match-making wizards and vampires together to find the best pairs to make up the team," Franco suggested.

Josh unsheathed a dagger and studied the edge. "An intriguing idea."

"Killian or I would need to be with the strike team," I said.

"Why?" Felix asked.

"Because if the queen and consort surrender, we'll need to be there to make it official and to give them the terms of surrender."

Rupert shrugged. "Is that really necessary?" he asked. "Given they hate the Drake Family enough to break Cloister law and bring the wrath of all supernaturals down on their heads, they're not going to give up."

"I don't care," I said. "We *have* to give them the option of peace, first."

There were a few eye rolls, but my people seemed a little relieved.

"We'll create articles of surrender," Killian said. "But there are some hard stipulations we'll include—like requiring that they step down from their positions in the Night Court." He smiled widely, flashing his fangs. "I will not allow them to surrender, simply so they can rebuild their forces and try again."

"Yeah, that sounds about right." I exhaled deeply and pushed some of my blond hair out of my face. "They've proven they have no honor, so we should expect they will try a stunt like that."

"Celestina will research the various places where we can hold the battle and will test which one will be most advantageous for us," Killian said. "We will continue to hold strategy meetings, but our main focus will be training and practicing together."

"So let's get to it!" I grinned. "Who wants to blow stuff up?"

The House Medeis wizards cheered, and more than a few vampires looked pretty pumped at the idea.

The meeting broke up as everyone stood.

I watched Gavino make a break over to the wizards, dragging Julianne, Manjeet, and Tasha with him.

Mr. Baree offered them a smile and his hand, pumping each vampire's arm with great enthusiasm.

Great Aunt Marraine wriggled her eyebrows and playfully elbowed Gavino, making the pale vampire laugh.

"You'll oversee the training today?" Killian asked.

I slightly shook my head and shuffled around to face him. "Yeah, Celestina and I came up with a list of things they should do. I already have a few groupings of who I think might work well with who, so I'll be playing around with that today." I pulled my smartphone from the pocket of my black jacket and waggled it. "Since we have more vampires than wizards, I think in most cases I'll assign two or three vampires to a wizard."

"There will be some exceptions?" Killian asked.

"I'm figuring that will be part of our surprise strike team, but I'll have to wait for us to come up with an official strategy before I really settle on who works with who." I groaned and rubbed my face. "I can't believe we only have a week to pull this all together."

"We'll make it." Killian slipped a finger under my chin and tilted my head up so I looked at him. "And we'll protect your people."

I smirked. "Actually, I think it's the other way around. *We'll* protect *you*! We're the ones with shields, anyway."

A hint of a grin tugged at his lips. "I stand corrected. But you really think a surprise strike will work best?"

"After what the Paragon told us, yeah. I had a conversation with Leila, too. You know she's part fae?"

Up went his eyebrows. "Do you really think I wouldn't vet my neighbors? Hazel, I am hurt."

I rolled my eyes. "Whatever. She told me that because the fae will believe they are smarter, the fastest and easiest way to beat them would be to surprise them in a way they wouldn't expect, or with something they believe can't be changed." I hesitated, then added, "She doesn't seem overly fond of fae, and I don't think she's lying."

"She's not." Killian rubbed his chin as he thought. "It is in their psyche to think they are the most devious supernaturals. A surprise attack would shock them. But I don't know *how* we could surprise them more given that they already know about House Medeis's awakened power, and that wizards and vampires make excellent teams."

"Yeah," I agreed. "That is a problem." I sighed and picked at my cellphone case.

"We're going to keep *our* private practice session in two days," Killian said.

I peered up at him. "Are you sure about that? It doesn't seem like the best use of our time given what's going on."

"It's now more important than ever," Killian said.

"Okay." I shrugged. "If you say so. I'll drop by after this first training session to let you know what I think."

"Excellent. And allow me to lodge a suggestion?" Killian's eyes had returned to a shiny shade of obsidian cracked through with red, and his smile was too open.

He looked innocent, which instantly put me on my guard. "What?"

"If you truly wish to surprise the Night Court, perhaps it is best to test your various limits. If you agree, I'm sure I could arrange some surprise experiments—for science, of course."

I scowled. "You just want another excuse to throw me off the roof! Although I expect it will be something different, this time."

"It would be," he shamelessly agreed. "Or it wouldn't be nearly as fun."

"My answer is NO."

"I can guarantee there would be a significant morale boost among the Drake Family."

"Still no!"

CHAPTER TWENTY-ONE

Hazel

I was facing Killian down during our practice match with my shield raised between us. He tried to ram it, but it held steady—not even flickering. (That was an improvement.)

I jabbed a finger at Killian, and thick ice formed around his feet.

He crouched and jumped free, but I figured he would, so I pelted him with fist-sized chunks of hail. For once I was keeping up with him. (Yet another improvement!)

I blinked, and in that time Killian slipped out of the hail zone, charged around my shield, and stopped at my side.

I pulled in more magic, trying to create an electric charge that would travel up and down my body, but Killian grabbed me, flipped me over his shoulder, and firmly set me on the matted floor with just enough force to make me cough, but not knock the air from my lungs. (Despite being able to breathe, this was *not* an improvement.)

He lounged casually next to me, his hand loosely holding my throat.

I *still* wasn't able to override my instincts with Killian when he had his fangs out, eyes red, and a general glee of bloodlust emanating from him. So I flinched, my whole body cringing.

He was back on his feet in a flash, not even looking winded or at all mussed. The jerk. Though he looked uncomfortable like he always did whenever I cringed. "Surrender?" he asked.

"Obviously!" I snarled.

He chuckled a little, his expression relaxing.

I groaned and peeled myself off the ground. "I am never going to beat you."

"One day you might grow up big and strong." He took my hand and popped me to my feet. "Is anything injured?"

"Nah. You're always careful." I rolled my stiff neck and groaned again.

Killian tossed me a black water bottle. "I try, but you're getting better."

I scoffed. "Yeah right. What does that mean—I'm about half way to keeping you on your toes?" I grumbled to myself before I took a swig of water, successfully tilting the bottle too far so water dribbled down my chin and splattered my shirt.

Killian wiped his hands off on his exercise pants. "Your reaction time has sped up quite a bit, and you're figuring out what kind of magic most hinders me."

I gloomily set my water bottle down. "You still finish me off in seconds."

"Perhaps, but—as we have said before—I have years of experience."

I closed my water bottle and set it down with an aggravated thump. "I know, I know. That's why trying to beat you is like trying to strategize how to surprise the fae."

"Ahh, yes, I wanted to speak to you about the Night Court." Killian watched as I frowned at the water spots on my shirt. "You seem very insistent that we offer peace. Will you be alright if we have to kill Nyte and Ira in the end?"

"Yeah. I won't like it, but they essentially chose this." I frowned and stretched out my arms. "I want to offer them mercy, though, because I don't want to be like them. If they don't choose it, that's their choice. It was the same with Mason and Solene."

"What do you mean?"

"I offered both of them the chance to stand down and surrender. Solene wouldn't, and Mason did and then tried to kill me when my back was turned, making his choice pretty obvious. I had to kill them both. I didn't enjoy it—I won't *ever* enjoy it—but they had made their decision."

Killian nodded. "That's about what I expected from you. Given your moral code, you want to offer everyone mercy and forgiveness, but you won't tolerate it if they don't choose it."

"I guess," I slowly said.

"Next round," Killian said.

I scrambled to throw my shield up—whenever he cued the next match what he really meant was that it started two seconds before.

My shield flickered to life as Killian sprang at me, a blur I could barely track.

I swung my shield around to protect my back and created a cage of lightning around me.

Unfortunately, Killian was too fast and made it in before the lightning snapped into place. He hooked a foot behind my knees and pulled my legs out from underneath me, making me topple.

On my way down I released an inferno of blue fire, which heated the air and made me sweaty, but didn't harm me at all given it was my own magic.

Killian scooped me up and pushed me in front of him, shoving me into my own shield—which gave way, giving him the opening he needed to get out of the magic-flooded space.

Before I could mentally select a new strategy, he had me on the ground, a knee pinning my shoulder down.

I cringed, immediately making Killian back up even as his eyes glowed red. "Surrender?" he asked.

"Yes." I sighed and stayed spread eagled on the ground as my magic faded away.

Killian's shirt smoldered, and for once his skin had a little more color to it than usual—probably because I'd nearly barbequed him. Otherwise he appeared untouched.

It wasn't fair! I'd even made a lightning roof on my cage because he could have easily jumped in!

"Hazel?" Concern lined Killian's forehead as he crouched next to me.

"I'm fine." I forced myself to stand and tried to shake the frustration off.

I wasn't a bratty kid. I didn't *need* to win. But I wanted improvement—or some sign I wasn't going to be such a greenhorn in battle when I had my *entire House* following me.

But every fight with Killian followed a predictable pattern.

Fight, subdue, flinch, back-pedal, done. Again, and again, and again.

I needed to do something different, but *what?*

Leila's words about the fae floated through my mind.

You need to take something that they believe with every ounce of their being, and twist it on them.

Couldn't I use the same strategy against Killian? But what did he believe and take for granted? *He* had been the one that was insistent I had more magic, and that it could be used in unusual ways modern wizards never thought of.

"Do you need another break?" Killian asked.

"No." I sighed and rubbed my right wrist. "That last match was so fast I didn't expel much magic. I'm good."

Killian looked me over from head to toe—and not in a checking-me-out way, more like he thought I was enough of an idiot that I wouldn't notice if I was hurt. Or, more probable, he was worried he had overdone it. He seemed convinced I was terrified of him whenever we fought—wait.

That's it. That's something he absolutely believes. And while he does freak me out a bit, he seems to think I see him as a monster, which isn't true at all. But how do I use that...

"Okay then." Killian retreated back across the mats. "Let's go."

I powered up my shield, grabbed my chisa katana from where I'd left it on the side after a previous fight, and prepared for the usual—fight, subdue, flinch, back-pedal. And that's when I realized how I could get him.

Killian came at me again, his eyes glowing red and his predator smile on his face.

My heart sped up, but not from fear.

I shot off bolts of lightning and spread flames out around me.

Killian dodged my lightning, but I already had my katana up, guarding my left side—which was his favorite side to attack me on.

I stabbed my sword at his gut. He leaned back, but it passed so close to him I heard the tell-tale sizzle of the electricity that wrapped around the blade as it zapped him.

He darted out—the fire was too intense for him to risk skulking around me for long—and laughed.

I threw an ice chunk the size of a bowling ball at him, but he casually leaned out of the way, disappearing with his speed, again.

I pivoted so my shield was at my back, shut my eyes, and flashed a blazing, white hot light.

The light usually managed to affect a vampire's sight for a few seconds, buying me precious time.

When I opened my eyes Killian was shaking his head, his lips peeled back in a snarl of displeasure.

I pointed my sword at him, using the blade to more precisely fire off a lightning strike.

He ducked—dodging it entirely—then jumped, tucking his legs underneath him as he soared over my head.

I tried to lunge forward and escape, but he managed to flip midair and grab my shoulder and push, making me stagger.

I dropped my sword as I struggled to regain my balance, but he was behind me by then.

One hand to the neck of my black t-shirt, the other grabbing the top of my pants, and he literally hoisted me out of the fire zone I'd created, dropping me on a new section of mats.

This was it...

My back smacked the mats, and Killian knelt down next to me, his hand again gently resting on my throat, his smirk back on his lips.

And, of course, I flinched.

Killian's smile died, and he tilted his head back slightly, his muscles tensing as he was preparing to stand.

NOW!

I struck out with my hand, blasting him in the chest with lightning that used every drop of magic I had in my blood.

My fingers tingled with the force of the strike, and Killian fell backwards as if a truck had run him over.

My fists still glowed with magic as I scrambled to his side. I ended up having to rest my foot on his throat because I couldn't touch him with my sizzling hands. "Surrender?" I asked.

He gave me a tiny and pained nod.

I dropped my magic and panted for a few seconds before I realized what had just happened. "I won." I fell back on my rear and stared at my white shoelaces for a few shocked moments, then laughed. "I *finally* won!"

I hopped to my feet and did a victory lap around the mats. "I did it, I did it, I did it!" I chanted.

A quick glance at Killian showed he was fine. His t-shirt had a giant hole in it, but he was already slowly getting to his feet, and his skin looked unmarred.

That meant he was probably going to ask for another match, so I needed to capitalize on my victory time. I did the worst imitation of a disco dance ever and went back to hopping in glee. "I am a dirty cheater, and this would never count in real life, but I don't *care*! I wo—ahh!" I screamed when Killian intercepted me.

I thought he'd be upset—I had toed the line of honorable fighting and attacked even though he'd clearly gotten me. So I was pretty surprised when he swept me up in a hug with a deep laugh I could feel through his chest.

"That was brilliant." His British accent was on full blast, addling me like a vampire falling on my head. "Have you been planning that this *whole time*?"

Killian spun in a circle, so I grabbed his shoulders for stability. "No way," I said. "I just realized I could use it."

A bit of his smile faded. "Then you really are that scared of me?"

"No, not really."

His expression was unreadable as he held me high enough so we were eye to eye. "But you cringe."

"Killian." I rolled my eyes in irritation. "To end the match you routinely put your hand on my throat when I'm running high on adrenaline. *Of course* I'm going to flinch! No matter who I fight, I'd flinch! That is basic human instinct!" I released my grasp on his shoulders so I could poke the furrowed spot between his eyebrows. "And might I remind you, I've only been training with you Drakes for about half a year! It's going to take a lot more experience to override base instincts. But when I tried to tell you that, did you believe me? *Nooo!*"

Killian slightly shifted his grasp on my thighs so he could boost me up higher and I didn't slide down now that I wasn't clinging to him. "I'm well aware vampires are terrifying."

"You are," I agreed. "But I know you. And I know even when you go all out and your eyes are glowing, you'd never hurt me."

His exhale was deep but ragged. He slipped his arm under my

thighs, freeing up a hand that he gently pressed between my shoulder blades, scooping me into a hug.

He leaned the side of his head against mine, his lips brushing the spot just below my cheek, and I felt the last of my reservations fade.

In this moment, I felt more from him than I had when we'd kissed.

He wasn't hiding behind a smirk or a cold expression, and his relief was so sharp I could almost taste it. He was that happy that I trusted him.

I slung my arms over his tensed shoulder and hugged him. We'd come so far. He still manipulated things, but he was trying. And despite our differences, I knew I trusted him with my life. And yeah, I loved the jerk. Ugh. That was going to be *so much fun* to sort through once the war was over.

And in that moment, it hit me.

"Killian." I pushed away from him and scrambled, trying to get him to set me down.

"Is something wrong?" He loosened his hold, and I slid down his front, my hands shaking.

"No, everything's fine. But I know how we can surprise the fae and rip them a new one."

He tugged at the massive hole in the center of his shirt. "Really?"

"Yep. And you're going to *hate* it."

CHAPTER TWENTY-TWO

Hazel

My heart pounded in my throat, and I thought I might throw up.

I attempted to stare impassively at the barren field Celestina had selected for our war with the Night Court, trying to appear nonchalant even though the sight of the Night Court forces scared the magic out of me.

Spread out before us was a massive army, so thick with troops that it looked like a black shadow had fallen over the field.

A silver line near the back of the shadow marked out the Night Court fae nobles in their enchanted armor. Just before them—in black and muted purple tabards—were the bulk of the fae fighting forces, guards and soldiers standing in organized formations.

But spread in front of and wrapping around the sides was a thick band of fae citizens. These fighters made up about half of the Night Court's forces, and they weren't all humanoids like the nobles and soldiers. There were trolls, hobgoblins, a few sparks of light that were probably pixies, a hydra, and more.

Given only about twenty wizards from House Medeis were fighting and Killian had decided on roughly sixty Drake vampires for his forces, the fae outnumbered us at a ratio I didn't want to think of.

Momoko rested a forearm on my shoulder. "Someone has the numbers advantage."

Felix put his hand on the top of my head. "I think it's despicable. Almost the *entire* Night Court is here, including the fae that can't fight like the pixies and brownies." His lips pulled back in an almost vampire-like snarl as he used his free hand to point to the short statured brownies, who were visibly shaking on the front lines. "What a coward. Queen Nyte is planning to use her people as fodder. What a vile woman!"

I inhaled deeply, already tasting the floral, rose-bathwater taste fae magic oozed, and I felt a little better.

Momoko and Felix might look terribly casual considering I was their Adept, and the average person might think by their body language they were purposely underlining my shortness. But it was the opposite. Their blazing warmth grounded me. My heart slowed down so I no longer felt like it was going to rip out of my chest as their familiar presence and tangy magic floated around me.

I held out my hands. They both shifted to put theirs in mine, and I squeezed.

Thank you.

They squeezed back.

You're welcome.

This was what being part of a House meant. Support and love...and standing with each other when it was time to fight.

I was asking my people to risk their lives in this. Most fae magic didn't affect us, but based on the sword the Night Court had busted out in their attack at the Cloisters, there was a pretty good chance they might have something old and powerful enough to hit us. (If we hadn't used our shields in the cloisters, the bolt from the sword could have done some damage to us.)

And they had a lot of weapons besides their magic in their arsenal...

I squinted briefly at the sun—it was a deep orange, the first hint of sunset. It cast an anemic light over the field, and it was so cold a few snowflakes dusted the ground.

"We figured she'd do this," I reminded them. "She's obviously desperate to take out Killian. I think she blames him for the downward spiral she created in her life since killing her husband and then pettily trying to get Killian back for blabbing. She was willing to drag her entire Court down with her. I don't think it's that surprising that she's willing to waste their lives, too. But that's why we have our strategy."

Momoko grinned. "I hope I get to see her face when she realizes what's going on. It's going to be *rich*!"

"I'm just glad we don't have to be out there, listening to her drone on." Felix pointed to the spot where Killian and Great Aunt Marraine stood together, talking with Queen Nyte.

Both parties had three guards at their backs—to make sure no one tried anything before the duel started. Officially they were meeting to discuss laws of certamen and the terms of surrender for each side demanded in case of defeat—basically a lot of political-esque talk I was not at all sad to miss.

I smirked. "She looks a little upset."

Queen Nyte was furious. Her beautiful face was twisted in an ugly roar, and her willowy build looked more skeletal in her rage.

Celestina joined us, her hands tucked behind her back. "The Eminence must have gotten to the part where surrender from the Night Court means she and dear Consort Ira have to abdicate."

Queen Nyte held a harp that glowed purple with magic, and she started to raise it until the nobleman accompanying her furiously patted her hand and then pointed to the chairs set far back from the field.

There sat Pre-Dominant Harka, the Paragon, and the Elite—today's witnesses to make sure everyone followed the letter of the law. Behind them, ready to *enforce* that law, was a band of werewolves, and a squad of House Bellus wizards. And there was a weird shadowy presence behind the Paragon—almost a black hole, except I could feel how it radiated magic, the same old and ancient flavor I'd come across a few times since Mason's attempted coup.

If Queen Nyte tried anything dishonorable, they would mete out justice, and they'd make what Killian and I had planned look like a tea party.

I flexed my fingers and flipped up the hood of my white jacket—it was decorated with House Medeis colors of blue and gold, and was made out of the same breathable but sturdy fabric as my special workout clothes Killian had gotten me.

All of House Medeis was outfitted in similar jackets—complete with loose pants made of the same material.

Personally, I thought it was stupid to wear white in a fight—these clothes were going to show every fleck of dirt. But Killian had bought them for us, and I knew from experience that the fancy material made a big difference in keeping the wearer from getting banged up, so I wasn't going to complain.

"We'll start when Killian returns, right, Celestina?" I asked.

Celestina slightly bowed her head. "That is correct. I actually came to tell you all Drake forces are ready. We will move into position on your order."

I glanced at her. "I'm not the Eminence. The Drake Family doesn't answer to me."

Celestina dropped the formality long enough to snort and raise one of her sculpted black eyebrows at me in a decent Killian impression. She was no nonsense in her black suit, her hair secured in a tight braid as she scowled at me. "Please. I'm not a seer, but the future is *obvious*. You—"

"Okay, okay," I hurriedly interrupted her. "We'll get into

formation." I spun around to address my wizards—a blob of white at my back. "House Medeis, take up your positions!"

Celestina sighed. "It would figure you are as inventive at getting out of unwanted situations as you are at wielding your magic."

"You're the First Knight," I said. "Your job description is bossing the rest of the Family around."

She shook her head at me, but raised her voice. "Drake Family, move into your places!"

The vampires glided into their spots, filing in behind the House Medeis wizard they'd been assigned to during our practices.

Celestina, however, was still shaking her head when Josh joined us.

He was definitely the most prepared for the battle. Two swords were strapped to his waist, and I saw at least two visible handguns, but he probably had an armory hidden under his suitcoat.

He stopped at Celestina's side and respectfully tipped his head. "Should this be the day I leave this mortal world behind, taken by the skeletal hand of death, I wish for it to be known that I have very much enjoyed fighting with you, Adept Medeis, and meeting all of House Medeis. Also, my list that dictates who receives what weapon is under the largest pillow on my bed."

I shivered. Not from the cold—between nerves and the magic flooding my system I was so hot I was almost sweaty—but because Josh's words hit a little closer to home than I would have liked.

"We're going to make it," I said. "There will be no casualties because this fight will be over *fast*."

We'd designed our strategy for swiftness, planning to use all our forces to slice straight through the army to reach Nyte and Ira.

We could do it because of us wizards—with our shields we

could forcibly push open a path. But it was gutsy because we couldn't hold out for long. Once we reached the queen and consort, Killian and I had to end it fast, or it would become a bloodbath.

There was a risk we might run smack into a fae capable of creating a shield, or someone would set off an artifact, but Killian had brought his mints that collapsed wards and killed magic, and had distributed some amongst his people, so we had accounted for that potential hiccup as well.

Felix cracked his knuckles as we watched Great Aunt Marraine and Killian turn around and head back toward us. "As confident as I want to be, I'm a mess of nerves," he said.

"We'll win." Celestina's eyes glowed with a fierce kind of surety. "With our races united, the fae don't stand a chance."

"I agree," Momoko said. "But I'm still nervous. This is our first real fight."

"I object." Josh spared her a glance from the firearm he was inspecting. "You fought brilliantly at the Curia Cloisters."

"Yeah, but we didn't expect that. It was…" Momoko shivered.

"You've proved yourself," Josh assured her. "The Drake Family will protect you today."

"Indeed," Celestina grimly said. "We will see to it that not one House Medeis wizard is harmed."

Felix stood straighter. "And we'll make sure that no Drake vampires are hurt."

Killian and Great Aunt Marraine were close enough to hear us, so I shouted to them, "How did it go?"

Great Aunt Marraine chuckled. "That queen is angry enough to spit nails! His Eminence got her nice and riled for you."

"She didn't, unfortunately, agree to surrender, so the certamen is on." Killian drew a dagger from his suitcoat. The hilt was a little plain, but the blade had a beautiful edge and almost glowed in the dimming sunlight. "And with our light disappearing, it would be in our best interest to begin the battle as quickly as possible."

"I'll go inform the Elite and the others." Great Aunt Marraine snapped shut the leather-bound folder that contained the terms of surrender. (She was going to sit the fight out and stay with the Elite and the other officials. I wanted her to stay behind at House Medeis, but she *insisted* otherwise.)

Celestina exchanged glances with Josh. "We will move into position—unless you had new orders, Your Eminence?"

Killian tapped the dagger against his thigh. "No. We stick to our strategy." His smile was feral, and his eyes glowed as bright as the sun. "We'll blow them away with our *surprise*."

The First and Second Knight saluted Killian, then headed off to join the others.

Momoko then Felix hugged me.

"We'll be right behind you," Momoko reminded me.

"And ready whenever you need us," Felix added.

"Thanks, guys." I tried to smile as my stomach gurgled with nerves. "Be careful."

"You too!" Felix waved as he and Momoko also drifted into their spots.

Momoko was at the back with Celestina, Julianne and—lucky her—Rupert filing in behind her.

Felix only had Gavino and Josh, but he'd be near the front of our forces—directly before Killian and me when we made the push.

Killian sauntered closer to me and took my hand in his. "Are you ready?"

"I feel like throwing up."

He tugged on my hand so I leaned into him, thumping against his chest. "I'm sorry. I know this will be hard for you."

I grabbed the lapels of his suitcoat to give myself an anchor to hold on to. "It's tougher knowing I'm bringing my House into this. But this is for us, too. After all we've done, Queen Nyte won't let us merrily skip off."

Killian rested his free hand on my lower back. "We'll win."

I snorted. "After what we've done? Heck yeah we will!" I tried to swallow, but my metallic-tasting spit refused to go down. "We're in this together."

His loose hug tightened for a moment. "Yes."

That simple reply put more steel in my spine than any pep talk could have.

Killian was with me. With the two of us teaming up, it would take *a lot* to defeat us.

We would win this fight, and we'd make sure Queen Nyte wouldn't hurt a Drake vampire or a Medeis wizard ever again.

I took a deep breath and stepped back. "Let's do this."

Together—our hands still linked—we took our place behind the front row of wizards and vampires.

Great Aunt Marraine had reached the sidelines by now and was passing over the leather folder to Elite Bellus for inspection.

With the paperwork settled—I know, meta much?—we waited for the signal from the officials.

"Keep to the strategy." Killian's usually muted British accent was clear and crisp today. "We push hard and breach the Night Court's forces all the way to Queen Nyte and Consort Ira. Then Hazel and I will handle it while you keep the fae off us."

"Sir!" The vampires all saluted Killian in perfect unison, and I felt the weight of their red eyes when they looked expectantly at me, along with the wizards from my House—who were all white-faced with strain.

"Stay safe," I shouted. "Work together and keep an eye out for one another. No one gets left behind."

The Drake vampires saluted me, and my wizards let out a few smatterings of applause before their expressions turned grim.

We waited in silence until the Paragon and the Elite stood up together.

Elite Bellus tossed a fireball into the sky, signaling the start.

We moved as a group. The vampires kept to a slow jog as my wizards squared their shoulders and drew on the magic in the air, their black wizard marks surfacing on their jaws and cheeks.

Killian and I ran side by side as our forces arranged themselves around us in an oval shape, keeping us on reserve until we faced Queen Nyte and Consort Ira.

The fae shouted, roared, and yelled as they stormed toward us.

Our people were silent—every fiber of their being concentrated on the battle and their role in it.

I could see Queen Nyte and Consort Ira—not because they particularly stuck out since they were also dressed in silver armor, but because of the giant, dome-like shield that sprouted around them and flickered green like newly awakened grass.

I guess it's a good thing Killian brought his mints!

"Brace yourself," Killian shouted, shattering our silence moments before the two sides collided.

Iridescent blue shields sprouted in front of my wizards, stretching high above our heads and sizzling as they locked into place, connecting with the neighboring shield to create a solid wall that enclosed our forces.

The sun hovered above the horizon now, and with the shields up we were officially on a timer.

"Hold your positions!" Josh shouted. He was leading the front lines as Celestina brought up the back, guarding our weakest point.

Once we infiltrated the fae forces, we'd be surrounded. If any of the shields gave out, it was over.

Felix and Leslie—the two wizards directly in front of me—crouched, making sure the shields extended all the way to the ground.

"On your mark," Felix said.

"Momoko, now!" I yelled.

Momoko—the only wizard who hadn't put up a shield besides

me—pointed a finger to the sky, and fireballs exploded in front of us with pinpoint precision.

Since the first layer of fae were those untrained in combat, they fled, tripping over each other. I saw eyes wide with fear and heard screams as they parted for us, but I smiled grimly.

I'd rather have them afraid and *alive* than watch the vampires cut through them like fodder to get to Nyte.

"Push!" Killian yelled.

The House Medeis wizards relentlessly marched, their arms pushed out in front of them and their teeth gritted as they knocked fae out of the way and plowed ahead.

We made it all the way to the fae soldiers, where we rammed into a protective barrier they'd raised.

Josh unsheathed one of his swords. "Formation two!" he shouted. "Formation *two!*"

Felix and Leslie stepped apart, creating a tiny gap between their shields.

Killian casually tossed a mint, which hit the fae barrier.

The magic of the barrier rippled, then crumbled.

Vampires shot out of the tiny opening between Felix's and Leslie's shields, falling on the unprepared fae troops. They moved like quicksilver, overwhelming the soldiers with speed.

They didn't actually kill that many fae—that would slow us down and make it harder to push past the bodies.

Instead they ran through their ranks, causing unrest and raising the alarm.

I saw Julianne run dangerously far from our protective circle and kick a soldier, slamming him into two of his comrades, before she zipped back.

Josh pistol whipped one fae and slammed his palm into the nose of another, then caught them both as they fell and tossed them at their brethren.

In their confusion under the wide-spread attack, the fae

soldiers gave up ground, allowing Felix and Leslie to push ahead, leading us deeper into the army.

"Stop them!" Queen Nyte screamed, her voice as sharp as shattered glass. "Nobles, *march*!"

The silver line of armored nobles moved forward, pushing through the fae soldiers to meet us.

"Fall back!" Killian ordered.

Josh, Julianne, and the other vampires returned, slipping back into the protective circle of shields.

As soon as the last vampire zipped through, Leslie and Felix slammed their shields together, closing the hole.

"Momoko, try lightning this time," I yelled as the nobles marched forward, magic runes on their armor glittering as their weapons started to glow and the scent of fae magic grew overwhelming.

"Gotcha." Momoko took a deep breath, her eyes fixed on the fae nobles as her wizard mark darkened.

Lightning struck the leading nobleman, then raced up and down the line of armored fae.

It didn't electrocute them—it looked like their armor was spelled against that—but it snuffed out a few of the glowing weapons, tossed a couple of fae as if they were dolls, and made some of the gems encrusted on a few nobles' helms explode, toppling them over.

"Formation two-B," Killian said, his voice ringing above the panicked cries of the fae and the sharp sizzle of magic.

On Felix's other side, June and April stepped apart, creating a new gap.

Once again, vampires sprinted through the hole, flooding the area in front of us and falling on the fae nobles. Unfortunately, the nobles were better outfitted and armed with magic weapons.

The two forces clashed.

Josh pounced on the leading fae, the blade of his sword singing when he blocked the first strike.

Manjeet and Tasha fought back to back, fending off the attack of three nobles. Whenever they struck at one of the fae, two more fae would attack, driving them back.

It was a similar situation everywhere I looked. The armor prevented the vampires from hitting any weak spots, and the fae drew on magic to make themselves stronger.

For a moment, it appeared that the fae might overwhelm the vampires...Until Gavino shot a fae in the foot, revealing that the armor was spelled against magic and bladed weapons, but not bullets.

At about that time, all around us the regular fae forces and soldiers started to recover and reform their ranks. They rammed the shields, but the House Medeis wizards held strong, sweat dripping down their faces.

I wanted to tap my magic so badly my blood boiled, but I gritted my teeth and stood with Killian.

I glanced at the sun, which was now brushing the horizon.

We didn't have long. But through the fighting nobles, I could see the green shield that protected Queen Nyte and Consort Ira.

"House Medeis, keep pushing ahead!" I shouted. "We're almost there!"

The wizards pushed with renewed vigor.

"Medeis!" Mr. Baree yelled.

"For the House!" Mrs. Yamada shouted.

"For the Drakes!" Felix roared.

They leaned into it, pushing with every muscle in their bodies.

Every part of me screamed for magic, but I unsheathed my chisa katana and walked with Killian as we closed in on the barrier.

Manjeet and Gavino forcibly shoved fae out of the way, driving them to the sides so we could inch forward.

Soon we were twenty steps away, then ten, then five.

Killian stepped in front of me, a smirk on his face as he flicked a mint at the barrier.

Even over the screams and clangs of weapons, I heard the click the mint made when it hit the barrier...and was pulverized.

My heart froze. "It didn't work?"

Killian frowned. "It seems a direct application might be necessary." He slipped through the gap, scooped a handful of mints from his tin, then slammed his fist into the barrier.

Magic sparked around his hand, glowing white hot as he pressed the mints into the barrier's surface.

I watched in shock as he dug his fingers in, making tiny hairline cracks in the shield.

Just how powerful is he?

His shoulders were tensed, and I couldn't imagine the kind of pain he had to be in. But he kept standing, even as magic swirled around him, crawling up his arm like a creature trying to devour him.

The mints fizzled and boiled in the space between his hand and the barrier, and there was a loud, roaring noise that sounded like a dragon.

The earth shook, and the top of the shield cracked so it looked like a huge animal had raked its claws across it.

The heat was unimaginable, and I thought I could smell burnt flesh.

"Killian!" I screamed.

He ignored me and kept his hand planted. He curled his lips back in a smirk and bared his fangs as more cracks spiderwebbed out from where his fingers dug into the magic shield.

The mints exploded into tiny fires.

A shockwave burst from the barrier, and it shattered.

Shards of the barrier were flung over the field, pelting the area —though they bounced harmlessly off our shields. Another roar, and they disappeared entirely.

I sprinted through the hole between April and June, ignoring the shouts of my friends. "Killian!" I skidded to a stop next to him, carefully holding my katana in one hand while I rested my other on his elbow.

His arm was a mess. The sleeve of his suitcoat and his dress shirt had tattered, revealing bloodied flesh.

Killian flexed his fingers—which were also covered in blood. "Give it a moment, I'll be fine." His smile was feral again as he shifted his attention. "I'm in well enough health to bid my respects to the *honorable* Queen Nyte and her *courageous* Consort Ira."

With the barrier fallen, it gave me my first good look at Queen Nyte and Consort Ira.

Nyte was in a state of shock. Her coppery skin was an ashen color, and she had drawn her hands up to her throat—one of the only visible pieces of skin since she was armored from her feet to her neck. But apparently she hadn't given any thought to wearing a helm for her *head* like her nobles had.

Consort Ira, however, was furious.

His jaw was locked, and I could see the muscles on his neck throb as he, too, had gone for vanity over practicality and wasn't wearing a helmet either.

"You think you've won?" Ira spat. "We haven't even *begun* to fight! All you've done is manage to get your troops surrounded. We're going to kill *all* of you."

I wanted to unleash a fireball and strike him where he stood.

The two monarchs' matching armor—silver plate armor with runes and black and purple crystals embedded into it—would protect them from any light attacks. Although it appeared to be similar to the armor the nobles wore, it was undoubtedly a level above in power, which meant guns weren't going to be much help.

The armor looked heavy, but the best fae armor was really light because—surprise—it was actually made by the elves, and had been guarded jealously by the few fae who could afford to own it.

That also meant it did an excellent job at protecting them.

Weapons were pretty much useless. Magic was the best way to go, but I needed to make sure when I went for them, I had the perfect shot, which was where our plan came in.

So even though instinct screamed at me to bust out my magic, I forced myself to smile. "That's cute. You think you can overpower us wizards with your *borrowed* magic?"

Ira didn't like that.

He hissed—like a freakin' snake. Or a vampire.

"Enough!" Queen Nyte had recovered from her surprise. She held her harp, which glowed black and looked pretty ominous and was very obviously magical. "You will pay for your impertinence!"

CHAPTER TWENTY-THREE

Killian

I am aware I occasionally lean on the cliché beliefs about vampires to magnify my image—we have a mysterious aura I find very useful in dazzling pesky humans who want me to do things like get *permits* and other stupid red tape items.

But, truly..."you will pay for your impertinence"? How trite can you get?

I glanced at Hazel. Based on her posture and the way she rubbed the hilt of her sword, she wasn't very impressed either.

I leaned over and murmured in her ear, "Order the troops."

"Yeah, yeah." She backed up a few steps and raised her katana to a guarding stance. "Formation release!" she shouted over the din of the fight. "Adjust to formation...*companion!*"

I flexed my fingers again. My arm had mostly healed—breaking the barrier had hurt, but we couldn't have Hazel break it and give our biggest strategy away.

I pulled out my dagger as I strode toward the fae monarchs, studying their armor as I weighed out the best way to subdue them.

Queen Nyte laughed. "I have waited so long to visit misery upon you, Killian Drake. You ruined my life when you—" She cut off in a very undignified squeal when I, using my vampire speed, rushed her and tried stabbing her under the armpit—which is typically a weak spot in armor.

Unfortunately she was wearing elven chainmail under her plate armor, and my strike glanced off without any harm.

She plucked a string on her harp, but I leaped back before her black magic could reach me. "Don't you want to know why we've done this? Why we will endlessly hunt you for the shame you brought upon me when you revealed—"

I interrupted her before she could go any farther. "I am not interested in your motivation. I don't care about how you *feel* about me. You are deluded and foolish, which is all I need to know about you."

Queen Nyte released that awful, high pitched shriek that made her sound like a harpy.

I glanced back at Hazel, confirming she stood a little behind me with one of her wizards—Leslie, I think—guarding her back with a blue shield.

As ordered, our forces had broken up the enclosed oval shape, and were now scattered around us in a crescent moon formation, keeping the nobles and soldiers from interfering.

Two or three vampires worked with a single wizard, as we had decided in our strategy meetings. The wizard provided protection while the vampires orbited around them, taking out targets and retreating back to safety while another took their place.

It appeared to be working, but we were almost out of sunlight, and I knew all the wizards didn't have Hazel's stamina. Some of them were approaching their limit.

I needed to end this fast.

When the fae queen finished her temper tantrum, I shifted my gaze back to her. "I suggest you guard yourself."

I lunged for Queen Nyte again, this time aiming my dagger at her throat.

She plucked another string on her wretched harp—it was her source of royal magic, if I remembered correctly—and misty black magic surrounded her.

"No plea for our surrender?" Consort Ira sneered as he raised his sword—which was wrapped in red colored magic.

I shrugged. "You won't listen until I have my hands around your throat."

Since I had no desire to attack Nyte while she was sheltered by magic, I cut around to Ira's open flank and kneed him in the side.

Slamming into the plate armor made my knee bones grind, but he staggered, so when I kicked him with my heel in the same spot he went flying, smashing into his queen.

Ira recovered first.

He ran at me with his sword raised and mouth open in an entirely unnecessary battle cry.

I zipped around to his back and hit him at the base of his skull with the hilt of my dagger.

He dropped, but before I could pounce on him, Queen Nyte played a few notes on her harp, and the ground beneath me swirled black.

I jumped back, but not before a tendril of the black magic flicked against my leg.

Pain shot through my entire body, setting fire to my muscles. It thankfully didn't last long. By the time I landed it was back to a dull ache, but I needed to avoid getting hit by that in the future.

Ira made another wild charge at me, swinging his sword.

When he raised his blade over his head I dropped my dagger and caught his wrists. I twisted one to the side, and forced the other painfully behind his back in a way that would do some serious damage if he didn't drop to his knees.

His moans of pain almost drowned out the melodic tune Queen Nyte plucked on her instrument.

I shoved Ira to the ground, snatched up my dagger, and backed away as fast as I could, narrowly missing the thorny vine that sprouted where I'd been standing.

In that moment I wished I'd brought a sword, but I was most skilled at a two-handed sword, and I'd need both hands for what we had planned.

So I exchanged my dagger for my handgun, racked it, clicked off the safety, and shot Queen Nyte in the chest.

As expected, her armor was a level above that of the Night Court's nobles. The bullet didn't punch through, but it startled her so she screamed.

She used her harp to raise a barrier, blocking any shots I might take at her head.

I emptied a magazine; the bullets ricocheted off her shield, but it kept her distracted as I approached Ira—who was still down.

He finally revealed his fighting skills, though. Ira waited until I was almost on him, then sprang up, stabbing me in the shoulder with a dagger while I was watching Queen Nyte.

Pain stabbed through my muscles. I grimaced, but I didn't move, even when he pulled the dagger from my shoulder.

I slammed my head into his, granting me the satisfaction of hearing the tell-tale crack of a broken nose.

Ira toppled with a whimper.

I slipped my gun back in my suitcoat as Queen Nyte screamed "Ira!" and dropped her shield in her dismay.

I tried rushing her, but she got the dratted thing back up just in time. I slammed into it, and for a second my vision was hazy before my vampire abilities kicked in, healing both the stab wound and whatever head injury I may have sustained.

Ira must have finally learned his lesson. When he staggered to his feet—blood dripping from his nose—rather than attack me, he flicked a dagger at Hazel.

I shot across the battlefield, catching the dagger midair. But when he used what appeared to be a thumb-sized rock sculpture to shoot a bolt of yellow magic at her, I dove to the ground to avoid getting hit.

Hazel had promised her people would protect her in case Queen Nyte and Consort Ira used a spell or charm that was one of the rare ones actually capable of harming a wizard. I could only hope her wizards would be as diligent as she believed.

I flipped to my other side, everything in me relaxing when I saw the big wizard—Mr. Baree—standing between Hazel and the crackling yellow magic. It collided with his shield with a thunderous crash, but he didn't even flinch.

Hazel's blue eyes almost seemed to glow in the twilight as she stood behind Mr. Baree, her hands convulsively tightening on her katana's hilt.

This strategy was perhaps hardest on her—mentally speaking. Although physically, that might soon be true, too.

A fae noble managed to push his way through Mrs. Yamada and Mrs. Clark.

Hazel threw a dagger at him—probably provided by Josh—but missed by a mile. "We have a runner!" she shouted.

The fae noble made a dash for me, but before he could reach me, Celestina was there.

She picked him up off the ground as if he were a child and tossed him back into the fray.

"Thanks, Celestina!" Hazel shouted.

Celestina winked. "Don't mention it!" She slipped back into the fight.

Queen Nyte chuckled as she slithered up to Ira and leaned on his shoulder. "I see what's going on. You can't use your little wizard friends to attack us when we're in such close quarters, can you?"

It was true. If any of the wizards attacked the fae monarchs, it was almost impossible for them to avoid hitting me.

I ignored the gibe and rolled to my feet, glancing at the sky for an indication of how much time we had left. Night had almost fallen—only a sliver of the sun hovered above the horizon. Soon the wizards would be fighting blind.

I needed to end this *now*.

"Face it, Drake. Your numbers are too low to beat our forces, and unless you send some wizards in to be slaughtered, you can't catch us."

Yeah, we'll see about that.

I removed my dagger from its sheath in my jacket, then attacked.

I was on them in the blink of an eye and started with elbowing Nyte in the throat—she seemed the more dangerous of the two with that harp of hers.

She gurgled and hit me with her harp. It radiated so much magic that smashing it on my shoulder gave me a bad enough zap that my fingers twitched.

Ira pulled back, preparing to stab me. Unfortunately for him, I got my dagger between his wrist and the elongated hilt of his sword, then twisted it.

It bit into his wrist, and he loosened his grasp on the weapon with a cry.

I dropped my dagger and plucked the sword from his fingers. I gripped the naked blade in my hands, wincing when it cut into my skin, but smashed him in the gut with the hilt, making him double over.

I applied my knee to his head—which hurt a lot less than kneeing his armor—and he collapsed.

I chucked his sword across the field and kicked my dagger a few feet away so he couldn't grab it.

Nyte recovered around then. I heard her strum the first note before I whirled around and grabbed the harp by its intricately carved frame. It felt like I was holding a live wire, but I doggedly held on—this was my chance.

Ira was gurgling somewhere on the ground. I nudged his shoulder with my foot, then put a foot on his chest and pushed, pinning him in place like a bug.

The magic from the harp was starting to haze my vision, so I lashed out, grabbing Queen Nyte by the throat with my free hand.

She kept one hand on her harp and scratched at my wrist with the curved nails of her other hand, but I had them both stationary and in place.

Using every ounce of my vampire speed that I could muster, I let go of the harp and grabbed her wrist, holding her arm high above her head so she couldn't strum the instrument.

I exhaled, relieved.

"You think you won?" Queen Nyte sneered. "You can't hold the both of us long. We'll break free before one of your underlings is able to come help you."

"Hazel," I called.

She trotted out around Mr. Baree's shield and slowly approached us. "This is your last chance, Queen Nyte and Consort Ira," she said. "Surrender now."

Queen Nyte spat at Hazel. "You think we'd accept your demands? You overestimate your own skills, *wizard*. If you harm us, you'll hurt the Eminence."

Ira was grabbing at my shoe, trying to force my foot off him.

In a few seconds he was going to succeed. "Do it," I said.

"My offer is your last chance," Hazel said. "Surrender now, or die."

"We'd never choose a *wizard's* mercy," Ira sneered as he almost succeeded in pushing me off. "Our bones will shatter before we surrender to you. You ought to be preparing yourself, because we will destroy your House!"

I could tell the second the honor and valiance that drove Hazel took over. She blinked, and the blue of her eyes was darker, her face showing no regret as she stabbed her katana into the ground. "Very well, you've made your choice."

I grinned savagely, and Hazel started to gather magic to her.

CHAPTER TWENTY-FOUR

Hazel

I opened myself to the wild magic that stirred the air, and it flooded me—almost *painful* in its enthusiasm.

Since the start of the battle, my heart had screamed at me to take up my magic, to protect those I loved.

Now, it was *finally* time.

Queen Nyte must have been able to tell I was filtering magic through my blood, because she stiffened.

"You're going to use magic and hit your ally?" she demanded.

Blue magic crested around me like a wave, glowing brighter and brighter as it transformed into crackling lightning that flickered wildly in a mad dance at my feet. "Yes," I confirmed.

"You'll kill him!" Ira shouted. He was clawing at Killian with frantic panic, but Killian was able to keep him down.

My wizard's mark—powered by the sheer amount of magic I was daring to build—burned my cheek with such strength it stung. "Actually...I won't." I smiled, delighted *I* got to be the one to deliver the bad news. "You see, my magic *can't* hurt him."

Queen Nyte turned ghostly white, and she shifted her gaze to Killian.

He smiled at her…a wizard's mark identical to mine surfacing on his skin one beautiful flourish at a time.

"You drank from her." Ira stopped struggling, frozen in his shock. "You drank her blood, and now you're immune to her magic."

"But you *never*—you can't!" Queen Nyte strained, trying to pull her neck from his grasp. "You don't *trust*! You're the most paranoid monster alive!"

Killian laughed. "Do you see, now, where you made your fatal mistake?" His eyes glowed a frightening red, the kind that stirred fear deep inside your soul. He leaned close to Queen Nyte and snarled. "You shouldn't have underestimated what the love of a wizard could do." He abruptly broke off and roared to our joint forces. "Formation, protect!"

As one, the wizards and vampires moved back together, falling into a tight cluster sealed off entirely by my family's blue magic shields.

"No," Queen Nyte thrashed. "That's not possible! You'd *never* drink from someone! Never!"

I was holding in so much magic it felt like I was on fire. My limbs ached from the concentration of magic, and my fingers were starting to go numb.

"This can't be! Never, you're too soulless to do it!" The queen of the Night Court and her consort struggled to get free, and when Killian's red eyes met mine I unleashed my magic.

It was like a lightning storm went off.

Gigantic bolts thicker than cars struck the battlefield, sending frozen chunks of turf and dirt flying as it struck deep into the earth.

Bolt after bolt hit Killian and the two fae monarchs, shaking the earth and splitting the air with deafening rumbles that vibrated in my gut.

The air was so heavy with the electric tang of my magic, I could barely breathe. It was physically heavy.

And still I poured more and more magic into my attack, which was getting hard to control because there was just *so much*. I had to cling to my sword to stay standing upright.

Killian was a black blob in a sea of white lightning. A few of the magic-unleashed bolts actually went wild, striking the area around Killian and me.

One struck our forces, but my family's shields held strong.

I knew Nyte and Ira had to be dead, but part of our strategy was to use this moment to scare the rest of the Night Court into submission. And it seemed like it was working. As I poured more magic out, the Night Court forces scattered.

When I started to see white—not because of all the lightning, but because I was getting really lightheaded, I finally stopped.

My wizard mark pulsed with pain, and it was hard to stand. But when I blinked the fatigue from my eyes, I saw Killian—unruffled and perfect, with the exception of his torn sleeve—standing in the crater my magic had created.

Queen Nyte's and Consort Ira's bodies were at his feet, and for a moment I was sorry it had come to this.

But we had spared so many lives of innocent fae with this strategy, so while I was sorry it had happened, I wouldn't regret what we'd done.

I twirled around, and as we had planned, Felix, Josh, and Gavino had singled out the highest-ranking noble present. (It wasn't a hard job—his helmet had extra flourishes and a glowing circlet of magic etched into it, the perfect shining beacon.)

"Adept, Eminence, we have found the fae in charge after Their Majesties," Felix said.

I was glad my wizard mark still burned with the leftover magic from my attack, because I didn't think I could summon even a single flame of magic at the moment, but I wanted my mark out as a reminder.

"Do you, as a lord of the Night Court, accept our mercy on behalf of your brethren and admit defeat?" I asked.

Momoko—standing off to the side—threw a couple more lightning bolts, which only raced across the sky but still made the fae grimace.

"We do," the fae lord said.

Killian raised an eyebrow. "You do *what?*" he specified, his voice icy cold and dangerous.

"The Night Court admits defeat and surrenders!" the fae lord quickly replied.

I smiled. "Excellent! In that case, House Medeis, stand down!"

"Drake Family, disengage," Killian shouted.

Our people pulled back from their pursuit, and as if on cue, at the far side of the field, the Paragon waved a white flag, signaling the battle was officially over.

The Night Court still crowded as far away from us as they could get, but it was over.

The Drake vampires were offering each other curt nods and a few smiles and back slaps, until Momoko hugged Celestina and it became a free-for-all hug fest that involved most wizards chasing down slightly panicking vampires.

(My favorite, I think, was when June snuck up on Rupert and gave him a hug. He squealed like a pig, but sat through it like an obedient dog.)

Something in me loosened, and I shifted so I could see Killian again.

My wizard mark was still stark on his face—the edges actually glowed a soft blue light.

Huh, mine must be doing the same.

Killian crossed the gap between us in a second, steadying me when I staggered.

"You know," I finally let go of my katana and shook out my numb hands, "it is disgusting you look this good with my wizard mark when you are clearly a vampire."

Killian gave me a crooked grin, which actually made him look a lot younger and less perfect. "If I made an inappropriate joke here about your blood and my looking good while on it, I assume you would stab me."

I glanced at my katana, which was still staked in the ground. "I don't think I'd have the energy for it," I admitted. "My arms feel like noodles. That was about a thousand times worse than shielding you all in the Cloisters." I leaned slightly so I could peer around his side, still barely able to believe it was all finished. "It's over?"

"It's over," he confirmed. "We won." He tugged on my arms, and I happily tilted forward, letting him take my weight.

"Thanks for trusting me," I mumbled into his suitcoat.

"I should say the same." He slid his arms around my lower back so he could better stabilize me. "Are you feeling okay?"

"Yeah, just a little light headed." I tilted my head up so I could suspiciously look at him. "Unless the Elite or Paragon is heading this way. Then I feel awful."

"Because they're going to grill us?"

"Exactly."

Killian chuckled. "Once word gets out, we'll have to face a lot more than just those two."

"I know." I leaned back so I could smile up at Killian. "But just think how long we can drag out telling everyone. We can exclusively own the supernatural rumor mill for the next month at least!"

Killian leaned down and brushed his lips against mine. "I think we can make a few more scandals that will last much longer than a month," he murmured before delivering me a knee-knocking kiss in the steaming remnants of the battlefield.

CHAPTER TWENTY-FIVE

Earlier That Day...

Hazel

I followed Killian down the hallway. We were heading to a room in Drake Hall I hadn't ever seen before, the place where the blood donors fed the vampires.

It was in the basement and highly secured. Killian said some vampires would be standing guard at the doors once we got inside, but I was so glad they weren't there yet. This whole thing felt twenty degrees of awkward.

And, apparently, I was the only one feeling it.

When Killian reached the unremarkable wooden door at the end of the hallway, he unlocked it with an elaborate gold key and stepped inside.

I, however, hesitated in the doorway. "Are you sure you want to do this?"

"If you're worried I won't be able to actually drink your blood, it shouldn't be a problem. We've already established you smell... amazing to me. The greater issue is whether you trust me enough that the magic in your blood doesn't taste rancid." He flicked on a light switch, illuminating the room.

It was more...average than I thought it would be.

It still had all the same expensive and comfortable furniture the rest of Drake Hall had—imported Turkish rugs, fancy wall sconces, and elaborately framed portraits.

The plate of fruit and reusable water bottle placed on the coffee table were a bit out of place. But they were probably for me.

Killian had explained that usually blood donors were immediately escorted out after a vampire fed so they wouldn't see how helpless the vampires became. It was going to be the opposite for us.

They were locking me inside the room with Killian—it would be a big security risk to open the door if someone ever found out what was going on, and, frankly, he was safer with me at his back since I could blast anyone who tried to attack us, and my magic wouldn't harm him.

If this all worked.

I still wasn't certain Killian really trusted me enough to go through with this.

"My blood will taste fine." I wandered up to the plate of fruit, noticing it contained all my favorites. (How...*thoughtful?* And a little weird, honestly.)

"You can't know that for sure." Killian swung the door shut. It creaked on its hinges, and I heard the lock click into place.

I didn't love the idea of being locked *anywhere*, so the noise made me a little uneasy. "Of course I know for sure," I said. "I trust you, and I can just feel it that my magic isn't going to reject you. And I wasn't actually referring to my blood or any of that, I meant are *you* sure *you* want to do this? I know what this means... can you actually do it?"

Killian shed his suitcoat and pulled his tie off, tossing them both on a padded chair before he started rolling up the sleeves of his dress shirt. "You mean after everything I told you about how helpless we become and how easy we are to kill, can I really stand putting myself in a position where you could off me?"

I rolled my eyes. "I was trying *not* to be indelicate, but since we're abandoning thoughtfulness, yeah. How are you going to be able to do this? Having you drink from me and then using my magic on Queen Nyte and Consort Ira while you hold them down is the best sucker punch we could ever come up with because your unwillingness to drink from a donor is an image you've been building for decades. Or centuries, even. But can you actually set those hundreds of years aside for this?"

Killian considered me—his eyes were their usual obsidian-red shade at the moment. "Could I do it for the battle? No. However..." He crossed the room in the blink of an eye, joining me by the coffee table.

Slowly, carefully—as if he was afraid he might break me—he raised a hand and brushed my right cheek. "For you? I will." He smirked. "And I am not planning for this to be a one-time thing."

That news floored me. I reared back in surprise. "Wait, for real?"

His smirk lost that usual edge of arrogance he always had. "Yes...seeing how much I trust you, why would I limit it to just this once?"

"Because of everything you've told me! Even if you trust me, even if you know I won't hurt you, it's still a risk every time. And after the fight *everyone* will know that you drank from me, so it's not like we'll even be able to keep it a secret and—"

"You are right, I know you won't hurt me," Killian interrupted. "You're too good for that, and you continue to be a virtuous idiot."

"Yeah, but..." I trailed off, unable to grasp the immensity of what he was saying. "*Why?* With this fight it makes sense, but we'll never be able to use this again. Supernaturals will know. What's the point?"

"Because it's the only way I can prove how much I trust you," Killian said.

I stared up at him, trying to puzzle through what he meant. "I don't get it."

"I'll never be able to tell you *everything*," Killian said. "Even if I trust you with my life, there are politics in play I don't want you to have to know about. But I can drink your blood, and prove to you time and time again that I don't just trust you enough to drink your blood, but I trust you with my life when I'm weak."

The red in his eyes flared to life like hot coals, and he intertwined his fingers with mine.

My heart spasmed in my chest, but it was his explanation that floored me. This was about *us*? That's why he was doing it?

"It's the greatest reassurance I can give you." He took a step back to give me breathing room, but he kept my hands enfolded in his. "Will it be enough?"

It wasn't exactly what I wanted…but I was realistic enough to recognize he was right. No matter how much we trusted each other, there were certain things we couldn't share.

I had become obsessed with trust after Mason's coup and my parents' hiding so much from me.

But demanding absolute clarity wasn't possible for us, particularly since he was the Eminence and there was a slight possibility I might one day be the Elite.

If he drank my blood, though, I'd know. It was a physical symbol of our trust. There was no way for him to manipulate it, and even with my belief in all things right, my magic wouldn't passively sit by if it thought there was a problem.

This was how I would always know, and always have something to lean on.

Killian Drake was manipulative, powerful, and lethal. But he was willing to risk it all just for us.

"Are you sure?" I repeated the words I'd uttered when we first came in here. "Even with all the risks?"

The smallest smile tugged at his lips, and he leaned down so we were almost eye to eye despite our huge height difference. "Of course," he said. "Because I've found something I love more than my survival."

I couldn't help myself. I threw my arms around his neck and kissed him.

Yeah, I kissed Killian Drake.

And it was even better this time.

That electric tingle was still there, pulsing at the pads of my feet. But everything clicked together in a way it hadn't before. It was still overwhelming and passionate, but I could feel magic breezing through my body.

Killian wasn't a wizard, but this felt so perfect I couldn't imagine anything better.

"Can I interpret this as a yes?" Killian murmured into my ear. "A yes to everything?"

"Yes," I echoed. "But we still have *a lot* to talk about, and it will have to wait until after the fight."

"What do we have to talk about? Unless there are body parts of yours that require permission to touch besides your apparently blessed-and-sanctified-butt that must be protected at all costs?"

I wriggled out of his grasp—I couldn't let myself get too hopped up on his vampire pheromones or I'd forget why we were here in the first place. "There's that." I swiped up the water bottle and took a massive slug. "But there's also a lot of details we'll have to work out. Like what kind of schedule we'll be on so we can make this work, how do we integrate our households, and, most importantly, how are we going to explain this to House Medeis without making it angry enough to inflict ice-cold showers on us for the rest of our lives."

"*Oh*." Killian paused and folded his arms across his chest. "Yes, that is a fair point. Fine. I'll wait. *Even longer*." He rolled his eyes to show what he thought of the idea.

I took another slug of water to give myself something to do, then wiped droplets off my chin. "So...about feeding you. How do we do this?"

This was the part that actually made me a little squirrely. Killian wouldn't hurt me...but I was going to be pretty vulnerable while he drank.

Thinking of possible feeding methods, something in my stomach flopped. "Do you have to drink from my neck?"

"No," Killian scoffed. "You're tiny. If I fed off your neck and collapsed on you, you'd suffocate."

"I think I'm strong enough to push you off," I shook a finger at him. "I might have to push you onto the floor, but that's a sacrifice I'm willing to make."

Killian gave me a flat look. "You dropped Gavino on *your head* while fighting him. Seeing how I'll be too out of it to help, we're going to take precautions. Your arm will work fine—specifically your wrist."

I honestly felt a little relieved by that. It was a lot less intimidating to offer out my arm than my neck. "Okay."

Killian made an inspection of the three couches that were in the room. "Besides, this isn't one of those horrid romances we try selling the humans to convince them we're not going to eat them."

"You're right. It's just dinner," I joked.

"Not at all." Killian turned slightly so he could face me. The set of his mouth and eyebrows were serious. "It's much bigger than that."

I cleared my throat, suddenly feeling awkward under his glowing gaze. "Right. So how is this going to go down? Or, what I really want to know, is how much is this going to hurt?"

Killian slid his hands in the pockets of his pants. "There will be some discomfort when I first bite," he said. "But it will fade after that. I'll dampen my pheromones so you don't get groggy off them—it was one of our original survival techniques when blood packs weren't available and we *had* to feed off humans."

I relaxed—I should have known Killian was going to be thoughtful about this. Giving him blood or whatever I should call it was maybe going to be a little embarrassing, but I'd be fine. "That would be great, thanks."

"I won't take enough to harm you." He looked around the room once more, then sat down on the blue leather couch in front of us. "I physically wouldn't be able to drink that much. Blood from a living being is extremely rich, and with all the magic in your blood I'd probably get violently ill."

"Killian." I sat down next to him, one leg folded underneath me, and set my hand on top of his. "I'm not worried that you're going to harm me."

He slowly nodded.

I smiled and held out my arm.

He touched my wrist as he slightly maneuvered himself so he wouldn't be in danger of falling off the couch.

After a moment, he slowly raised my wrist, and kissed me there.

My heart gave an unsettling twist.

He was right—it wasn't romantic. This was far too stripped down for anything like that. This was the same kind of raw connection I shared with my family and House.

I was nervous, and I could sense that Killian was just as tense as I was.

This won't work. We need to relax.

So, of course I opened my big mouth. "This is super unsanitary."

Killian exhaled loudly, his breath feathering my bare arm. "Did you get a nursing degree in the past few months that I am unaware of?"

"No, but you're going to *bite* me," I pointed out.

"Vampires have microorganisms in our spit and bodies that clean out things like bacteria and pathogens," Killian said. "My spit is not contaminated—I'm more likely to get sick on your blood than the reverse."

"Oh, so you're like a dog," I said.

"*What*." Killian sat back in the couch after that, a look of disbelief etched on his handsome face.

"You know there's a saying that a dog's mouth is cleaner than a human's," I said.

Killian dropped my arm entirely and rubbed his eyes. "First of all, I can't even begin to deconstruct how wrong that is."

I couldn't hold my laughter in any longer. It erupted from me. "Killian, I'm *joking*," I said. "I was just lightening up the moment."

"You have an inappropriate sense of humor." Although his words were critical, the lines of his muscles were more relaxed.

"I don't know why you were expecting anything different," I said. "I beat a wizard senseless with a dictionary."

A tiny smile pulled on his lips. "Thank you." He leaned forward and kissed my forehead. "We'll be fine."

He raised my wrist to his mouth again, glancing at me when I didn't object, and then bit.

It stung a little like a shot—a momentary pinch of pain. I felt it when his pheromones or microorganisms in his spit or whatever it was kicked in. The pain faded away, and I felt just a tiny bit bubbly—like I'd just downed a shot of espresso.

Maybe that was adrenaline, though?

I couldn't feel his teeth anymore, just the gentle brush of his lips—although I had the nagging sensation that I wanted to itch the spot where his mouth was.

But after a few seconds, I realized something was very, very different.

I didn't feel hot.

Wizards ran hot due to magic, and since I'd unsealed my magic my body temperature spiked into sweaty at the drop of a hat. I was *always* hot.

Except the spot where Killian's lips brushed my wrist was... cool. Like putting your feet in a lake at sunset.

Even better, I could feel the sensation ripple slowly through my body. The uncontainable heat slowly faded, leaving a cool, calming sensation behind. I felt...*balanced.*

That sensation was why I didn't freak out even though the feeding process took a lot longer than I thought it would.

I assumed it'd be a minute maximum. It was closer to five before Killian licked the spot (like a dog—but I wasn't going to push my luck twice in such a short span of time) and my blood clotted.

I don't know if it was the vampire spit or what, but the bite mark scabbed over within seconds.

I was so busy marveling over my arm I almost missed it when Killian fell back against the couch, his head sagging on his neck. "You taste so much better than I thought." His British accent was so strong I could practically poke it, and his eyes were lazily lowered to half-mast.

"I taste like Christmas dinner, good to know," I said.

Killian snorted. "No. You taste like *sunlight.* I didn't know how much I've missed it—how it used to feel. Now it just dulls the senses...You let me experience something I'd forgotten, something I thought I'd never have again." He flicked his eyes in my direction as he sagged deeper into the couch. "In more than one way." He tried to brush my cheek, but the high of drinking fresh blood must have gotten to him because he couldn't quite raise his hand high enough. "And that's all there is to it." His words were slurring together more—he probably didn't have long before he was going to pass out.

I glanced down at my arm—which now held no sign of the bite mark, not like it mattered, I would wear a coat for the fight anyway. "You don't need any more?"

"No," Killian said. "But if you leave me, I'll come find you."

"I'm not going anywhere," I said.

"Good." He shut his eyes and exhaled, and for the first time since I'd set eyes on Killian while running from Mason, he relaxed.

Every muscle in his body loosened, and he yawned widely, resembling a cat.

One of his shoulders dropped, and he jerked in the couch.

"Here, just lie down." I stood—pleasantly surprised when I moved that I didn't feel any ill side effects from the process—and crouched next to the couch.

Killian obediently stretched out, his long limbs draped over the cushions. "It won't be too long," he said.

"Yep. Just sleep it off. When you wake up we'll finish preparing to face the Night Court." I brushed some of his hair out of his face.

He didn't move or reply.

I waited several more seconds before I realized he was sleeping.

I studied the fearsome Eminence who I'd gone through so much with, and who had stood by and believed in me when my own people wouldn't. He was terrifying, and yet he'd just given me the greatest gift he could have given: his trust. "Thank you, Killian." My heart brimmed with joy, my body still felt blissfully cool, and I'm sure I grinned like a moron as I lightly brushed my lips against Killian's. "I love you."

Killian

WHEN I WOKE UP, I knew something was different.

Hazel was using her magic.

Even before I cracked my eyes open, I *knew* it. I could feel it in the air—a side effect of her blood, probably.

Since the magic in her blood would protect me from her powers, it made sense I'd be able to feel it.

However, for a second, it put me on edge.

Why was she using her powers? We were locked in a saferoom. There was no reason for her to be flinging magic around...unless?

She's practicing, you paranoid numbskull, I realized, relaxing again.

I trusted Hazel with my life, but I wasn't going to overcome years of guarding myself in just a few days. Besides, this was the first time I could actually remember feeding. I'd been on bagged and bottled blood for so long I couldn't even remember what it was like previously.

The first *public* and successful blood transfusion was done in 1840, but vampires had long figured out ways to extract blood even before then. It was safe to say I hadn't fed on a human in centuries.

Enough. It's fine. I trust her, and she's probably...

I opened my eyes, and everything in me ground to a halt.

Hazel was standing a few feet away from the room's entrance, her fists engulfed in blue flames as she stared at the door, which she had fortified with a massive blue shield forged of magic.

She peered up and down the wall, her wizard mark a stark black flourish on her skin as blue pulses of magic rippled from her as she stood watch.

That's what she was doing, guarding me.

Even though she didn't agree with my paranoia, even though she believed better in everyone...she knew that feeding like this preyed upon my worst fears, and so she was protecting me even when I wasn't awake to see it.

Her magic heated my body, and I could feel in my bones that she was using it as a sort of rudimentary warning system. If someone attacked the room, she'd feel it, and she was ready for them.

And in that instant, I knew she was *the one*.

The one that came rarely in a vampire's lifetime, and sometimes not at all. The one who I would love for all of my existence, and trust to guard my back, fight at my side, and laugh with me during the day.

She was more than I imagined, a dream I hadn't thought could exist for me.

And as I stared at her, she turned around, a smile brightening her face.

"You're up!" Instead of coming over to my couch, she grabbed the shiny silver plate her fruit and water had been placed on.

"Yes." I cautiously sat up, blinking as I tried to adjust.

Hazel's blood had been a daydream to drink. But now that it was actually flowing through my system, I felt...*alive* again.

"You're feeling okay?" Hazel flipped the plate a time or two in her hands.

"I feel wonderful," I admitted. "Everything seems...*brighter*. Do you live like this all the time? With your magic, I mean."

Hazel tapped her chin with the plate. "Maybe? I can't say what living like a vampire is like, so it might just be a side effect from drinking fresh blood."

I shook my head. "I don't think so. I don't recall feeling quite this...alive. And I can tell I feel stronger—not just physically, but there's something about the magic in your blood. It's amazing." I eyed her in concern. "I can see, now, why your temperamental blood is a necessary survival technique. We're going to have to take special care of the rest of your House to make sure no one goes around getting any ideas..."

"It'll be fine," Hazel said. "My people won't trust just anyone. The stink of their blood will drive away any vampires who get any bright ideas."

"Perhaps," I said, unconvinced. "Regardless, Queen Nyte and Consort Ira will regret the day they crossed the Drake Family and House Medeis."

"Funny you should mention that." Hazel laughed nervously. "We need to make a slight adjustment to our battle plan. I'm not going to be able to use any magic until it's time to fry Nyte and Ira."

I rubbed my jaw, and rested a hand on Hazel's hip when she drew close enough. "Why is that?"

Hazel handed me the reflective plate. I glanced down at it and did a double take.

Spreading up my forehead, down my cheek, and crawling down my neck was a black wizard mark. It had the same flourishes and swirls as Hazel's, a perfect twin.

"I'm pretty sure they're going to figure out fast what our secret is if they see your new decoration." Hazel extinguished her magic.

It took a while, but our marks faded at approximately the same time. I pressed my lips together, thinking, and passed her back the plate. "We can deal with it."

Hazel tapped the plate on her thigh. "You think so? It means I can't fight *at all* until we get the monarchs."

"I half expected something to happen," I admitted. "Not this exactly, but something. A vampire hasn't fed off a wizard for so long, it's only natural that there would be side effects that were lost in history. I had prepared for worse."

Hazel exhaled. "Good. I think we'll be okay, too. But I didn't know how much it would mess stuff up."

"Hardly at all."

"Great." She looked down at me, then hesitantly reached out and pushed a bit of my hair off my forehead in a sweet gesture that simultaneously warmed me and caught me a little off guard. "Are you ready to head out? We'll need to tell everyone about this change in plans."

I stared up at her.

No, I wasn't ready at all to leave.

Hazel was *the one*. There was so much I wanted to talk to her about, so much I needed to tell her...including the fact that as a vampire feeding off her, I could significantly extend the length of her life if I wanted. (And oh, did I want to.)

Since I'd be drinking her blood, it wouldn't be too difficult to flip the magic switch for a chemical compound I could secrete in my spit to give her a longer life.

In the past century—and even before then—we vampires hadn't often used this particular ability of ours. The last thing we wanted was people chasing us down in the search for eternal youth. But I'd bend the rules for Hazel.

I didn't want to tell her about my plans, though.

It would be ideal if she didn't realize what I was doing until she was forty and was still getting carded.

But...with the warmth of her blood pushing its way through my cold body, and remembering how she had stood guard in front of the door, I knew I needed to tell her. And sooner as opposed to later.

However, I was going to stack the deck in my favor. I could drop the near-eternal-youth bomb at a time when she was so happy she wouldn't be able to refuse. Or maybe I could use it as a bargaining chip?

Either way, I'd have to come up with a way to tell her. But I didn't think it was necessary to do so right now. Particularly since I'd need to do a little more research to figure it out, first.

So I smiled. "Yes, I'm ready to leave." I stood, and it again took a moment to adjust to the subtle difference in the world.

"Great. I hope you remember the knock we're supposed to use to warn them we're coming out. Josh made it overly difficult, so I had no hope of memorizing it," Hazel grumbled.

I took her hand, moving at more of an amble so she didn't have to hurry to keep up as we made for the door.

"No need to fret. I remember it." We reached the door and I paused, my knuckles hovering over the door as I recalled a very important detail I'd almost forgotten in the high of drinking her blood. "Oh, yes. Hazel?"

"Hmm?" Hazel looked innocently up at me.

I couldn't help the roguish smirk that took over my lips. "I love you, too."

"*You were awake?*" she shrieked, her voice possibly piercing enough to be heard through the solid door.

"Of course."

"You, you, you sea cucumber!" She blushed bright red as she puffed up like an angry cat.

"Did you miss the part where I said I also love you?" I asked.

Hazel made one of those amusing noises she emitted when she was so embarrassed she couldn't speak.

Yep. She's going to have a very long, very full life, I thought with satisfaction.

"Since you love me as well, I assume that is the long-awaited permission to touch your rear without getting stabbed?" I asked.

Hazel recovered enough to snap, "Open the door!"

"Fine, fine," I agreed. "Just one more thing."

"*What?*"

I swept Hazel up in a tight embrace as I kissed her.

She didn't step on my foot like I thought she might. Rather, she stood on her tiptoes and grabbed the front of my shirt for balance.

I'd always known together we could trounce Queen Nyte and Consort Ira. But it was then that I knew we'd be fine. No matter what I had to do to appease her House, and what we had to tell everyone.

Or at least, we'd be fine until I had to tell her about her lengthened life. That was going to be a brand-new breed of fun.

EPILOGUE

Hazel

"As you can see, our founder has successfully built intermingled apartment buildings throughout America. By encouraging various supernaturals to take up residence and rent there, it fosters a comradery between races normally not seen, and gives the supernatural community a rally point to gather around."

I listened with great interest as the presenter switched to a new slide in his powerpoint presentation, appearing only a little intimidated as the four members of the Midwest Regional Committee of Magic stared him down.

I was pretty sure he was a wizard and not a regular human, but he wasn't wearing anything that put him with a particular House, and he hadn't used magic so I couldn't be sure. "We believe Magiford would be the best choice for our next building project, and the perfect location so we can expand into the Midwest as it succeeds." He gestured to the map on his slide for emphasis, then flipped to a new cue card on the podium he very strategically hid behind.

Killian had his arms folded across his chest and was leaning back in his chair with the air of a king. "I don't like it," he announced.

The presenter winced.

"You don't like anything that could help any supernaturals besides the vampires," Pre-Dominant Harka grumbled.

"I am inclined to agree with the Eminence." The Winter Queen of the Midwest was the fae representative on the Regional Committee of Magic at the moment. Her full lips were pressed in a straight line, and the light blue of her eyes seemed almost gray as she studied the gulping presenter. "Though perhaps not with such...dedication. I am merely concerned that such a building will lack the safeguards that intermingling will require. For fae alone it will be a problem as all the Courts do not get along. If citizens of opposing Courts were to cross paths..."

The presenter actually brightened. "Oh! The safeguards I mentioned in my presentation are only the beginning. The founder invests heavily in extensively warding all properties using both fae and dragon shifter magic."

That got a whistle from the Elite. "That must cost a pretty penny. Dragon shifters aren't known to lower themselves to grunt work like that unless they're paid a king's ransom." He murmured to me, given I was seated in a chair directly behind him, but Harka and Killian probably heard him as well given their stronger senses.

"There are additional safety measures in place." The presenter ruffled through a leather briefcase, then passed out packets of the additional precautions to the members of the committee. "Including a non-aggression spell that will dissuade any renters from being involved in physical or magical fights."

I peered over Elite Bellus's shoulder, getting a glimpse at some of the additional measures—including a magical and human-grade security system, some elven artifacts, and enough costly spells to bankrupt a millionaire.

Seriously, who can afford all of this for an apartment building?

"This seems like a lot of money to invest." Elite Bellus put his paper down. "I was under the impression that the apartments were meant for the middle class. Are they luxury apartments?"

"Not at all," the presenter said. "Our founder is more interested in promoting goodwill between supernaturals and humans—and offering safe spaces for those who might normally be excluded—than in making money. These buildings are considered something of a hobby for the founder."

"Did you get reports on this founder?" I whispered to Elite Bellus.

"When they first approached us with the request. Everything checks out," Elite Bellus whispered back. "I even reached out to a few wizard Houses in the communities where some of these apartment buildings have been built. It seems like the presenter is telling the truth. All of this is done for the good of the supernatural community."

"Huh." I leaned back in my chair, impressed.

"I'm still against it," Killian said flatly.

"Why?" Pre-Dominant Harka asked. "The builders are taking on all the risk, and they've already gotten a building permit from the humans."

Killian narrowed his eyes. "It's too dangerous."

I loudly snorted.

The Winter Queen was still paging through the various safety precautions. "I disagree. It seems to me it might be the safest place for our stragglers—provided everything is kept up to code and all of these proposals are followed." Her voice had more than a little frost to it at the end.

The presenter did his best to smile. "We strictly follow every proposal we make," he assured her.

Killian shook his head. "I don't want any young Unclaimed flocking there. They'll be easy targets."

"Wouldn't it be safer?" Elite Bellus asked. "If—"

"No," Killian said.

I sat on my hands and had to resort to bulging my eyes so I didn't visibly roll them.

Elite Bellus turned around to eye me. "Do you have something to say, protégée?"

"Nope," I said through clenched teeth.

"The apartment is *built* for the loners of our society." Pre-Dominant Harka ran a hand through her hair in barely veiled frustration. "They'd be safer there than anywhere else in Magiford. Frankly, I'd rather any Lone Wolves stay in a place like this than roam alone."

Killian's black eyes looked dark and cold. "Then it's a good thing you're the leader of the werewolves and not the vampires so you can sacrifice your own people."

Harka growled, a spark igniting in her eyes. "What did you say?"

Killian smirked. "I said—"

"That's enough!" I declared. I leaped to my feet so I could stand next to the Elite's chair and slap my hands on the table. "It will be far safer for the Unclaimed to live in an apartment like this—not only because they'll be surrounded by supernaturals, but because they'll have a place to flee. These wards won't just protect your precious Unclaimed from anyone in the building, they'll keep invaders out as well. You aren't going to be able to provide a better housing situation for them, and if you refuse to give them any choice in the matter, things are only going to escalate with them."

I was a little out of breath by the time I finished my lecture, but no one looked at all bothered by my outburst.

Killian sagged back in his chair. "Fine. I'll vote for it as well." He gave in way too easily, which meant this had been a bit of manipulation on his end.

Of course.

"In that case, let's hold the vote." Pre-Dominant Harka

snapped up so she was sitting straighter. "Thank you, Adept Medeis," she added.

I plopped back down in my chair, aware I should be embarrassed, but this had happened more than a few times during committee meetings.

Elite Bellus gave me a thumbs up and returned his attention to the meeting when Harka called out her vote.

He didn't turn around to face me again until the meeting wrapped up about ten minutes later.

"Well done, protégée." He beamed at me. "I was wondering when you were going to muzzle your vampire."

"I don't muzzle him," I protested.

"You do," Elite Bellus said. "I swear he's gotten more stubborn since I brought you in as my trainee, but you can at least verbally shake some sense into him so I suppose it doesn't matter much."

"I don't know about—"

Elite Bellus ignored my protests and plowed over me. "Turn in your notes to my secretary, and then you're free to go."

"Okay," I reluctantly agreed.

Elite Bellus grinned at me. "Cheer up. You've got the makings of a great Elite since you won't take guff from anyone."

"I'm still not sure how *legal* any of this is given who I'm dating," I grumbled.

"It's fine," the Elite assured me. "No one in the Midwest cares anyway. Have a great evening!"

"Thank you." I started to gather up the copious notes I'd taken, when I remembered something I needed to discuss with the older wizard. "Oh, Elite—" I started after him, but an arm snaked around my middle and dragged me into the shadows.

"Fraternizing with the enemy?" Killian asked.

"I'm a wizard," I pointed out.

"True." Killian edged just so his back blocked us from the supernaturals mingling around the center of the room. "Indeed. Well done speaking up in the meeting."

"Yeah, about that—you could have just been honest and approved the building like you wanted to," I said.

"Why do that when I can convince the committee I'm so head-over-heels for you, I'll let you push me around? It makes them *so much easier* to manipulate and test."

"That's the other thing. You really need to stop picking on the other leaders just because you're trying to push them to stand by their decisions," I warned him. "One day it's going to backfire on you."

"I doubt that." Killian kissed my neck. "You can head back to the House first—I still have a few more Elders I have to speak with."

"Gotcha. Don't let them ramble on for too long."

He chuckled. "You didn't fall in love with me because of my patience."

"True." I tugged his suitcoat straight. "See you then."

"Yes." He scooped me in for another kiss—I heard some of the fae who saw us let out a twittering giggle.

My face was a little red when we parted, but I made my back straight as I left the assembly hall, even though a few werewolves grinned at me, and more than one wizard cheered.

As the Paragon had predicted, Killian and I—or rather our relationship—had become a mixture of gossip and fairytale. Mostly people were content to just whisper about us, but I was still shocked by the occasional supernatural who approached me to wish me luck in taming Killian Drake.

Usually around then Killian popped out of the shadows just in time to frighten whoever was unfortunate enough to suggest such a thing, and inform them he was the one they should feel sorry for because I had a magic, sentient House at my back, which made arguments *spicier*, according to him. (Not that he was wrong. The first time we had a fight in House Medeis, the House locked him in the gym.)

I shook my head as I made my way through the Curia Cloisters.

When Mason chased me out of House Medeis, never in a million years had I thought this was the sort of future that awaited me.

I'd be lying if I didn't admit that once in a while I woke up and my parents' death hit me all over again. Sometimes I ached to sit down and drink tea with my mom again, or hear my dad laugh just one more time.

But in interacting with the long-lived Drakes, I'd come to understand that grief never disappeared. It just faded slowly, bit by bit. One day I'd be able to think of my parents without wanting to cry, and for now, that was good enough.

I had my family, I had Killian, I had the Drakes, and I even had my House. I was unimaginably happy.

―――

THE NEXT DAY I threw my gym bag in the trunk of the black SUV. It was late afternoon and the sky was painted brilliant hues of gold, baby blue, and pink.

"Are you ready?" Killian asked, crowding me from behind.

I pressed my lips together as I mentally reviewed everything I'd packed—today was our scheduled day for Killian and me to make the switch from House Medeis to Drake Hall. (We usually shifted back and forth between the two buildings every two weeks or so.)

I snapped my fingers. "Nope," I said. "I forgot my gym shoes."

Killian made a noise in the back of his throat. "I don't know why you won't let me purchase a full wardrobe to leave at your room in Drake Hall."

I walked backwards, away from the car. "Because that's not practical, and nobody needs that many clothes."

"Whatever, peasant," Killian said. "Don't take too long."

"I just have to run and grab them from my bedroom. I won't be long." I waved to the five-car motorcade that was waiting to escort Killian and me as I jogged back to House Medeis.

Rupert was driving the car Killian and I would ride in. When he saw me he stuck his hands on his hips. I gave him an obnoxious wink, and he dove behind the car.

"Brat!" he called after me.

I cackled as I jumped a bed of budding tulips.

Spring had arrived. A few more weeks, and we'd be at the anniversary of when I officially entered servitude to the Drake Family—not that it had lasted long.

I jumped up the porch stairs and affectionately patted the doorframe as I slipped through the front door.

I almost slammed into Great Aunt Marraine, who was making a beeline for the outdoors. "Oh, my! Did you forget something, Adept?" She wobbled a bit when I darted around her.

"Yeah, my shoes." I pounded up the stairs, waving when I passed a clutch of vampires meandering down the hall.

Shortly after Killian and I decided to go official, it became pretty obvious why the House had added an extra wing on when I Ascended.

It wasn't because it expected a huge uptick in wizards applying to join—though we had gained about a dozen new members since then.

No, the extra wing and all the bedrooms and sitting rooms with no windows weren't for us wizards...they were for the Drakes.

About twenty-five Drake vampires had moved in, making House Medeis their residence. Some of them rotated back to Drake Hall with Killian and me, or on a monthly basis for training and to receive their assignments. Others—specifically Killian's minions who worked at the Curia Cloisters—made House Medeis their permanent home.

The reverse had happened, too.

Roughly eight House Medeis wizards flip-flopped back and forth between Drake Hall and House Medeis. Again, some of them rotated with Killian and me, but sometimes they did whatever they wanted, like Momoko and Felix.

When I popped out of the stairs and zipped down the hallway, making a break for my room, I almost collided with the two of them as they sprinted for the stairs.

Seriously, why was everyone in such a hurry?

"Woah, hey." I paused long enough to smile at my childhood friends. "I thought you two weren't coming with us today."

"We're not," Felix said. "We just wanted to say goodbye."

I tilted my head and frowned. "You said goodbye when I came up here to grab my gym bag."

"He meant we wanted to say goodbye to *Rupert*." Momoko smirked.

Rupert was one of the vampires who had surprisingly requested a room in House Medeis and ferried back and forth with Killian and me.

I was honestly shocked, particularly because it had become something of a wizard hobby to pick on him by constantly trying to hug him—something he wasn't fond of.

I laughed as I took another step toward my room. "Can't let him escape unscathed, huh?"

"Nope!" Momoko said with pure satisfaction.

"Oh, we did want to tell you, though, we're thinking about offering to be blood donors," Felix said.

I paused midstep. "Say what?"

"Yeah, I think I trust Celestina plenty for my blood to taste fine, possibly Josh, too." Momoko scratched her side as she thought.

"I haven't picked a candidate yet," Felix informed me. "But I know I want someone who is the vampire version of a gym rat. If I feed them I bet I could bargain for some extra weightlifting lessons."

"Why do you guys want to be blood donors?" I asked.

Momoko pressed her lips together. "Because, frankly, it's not fair how much better of a team you and the Eminence are since he's immune to your magic. I figure if a couple of us wizards donate blood, we'll get elite vampire buddies to fight and train with too."

"Even though we haven't had to fight since the Night Court surrendered?" I asked.

"Hey." Felix jabbed a finger in my direction. "You told us that we trained to be prepared!"

"Yeah, I guess," I said, bewildered.

Momoko grinned. "It's not as big a deal as you think, Hazel," she said.

"And we're not the only ones thinking about it," Felix added.

"Okay." I nodded. "If you guys are really serious about it, let me know."

"Right-o!"

"Now if you'll excuse us, we have a red-haired vampire to embarrass." Momoko's grin turned positively wicked. "Oh, Rupert, our darling!" she sang at the top of her lungs as she and Felix scrambled down the stairs.

I couldn't help but shake my head as I zipped into my room and fished my gym shoes out of my closet.

Being with Killian had a lot of ripple effects I hadn't anticipated—vampires were living with us, other supernaturals were very eager to support us...and it seemed like my own family was going to fundamentally change as a result.

But, really, all of it was positive change.

And even though Killian and I were breaking something of a soft taboo...I couldn't help but feel like magic itself approved.

These last few weeks, I could have *sworn* I'd gained an extra flourish and a new loop on my wizard mark that hadn't been there before. But maybe that was just wishful thinking.

I ran back down through the House and burst onto the front

porch, a little surprised when I realized about half of the House—wizard and vampire alike—was standing on the front lawn.

I paused on the sidewalk, my shoes dangling from my fingers. "Is everything okay?" I cautiously asked.

Josh and Celestina were closest to me.

"Of course," Josh said. "It's just—"

Celestina slapped a hand over his mouth, her expression tight. "The House swallowed the Eminence again." She pointed to a mound of bushes, brush, and budding leaves that was about the size of two cars, and woven so thick I couldn't even see Killian.

"Dang it, what did he do?" I dropped my shoes and ran for the bush-ball, but no one answered me, even when I got close enough to touch the greenery. "I'm sorry," I said to the House. "Whatever he said he didn't mean it. Could you let him go?"

I didn't feel any anger from the House. It didn't even sulk. Instead, I felt...*excitement*?

It opened up a hole in the bush wall, one small enough that even I had to crouch down and shuffle a little to get in.

"Killian?" I called. "Are you okay? And what did you *do*?" My last word came out as more of a snarl, but any follow up lectures dropped from my mind when I finally made it in.

Instead of being filled with prickers, poison ivy, and other landscaping torture devices, as I had expected, the gigantic sphere was blanketed with wall to wall flowers.

Directly behind Killian was a lilac bush that was blooming unseasonably early—same with the pink and red roses that carpeted the floor. White and yellow lilies dripped from the ceiling, and blue hyacinths ringed the walls.

I blinked, my brain processing too slowly to comprehend what I was seeing. "What's going on?"

"You're my One," Killian said bluntly. "You're my sun when I shouldn't be allowed any. I will never love another like I love you, and I'll never trust another the way I trust you." Killian held out a tiny black jewelry box. "So I thought we should make things permanent."

As I stared open mouthed, he added, "I considered asking you at Drake Hall, but I was pretty sure your pain-in-the-ass House would never forgive me."

I didn't need to hear any more.

I released a choked laugh and flung myself at Killian.

We kissed, and surprisingly it was Killian who pulled back first. "May I interpret that as a yes?"

"Of course!" I laughed.

"You haven't even looked at the ring—which I spent a long time picking out," Killian said. He flicked the box open, revealing an unusual engagement ring.

Instead of the traditional diamond, Killian had picked out two colored gems arranged to almost resemble a flower. One stone was a deep, blood red color, the other was the distinct shade of Medeis blue.

"It's your House blue, and red for me, the vampire," he told me as I smiled at it through wet eyes.

"Thank you," I whispered.

He threaded his arms around me. "Of course. It's you and me, forever." He kissed me with enough passion to actually make my knees weak and my heart thump.

"I love you Killian Drake," I said when we parted.

"I love you Hazel Medeis," he said.

Faintly, through the protective shell of greenery the House had made, I heard Great Aunt Marraine. "What'd she say?"

Killian sighed. "I might have also asked you here because your family is worse than termites," he added.

I laughed. "We should tell them."

Killian kissed my temple. "She said yes," he called out in a raised voice.

The flowers and brush dropped away, and our friends and family that had gathered on the front lawn cheered and hooted.

I shyly leaned into Killian, until I finally recalled his specific wording. "Wait, forever?"

"Ahhh, yes. I've been meaning to tell you about that." Killian beamed down at me. "You're probably going to live as long as I do."

"*WHAT?*"

The End

If you enjoyed Hall of Blood and Mercy, please check out Leila's Story in the Court of Midnight and Deception series on Amazon.

SINCERELY, HOUSE MEDEIS

A Hall of Blood and Mercy short story

House Medeis *hated* Killian Drake.

It took a lot for a building—even a magic one—to harbor such passionate feelings against a mere being, but from the corners of its foundations to the support timbers in the rooms, House Medeis hated the Eminence of the Midwest, the upstart vampire Killian Drake.

The animosity started when Hazel Medeis lived in Drake Hall.

The Traitor, as House Medeis had labeled Mason, was stomping around fancying himself the Adept, but House Medeis knew better.

Even if Hazel Medeis hadn't Ascended, she was the Adept. And as she expanded her power base and worked on her magic, House Medeis was able to stabilize itself, at least enough so it could bear the Traitor sauntering around while it waited for the true Adept to return.

It was through the tiny, fragmented bond House Medeis had formed with Hazel that the House first became aware of *Killian Drake*. Ew.

But House Medeis was, above all else, *a house*. It didn't understand the finer points of Hazel's relationship with the vampire. It just knew the vampire got to have her when House Medeis didn't.

That was enough to forever put him in disgrace—at least, as far as the House was concerned.

So, when Killian visited the House and dared to *shoot* it, House Medeis gleefully swallowed him whole. And perhaps it should be confessed that it didn't just lock him in the basement closet, it proceeded to dump a trash bin, a dead shrub, and a stack of bricks on him as long as he was stuck there.

"Fine. I get it, you're angry you miserable chunk of magical wood." Killian narrowly avoided taking a brick to the face. "You'll protect her, that's all I wanted to confirm. Now let me out."

The House used a blip of magic to inspect its boundaries, found what it was looking for, and sucked it into the ground. A moment later, it deposited a thoroughly dirty and *angry* black cat on Killian.

Killian proceeded to growl in several old, archaic languages the House didn't understand.

The cat hissed and backed itself into a corner.

Killian ran a hand through his hair, pulling out a leaf the dead shrub had left behind, then crouched by the locked door and returned to picking it. "Hate me all you want—I don't care what a *house* thinks of me. But if she gets attacked while on Medeis land without me, and doesn't survive, I'll burn you down, salt the gardens, and turn the lot into a cemetery for everyone I kill in retribution."

The House was irritated now for different reasons—how *dare* the pasty vampire think Hazel, much less the House, could ever be defeated on Medeis land!

The House cast around the kitchen, trying to pinpoint the location of the knife block as Killian kept tinkering with the door.

"She loves you too much. I don't care that I'm sharing her— even if it's with a *house*, though it does dent my pride to think that

I rate equal with a building—because her loyalty for you sparks her independence. As a vampire, it's my nature to be possessive, but I can't be so with Hazel. She'd cut herself out of my life without remorse if I tried; she's meant for freedom."

The House stilled.

"I'm not going to steal her from you. She'd never let me, and though I wish I could, I won't." Killian stared at the door—the House recognized his expression as one of frustration, for it had seen the furrowed eyebrow look many times before. "Hazel is a wizard. She can do lots of wonderful and beautifully terrifying things because she's a wizard. And part of being a wizard is her connection to her House."

It occurred to the House it had never heard anyone refer to power—like that which Hazel wielded with her brutal fighting methods—as 'beautiful'. This made the House wonder just how likely was it that Hazel Medeis would find a suitable partner to share in the exploits of House Medeis that would not be in awe of her, or frightened by her lovely abilities?

"I like who she is, not who I could make her become," Killian continued, apparently content to rage passionately about his affection for the Adept as long as he was stuck. (*Boring.*)

But as little as the House wanted to admit it, it knew Killian was going to be a part of Hazel's life.

It hadn't increased in size on a whim.

It had grown a floor to house all the new wizards that would join House Medeis as a result of Hazel's policy changes. It had grown a brand-new *wing* to hold all the annoyingly silent, ghostly vampires Killian Drake was sure to bring.

Provided he didn't succeed in stealing her back and taking her off to his stupid Drake Hall.

Killian took advantage of the House's inaction and finally succeeded in picking the lock. He propped his dagger in the doorframe so the House couldn't slam it shut on him, then glanced at the hissing black cat.

"Are you going to take care of the animal?"

Sulking, the House opened up one of the basement storm windows.

The cat pricked its ears, then scrambled out of the corner. It hopped onto the washing machine and jumped through the open window, its tail puffed as it scrambled across the lawn, leaving the lot behind.

The House let Killian pass unmolested through the basement, though it considered swallowing the staircase so he couldn't get up—until it remembered he was a vampire which meant he didn't have the same physical limitations as a wizard. Another strike against him.

Killian paused at the base of the stairs. "I'll do everything I can to protect her."

The House creaked.

"She's going to be put in danger because of what I've done. I'm selfish enough that I don't want to do without her. But I'll pay whatever price is necessary to keep her safe."

...Perhaps it wasn't so bad that he didn't have physical limitations after all.

Still. The House didn't have to *like* him. So, on principal, the House weakened the wood of one of the stairs, so when the vampire stepped on it, it broke under his foot.

The pipes of the House gurgled in its amusement as Killian Drake released another string of heated words in various languages.

An uneasy understanding was reached between a vampire and a House that didn't like each other. Very well, it could manage that.

It was finished.

The fiends that had attacked Hazel Medeis had been taken care of. She wasn't in danger anymore.

The celebration lasted three days. Vampires and wizards alike shifted through House Medeis, laughing in their joy. There was also a lot of hugging—mostly from the wizards squeezing each other and some deeply surprised but not-protesting vampires.

And when the dust settled, House Medius understood two things very clearly.

1. Hazel loved and had chosen Killian Drake.
2. As a vampire, Killian Drake could never be an Adept with her.

He wouldn't enter into the bond Hazel shared with the House, unlike Hazel's parents, Rand and Rose, and Rand's parents before them, and his grandparents before them.

Mason's brief takeover had frightened the House. But knowing that Hazel would be connected with someone who could never share in the comradery of a Wizard House, someone who couldn't understand the flow of magic...that made it terrified in a wholly different way.

Hazel was the first in generations to understand the true role of wizards. If she left House Medeis...

A month after the fiends were defeated, Hazel and Killian returned from a recent visit to Drake Hall.

The House listened with curiosity as Hazel shooed everyone—wizard and vampire—out. Not just out of the rooms or out of the house, but off the *property*.

Those who weren't at work hopped into cars and drove off, leaving Killian and Hazel as the only two beings remaining.

Uneasily, the House tracked their progress as the pair made their way to the top floor, then opened a closet door, and started climbing the ladder that led up to the tower that held the Beacon.

Hazel went first, pushing open the trap door and limberly pulling herself up. She smiled brightly as she stretched out her hand, tapping a gentle finger against the blue and gold tinted light of the Beacon.

Behind her, out popped Killian.

The House rattled its shutters and made the weather vane on one of the opposite turrets spin. Why was Hazel bringing the vampire up to such a special place?

Hazel smiled up at Killian as he draped an arm over her shoulder. She leaned against him, but kept her hand hovering just above the Beacon.

"House Medeis, we need to talk."

No.

No, no, no, no.

The House creaked its wooden floors, and the whole lot might have rumbled.

Its fears had been realized. Hazel was going to leave for the big, shiny vampire mansion. She wasn't going to live at House Medeis anymore. She was going to live there with *Killian Drake*. And—

"Since it seems Killian and I are going to be romantically involved," Hazel began.

"It *seems*?" Killian said.

"We want to let you know that we're dedicated to splitting our time between Drake Hall and House Medeis. There will be changes—I know you built the wing for the vampires, but now they won't just be guests. They'll be moving in."

Killian gestured with his free hand. "Permanent rooms for Medeis wizards will be made available at Drake Hall as well. Even though Hazel and I will rotate between Drake Hall and House Medeis, there will be vampires and wizards permanently stationed at both locations."

Hazel gulped. "I hope you'll work with us on this." She let her fingers sink so she caressed the Beacon again. "It's a lot of change...and things will be different. You'll always be my home. But...do you think you could be *our* home?"

It took House Medeis several moments to understand exactly what Hazel and Killian were proposing.

They wanted to meld the two households.

They weren't going to abandon one building for the other, nor were they going to adopt all the old traditions—like an Adept couple would.

For a moment, House Medeis didn't know how to react. And then it felt the warm bloom of magic around the couple.

A wizard and vampire were together. Such a thing hadn't been done in a long time.

And the magic—wild and free and *dying*—swirled around them, fresh, new, and bright.

House Medeis existed to protect the wizards living in it. And it knew the inevitable death of magic was the greatest threat they faced.

But maybe...*perhaps*...all hope wasn't lost.

Hazel pressed herself closer to Killian and anxiously glanced up at her vampire.

Killian Drake kept his shoulders straight as he stared at the Beacon, waiting for the House's reaction.

House Medeis tapped some of the fresh magic wafting off the pair, and got to work.

The front lawn was covered in snow, but with a little bit of magic, and some shuffling of the gardens, bright red tulips bloomed, popping out of the snow in a stark smear of color against the white ground. The tulips had been rearranged so they traced out a giant heart on the front lawn.

Hazel laughed and pressed her face into Killian's chest as he hugged her.

And once again, from the stone of its foundations to the timbers of its roofs, House Medeis felt something. But this time, it wasn't hatred. It was the knowledge that things would be different.

For starters, there was going to be a vampire in House Medeis. But perhaps that was for the best.

Because House Medeis *hated* Killian Drake...but it held no such dislike of Celestina Drake, Josh Drake, that funny red-haired vampire who complained loudest about the wizard hugs even though he seemed to get the most, or any of the other Drake vampires!

The End

IF YOU ENJOYED THE HALL OF BLOOD AND MERCY SERIES CHECK OUT LEILA'S STORY!

The Court of Midnight and Deception Series

Book one: Crown of Shadows
Available on Amazon!

The fae of the Night Court are desperately searching for a new monarch to crown before the Court collapses.

I couldn't care less.

I've done everything I can to bury my fae blood and embrace my human half. That changes when some fae nobles show up on my doorstep and announce that I'm the next Queen of the Night Court.

Becoming an unwilling fae queen? Check. Inheriting a terrible mess? Double check.

The Court is almost bankrupt, my citizens' favorite hobby is backstabbing one another, and I don't know who I can trust since someone keeps trying to assassinate me.

Speaking of assassins, I get introduced to the best in the business—a fae lord nicknamed the Wraith. His deadly profession means he fears no one. The only reason he doesn't kill me on the spot is he's also a member of the Night Court and the Court's magic protects me. But that doesn't prevent him from trading verbal barbs with me whenever we meet.

And if cat herding all these uncooperative fae and chatting with assassins wasn't enough, I'm required to get married as part of some archaic Court law. This "queen" gig is the worst!

Supposedly I can choose anyone to marry, but with all the infighting I need someone who is neutral and won't provoke more political power struggles.

So, why do I keep thinking of a certain assassin?

Court of Midnight and Deception is an urban fantasy trilogy featuring fae, werewolves, vampires, and wizards. It's packed with humor, adventure, and a sweet, slow burn romance between a reluctant fae queen and the assassin who tried to kill her.

OTHER SERIES BY K. M. SHEA

The Snow Queen

Timeless Fairy Tales

The Fairy Tale Enchantress

The Elves of Lessa

Hall of Blood and Mercy

Court of Midnight and Deception

Pack of Dawn and Destiny

Gate of Myth and Power

King Arthur and Her Knights

Robyn Hood

The Magical Beings' Rehabilitation Center

Second Age of Retha: Written under pen name A. M. Sohma

ADDITIONAL NOVELS

Life Reader

Princess Ahira

A Goose Girl

ABOUT THE AUTHOR

K. M. Shea is a fantasy-romance author who never quite grew out of adventure books or fairy tales, and still searches closets in hopes of stumbling into Narnia. She is addicted to sweet romances, witty characters, and happy endings. She also writes LitRPG and GameLit under the pen name, A. M. Sohma.

Hang out with the K. M. Shea Community at...
kmshea.com

Made in United States
Troutdale, OR
07/11/2023

11128623R00182